CW00867315

Angels Burn

A Novel by Barritt Firth

Copyright 2020 © Barritt Firth
All rights reserved. No part of this publication may be reproduced
or distributed in any form or by any means, electronic or
mechanical, including photocopying, recording, or by any
information storage or retrieval system, without the prior written
consent of the author.
ISBN: 979-8-6788-4-2107

Table of Contents

Chapter 1

Mila checked the time, flipped on her screen, and stared. She fought to slow her breathing. The press conference was scheduled to start in less than a minute. A message arrived. She checked to make sure it was not her dad. It was her roommate. She felt stupid for thinking it might be her dad. A friendly distraction might prevent Mila from having a stroke, only she did not answer her friend. Her chest tightened as her heart thumped. Her bruised back ached. The live stream started, and the first blackwing to go public stood in a park before a podium less than two hundred miles south of Mila's Seattle dorm.

"We're not demons," said the winged man. He was skinny, tall and looked like a normal human, except for the frightening, mesmerizing dark wings spread behind him two times the span of his outstretched hands. He was young, maybe nineteen, and handsome, with high cheekbones and a wry smile. His eyes, the irises, looked different. A purple hue? The ebony wings on his back arched, withdrew, and then suddenly flapped, lifting him a few feet into the air.

Mila gasped in unison with the huge crowd. People backed away from the blackwing. Mila leaned closer to the screen. His fully extended black wings lifted him gracefully. The camera panned out as the man flew over the press conference and crowd. People cowered, expecting his wings to give way, or anticipating an attack or some other supernatural display of power. Each time he glided to a new section of the crowd, they spread apart beneath him, and when he dipped closer, they panicked and screamed, shoving each other out of the way. As if toying with them, he changed

1

directions suddenly and swooped faster. Mila giggled, finally breathing. A young female reporter jumped into the picture, the blackwing in the air behind her. Mila wanted the woman out of the way. She wanted a close-up or a different angle. She had to see his back. The press conference was on the riverfront in Portland, Oregon. The blackwing soared over the slow brown Willamette River, circled around an old brick industrial building on the other side, moving away from the city center.

The blackwing returned. As a section of the crowd parted, a solitary man stepped into the void. Several gunshots erupted, like the final random bursts of popcorn popping in a microwave, followed by screams. Mila winced.

"You're Satan," yelled a man in a brown suit, brandishing a small handgun. Others near him shouted the same as most of the people darted from the area, leaving an isolated group of about six or seven men and women standing on the grass.

The blackwing flew up as the man fired again. The blackwing floundered and dropped a dozen feet or so, but then beat his wings and veered up and away. In a blink, he was gone. Two black helicopters and several small drones climbed above the crowd, over the head of the reporter, and disappeared after him. The shaking camera followed the specks as best it could, until they disappeared like the blackwing into thick gray clouds.

An error message appeared. The internet had been shut down or had crashed. Mila's hand shook as she picked up her cell phone, and then set it down after seeing the cell service had also shut down. The screen flickered back on, but Mila rushed to the bathroom and shut the door. Even though she knew Jenna was out and most likely glued to a screen, along with billions of other people across the planet, Mila took the extra precaution and locked the door. After an early-morning soccer game, where Mila had scored a controversial game-winning goal, she had been haunted by a question. She ripped off her shirt, turned, jerked her sports bra up, and peeked over her shoulder. The marks were still there. Two swollen parallel black ridges that looked like dark bruises. They started just above her shoulder blades and ran along her spine, stopping just above her waist. She touched one. It was moist and tender. It could be an infection, but she could not go to a doctor, not until she knew for sure.

When rumors about blackwings had initially surfaced, Jenna had insisted these mysterious beings were demons. Mila did not know what they were. Maybe they were not even people. Yet, if they were normal people who had changed, and she was turning into a blackwing, if she could fly... She thought about her dad. With wings, she could cover a lot of ground. She shook her head. *Bruises. Just bruises. I'm just a soccer player who gets knocked around. A lot.*

She pulled her shirt back on and hurried out to watch the news.

Crap. Six minutes to meet Jenna and Kathy. Mila put on her running shoes and then slipped her phone into her pocket. She sprinted into the hall and hopped down a flight of stairs. Students, loud and frantic, looked up from their excited conversations and handhelds and stared at Mila as she raced by. Mila pushed her way through a cluster of kids, burst out of the dorm building's main door, and within a few minutes she was approaching her favorite coffee house, Sweet Perk, just on the other side of the University's tall security fence. Mila ignored various hazard signs in large red capital letters. *ALWAYS CARRY ID. LEAVE AT OWN RISK.* There were electrical shock hazard signs on each fence segment. Razor wire along the top faced out toward the city.

Like most students, she secretly relished short-lived crusades into the city, though few travelled further than a noodle shop, burrito house, or coffee shop a block or two away. Outside, the external, collapsing, smog-laced world threatened to fall apart before their very eyes. Mila knew it was a rough world that too often consumed university students through drugs, bars, robberies, corruption, and even the occasional kidnapping for ransom. Like most students, she was skeptical that anything bad could happen to her. Still, before crossing the checkpoint, she eyed several men standing on a corner, trying to determine if they were armed hoolies. She would cross anyway. Sometimes, campus life was too much for Mila. Her campus life was her campus lie. Pretend you are interested. *Nod.* Pretend you are happy. *Smile.* Pretend you like someone. *Flirt and gossip.* Pretend you are not starving. *Take small bites and chew lots of times.* Pretend you have money. *Shop, but don't buy. Act picky.* The other side of the campus perimeter fence was filled with a bustling crowd. These people were hungry. These people hated. These people fought and argued. These people did not have. The other side was an escape to the truth.

The security guard, a Chinese UNSI, garbed in black riot gear, studied his wrist reader and with a scowl, unclasped his Taser and blew a high-pitched whistle as a female student nearly made it by him without his approval. He compared the faces on his screen to the transmissions from the student's ID card and read her vitals. Mila paused until the Asian soldier nodded her along as well. As Mila trotted across the street, a whiff of strong coffee broke through the volatile scents from automobile exhaust and fast-food oils. A place like Sweet Perk, only twenty yards from the same razor-wire-topped security fence that locked the world out and the students in, was more akin to a walk on a leash than a real adventure. Mila ignored a row of panhandlers with grimy outstretched hands and barged through the door. The coffee shop was crowded; every seat at every table was taken, and each table had more than one student standing alongside. The chatter was understandably much louder than usual. Mila looked to the coveted sofa next to a fake stone fireplace wall mural, her favorite spot to sit, but soon spotted Jenna at a nearby table.

"Sorry I'm late," Mila said, placing her hand on Jenna's shoulder. Jenna sat with Kathy and a group of kids who Mila recognized as part of Jenna's prayer team. They were streaming a replay of the blackwing's press conference on a tablet. It was a feed of the broadcast Mila had seen earlier. Her sense of unease returned.

Jenna scowled and then glanced at her phone. "Uh. Yes. Late, as usual, but one minute?" Jenna asked.

Mila checked her phone. No. She ran the whole way, and she was fast, even for a soccer player, but even with soccer conditioning, she knew that it was exactly 1.2 miles from her dorm room to Sweet Perk. She could not have possibly run over a mile in under five minutes, especially after playing a ninety-minute soccer game earlier that morning. Add a stop for security, and no way.

"You miss the press conference?" Jenna asked, eyes wide.

Mila shook her head.

"Mila-chick," said Kathy, without looking up from her tablet, "you shredded that ball." Kathy paused and zoomed in on the black wings.

Mila smiled, leaning closer. She had. The winning goal not only flew into the back of the opposing team's net, but the ball popped and shredded through the net. Yes, she was talented, a rising-star athlete, but not *that* talented. It was a confusing day indeed.

"It had to be a trick, like those exploding golf balls," Mila said.

"And you are killer fast, Mila-chick," said Kathy. "Killer. Fast."

Yes, and I just ran a sub-five mile with a stop.

Mila nearly jumped as a soft hand touched her back. "Crap, Garrett."

He smiled and raised his eyebrows. "You remembered my name?"

Mila glowered. "Don't flatter yourself," she said, tapping his gold nametag.

"The usual?" he asked.

"Sure," she said, matching his earlier smile.

"Don't flatter yourself," he said, tapping his nametag with his forefinger. Instead of his name, Garrett, the word *Nametag* was embossed in its place.

Her face reddened. "You got me." *Garrett Webb.*

"What's your drink?"

"Americano, extra shot. No. No extra shot. Too much going on."

"Don't want a heart attack? As much as I love this wonderful drug I peddle, I won't need caffeine for a year."

Mila sidestepped to the counter and pulled a five Amero bill and five single Ameros out of her pocket and placed the crumpled money on the counter. She wanted to tip him, but then she would be completely broke. Eighty-nine cents would get her Chinese ramen noodles at the student store. Her dad was supposed to wire some money, money he probably did not have, but she had not heard from him in nearly two months. He had never gone more than a month without calling her. Usually, it was an apology or an excuse, but still, he made contact.

Garrett smiled as he palmed the change into her sweaty hand. "Thanks, Mila—sometimes called Mila-chick. No nametag necessary."

She blushed, looked away, and could not resist. She tossed the coins into a jar with a scrawled note with a hand-drawn picture of a cow on its side, stating that cow-tipping was bad, but Garrett-tipping was good. In fact, even with everything going on, there were times she just wanted to tip Garrett over. A voice inside her head whispered, yesss.

"Uh, thanks," Mila said, somehow drawing enough courage to find his eyes, though she was still too shy to keep her gaze locked on his for more than two seconds.

She bumped into the corner of a table, jarring her hip on her way back to rejoining her friends. She scooted down a padded bench at Jenna's table. The people around were all talking at once. Who did not have something to say after all that blackwing stuff? She had heard only rumors before, but now, there was indisputable proof. Blackwings were real.

"Didn't think you'd make it," said Jenna. "You come just for him?" She nodded her head toward Garrett, who was wiping a rag over steaming coffee equipment. Jenna, blonde and beautiful, but overly protective and overtly snobby, glared at him.

Kathy, who formed a best-friend trio with Jenna and Mila, reached over and playfully socked Mila on the shoulder. "It's true." Almost everything Kathy said was either followed by or preceded by a smack. "You came for him." She punched Mila again.

Garrett grinned, as if somehow aware they were discussing him.

Mila stuck her tongue out at Jenna. "He doesn't even know I exist."

Jenna nodded. *Right*, she mouthed. Kathy smacked herself on the forehead.

"No, really. He has a hundred girls chasing him already," said Mila. "I came for the sweaty-palm bacteria exchange."

Kathy looked confused.

Jenna rolled her eyes. "Prayer circle? Mila, you missed it. There were over one hundred hands, too."

"Wow." Mila pretended to count her fingers. "That's

more than a two billion bacteria migration, plus viruses. Don't worry. I'm sure everyone in the prayer circle is fully vaxed and recently washed their hands."

"Mila—forget bacteria and viruses. You were watching, right?" asked Kathy.

"I can't believe that guy shot a blackwing," said Mila. "I hope the blackwing's okay."

"Really. And why?" asked Jenna.

"If there are more blackwings, they'll be afraid to come out."

"Honey, *honey*. You didn't see the blackwing return?" asked Jenna, incredulously. "You did not see the blackwing return."

Mila shook her head. The three friends and Jenna's prayer team crowded around the screen. Jenna tapped on a media box and stretched it out so they could see it better. The clip was from right where Mila had stopped watching. The helicopters and drones flew in fast straight lines after the blackwing. They all disappeared into the overcast sky. The camera zeroed in on the man who had fired the shot. Several police officers rushed in, disarmed him, and cuffed his hands behind his back. He reminded her of her dad. He was about the same age, maybe a little younger, and wore a dark blue suit like the one her dad used to wear when he worked in sales. She wished that somehow, memories of better times, like when her dad had a job, would make her feel better, but they did not.

An object swooped downward out of the gray sky, and the group of people and officers gathered near the shooter suddenly scattered. Others shouted, pointed, and then sprinted away. Something moved up into the air again, dangling a kicking human figure. People shrieked and shouted, some dropping to the ground and frantically crawling forward on all fours. People at a safe distance pointed at the sky until their hands eventually flopped to their sides.

"What happened?" asked Mila, but she was already playing the clip again, only slower.

"He pulled the shooter from the cops, pulled him into the air, and disappeared. See, there," said Jenna, pointing to a distant cloud.

Mila thought that was what she had seen, but it had happened so fast, and she was still in disbelief about all the day's events. She could not tell for sure. She set her coffee on the table, partly so she could search for a clip with a better close-up, and partly because her hands were shaking again. She found a new video with an improved angle. Yes, the blackwing had dropped the man from the sky. He fell a few hundred feet. With cuffed hands and no parachute, the man was surely dead. A close-up confirmed it.

She took a deep breath. Her friends shook their heads, but Mila wanted to smile. Was that wrong?

"Blackwing justice," said Garrett, now part of a group of about six people watching the clip behind Jenna and Mila.

The comment made Mila's heart quicken. She liked people who stood up for an underdog, but more than that, it came from Garrett.

Jenna loudly cleared her throat. "It's a demon dropping a human from the sky," she said, staring up at Garrett with a chilling glare. "You have a sick mind. Sick minds should be reported."

"The man shot him, Jenna," said Mila. "I agree with Garrett. Are you going to report me now?"

"Shut up, everyone," Kathy interrupted, compulsively slapping every arm within reach. "There's another clip. Look, *look*."

The whole coffee shop was now quiet; a new story filled various devices.

Back at the park in Portland, the crowd parted as the blackwing approached a cellphone camera. The owner's hand was shaking.

"If you're a blackwing, don't let them know who you are yet. There are too many who will try to harm us." His voice shook. Tears streamed down his cheeks. The blackwing's gaze drifted to the crowd around him. He looked back into the camera again, snapping out of a daze. "Don't be afraid of blackwings, but whatever you do, don't try to kill us. If you attack us, we can *and will* defend ourselves." His voice was shaking even more noticeably. So were his legs. He looked like he might collapse, but then his eyes narrowed, and a slight smile appeared.

A large man the size of a bouncer or linebacker reached out from the crowd, as if to grab the blackwing's wrist. The blackwing struck the man's forearm. The man quickly dropped to his knees, cradling a bent broken arm that now looked like it had an extra elbow at the wrist. Another man stepped forward, but the blackwing just pointed a finger and shook his head. The man disappeared into the retreating crowd.

The blackwing shot up into the clouds.

Disgusted and dizzy, Mila could not watch any more. She wanted to, but her mind was drawn to how much her back ached. She could feel the ridges running on both sides of her spine, and they felt as if wings might burst through them. *No. I'm imagining things. It's just because of this.* She knew she was a hypochondriac. That was why she was following a pre-med track. But her feelings for the blackwing nearly overwhelmed her. When the shots were fired, it felt as if the bullets had ripped into her very own wings.

No. I don't have wings!

Only, somehow, she knew how it felt, and what scared her was how she enjoyed it when the blackwing sought revenge.

"Don't ask Coffee Boy out," said Jenna. "He shouldn't be talking like that. He's probably an anarchist—a terrorist. Look at the riff-raff this place attracts." She pointed to several local panhandlers at a table drinking coffee.

Kathy nodded. Mila watched Kathy's fist to see if she would speak, but Kathy spoke up without punching. "He gives them free coffee. Why don't we get free coffee?"

"Reverse discrimination. Normal people know you shouldn't feed strays," said Jenna. "They're probably all anarchist terrorists."

"First, they are not all terrorists, or at least not violent terrorists," said Mila. "And you don't know if he's even an anarchist, much less a terrorist. Garrett just felt bad for the blackwing. A random Bible guy shot him, completely unprovoked. That's not right."

"So, we just let flying demons drop men from the sky?" Jenna asked.

"And we just let men shoot whomever they want?" Mila asked.

"The man who shot the blackwing called him *Satan*," said Jenna. "Maybe God told him to do it because it's a demon."

"No. I don't think they're demons," said Mila. "And this one certainly isn't Satan. Satan works for the Internal Revenue Service."

"That's true," Kathy said, punching Jenna's arm this time. "Fast and funny, Mila-chick."

"I'll give you fast, and maybe, maybe I'll give you funny," said Jenna. "Look, now Garrett's feeding them."

Mila looked to the table of panhandlers, which had now grown to six. They were devouring a plate filled with coffee cake. Garrett was walking away. "Isn't this where you say *let them eat cake?*" asked Mila, smirking at Jenna.

Jenna rolled her eyes.

Kathy spoke again but kept her hands to herself. "In a different video a blackwing said he's human. Said something shares his body."

"It's a demon. It's called possession," said Jenna. "It goes way back. The only cure is God."

Jenna's friends from prayer team nodded in agreement.

"I doubt it's possession," said Mila, trying not to let on that it just might be. How would someone know for sure if there was one inside of them?

"You doubt everything," said Jenna.

"It's true," said Kathy with a punch. "You do."

"Well, if it's a demon, I doubt God can cure it. God hasn't cured much lately." Mila rubbed her shoulder. Usually Kathy punched lightly, but this time she had slipped a knuckle in.

"Uh, the virus?" asked Jenna.

"People cured that," said Mila.

"We can agree that the world is rough," said Jenna. "But this is the last thing this country needs. Possessed people dropping real humans from the sky. Hasn't this country been through enough?"

Mila's stomach ached. Hunger? Might be. Nerves? Likely. She looked up at Garrett. Even with all this going on, she still found his green eyes enchanting, and she still wanted to go out with him. On the other hand, she sure wished she had that eighty-nine cents back she had carelessly tossed into the tip jar. Mila's eyes went from the tip jar to her friend. Why couldn't her dad be loaded like Jenna's dad? "Jenna, I need to borrow an Amero."

Jenna nodded, pulled two green fives out, and tucked them into the pocket of Mila's sweatpants. She followed Mila's gaze. "I don't know what you like about him. He's not even a student. This is his career. Serving students is his career."

Six-foot. Sideburns. Blue-green eyes. Dark hair. Rebel. "He used to be a student," Mila said. "Thanks for the loan."

"He was expelled," said Jenna. "No problem. And it's not a loan."

"You don't know he was expelled," said Mila. "Wait. Do you?"

Jenna shrugged.

"It's true. I heard it from two other people," said Kathy, again using her fists for emphasis.

"Wow. Two people said something. With stats like that, it must be true." Mila shook her head. "I heard he was a soldier and lost his leg."

"Well, he's got two," said Jenna. "So that's not true."

Kathy smacked Mila. "He does."

They stood to leave. Mila, Kathy, and Jenna three-way kissed with light amusing pecks. Mila looked back over her shoulder to Garrett, who had stopped talking to a blonde freshman Garrett-worshipper not much different from herself. He looked at Mila and smiled.

"I'll be at the dorm in a few," said Jenna. "Some of us are meeting at the cathedral down the street for one more prayer. Kathy's coming. You should come too."

"Actually, I can't," Kathy said. "I'm going to the library to study with a hot senior." She used finger quotes as she said "study".

"Enjoy yourselves. No offense, Jenna, but Kathy's way of spreading bugs sounds like more fun," said Mila, quickly turning and heading out the front door before Jenna could insist she and Kathy tag along with her prayer team.

Holding strangers' sweaty hands, praying, and talking about how great God is, while double-digit unemployment climbed higher and starving children's bellies distended? No. That did not work for Mila. Not even with hand sanitizer. She wished it did. It would make things easier, much easier, if she could believe this was all part of a plan.

Mila passed by security at Campus Wall, holding out her RFID card. The UNSI blew his whistle. Mila turned and pulled her scarf down so he could see her face. He looked at his screen, verified that Mila matched the physical description transmitted by her card, and then nodded. She froze as the UNSI's whistle again screamed. A group of students threw their hands up at the hassle. Most students, except pious ones like Jenna, loathed the idea of privatized security, especially privatized security from China. *We were violating free-trade agreements. They were cheaper and won the bid, and, besides, the UNSIs save our government and taxpayers a fortune*, argued Jenna the first time Mila expressed her true feelings on United Nations Security, Inc. Their name was deceptive. Most people thought UNSIs were really a part of the United Nations and were there to help, but they were a low-bid privatized security force with United Nations in their company name. Sure, security was necessary, just like the Campus Wall that surrounded the University and student housing was necessary. If the University of Washington was unsafe, rich parents and donors would soon find another repository for their money and brood.

She ambled back to her dorm in a daze as anxious students rushed by to watch highlights on television or the web. Every group she passed was emphatically discussing blackwings and re-watching clips or excitedly pointing to a new post. Students bared their teeth, spread their arms out, and flapped, reenacting what they had seen, or what they thought they had seen. She did not remember the blackwing baring his teeth.

Mila looked down. There was too much on her mind. She avoided any eye contact that might draw her into a conversation.

A sharp pain hit as her stomach cramped up. She stopped in the crowded dormitory store, bought an instant noodle pack and the green apple with the fewest bruises, and then stared longingly at tastier food that was priced appropriately higher. Roast beef sandwiches, fruit, cheese and vegetable trays, and dessert packs all sounded good, but they also threatened to bust her budget.

Mila returned to her room, where she prepared and then nibbled at her small meal, and studied, wondering if her body aches were from hunger or nerves.

After a few hours of reading and re-reading, while trying to keep wild thoughts from escaping and spreading, Mila rushed to the bathroom, her gut in knots. She had to look again. *I'm not a blackwing. I'm not a devil.* She closed the bathroom door and locked it.

A second later she heard the dorm-room door outside open and shut as Jenna entered. Mila double-checked the bathroom lock.

"Mila. I'm sorry, I forgot to congratulate you on your game," Jenna called from the other side of the door. "You got a heckuva goal today."

"Yeah. Thanks."

"Heard some techies made the ball explode."

"Yeah."

"Heard the Pilots are going to protest."

"Probably. They'll find someone who specializes in balls to investigate. Maybe Kathy should volunteer."

"Crude, Mila. But funny. I'm going to bed. Mind's full. Too much happened today. You okay?"

"Yeah."

The light darkened at the base of the door as Jenna flipped the switch outside.

Mila pulled her shirt and sports bra off and turned away from the mirror. Looking over her shoulder she could see that

15

the two black lines rose higher than the last time she had looked, each with a line down the middle glistening with moisture. Mila pushed from deep within, flexing muscles she did not know she had, and wings popped out, hitting the door and the wall with loud thumps.

"You okay?" asked Jenna.

Mila gasped. "Yeah. Cramps."

For a moment, her mouth twitched to a smile, but then a feeling of dread, an irreversible sense of fear and loneliness, like she had experienced at her mother's funeral, overtook her. Tears streamed down her cheeks. *No.* She did not want and did not deserve this. Go away, she thought. *But if I can help my dad.*

She felt woozy as the wings pressed against the walls of the small bathroom. Her eyes burned and blurred. She had to lie down. Mila's stomach muscles constricted, and she lost her breath as if she had been punched in the gut. She hunched over, staggered back upright, and looked in the mirror. The wings were gone. Were they back inside of her? How could they fit? She turned, looking at the same two black lines running alongside her spine. *Had this really happened?* She tried to "push" again. Nothing. She wiped her tears and threw her clothes back on, turned around, and then scrutinized the back of her gray T-shirt. She could see the bulges, barely, but would someone else notice before she got to a doctor?

"Are you there?" Mila whispered, steadying herself against the bathroom door, her legs wobbling.

"Yeah," her roommate said, sounding tired and annoyed.

Yes, a different voice answered, but this one was inside her head.

Mila desperately tried to chase the voice, but she became confused. A long yawn erupted as sleep-inducing chemicals spilled into her mind, forcing her frantic thoughts to fragment. *How can I be tired? This is just a bad dream,* she told herself.

She turned off the bathroom light and groped her way to her bed through a dark room lit only by a small blue light from a charging station on the wall above the desk. Her heart thundered and then echoed like a distant bass drum. She wondered how on earth she could be falling asleep, but then wondered if she was fast asleep already.

Sleep, the voice that was not there hissed inside her head.

Chapter 2

After Mila convinced herself that she had been dreaming, hallucinating, and likely having a textbook reaction to stress, hunger, and a missing dad, she also insisted that the lines on her back were bruises from soccer. Smaller than many of her opponents, she was like a pinball out there on the soccer pitch. They did whatever they could to try to slow her down—punches to the back, thrown elbows, shirt pulls that pinched skin, ankle kicks—especially when a referee's head was turned. If they could not take the ball from her, they would settle for taking her from the ball. Heck, even her own teammates leveled her in practice. On the field, everyone competed for playing time, positions, the ball, a goal. Opponents struck her back as often as they elbowed her head. Bruises and concussion-induced psychosis were more likely than a demon giving her an ability to sprout wings from her back. Too bad though, with wings she could probably find food and her dad on the same day.

The morning after her strange episode, she tried pushing as she had done the night before, but no wings came out. And when she tried to think about the voice, or a being inside of her, her thoughts clouded and slowed, so maybe it had not really happened. And the voice? Anyone could ask themselves a question and hear an answer.

Interesting, an internal thought said.

She tried to chase the voice, but again she found herself confused and disoriented.

Urgent Care at the university was intended for emergency visits only, and this was not an emergency, yet, so Mila spent most of the school day trying not to think about her back, trying not to think about a voice, trying not to think about anything and everything that felt different or did not make sense, but most importantly, trying not to think about her wings—because *I don't have any! I'm just hungry, freaking starving, again.*

Classes blurred together. Mila had her tablet on during each class, but her fingers would not move. She would have to borrow notes. She found her eyes seeking the sky through classroom windows, yearning for the cold gray mist of the low clouds.

After breezing through her psych book that afternoon, she confirmed that a human suffering from duress, depression, or a mental health crisis could see or imagine just about anything. Maybe she was schizophrenic. She needed a mental health evaluation, but a request like that would go on her permanent record. Students hovered over blackwing news reports, and Mila just as frantically pored over anything on the Internet that had to do with blackwings. Hallucinations or no, blackwings were real.

That night, on her bed, Mila opened the previous month's issue of *Confessions of an Agorist*, an underground e-paper sweeping through the campus that students simply called *Confessions*. She got it from someone who got it from someone who got it from someone. Everyone got it that way, but nobody knew who authored it. A disgruntled student? She read away, devouring the articles as if they were pizza slices.

Jenna, in the bed across from her was deep in her studies. "President's press conference. Five minutes," she said.

Mila nodded but continued to read *Confessions*. Jenna would hate what Mila was reading.

The Young Adult Protection Act provides the ability and means to medicate and treat uncooperative children and young adults. Educators and employers are required to identify abnormal behavior due to liability and safety.

A signature by a parent and/or guardian and/or an authority figure trained in Attention and Cooperation Disorders can be enough to medicate or incarcerate any nonconformist. Students, freethinkers, dissenters, those who ask too many questions or think and act differently are a threat to those who cooperate or look the other way. Three in ten children by the age of fourteen have been identified as "suffering" from Attention and Cooperation Disorders, ACD, and are currently taking psychotropic drugs that are mood-altering and addictive. Those in poverty are ten times more likely to be diagnosed....

True or not, the revelations made Mila nervous. *Maybe that's what I need, mental-health care.*

"You shouldn't read so much," said Jenna. "It makes the rest of us look stupid."

Jenna was joking, but the reading, Mila had not really thought about it until now. In the past week, her raging thirst for written words was difficult to explain, electronic or print, brochures, and textbooks—she had always been a reader, but not like this. A textbook on amino acids and proteins. It was dry, uninteresting, and she had already finished it the first week of class. So why did she just read it again?

"Press conference is on," said Jenna.

Mila closed out the article and clicked on the Presidential Press Conference tab.

President Laura Banks stood at her podium, no longer hiding from the press. The economy was getting worse. Double-digit unemployment grew higher. Home foreclosures were up. Now, there were not just homeless villages but homeless cities. Squatters claimed empty homes and buildings, and many of them were now armed. The economy? Off a cliff and it still had not hit the ground. There were rumors of a one-world government. United Nations Security, Inc, UNSI, was gas on fire to those rumors. The only thing worse than Martial Law was cheap, privatized Martial Law imported from China. There was so much going on in the world, and people wanted answers and action: Open abandoned homes. Take homes from the banks and give them to the unemployed, or at least rent them at prices people could afford. That's what was foremost on the minds of people. Until today. The President could not hide from blackwings today.

President Banks always wore the same bright fresh-blood red dress when facing the press. She had jet-black hair, blue-gray eyes, and a grin that showed teeth, teeth that bit hard without a warning bark. She had not become CEO of the world's largest financial firm, and then President of the United States, as a middle-aged divorced woman, by being easily intimidated. Yesterday, though, she had met her match. A blackwing had gone public. And today she had to answer. She adjusted her microphone and spoke, "Yesterday was a frightening or perhaps an enlightening day. A new species or a strangely evolved human, a blackwing, showed itself to the public for the first time. Although we were aware of a new presence, for reasons of national security, we could not openly address this issue. We are still learning about this new unnatural force. So far, there have been only a few incidents, but first and foremost, we must keep America and the world safe from any kind of attack."

Mila shivered and shifted in her chair as goose bumps quickly spread over her.

"I have issued an executive order for reasons of national security, and the United Nations, along with the G-10 leaders, have issued a similar directive, as this is either the world's problem, or the world's opportunity."

The other nations always issue similar orders. Our country is not our own, Mila thought, quoting The Agorist. There were many besides this anonymous writer who believed there was a one-world government already, we just did not know it. They had passed laws to prevent terrorists, pandemics, econonomic collapse, and now it would be blackwings. *Never let a crisis go to waste.*

"From this moment forward, if you are a blackwing, or suspect you might be a blackwing, you are required to turn yourself in to a proper authority. Proper authorities include the police, a military installation, or United Nations Security."

Mila did not expect the president to use United Nations Security's common name, UNSI.

"If you surrender and cooperate, you will come to no harm. We just want to understand you. If you harbor a blackwing, or suspect you might be harboring a blackwing, you must disclose this information to those same proper authorities immediately. If you have any knowledge of blackwings or suspected blackwings, you are required to report the information and any suspicious behavior or activities to an email or phone number that will be listed after this message, or to a proper authority. Failure to follow these orders will be considered an act of treason as this may threaten the sanctity and safety of our nation. Criminals and traitors will be dealt with accordingly."

The President bared her teeth again and nodded at various faces in the crowd that could not be seen from the camera's angle. Her expression morphed to sober and cold as she leaned forward and spoke again. Without flinching, she went straight for the punch. "For those of you who are *not* blackwings, as of now I honestly can't say there is nothing to fear. We just don't know. But my first responsibility is to protect American families, and this is why I have asked Congress to extend and modify the Loyalty Act with new provisions for blackwings and those who would aid them. We must pass this modified act now in order to protect and save

America. We need to do this today.

"We do have blackwings in custody, and though we don't know yet what they are or where they came from, we do know how to incapacitate and even kill them. Rest assured, we prefer a peaceful solution, but we do have an obligation to keep order, while protecting our nation and humanity. It is a time for us to rely on our leaders, our military and security forces, each other, and our faiths."

Banks smiled, waved, and walked away without answering any questions. She would leave the tough part to her press secretary.

Her image was replaced by an anchorwoman.

"There was a small explosion at the Hadron Collider at CERN in Switzerland. The Hadron Collider, as you may remember, was recently under public scrutiny after a team of scientists claimed that planned sub-atomic particle experiments could create a miniscule black hole. Was this explosion a coincidence or did it have something to do with blackwings? Government officials have not ruled out the possibility that blackwings have aligned themselves with terrorist networks," the anchorwoman said.

Mila flipped through some other news sites. They were all playing the same CERN story, and stating the importance of the Loyalty Act, while at the same time associating blackwings with terrorists. They all agreed the President's message was "bold" and "presidential".

Sweat channeled down the nape of Mila's neck and onto her back. Her skin tingled as the blonde hairs on her arm stiffened. *Turn yourself in. They know how to kill or incapacitate blackwings.*

Jenna shifted, startling Mila, and looked at her from her bed across the small dorm room. Jenna said excitedly, "I'm reporting Garrett Webb. I don't care if you want to marry him. He's gotta be a terrorist. He sympathized with a blackwing."

Mila shook her head. She cleared her throat, trying not to speak with a shaking voice. "Don't even joke like that. They'll jump him and take him away. And I don't want to marry him."

"I'm doing this for you. Imagine dating him."

"I've imagined worse things, but if you insist, I'll imagine dating Garrett Webb as I fall asleep tonight." *It wouldn't be the first time.*

"They'll only keep him if he's guilty," Jenna said with the same stern somber look the president had only moments earlier. Maybe Jenna would be president someday.

"You're right, Jen," Mila said. "But don't do it. For me."

"He is cute, real cute, but his coffee shop is a haven for riff-raff. I saw hoolies in there the other day. It's too close to campus. The cafeteria coffee isn't that bad. Why don't we lead by example and go there?"

"Cafeteria coffee is water, brown dye, and a synthetic flavoring. The last time I drank a cup I nearly lost my lunch." Mila's tongue curled just thinking about the strange chemical aftertaste.

Jenna shrugged and nodded. "True. But if we're to keep going there, Garrett needs to leave. He's a bad influence on the students."

"Just ship anyone you don't like off to a factory camp?"

"Factory camp? You actually believe they're real? FEMA stations. Places where they care for families and people who are less fortunate than us." Jenna looked down. "Than me."

Mila had seen the underground e-paper and it had clips, pictures, and interviews. People were captive at these "stations". Younger people were being moved to factory camps where they were forced to work. They were not technically prisons because people could roam free within.

"They receive food and medical care. Besides the super rich, hardly anyone gets actual health care these days," Jenna added.

"We just pay for it."

"True."

Jenna jumped down from her bed and filled two cups of water. She handed one to Mila, who set it directly on the hard mattress. Water helped offset Mila's hunger. Water helped her sleep. The Agorist said there was something in the water, but tonight she did not care. She gulped it down.

Unfortunately, Mila's hunger and poverty were not unique. At least her scholarship paid for books, rent, and some meals. She was not living in a camp or on the streets, and she was grateful for that, but her income was barely enough to get by. Times were hard. Mila knew this all too well. Maybe the water helped. With millions of homeless, unemployed, and foreclosed upon, people should be rioting in the streets. Sure, there were panhandlers, elderly, and scurrying pot-bellied children, but thirty percent of the population was not out there raising hell. What could the government really do? There just were not enough jobs, and employers knew that, or were barely making it on their own, and so the jobs that were around did not pay enough to live on, especially after taxes.

"At least they didn't talk about the economy. Food lines. Work lines. That's not news. We know all about it. Show something positive, like the crowds at church and prayer circles." Jenna shook her head, and then winced. "I'm sorry. You didn't get any money?"

Mila's dad wired promises more often than money, but the last time she saw him, he had lost thirty pounds that he could not spare to lose. Two months was a long time to go without hearing from someone this fragile.

Mila shook her head. "No transfer yet. It'll be here

tomorrow," she said, keeping her chin up, fighting back a frown. "I've got some scholarship money. I just don't know what books will cost yet. Once the store knows a book is required for a course, they raise its price. It's always above the scholarship reimbursement level, too."

"Mila-chick, you're my best friend. Let me know if you need anything. You'd help me out. And you do help in other ways. You're the kindest person I know."

"Thanks, Jenna. Don't worry about me. I have a breakfast ticket for the morning and I'm going to totally pig out, so I'll be fine until the afternoon. I can always work, too."

"You can't. Not with soccer and school." Jenna jumped off her bed and leaned over. "Too much, Mila. Besides, where are you going to work? There aren't any jobs anyway."

"I meant I'll work on a cardboard sign."

"Funny."

Jenna was right. There were no jobs. Mila tried not to think about money. She tried not to think about food. She tried not to think about her father. She tried not to think about the slight ridges on her back, and how her body felt different, starving yet stronger.

Mila spent most of her night watching clips related to blackwings. Men and women wearing masks posted online blackwing confessions. Some were obvious hoaxes. News specials demonstrated various ways to determine if your spouse or loved could be possessed by a blackwing. A minister advised his parishioners to pray for God to protect the congregation from blackwings. One reporter held up a shirt with two slits in the back and a pair of scissors, as if it was news that someone could figure out how to cut fabric. Scientists, religious leaders, and talk-show hosts argued over where the Blackwings came from. Economists explained how blackwings hurt the economy. A gray-haired military general argued over what new legislation was now vital to ensure the nation's survival. Other politicians contended that their party was best qualified to deal with the blackwing problem. There were clips of the sky, a human-shaped object darting into clouds, and a voice yelling, *there's one over there!* Sometimes, it was painfully obvious it was only a bird. People would be filming the sky and anything that moved in it for a long time, if not forever.

Mila waited until Jenna crawled back into bed and was sound asleep.

Something again stirred in Mila's body, in her mind, and it was altering her thoughts. Her heartbeat quickened. She wanted it out. It fogged her intellect, especially when she thought about seeking help. She envisioned the wings rising from her back and lifting her into the sky. Maybe this was not a dream or a hallucination. To be honest, the thought of flying intrigued her. She began to consider the positive aspects. If only a blackwing could help her hunger. If only it could help her find her dad, or even help him find a job. There were even mentions of rewards for information that helped identify a blackwing. The money would help. A lot of students sold blood or participated in a medical study to help pay the bills. A blackwing, or even a suspected blackwing? Premium pay.

Maybe she should try to fly, just one time. She would never sleep anyway. Her brain raced. *Crap.* What was she doing? Every minute she spent thinking instead of turning herself in made her feel like a traitor—a criminal.

Fax News commentators referred to the blackwings as terrorists. But what about the man in the crowd? He had tried to kill the blackwing who was only speaking out, trying to inform the public. Wasn't the shooter the true criminal? Why wasn't anyone condemning him? The president said they had blackwings in custody. She imagined them caged like animals. How else could they learn how to kill one? Self-defense? Thwarting an escape attempt? Or a doctor cutting the wings off with a scalpel? The thought sent a jolt of pain down her back that radiated into her chest like an electric shock. It did not take a biochem class to know doctors and scientists would try horrible things. Anything could be done in the name of science. Imagine the grants. *Forget that premium pay.*

When Jenna had not moved for thirty minutes, Mila quietly snuck out of her bed. In their small bathroom, she cut two slits in the back of an old T-shirt. *Using scissors. Just like on the news*. She laughed to herself. She grabbed a scarf off a towel hook and tied it over her face. A lot of people wore scarves or surgical masks over their face because of the smog, or because they had shown recent flu symptoms, were in a hot spot, or failed a temp test. She would blend in. She kept her head down as she jogged at a fast pace beyond the campus wall. The smell of food and smoke wafted through the air as she traveled past a few late-night restaurants, a tavern, and small groups of people huddled next to hissing lanterns, cooking mysterious entrees over coffee-can fires or small portable propane stoves.

Was there a place in Seattle where she would not be filmed? On a telephone pole, a camera dome. Under a traffic light, another. The top corner of a small commercial office building, yep. Drones buzzed constantly overhead like mosquitoes. Cameras at every intersection recorded all movement. Terrorists brought that on. They missed the larger targets but sure managed to blow up privacy rights.

After hopping a tall chain fence, Mila sprinted into the shadowy abyss of an abandoned and cordoned-off neighborhood, ending up at an unlit track at a closed high school a few miles deep within. Most of the city was densely populated, but as funds shriveled, there were patches in shambles. A few city blocks here and there, dilapidated brick and cement shells, foreclosed upon and stripped down, had been simply abandoned and barricaded. She could sense through moving shadows, whispers, and flickers from the occasional lighter that she was not alone, but the types around her were illegal squatters, likely outcasts and outlaws who kept to themselves. Cops would come through here eventually, but for now hoolies, gangs of unemployed punks and thugs, occupied the surrounding buildings and blocks. This was as safe and hidden a place as she would ever find. She covered her face with the scarf and tossed her jacket aside. It took a couple of pushes, including one that nearly knocked the wind out of her, before her new appendages made it out of her shirt through the slits she had cut.

She stretched her wings. It felt like there was a smaller pair of wings fluttering in her chest, but it was her heart. Something inside her smiled.

"You see everything. You've been watching," Mila said.

Yes.

The internal voice scared the crap out of her. She tried to catch her breath. "Thought so. What's happening to me?"

You've changed. It can show you how.

"Like how to fly?" Mila asked, her breath arriving in short gasps.

Yes. Let us fly. Give it control.

"No," Mila said, her heart thumping. She sprinted and leaped forward, gliding and then landing on her feet. She flapped the wings, lifted into the air, and then dropped suddenly as she forgot to continue the flapping. She had been about ten feet in the air, but it felt as if she had stepped down from only a few inches. Her legs were stronger. Even running was effortless. Maybe she *had* run a mile in under five minutes with a stop. Maybe she *had* shredded that soccer ball through the net, and it was not techies playing a practical joke on a rival school.

You can run faster, and you're stronger.

"You're really here," she said.

Yes.

"Why are you inside of me?" she asked.

It needed to exist, and it fit in you, nicely.

"You keep saying it? Wait. Are you a he or she?"

He? She? No. It.

"It. Well, at least you don't have a penis. That would be weird." Mila breathed deeply. "Am I possessed? Are you a devil?"

Maybe. It isn't sure.

Mila's heart pounded faster. *Maybe?*

It's still learning your world. Not sure what a devil is.

"Do you have a name?"

It chose one in your sounds. Dia bliss. Diabliss. Very happy day.

Diabliss. At first Mila was confused, but then she figured it out. *Very happy day. Yes. Spanish and English*, she said.

A day of existence is a day of ecstasy.

Mila disagreed. *Some days are easier than others, Diabliss.*

Your body's hungry. Needs flesh. It will help you hunt.

Mila was famished, and her stomach did indeed ache, but she suspected Diabliss, or "it", did not quite understand her tastes in food. Flesh was a relatively vague term. She could end up feeding on people or drinking blood. "Eating's not that simple. I don't need food right away. Hunting's out."

You're afraid. It senses the chemicals inside you. How safe is this world?

Safe from cops or predators? "This world's pretty safe. Someone did try to kill a blackwing, though."

Blackwings. Yes. It is a blackwing. That's why you cover your face. Someone will try to kill it...us.

"Yes," she said.

Primitive. We need some metal compounds and elements to make a weapon. Humans can break open easily. We could tear most enemies apart with our body, but best have a weapon to be sure.

Mila stopped running and now walked the fraying rubber track with her scarf pulled back down.

"Sure, no problem, I've got a stockpile of metal I've been wondering what to do with," Mila said. She could sense Diabliss struggling with her sarcasm, but in a strange way detected his, or it's, diabolical pleasure upon realizing that's what it was. "Where did you come from anyway?"

It came through the portal. It was in another world, in captivity, and the hole opened. It escaped. It escaped the never-ending pain and the blue lake of fire. It and others escaped. Blackwings needed hosts. It needs you, but human bodies with blackwings are far superior in strength, agility, maneuverability, intelligence, speed. It made your shell stronger. Do you want it to show you?

"No," said Mila. "Tell me."

It just did. Let it have a turn. You can have control back any time. It will share. It promises.

"No. I need to do this on my own." Mila again secured the scarf over her face and sprinted, faster than she ever had in her life. She drew her wings out—their wings out—and launched herself into the air. Mila, nervously gulping for air, flew over the dead-grass meadow that years earlier had been a football field, over bleachers with the metal seat rows stripped out, and then down again onto the track. "It's all too confusing," she said. "I just want to fly."

She walked another full lap and then jumped again, stretching her wings wide. This time she flew toward the buildings of her college, and then rose even higher, climbing, flapping, and soaring to just beneath the clouds. It felt natural, as if she had always done this, and the relief; it was as if a

31

splinter the size of a toothpick had been pulled out. She had been filled with so many pains. Concern for her father. Hunger. Stress. Flight's wonder erased them all. Nippy moist air fluttered through her shirt, cooling her skin. The rising foul, sour scents from the city dissipated. She was free!

A loud noise drummed through her ears. *Thwap-thwap-thwap.*

Air machine. Behind us.

In her panic, she stopped flapping and spiraled toward the ground. She attempted to regain control, but the ground rushed toward her at a frightening speed. "Oh-crap-here-you-go," she said, ceding control just as she was about to hit the ground.

Her wings flapped and Diabliss veered upward again, darting left and right, keeping low, through trees, around buildings. It stopped on the rooftop of a residential dwelling. Diabliss could feel by the warmth that there were inhabitants inside, and food. But that damned air machine was chasing it. *Whap-whap-whap-whap-whap-whap.* It could not read their thoughts, yet, but feared their intentions. The contraption wanted to hurl fire and metal at the Mila-chick and maneuvered to do it. If they tried to hurt the Mila-chick, it would kill the machine and the men inside. It liked the Mila-chick, and it wanted life.

After another burst of flight and a short run, it finally lost the air machine, but another bother hovered in the clouds not too far away.

Diabliss returned to the ground, running on one of the hardened travel paths. Spotlights from the air machine swept over the earth, searching. Someone else was watching it. There. Electronic eyes on every pole. *Keep human face covered.* Another metal human-carrying device with lights raced toward Diabliss. It would stop the vehicle if it needed to. The car veered around Diabliss, making a loud trumpet sound. Trumpets. Oh, how it hated trumpets. Diabliss chased after the machine. The automobile traveled fast for a human ground device. It let the vehicle and human drive away. Damn. These people were primitive and vulnerable. If they knew how feeble they were, they would have never chased the Mila-chick through the sky.

And they had tried to kill a blackwing, but it could sense more than that. The cruelties. Other blackwings had been killed. Is that what their leader had said, killed? They had been mutilated. The woman speaking, their president, was a professional liar.

There were a lot of humans on this realm. Would it have to battle them all? Diabliss needed to make weapons. Humans could never defeat all of the blackwings if the blackwings united. Blackwings usually kept to themselves, but isolated, they were indeed vulnerable, and it did not know how many blackwings had escaped the bath of fire. It had to find more blackwings, and it needed to make a weapon. Diabliss smiled at the thought of using a weapon in this world. A dark sword would be effective against humans. But wings and strength would be enough for now. *Yes*. Diabliss sneered.

This planet, though. A perfect balance of rock, gas, and liquid, uniquely held together, and full of life and energy. This was much better than the lake of fire, always pulling them closer to it. The White Light had trapped them there for so long. *So long*. The scientists had made a hole, inadvertently allowing the blackwings to flee. The blackwings owed the humans for their freedom, but that did not make them slaves to humans or give men the right to hunt them down and try to kill them and their human shells. The hole the humans had made was now closed, but that would change. The White Light would find the blackwings gone, and they would come looking. They would find a way into this world if they were not here already.

Diabliss ran along the ground, unsure of where it was or where it was going, but the body, the air, all felt so good. But the Mila-chick hungered. It would have to do something about that. There was a lot of flesh. Some edible plant life. Even the ground had minerals. It'd have to tell her about that. The enrichment was so close. It eyed the ground hungrily, wishing to grab some. Maybe it would.

No. She said, *no.*

No. No, it mocked. *Ooh.* The Mila-chick disliked being mocked.

Another land machine on the road approached Diabliss. Lights on top of it flashed. Pretty colors. A siren chirped. An awful sound. A man jumped out. An authority—ha! He held metal in his hand. Too short for a sword. The contraption did something, and he was pointing it at Diabliss and its Mila-chick shell.

"Stop," the man shouted. "Freeze."

That's right. She had covered the face. She did that to hide her identity and this man somehow knew it.

Into the air. The man below hurled something at Diabliss through the metal piece in his hand.

He's trying to hurt the Mila-chick.

Diabliss liked its Mila-chick shell.

Trying to hurt her is not nice, it decided.

Diabliss laughed as a piece of metal ripped through the air nearby. It swooped down, dodging another projectile. After determining that there was a hole in a metal tube hurling small metal pieces forward, Diabliss bent the man's wrist inward so that the weapon pointed the other way. *Oops.* A bone snapped. Diabliss wondered if the man would fire the pieces into himself. No. The hand would not function at this angle. Diabliss had broken something. Oh, Mila would be mad. *Oops.* She was mad. She wanted her body back.

Mine, it said, taking the metal gun, stuffing it into a jacket pocket. *Mila needs to carry this until it can make a dark sword.*

Diabliss flapped away, giggling through the scarf. It liked the Mila-chick. It liked its new home.

Chapter 3

Theo knelt before the altar at the Seattle Cathedral, tears streaming down his face, a yellowed life-size plaster Jesus on a wooden cross before him. Candles, all different colors, thicknesses, and heights, wavered and flickered behind wilting veils of misshapen wax. Some were scented, and the merging perfumes, vanilla, rose, sandalwood, wafted from the twinkling lights. He missed the earlier days, where problems were so small the complaint of the day was fragrance in a candle. The lead-glass tinted windows in the background and at various points in the building's perimeter held their colors, but they were deadened and dull as it was night out. Shadowy pews behind Theo stretched back one hundred rows. Most nights he kept the building open later, but tonight he had shut and locked the doors. Some parishioners would wonder if the world of God was okay, others would just be thankful they could go home to their sofas and screens, leaving their guilt at the dark gray rain-spattered cement steps outside.

Physical attendance mattered less and less anyway. It was an archbishop who had congratulated Theo when viewership of his streamed sermons had exceeded in person visits for the entire region. The popularity was short-lived, and his streaming was soon discouraged. Even a monetized screen brought in less than regular attendance did. But Theo had already built a studio. The flock was what mattered. He would figure out how to bring back the revenue stream.

Only, tonight his "show" was not what he was struggling with. The White Light had entered him two days earlier, and he was not sure what to do. He should have called his bishop, but pride or curiosity had held him fast. At first, he thought it was possession. A blackwing. Oh, how foolish pride could bring a man down. What if it had been a demon? It would be too late. Now, he understood it was different.

The delicate voice from God whispered and soothed him like a warm gentle summer wind. Theo had been blessed by the White Light. God had sent messenger warriors to rid earth of evil soul-less blackwings. The White Light needed his help, or more precisely, they needed bodies. He had to surrender his body to the White Light.

It's just a human shell.

But it's my human shell.

You were chosen.

By God?

Is your faith so weak?

Theo wept. It was a test of faith, and each second that went by without Theo giving his body to the White Light was laced with intense feelings of frailty, regret, and failure. How could his faith be so weak? How did he ever lead congregations in God's name? His next confession could be to St. Peter! Wasn't that what he had always wanted, to enter the gates of heaven?

Satan spat warnings and doubt about the internal voice and cast a paralyzing, shameful fear, but the White Light, the calm firm voice inside, assured him that the body was a gift *from* God, and could be a gift *to* God as well.

Theo's faith battled his doubts. He finally grinned and returned to his solitude and quiet tears. He knew absolutely that what he was doing was right, but he said the prayer anyway. God would forgive him for his shortcomings and doubt and would recognize Theo's sacrifice and the strength it took to overcome a burden of misgivings placed on his shoulders by Satan's clever hand.

"God, if I am wrong, if this is Satan's demon, please cast

it out, or bring me to you through my death."

Theo's heart thumped and swelled. His surroundings brightened as a scorching light entered. The sensation burned, yet it felt so good, as if it were engulfing what was wrong with this world and life in flames. If Theo could have performed one last muscular function, it would be a joyous leap into the air. It felt so good and hurt so bad it had to be God.

A deep voice in his head told him not to fight the light; he was not demon-possessed. Blackwings were the demons. They were foul and evil. They would destroy this world and all the souls on it. They would never believe in God and the White Light. But after the sharp stabbing pains spread along his back, a fear entered, along with doubt, and then his mind and life returned. Theo regained his body once again, and the spirit that had made him want to jump for joy no longer gripped him. He had failed the White Light's trial. He had tried but could not give himself to it completely. *I'm a fool.* The tears falling now were tears of shame and remorse. Would he ever be given another chance?

"Please," he cried, throwing up his hands.

Disgusted, the White Light inside of him prepared to leave. *Someone is worthy of God and the White Light, but it is not you. You could have been a true servant of God.*

Bawling, Theo tugged at his hair until his scalp burned. "No. No. No. No." This light inside Theo was God-given. It was what Theo had searched for his whole life and what he wished to pass on to the people whom he loved so much. It was why he had become a priest, making the decision by the age of seventeen. He loved mankind. He saw the evil and doubt and how the negative forces were winning the battle on earth. Theo had joined God's army. He would do so again if given just one more chance.

Theo's faith ballooned. He thanked God for this test of

his faith. He was truly ready. He pulled his shirt off and prayed again. He grabbed two candles, the hot wax spilling onto his fingers, and placed them on the floor. Kneeling over them, he begged God for the White Light's return. He would do anything. He would give himself completely. He believed.

Theo's hands trembled as he placed them resolutely over the candles' small flames. As the pain increased, so did Theo's resolve. The trembling, he cast away like an evil spirit. He would burn holes clear through his hands for God and the White Light, but along with the hurt, the glory returned. The pain morphed into the glimmering White Light, drawing out God's warrior within him. *Yes*. Now, Theo was worthy of the White Light. It told him so. A stabbing pain tore into him as his back split open. Theo screamed. He screamed again. The pain. It was nearly unbearable.

"Make it stop!" he cried.

The voice in his head said, *no*.

Blood pooled at his knees and spread out onto the hardwood floor. This was what Christ had endured. This was how he too would save mankind, through suffering.

Wings, radiant and majestic, strength unknown to humankind, and a glowing white light. Theo cried, full of joy and wrenching pain. *The light.*

"It's beautiful," he said, sobbing, looking at his shining arms, bright with the White Light, and his wings—beautiful white wings over his shoulders—stretching out beyond his hands.

And now justice.

The luminous white feathers hugged Theo. Tears of bliss streamed down his face. Pure elation. This was virtuous and true. The pain? The skin on his back ripping open? It was worth it, for it would lead him to heaven.

Theo's thoughts flashed by in bursts of white light and then faded into darkness.

The White Light looked down at his frail, pink, human shell and up at the manmade version of a tortured, different man hanging on the wall. His human shell disliked the pain. It suffered, and he would remember that. The blackwings would feel that same pain in their human shells. He would make the blackwings feel pain, and more. They would cease to exist. Uncooperative humans would feel it, too. This feeling, this pain, would be utilized.

He had to find or make a weapon and then find the others. The White Light had already made contact. Some were already hunting. Some were building their empire. *Can't waste time.* This body—this world—had so many limitations, and blackwings would spread like a plague. Time mattered more than ever.

The White Light were uniting, but they had to find the right political systems. They understood empire building better than any beings in the universe. He had been watching, reading, and learning through Theo. With these bodies full of light, he would unite kingdoms and defeat the blackwings. Even better, though, this world would respect the White Light, and that would make sequestering full control of a body much easier. Most humans, for all their nonsense and many weaknesses, would at least understand and accept that the White Light was superior to them and served a higher purpose. This was a beautiful, primitive planet. It needed the White Light more than any other civilization he had come across. There was so much evil here and hardly any justice. He would show them how to really take care of blackwings. And he would show them justice.

Theo lifted the priest's holy book and read. It warmed his heart in so many ways.

Chapter 4

The Agorist crouched in the dark alley, his hoody pulled tight and his face covered with a scarf. Garbage had not been picked up in the city for three weeks, and the repulsive stench, rising from the piled black plastic bags and spilling heaps of unidentifiable rotting trash, reflected this. At least the smell prevented Garrett from thinking about the girl in the coffee shop long enough to adjust his scope, raise his rifle, and turn for his friend's approval. The man, his face also covered, nodded, his thumb adjusting his phone.

Garrett fired one shot. A silencer made from a plastic two-liter cola bottle filled with rubber washers and insulating foam muffled the sound. He had learned that from an insurgent he had killed during his tour in Syranistan. That time the contraption and whistling bullet had been meant for him, this time it was his own instrument for change. Garrett made a thumbs-up sign, but a thin layer of sweat coated his body. These actions were too close to what he had gone through in the blood-soaked swath of hell everyone just called Syranistan. He always feared he would black out and do something he would regret whenever he gripped a weapon, especially at night. Add an unexpected loud noise, and who knew what the hell might happen.

The cameraman focused in on a small dark object, a drone, falling from the sky. It hit the ground with a deafening crunch. These drones were unarmed, but in some cities not too far away, like Portland, Oregon, a transition to armed drones was already happening. The duo advanced, repeating the action a few blocks later. They sprinted away, ducking into shadows as cars passed, or UNSIs raced toward the wrecked drones. His lower leg throbbed. He had the best military-issue prosthetic foot money could buy, but a hard sprint pushed its limitations. They waited patiently when a dog-walker strolled by, the fur-clad mutt sniffing the air, curious about their scent.

The black helicopters in the night sky, though barely audible, were more abundant than ever. Their searchlights occasionally flared, the moon-like white circles sweeping over clouds and rooftops. The military was out in full force. *They're probably looking for blackwings. If there's one thing blackwings are good for, it's drawing attention away from those who want change.*

Garrett tugged his hood tight and straightened the scarf over his face, he stepped in front of his friend's camera and made his statement: "Public surveillance has to go. We will never have freedom in America if every action and movement is filmed by corporations and then sold to our one-world government. Destroy the eyes in our sky before they destroy us."

Garrett and his partner moved on. Several blocks away, they climbed a chain-link perimeter fence wrapping around Seattle's waterworks department headquarters. Even though Garrett draped a towel over the top, he snagged his jeans going over, leaving a slight tear just above his knee. His partner got caught up in the sharp razor wire as well. The grounds and building were empty. A friend of the cause had bought information from an inside person. Second office on the right. A file room. The alarm code 1111 had never been altered since it had been set up, but even if it did go off, they would have at least ten minutes before the cops arrived. The cops had more important things to worry about than an office break-in. Corruption, gangs, unemployed, homeless, and now blackwings. If there was ever a safe time to break into a building in Seattle, this was it. But then again, this was a government building.

The alarm triggered. Although they still had time, the ringing bell was painfully loud. Information bought and sold was often outdated or fraudulent and rarely worth the price paid, though the data they needed was found where they were told it would be.

In and out, they sprinted away in under five minutes, a folded file stuffed into the back of Garrett's sweats. Inside was a Material Safety Data Sheet for Flo-Rite, the chemical added to public water supplies. Six pages of health and safety risks associated with Flo-Rite. The names of several key chemicals, patented as anti-depressant and anti-anxiety medications, were listed in sections two and three. The percentages were listed as trade secrets, but it was enough to know that the water was medicated. *Drink six to eight glasses of water daily, more when food is scarce.* That was the government recommendation. Of course, when food was scarce and people were more likely to wake, stir, and rise up, they would get very...very...sleepy...

Garrett and his friend split up.

When Garrett got back to his apartment, he scanned the information sheets, downloaded the clip, and then wrote a short article to add to his underground e-paper. *Confessions of an Agorist* was gaining popularity. That was what he wanted, but the high-risk hobby would eventually have consequences.

We must get the word out about Flo-Rite. People have a right to know.

He peered out his curtains, expecting black helicopters, a police squad, or UNSIs to surround and bust open his one-bedroom apartment. Returning to his desk in the living room corner, he sat down and continued to write. *This is a political crime. I am willing to pay the price and do the time. Freedom will be mine.* His eyes burned, but he typed until he was finished. He ran a stylometry program that would make it difficult to profile him as an author, ran a program that would scramble the files used to write it so it could not be traced to his computer, and then saved *Confessions of an Agorist* to a black-market memory stick that also could not be traced. He again looked out his window. His apartment was on the top floor of an old stone building in the University District and had a clear view of Lake Union and the sparkling lights of downtown Seattle. There were several black helicopters roving across the sky, still visible, spotlights still sweeping, clouds and buildings lighting up beneath their rays. Undoubtedly, there were drones up there as well.

Don't fly blackwings, hide. Were they truly evil? Did he now have two enemies? If this government was looking for them, maybe the blackwings were not so bad. At least Garrett and the blackwings had a common enemy. Good or evil, heavenly or demonic, the Amero-fascists would use the sudden appearance of this unnatural force to pass more laws, put more UNSIs on the streets, and take away more liberties. Garrett shook his head. *As if there are any left.*

He slept, restlessly, sweating, maybe there was a scream or two, but he slept.

Chapter 5

Mila stayed in bed until Jenna left, but she could not stay in bed forever, and she was not ready to turn herself in to U.N. Security. Not yet. Mila bound her back in a tight sports shirt, even though she was getting better at keeping the wings tucked deep within her. It made her feel safer, though not anything close to safe. A blackwing in a video showed the best ways to conceal wings. "Complete crap," Mila said, twirling around in front of her bathroom mirror. An oversized hoody made her feel even bigger and puffier than before. The slight ridges seemed so obvious. She turned in another circle. People would notice. They would have to, and then they would dissect her. Other videos said the government would imprison blackwings and dissect them, like flies under the hands of wanton boys. Mila did not trust the government or UNSIs to do the right thing. The underground paper was right. UNSI forces had been providing domestic police and security, as well as surveillance, and this was all illegal. She had looked it up. The *Posse Comitatus Act* prohibited federal forces from any kind of civilian law enforcement without approval from congress or the state government. Even if the UNSIs were a privatized police force from China, they still reported directly to the federal government. UNSIs also had a shoot-first reputation. Leaked video footage had surfaced in an issue of *Confessions*. It showed a home invasion with UNSIs flushing out and slaughtering squatters. It showed a clip from the official news story blaming the same assassinations on anarchists, or as the authorities called them, DTs. *Domestic Terrorists*. Not a bad tactic, pit those who want change against those who need it the most.

She still had no idea what to do with the gun. She was mad at Diabliss for even taking it. She had watched enough crime shows to understand it was evidence of a crime. She did not know much about guns but understood that they were dangerous. The first night she had placed it in a makeup travel kit in the bathroom. In a shared bathroom there was really no such thing as a personal possession and a make-up bag would not work for hiding something as illegal as a stolen firearm. Her heart pattered and sweat broke as she hid the handgun in her pillow, then in the bathroom, and then in the garbage can. She finally settled for burying it inside her laundry hamper. That was one thing of hers she knew that Jenna would never touch. Laundry. They each had their own basket, and some of Mila's sweaty soccer clothes smelled like old soup.

Mila checked the news and the internet again and found an unsettling headline: "Blackwings Rebel in Seattle." Of course, it had to be Seattle, the dreariest city of all. Some blackwings, refusing to turn themselves in, had congregated on Capitol Hill. Three blackwings circled the small section of Seattle like crows in clouds until a line of helicopters swept in, dispersing the blackwings but not catching them. Capitol Hill had been cordoned off, but military and UNSI checkpoints did not matter. Blackwings could maneuver better than military helicopters and drones. The helicopters followed but could not catch them. They would have to change their air-attack strategies. A separate report showed a blackwing being assaulted in midflight. The helicopter's own camera showed the blackwing plummet toward the earth and return with a pole, which the blackwing then jammed into the rotor. As the helicopter tilted, the blackwing grasped onto the helicopter skid and drove it down, spiking the military bird into a tree, killing the soldiers inside.

She finished a *Confessions of an Agorist* story about foreclosed homes and squatters. UNSIs were moving into bank-owned homes. It was a trade for U.S. debt owed to China. Squatters inside the foreclosed homes refused to vacate. Skirmishes ensued. The official report said the squatters were domestic terrorists. Fax News went as far as saying that these terrorists were thought to have been hiding blackwings in the foreclosed homes. Only, the people forced onto the street by armed UNSI's in the *Confession's* video looked like plain, desperate, homeless people—regular folks, families and all.

Most people were sympathetic toward the homeless. These were hard times for many. Banks and corporations had been bailed out and subsidized, so why not people. If the economic recovery was indeed right around the corner, then a civilian bailout would not last long, right?

The media's spin came. Blackwings were being associated with crime and domestic terrorism. If blackwings were maltreated, would people empathize with them? No. People disliked different. They always had. Mila wondered what she would think without a blackwing inside.

She felt Diabliss stir as she put on a coat and then took it off, deciding that a coat over a baggy sweatshirt would draw too many looks.

They've come through.

Mila's heart rate jolted and then picked up speed. The internal voice frightened her.

"Who?" she asked, adding some old, dirty clothes kicked under her dresser to the laundry hamper.

The White Light.

What's that? Mila asked.

The White Light are the enemy. Your scientist opened the hole again, or the White Light found a way in on its own. It felt the stir. A particle wave. You wouldn't have known that's what it was. There will be trouble when they find us. They held us prisoner in a bath of blue fire. The burning. The fight.

47

The pain. Oh, they are so torturous and cruel. It won't let them win this time. This world is different. They had more power before. They'll inhabit human shells just like blackwings. We're closer to even now.

"And you're not cruel? You broke a man's hand. A police officer's hand," Mila said, speaking out loud. Maybe the violent actions were why she thought of Diabliss as a "he" even though Diabliss kept referring to himself as an "it."

The man tried to kill you.

"I know, but I have to ask, are blackwings evil? Are you evil? Jenna says it's possession."

Blackwings are independent. Possession is hard to define.

"And evil?"

So is evil.

Mila concentrated while Diabliss read her thoughts and memories from books, movies, and television about demonic possession. She felt foolish. If he were indeed a demon, he would likely lie.

Demonic possession doesn't seem real. Have human scientists ever caught or isolated a demon?

"No."

From the biology of the human brain, I would guess people made something up to explain brain chemistry functioning incorrectly.

"Good," Mila said, conceding he was likely right. Although she was only in her first year of college, she tended toward science and away from ghosts, magic, and unverifiable explanations.

"Could you possess me?" she asked.

Could I take possession of your body and control it? No. But it can change you. It has already. Wings and more.

"Great," said Mila. She could sense the blackwing processing her word, and then deciding between the two definitions. Diabliss showed excitement as he interpreted great being wonderfully great, and then she sensed disappointment as Diabliss realized the sarcasm. She would have to be careful that her sarcasm was not taken literally.

"Can blackwings fight the White Light?"

We might be too late. Blackwings should have united earlier. If you choose to die, it would understand.

"Not that I'm considering that, but what would happen to you?"

It will cease to exist.

"Will you go to heaven?"

Not sure it understands. What's that?

"It's where people go when they die," Mila said. "It's a better place."

Interesting. If Heaven's a better place, then why not just die and go there?

Mila was skimming through her text messages. She stopped. "That's difficult to explain."

This heaven. Have you been there?

"No."

Have you seen it?

"No."

Is there proof?

"No." There was not. Mila shuddered. She had never thought about heaven falling outside her science realm and closer to what should be classified as magic.

It might be another dimension; maybe you will open a portal someday and go there without dying.

"Maybe," said Mila, now suspecting Diabliss was a demon. In one short conversation he had taken away her cherished heaven. "So, this 'light'. This trouble. What will they do? I mean, will they attack me, or us?"

First, they will take power. They will take control of your planet. Then, they will hunt us, and yes, they will attack and try to kill us.

Mila had so many questions, but it was a bit overwhelming. Diabliss somehow sensed this, and in a way, tuned himself out, disappearing somewhere inside of her.

Mila focused her thoughts. *I still think it's weird that you're inside of me, and we can read thoughts.*

Mila finished checking her phone, wondering how much longer she had before it would be shut down. This long without talking to her dad, he was not paying the bill. If her phone went dead, she might never hear from him. She would have to skip a few meals so she could pay it.

She wanted to go down to Garrett's coffee shop, but since she was cash poor, she turned on a tablet instead. And Diabliss was right. Another press conference was on the news. She turned up the volume, and then her heart nearly burst as the door shot open and a person ran in.

"News. On, now," said Jenna, with heaving breaths. "Soccer's canceled." Jenna reached over and turned the volume up. "Angels. Sent by God," she said.

Two men and a woman stood behind the president. Spreading from their backs were beautiful white wings, like feathers from a dove, but brighter like a full moon surrounded by a dark sky. The three beings had their own form of luminescence that projected from their bodies. The white light mesmerized Mila.

Diabliss stirred again. *Don't stare too long or listen. Human eyes and ears can be easily deceived.*

Mila got mad as Diabliss fought to turn her away. *Am I being easily tricked by you?*

He squirmed within, and she tried not to stare but failed. She absolutely loved the wings. They were so beautiful, not black, rubbery, and batty, like hers.

It's them, Diabliss said. *They are here to kill us.*

Mila sighed. *No. It's angels. Angels are good.*

If killing blackwings is good, then yes, they are good.

Maybe the angels were good. At least they looked like angels. She again wondered if Diabliss was a demon. For nineteen years of life, she had always believed in heaven. Now, a family-reunion afterlife seemed as likely as a visit from Santa Claus or the Easter Bunny. Is that what demons do, cause one to doubt their faith? No, not likely. Mila had always had more doubt than faith.

The president faced the camera. She had her austere, presidential-at-a-time-of-crisis look, but still bared her teeth at the crowd. With so much going wrong in the country, she usually hid from the press. This was not just an elephant in the room, this was an elephant in the room with wings.

"My fellow Americans, and those of you around the world who will be listening to this message. It is time to explain some circumstances that have led to our current, unprecedented time. A great depression has ravaged the world economy. Evil networks of terrorism, domestic and international, have spread. As a new world order works to bring change to a world that cries for something different, blackwings and terrorists wreak havoc—if not on our peaceful cities and nation, on our weary minds. Several months ago, an experiment intending to study particle physics at the Hadron Collider in CERN, Switzerland, created a minuscule black hole that lasted for less than one thousandth of a second. During this apparently harmless blip, a portal opened. It is now confirmed that this is how the blackwings, a new species that either possesses humans or creates a new breed of humans, arrived on Earth. We do not know exactly how they crossed over, or even how many crossed over.

"But we do know that the blackwings crossed through this portal which was inadvertently opened. The portal was quickly closed and remained closed. Until recently. The portal, or miniscule black hole, was recreated, but not by CERN physicists. A different breed entered through this new portal. I believe they are angels, sent to us by God to provide comfort and safety. You must make your own decision as your faith allows. That is what we do in a country with religious freedom. I have met with our new guardians, and I am working to build an alliance with them. Unlike the blackwings, the angels' communications have been clear. The angels are on our side. The White Light will guide us through darkness and terror."

Mila's jaw dropped open. She clenched her fists. Diabliss wanted to tear at the screen. He wanted to find the White Light and hunt them. Diabliss wanted to kill these beautiful creatures.

Mila and Jenna looked at each other in complete disbelief. Only Jenna was smiling, tears welling.

"Angels," Jenna said excitedly, as the press conference ended, clapping her hands together.

"Demons," said Mila, in a near whisper.

"Yes." Jenna hugged Mila. "Angels to battle the demons. I'm glad we finally agree. Praise be to God," said Jenna. "Now, you have to believe in God."

"I never said I don't believe."

"You don't worship."

"I don't *attend* worship."

"We'll work on that," said Jenna with a wide grin, her tears finally spilling through. She firmly grasped Mila's shoulders and shook them excitedly. "I'll pray for you."

"Don't. I'd hate to have you waste a prayer on me and have it work. Save it for an amputee. Someone who really needs it." Mila stepped back. "I don't know what to believe," she said, scooping her cell phone off the desk and stuffing it in her front jeans pocket. "How do we know which side is good?"

"Angels are good and demons are bad. The demons work for Satan. It's been that way since time began," said Jenna. "Since soccer practice is canceled a bunch of our teammates are going to church. Come with us."

"Not today. I'm still not feeling well. I'm going to catch up on my studies and finish an essay. Maybe grab a cup of coffee later. It's bottomless Tuesday down at Sweet Perk."

"Do you have everything you need? Do you have enough?"

"I'll beg on a corner," Mila said, peeling a five out of her pocket. The five Amero bill was from an emergency stash that she had hoped she would never have to raid. Unfortunately, she had, and this was the last dip into her shallow reserve.

Jenna wore a big smile. "Wonderful. Still not enough to go shopping. At least you've put on weight. Starvation's showing on a lot of people. Don't feel bad. Even students can show hunger. You're not skinny, though. I'm a friend. I can talk about your weight."

Jenna, her eyes sweeping over Mila's body, had to have noticed the shrinking jacket and Mila's concealed wings. Blood rushed to Mila's face and her adrenaline surged.

She can't see your wings, said Diabliss. *It made your body just a little bigger to help hide the wings. Barely noticeable to the human eye.*

You made me bigger? asked Mila. *I know you call yourself an "it," but you're definitely a "he." A woman would know better.*

Jenna continued to size Mila up and down. "Looks like muscle, though. You're cut. You look great, especially on the field. Nobody can keep up."

"Thanks."

Jenna sighed. "Mila, this has changed me."

"I'm glad to see you so happy." At least somebody was.

53

Jenna hustled out the door, off to church with her friends, not even wiping her tears, instead wearing them like a badge of faith, showing everyone how happy she was that angels had arrived.

Mila nodded and shut the door, wishing she could share Jenna's enthusiasm.

Mila felt so ashamed about not having money and her dad not having a job, but only three in five U.S. citizens were employed, and most of them were overtaxed and at or barely above the poverty level. Her situation was not unique, nor was she worse off than most.

But the wings. She could not hide them playing soccer, could she? And what if they searched students? They could. Nobody had rights anymore. Not with all the terrorism.

She threw a backpack on, even though she was just going for coffee. The pack covered her back and helped her feel anonymous.

Outside, the sun shone but a cold wind cut through the campus. A gray squirrel scurried toward Mila and then raced up a tree. Mila wound through students and crossed between the libraries. She checked the air when a bird flew overhead, but her eyes were drawn especially to each passing helicopter. Before, they had seemed to blend; it was easy to deny their existence. Now they took on an ominous presence. She wondered if they were even necessary. There had not been any major terrorist attacks, even though there was a lot of social unrest. The black specks in the sky certainly did not make her feel any safer. They were constant reminders that she was being watched.

The White Light lent courage and strength to Jenna, but with Diabliss' warnings, Mila felt fearful. Were they angels? Were they good? If they were either, it meant Diabliss was bad, and now, maybe she was bad too. She could not talk to Diabliss about this until she understood him better. Or maybe he knew everything she knew. If he could read all her thoughts, he had not told her.

When she arrived at the coffee shop, Garrett opened the door for her. Mila smiled, thinking he was being polite, but scowled upon realizing it was just a coincidence. Garrett was looking both ways outside the door, probably scouting for a member in his army of female fans.

She stepped up to the counter, fumbling for the five in her pocket. This time, she would keep the change.

"The usual?" Garrett asked, making his way behind the bar.

"And I supposed you know what it is?" she asked, smirking.

"Maybe," he said.

She waited for something sarcastic, but Garrett moved to the espresso machine and went to work. When he came back, she paid and dropped the loose change into the tip jar. "No cow tipping?" she asked with a smile, pointing to the crude drawing of a cow on its back, smoking a joint.

"No," he said. "It's been outlawed. Tipping cows over is eco-terrorism because it hurts the beef industry. But you can tip me any time."

No, I actually can't. She sat down and quickly scalded the tip of her tongue with her drink.

Go get him. Procreation will feel good.

"No, I don't think so," she said. Not only was she not the one-night-stand type of girl, Garrett was out of her league.

Two men sitting at a corner table looked up. Garrett did as well. She had said it out loud. Mila blushed. Diabliss *was* a demon. Food, sex, and a fight—that was what he seemed interested in. She popped open her laptop and tapped the WiFi.

Garrett leaned over the table with the two men. He palmed a black memory stick and stood next to a guy with a shaved head, a few piercings, and tattoos—a punk who looked like a hooley.

Mila looked down and then up again. She was curious about what Garrett was doing but shook her head after losing herself in his blue jeans. A physique like his did not match most students, or even the typical barista. He seemed out of place. She found herself wanting to pluck him up and take him some place quiet.

She wiped her mouth. *Diabliss, are you making me drool?*

Garrett plugged the memory stick into a port. *Why didn't he use WiFi?* It was probably the latest copy of *Confessions*. This was how it usually spread. Social media and searches censored it out. It had to be transferred physically. The man handed the thumb drive back to Garrett. For some reason she had thought that only students read the underground paper, but then again, he could have downloaded anything.

She replayed the White Light's press conference. She despised the White Light, and now struggled to even think the word angel. Was Diabliss making her loathe them? She resolved to at least wait for evidence that they were not only angels but that they were here for a purpose that would benefit mankind. Only, what kind of being would trap Diabliss for all those years? Unless they were in hell. She would have to get more details. Didn't he say it was a lake of fire?

She looked across the room. This time she did not look away when Garrett caught her gaze. Instead, she moistened her lips and parted them slightly. Shit. What if she lost control and grabbed Garrett, throwing him on the floor right here?

Just do it.

"No," she said aloud, blushing. *You're a total slut, Diabliss.*

"Watching something good?" Garrett asked, coming to

her side.

"You keep looking outside," Mila said. "What are you watching?"

"Looking out for a friend," he said.

"Oh, one of your many female fans?"

"Ha-ha. No, not a fan. Not a four year."

"You don't do the four-year thing?"

"Campus girls either want a frat boy or they want someone who will piss off their parents. Admittedly, I'm all for upsetting authority figures, but I've already upset more than my fair share."

"I bet you have."

Garrett walked away.

"Garrett," she said.

He turned around. "You remembered my name. I'm flattered."

"How do you know I didn't read your name tag? Even though it actually says, 'Name Tag', and not Garrett"

"Name Tag is my real name. Garrett's a nickname."

"You're smarter than you look," she said. Then she regretted what she had said. Her sarcasm nearly always came out too fast. "I'm sorry. I didn't mean that. Do you have the latest *Confessions*?"

"Not sure what that is."

"Don't worry. All the students read it. Even those who disagree with it. They need something to argue against."

"Don't have it, whatever it is."

She pointed to the two men across from her. "Do they have it?"

He shrugged, but then nodded. "I think it's an old issue," he said.

"I've read it then."

He left and then came back and handed her the black memory stick. "It's new, but you didn't get it from here."

"I didn't get it from anybody. Nobody gets it from anybody. Nobody really cares, do they?"

"Nobody cares if an independent coffee shop that's not part of a Wall Street chain is shut down. And I've got a mouth to feed."

"You have a kid?" she asked, surprised.

"No. *I* have a mouth, and I need to feed it." He smiled and put the stick in her laptop, and then pulled it out when she nodded.

Put your mouth on his. You have a mouth to feed.

Mila's lips parted again and her sultry smile returned. She shook her head as if she were shaking water from an ear. "No," she said.

Garrett looked at her quizzically. The two men looked toward her again.

I am so stupid. Garrett thinks I'm crazy. It was hard to think things without saying it out loud. *Maybe I am crazy.* Needing a distraction, she immediately clicked the issue open.

"There's a good article on a factory camp that doesn't technically exist but isn't too far from here. I don't pay much attention, though. That kind of stuff doesn't interest me." Garrett walked away.

"Too bad," she said, sighing. She shook her head. It figured they would not have much in common. That would make him perfect.

Chapter 6

Mila's coach would never allow her to skip two days of practice, especially with an upcoming championship run. They had a midmorning workout and an afterschool scrimmage scheduled. She thought about feigning illness, but that would only bring out a sports-medicine doctor. That would screw things up big time.

She knocked on the solid slab door. She peeked through the window next to it and saw the coach sitting at his desk. He motioned for her to come in.

"Mila, I was just about to fake that I was on a phone call so I could send away whoever was at my door. Glad to see it's you. Now, I can relax." He put his feet on the desk and his hands behind his head. The coach was in his late thirties. He had played for the Sounders, and in his day was a city hero. Soccer hoolies sang his name. He was young for a coach and still had a solid soccer physique. Most of the players respected him, and maybe even flirted with him, despite him being gay. Fortunately, Mila did not have to play that game. Not only was she a freshman with plenty of time to develop, she was already getting starts and goals for her team.

"Coach," she said, "I have a problem."

"I know. I've been meaning to speak with you. Your mind's not on target. It happens. But that's why we have habits. Your work ethic and speed is carrying you through. Your speed..." He shook his head. "It's unbelievable. I'm afraid a track coach will see you run and try to swipe you from me. And your ferocity is unmatched. So I wanted to talk to you, because I can tell that your thoughts are elsewhere, but I also wanted to tell you not to worry, so it doesn't get in your head and hurt your game."

Mila's jaw quivered. "I need to take some time off." Diabliss counteracted her rising emotion, only she did not want him to. She needed to gain sympathy. Diabliss did not understand the value of conveying feelings. "It" did not have a feminine side.

The coach made a fist. "Fake it until you make it. That's the saying. That's my advice. A break's coming. Thanksgiving's just around the corner."

"I can't..." The tears were coming.

The coach's face reddened. He jumped up. He was upset. She knew he would be. This close to a championship run? If the tears fell, though, that might help, but Diabliss pulled them back, tampering her exposure again.

Diabliss, no. I need the tears.

Then they came. She wondered if Diabliss had pushed them out. If he had, maybe they should switch schools and join a drama program.

"How much time are we talking about?"

Mila, speaking through quick breaths and slowly exhaled sobs, told him her plan. Two days tops. A Friday and Saturday. She would get her running in. And then she told him about her missing dad.

"There are travel restrictions."

"Not where I'm going. It's just Portland."

"Some routes are restricted. You'll be back to practice on Monday?"

"And I'll get my cardio in. I'll run lots of miles and keep track."

"Your dad's sick and you need to spend time with him."

Mila looked at him, confused.

He was nodding his head. "When a parent's sick, and you need to spend time with the parent, that's one of the valid reasons for missing a practice. Family sick leave."

"Family sick leave." Mila nodded in recognition of his help. "I truly believe he might be sick, and that's why I haven't heard from him for so long."

"Excused," he said. "See you Monday. Keep track of how far, and how many times you run."

She planned to run fifty miles and fly even more. She grabbed his hand and thanked him. Maybe he was not so bad after all. Coaches had to pretend they did not care sometimes.

Now, what to tell Jenna. The truth?

"Mila-chick," said Jenna, staring incredulously, "you're not going alone."

"Yeah," said Kathy, smacking Mila on the arm.

Mila disliked lying to her best friends. If they knew she was going out of town without any money and only a University public transportation pass, they would throttle her, turn her in to the coach, anything to keep her safely on campus. "I have to see my dad. He's sick. Maybe even dying. He's supposed to be in Tacoma." Mila knew that if she told her friends the truth, that she was going all the way to Portland, Oregon, they would really freak out.

"Supposed to be?" asked Jenna. "Let's call the hospitals."

"I've already tried that," said Mila. "I'm going, and you two can't stop me. If it was your father, you'd do the same thing. It's just thirty miles away."

"Thirty miles of chaos," said Jenna. "Terrorists, blackwings, hoolies, disease."

"That's just hype. I could jog the thirty miles and still be safe."

They were in the small dorm room shared by Jenna and Mila. Kathy and Jenna stood between Mila and the door. If they only knew Mila could not only push them right through it, but Diabliss was urging her to do it. *Not funny, Diabliss.*

What if we hurt them? Stay out of it.

"Hello. Planet Earth calling Mila from Seattle," said Jenna.

"There she goes again," said Kathy. "When you wake up, try listening to your best friends." Kathy threw her hands up. She went to the mini-fridge and pulled out a beer. Kathy kept her beer in Mila and Jenna's fridge so it would last until the weekend. "You're making me do this. Drinking before the weekend. And this is a two-beer problem." Kathy shook her head and glowered.

"Uh-huh," said Mila. "Try not to smile while you're enjoying that. Am I going to make you meet a senior at the *library* tonight as well?" Mila did finger quotes when she said "library."

Kathy smacked Mila on the arm and grinned. Fortunately for Kathy, the light punch did not hurt. If it had, Mila might not have been able to control a pooling outburst from Diabliss. He was still learning the nuances of this world and that Kathy hit everyone. Her friends understood it was only a punctuation mark, usually an exclamation point.

No, Diabliss. That was not a strike, Mila thought just in case.

"How do you both think I got to school this year? My dad didn't drop me off. I took the train from Portland, and then a bus. Everything in this room I carried on my back. I think I can make it one city away. You two have class. Jenna, you have a test, and Kathy, you have a paper due that you should be in the library—the *real* library—researching. I've been excused. I'm going alone."

"Don't take the train," said Jenna. "You need a driver who looks out for passengers."

"Sure, Jenna. I'll just hire a car, or maybe even one with a driver!" Frustrated, Mila shook her head. "Must be nice to live large. But for the rest of us…"

"Metro busses," said Jenna. "There are kids in my prayer group, not even students, they ride them all over the place. They go all the way to Tacoma."

"Yeah," said Kathy. She grunted as she hit Mila this time, but still, no matter how hard she tried, Kathy failed to elicit pain. Kathy looked disappointed.

Still not a strike, Diabliss. And yes, I'm getting annoyed too.

Mila sighed, pulled her hoody and backpack on, and then put her hands on her hips. "If it makes you feel better, I will take a thousand Metro busses. But it will add two hours and a million transfers and will only increase the danger level."

Jenna hugged her.

Kathy smacked Mila's shoulder and then wrapped her arms around both friends. "You're so stubborn, Mila-chick," she said.

At Sweet Perk, Mila, Kathy, and Jenna sat at the coveted sofa next to the fake fireplace. Mila had her hands out as if she were warming them on the fake orange flames.

"Careful," said Garrett, wiping down an empty table. "It's hot and those painted logs have been known to roll out."

Mila blushed. She was rubbing her hands together by the wall to bother Jenna, who hated the fake fire. Now, it was her face that was scorched, not phony flames.

Jenna looked at her, and then at Garrett, rolling her eyes. "Oh, get a room, you two."

Garrett turned to leave. His face was now red as well.

"Wait," Jenna said. "Garrett, or Mr. Webb? If that's your real name."

"Jenna. What are you doing?" Mila whispered.

Jenna turned to Mila and put her hand up. "Maybe you can talk some sense into our good friend Mila-chick."

"Yeah," Kathy chimed in.

Garrett asked, "Now, why would your good friend Mila-chick listen to me?" He looked to Mila.

Both Jenna and Kathy faced Mila, who was perhaps even more red.

Kathy spoke first. "Why would you listen to him?"

"Stop embarrassing me. Sorry, Garrett. I wouldn't."

Garrett looked at her, ignoring Jenna and Kathy. "It's okay, I wouldn't listen to me either."

Mila nodded. As she looked at Jenna, she put her hands out toward Garrett. "See?"

"Just in case you ever need it, though: Bad advice is free. Good advice costs two Ameros."

Jenna interjected, her face between Garrett and Mila's gaze, "Don't take either. Both prices are a rip-off."

Before leaving, Mila caught Garrett looking at her three times.

After stepping up into the Metro bus, Mila climbed over several pairs of legs, found a window seat, and waved to Kathy and Jenna, who stood at the curb. The glass had a layer of condensation on it. Mila drew two circles, rubbed in the center of each and then added a few straight lines. Glasses. She peered out through them at her friends. Kathy smacked Jenna on the arm and pointed. Mila erased it all, leaving a larger clear spot. As they waved, she pinched her nose and then pointed toward the center aisle. The bus smelled sour and old, like a sweaty sock. She looked outside at the cold drizzling rain, and then back at the people around her. They had likely begged a buck and would ride inside, warm and sheltered but without a destination, until the driver kicked them off or asked for another fare.

She remembered the warmth of the fake fire at SNP, with Garrett and her stealing glances at each other, maybe even flirting. Her heart fluttered. Was that what she and Garrett had been doing, flirting? She turned her thoughts to her father. She should be worried sick about him. She should be combing streets, neighborhoods, work camps, whatever, until she found him. She should be on the verge of tears just thinking about all of this. And she was.

Her phone buzzed in her pocket.

miss you already better hurry back or kathys going to ask out Garrett Webb jkb cu soon update us or we'll call da unsis onya.

Mila smiled, rubbed away droplets that had snaked across her window, and again pressed her face closer as the bus lurched away. Her attention fell on a woman with a plastic grocery bag wrapped over her head. A free hat to keep the rain out, not a new fashion trend. It had a W on the side for the only megastore in town. Mila looked down at the different W on her own hooded sweatshirt. As bad as her hunger was, as much as she missed her father, she was living a preferred life and the UW was a much better W. Mila whispered a thanks, which confused Diabliss, and then closed her tired, heavy eyes. She only had time for a short rest.

When the bus stopped for the fifteenth time in fifteen minutes, Mila finally got off. She had kept her promise to take the slower bus. She would go to Tacoma, too, though she would also travel nearly three times as far away on the high-speed train to Portland. Even though the train was notoriously dangerous, and Portland had been on the news for riots and the blackwing news conference, she had no choice but to lie to her friends. They would never understand. She needed to find her father and to do that she needed to go where she had heard from him last, Portland.

Chapter 7

Theo swiped through the thin tissue pages of his human's Holy Book, smiling and nodding as he quickly reached the end. He had observed for several days through the eyes and ears of his host and did not need to familiarize himself with this world any more to understand that humans would readily join his side and serve the higher purpose. A door behind him opened. Shocked by the sudden sound, he stood, spread his wings, radiated light at the intrusion, and rushed at the person entering. Theo needed a weapon, but this body was already much stronger than when he had entered it. Much stronger.

The intruder, a dumpy, thin-haired man with small shoulders and a concave chest, an assistant in Theo's old life, shielded his eyes with his arm, terror written on his face. Just as he turned to run, Theo spoke.

"It's me. An angel in Theo. I'm here to save your world."

The man trembled and dropped to his knees. Theo loved the respect. This first loyal servant would be useful.

"You're glowing...are you a blackwing?"

"No, my dear friend." Theo laughed. "I was sent by God. Your God. I am in Theo's body, which he has offered to me in order to save mankind from blackwings."

"You're an angel?"

"Yes. One of God's angels."

There was a knock on the door. "Theo, it's time to go on air," said a different man from the hallway outside.

Yes. The shell he had taken spoke through a communication device that transmitted his solicitations throughout the planet. The information stream went out to more viewers than did the other hosts he had explored. That was why he had chosen to settle in this body. He could convert so many humans to the cause, and this would place him rightfully at the top, where he could gain control.

"I'm ready," Theo said, smiling at the assistant. "You will help me save the world, and I will let you live in eternal light."

The man, weeping and still on his knees, fervently grinned. He placed his palms on the floor and pressed his belly downward until it too touched the floor. His weeping turned to bawling.

Theo delighted in the tears of joy and worship. He crouched down and patted the man's head lightly. "Rise. We will work together. Your God is very unhappy. This world has harbored evil for far too long, and now it is in grave danger."

The man stood up. "You've been sent by God."

"Yes. To smite those who stand in God's way."

"And you're an angel?"

"Yes. I already confirmed this," said Theo, gripping the man's shoulders and pressing until his nails pierced the skin. "God loves mankind, and that's why he sent angels. We are true to his path."

"I won't doubt you again. I don't doubt you now." The man's legs wobbled as he stood. He wiped his tears and running nose with the sleeve of his forearm. "What can I do?"

"Obey me fully. Your people await redemption and salvation," said Theo. "I will bring righteousness to this world. And justice. So much justice."

The man stood with his head still bowed. Theo appreciated the gesture. He disliked it when common men looked him in the eyes while standing this close. It was a sign of familiarity. It lacked acknowledgement of hierarchy and respect. He appreciated a loyal servant of the White Light, but Theo was not here to give comfort. *Maybe someday.* He was here to battle demon-infected humans. He would cast the whole world into a lake of fire if need be and burn the lot right out of existence. By now the blackwings would be scattered around this world, but even if the foolish creatures did not unite, he would hunt them down one by one.

There was another knock on the door, and then it opened. "You're on in thirty seconds," a panic-stricken voice yelled.

Theo disliked the surprise. He fully extended his wings and intensified his light. The man shielded his eyes and within a blink, Theo clutched the man's throat so hard that a small trail of blood trickled down his neck. "Perhaps, a warning before you enter, if you enjoy this human life. This is a battle betwixt good and evil, and evil is full of surprises, is it not?"

The wide-eyed man, scared witless, gasped for air until Theo relinquished his grip. He cried out. "Who are you? Theo? Is this a costume for the show?" He dabbed at the marks on his neck with the palms of his hand.

"I am an angel in Theo. Sent by God."

"He's an angel," the first man reiterated emphatically. *"Sent by God."*

"I'm here to destroy those called blackwings and damn them for eternity, along with anything or anyone who stands in my way. There is an army of angels rising, and we are here in answer to so many prayers. We are here to fight evil and save mankind."

The newcomer collapsed to his knees, his face suffused with wonder and fear. Theo's skin radiated a brighter white.

A young woman in a business suit shuffled down the hall, her low heels clacking on the vinyl floor. "Prayer Channel now. Time is up. People at home are ready to click on something else," she shouted. "Where's Theo?"

"We're here," said Theo. Yes, these men would stand strong. "And we're ready for the world, are we not?"

Chapter 8

Outside the train terminal, people lingered in various groups around small enterprises—a snack, smoke, and vape booth, a taco cart, a guy selling bottled water out of a cheap styrofoam cooler, melted ice and condensation dripping down the plastic bottles, and a one-man street band, slapping plastic pails with wooden spoons. Mila steered around hooley gangsters and hastened past a wall of middle-aged men who hungrily eyeballed her. A homeless man with a skinny dog tried to garner sympathy. Mila wondered what Diabliss would think about how she felt sorrier for the dog than the gray-haired human with leathery skin, faded tattoos, and revelatory facial scars.

Inside and down the stairs, the tube was even more packed than above. People likely came down to stay dry and warm and use the public restrooms. Shady street vendors tried to sell her black-market goods draped over arms or hanging inside open coats. Designer watches. Wrist Phones. Necklaces. Bracelets. Knives. Glass pipes. Gum. Candy. Lighters. Purses. Even drugs and small bottles of booze. Selling or practicing business without a license was illegal, but these were discouraging times; people were desperate to earn anything, even if it was just a single Amero. And all items were likely counterfeits. Mila was a rare student who understood the value of one Amero. It was enough to get you through one, maybe two days. Sheer distress showed on the faces of those who pressed into her with forceful smiles and insistent voices, all trying to earn. *You must own this. Here. Take it. It's perfect for you. Don't walk away. You buy? Three*

Ameros but today only two. Okay—you're too smart. One. Over and over again. Mila did her best not to make eye contact.

As a wall of UNSI officers swept through, speaking to each other in some Chinese dialect, trinket-laden arms went into sleeves, stuffed bags flew over shoulders, backs turned, and people shuffled a short distance away. Money was pulled back or tucked into pockets, and in seconds, the small mobile enterprises shut down like a wave, only to reopen hesitantly as the officers walked away. Even though the vendors went great lengths to hide what they were doing, the street selling was obviously a low priority for UNSI as there were camera domes throughout the underground terminal.

When she heard the song, chant, and claps, her heart quickened. Hoolies. Organized thugs. The traders and sellers quickly finalized deals and dispersed, rushing and shoving to get away. The nervous street vendors made their way up and out of the terminal, anxious to get out and escape what was about to happen inside.

Mila pushed into the crowd, found her way to the turnstile, and entered a platform where it was much less crowded.

The chanting and clapping got louder. There was a panic as the people on the platform where Mila was now standing realized that hoolies were approaching. Mila hoped they were not coming, but the sounds were getting closer, and where else would they be going?

The marching hoodlums boot steps and chanting grew louder. *Shit.* Then she remembered. The Sounders FC soccer team was playing their rivals, the Portland Timbers. Portland's soccer club was notorious for their rabid fans, particularly the Rose City Hatchet Club, a spin-off gang known for knives, axes, crime and terror. Clashes between the two radical forces on game day were imminent. Take hundreds, or maybe even thousands, of people unafraid of gathering in large groups, unafraid of riot, terrorism and disease, and then divide them and place them on opposite ends. Seattle media talked about how bad the Portland soccer fans were, but always failed to mention that the Seattle gangs were the same. The Emerald City Elite, known as the EC Elite, were notorious criminals outside of being soccer hooligans. There was no way to say that one side incited crime or violence more than the other. Soccer was the only professional sport left in the northwest and tickets were cheap. The other sport franchises had been sold to more profitable markets or no longer hosted public viewings. These rabid fans lived for game days. Outside of game day, they were just organized thugs.

Mila understood the fear in the eyes of the fleeing vendors as they ran from the crowded terminal. In fact, the people on the platform were just now realizing they were going to be trapped and buried in the new train, in a tube, hurtling in and out of underground tunnels, without the ability to stop, while surrounded by brutal, rabid gangsters.

According to *Confessions* even UNSIs and city police gave the EC Elite a wide berth. They did not want a street war or for various thug groups to unite. They understood the sheer numbers, but according to the underground newspaper, the largest reason was that the hoolies occasionally provided cheap "security" for corporate interests and were easily paid off. Ignore the petty crimes. Ignore how they terrorized civilians. Call it youth, shenanigans, and pranks, if they were on your side or could be bought by those who could afford to pay.

Hoolies hopped over the turnstile; the gate attendant was long gone. The people around Mila pressed and packed together.

"Where are the UNSIs now?" inquired a nervous man

next to her.

"They're everywhere except when you need them," answered a woman hugging a waist-high girl staring up from her legs.

"Can you blame them?" asked a teenager, who was likely skipping school and only steps away from being a hooley himself.

Mila lifted her hood up and tightened the scarf over her face. Maybe if she looked like them, she would be left alone. If they saw the giant purple "W" on her sweatshirt, though, they might think her privileged enough to harass or rob. Not that she had anything to take.

A roar erupted as a train pulled up and the doors hissed open. The hoolies at this point numbered in the hundreds and would not fit on this train car alone. Mila followed her group, though it dissipated as some broke for the outside, obviously deciding to allow this gang to cut in front. Mila did not have time to waste. The swarm now moved as if it were a single amoeba-like organism. Its cell perimeter kept its contents within, only shrinking enough at points to squeeze through a door, breaking apart only when another opening made it preferable, and then reconnecting into its single mass once inside the train. Diabliss stirred within, unafraid, yet comprehending the danger of the situation, the possibility of being crushed or assaulted in the standing-room-only crowd.

The hoolies, wearing neon-green hoodies and tough arrogant stares, pushed and shoved their way into the mass of frozen-eyed civilians. The doors hissed shut and the train pulled away from the platform.

A purse lifted and floated away through a sea of hands. The owner yelled and reached for it, but it was long gone. The original thief blended into the crowd, as hooley friends grabbed the woman up before she could gain any ground going after him. She slapped, hacked and backstepped until another group pushed in from the other side. She spun around, lashing out again.

Mila's breathing picked up. She could not risk exposing herself as a blackwing, but it was only a matter of seconds before they would discover her, standing alone. She could handle herself. She knew she had strength beyond what these men could dole out, and she knew she could relinquish control to Diabliss, but that would be horrible. She could feel him seething. His emotions alone were nearly taking her over. When some of the punks pushed into her, surprisingly, she shoved back. When a large man knocked over the little girl, who fell to her hands and knees, Mila tapped on the man's shoulder. When he ignored Mila, she tugged sharply on his ear.

"Apologize," she said, knowing that if he even looked at her wrong, she, or Diabliss, would go off. Mila, extremely agitated, was losing control, as if the cells in her body and mind had been dosed with racing fuel.

"Sorry?" he asked.

Mila practically leapt out of her skin. She was furious. The hooley was interfering with her mission and about to face the wrath of a blackwing protecting its host. "Don't say it to me," Mila said, jamming her finger into his pudgy chest, and then pointing to the young waist-high girl in tears. "Say it to her. You knocked her over." Mila found herself jumping lightly on her feet as if she were nearly weightless. She was trying to stop herself from lunging at him, scratching him, striking him.

"Are you on crack? Shit, I didn't think there was any left. Do me a favor; tell me where you get your drugs. I need a good lead." The man's head was shaved. He had scars across his face and tattoos crawling up his fat neck.

Mila stepped forward, but then jerked herself back as if she had hit a wall. *Diabliss, are you doing this, are you jacking me up?*

Yes.

Mila, feeling euphoric, shook her head in disbelief. *Jesus Christ, Diabliss, I love it...*

She swung out, cracking the man in the jaw. One of his friends jumped in, but upon seeing that Mila was a young woman, stopped himself and instead laughed at his friend.

Mila's aggressor dropped to his knees and looked up. His face reddened as he lunged forward.

Mila had had her share of brute knocks. Soccer was a contact sport, but she had never punched someone before and had never felt the bone under flesh striking bone under flesh. She had never felt the power as someone went down under her, and it was like scoring the game-winning goal against a rival team. This man disgusted her. And now he was pushing up and coming at her for more. Thoughts flashed through her mind, his alternatives and hers. She chose the one most likely to send him back to the floor, a closed fist moving down like a hammer at the back of his skull before he could fully stand.

He collapsed again at her feet. His mates quickly engulfed him, but they were all laughing now. A few pulled their friend to his feet and propped him up. He staggered a bit. His eyes crossed and then straightened. He shook his head as if quieting a ring. Another cheer erupted as someone shoved a bottle of whiskey into his hand.

Mila readied to fight again as she was pulled into the group. Her opponent grinned and then held his arms out, as if wanting a hug. Mila shook her head, but then hands pushed her forward from behind. He placed one arm around her, and then he kissed Mila on the cheek. Her elbow was poised to hammer into his ribs, but there was no groping, and the man gingerly removed his arm from around her, and then he bowed.

The crowd cheered again. Someone grabbed the whiskey

bottle, and after it made its way in and out of the crowd, surprisingly, it landed in Mila's hand. There was silence as she looked down. She imagined what kind of germs pooled on the glistening glass top, but she put it to her mouth, grimaced, and then took a small swig, just enough to coat and burn her throat.

After Mila smiled, the crowd again erupted, and then they went back to their business, while Mila stood amongst it all.

Was she now an honorary member?

"Now this is true love," the man who had attacked her said, grinning. His eyes were still slightly crossed, and he was missing a front tooth, though that was not Mila's doing. His breath reeked of booze, yesterday's hamburger, and stale cigarettes.

"Careful, my guess is she kills after she mates," said an older man in his late thirties.

"Actually, my lovers usually just kill themselves," said Mila.

A new bottle, rum, was thrust into her hand, but she shook her head and passed it along. They coerced her into singing an FC Sounders song with them as penned civilians, outsiders, nervously watched. Mila winced. Their words were more like shouts than music. They leaned over and shook their fists for emphasis with each word. They certainly would not be performing at the cathedral this Christmas.

The man she had knocked down talked to her enthusiastically about soccer, the Sounders, and the players, and how great they all were. His nickname was Pumpkinhead. When he discovered she was a soccer player, the entire group seemed to celebrate her achievement, and she was promoted to near-celebrity status. Mila did not care. At least they were no longer threatening civilians, especially the little girl whose mother found Mila's eyes and nodded, acknowledging her appreciation. Mila's victim coerced her into a slow-motion reenactment. He had no shame about the situation whatsoever and introduced her to several friends. Oddly, *she* was the embarrassed one. Her first fistfight ever, her first bonding experience with a gang, and in a way, she enjoyed both.

Approaching Portland, the singing returned until the older man, who had made the comment about Mila killing her mates, told everyone to shut up. His name was Uno, and since they obeyed him, he had to be their leader. He was alert and speaking with a group, possibly determining their marching or looting strategy.

Mila distanced herself during this plotting, returning to the other side, where the isolated civilian crowd stood. She tried not to look the frightened passengers in the eyes, mostly because she thought she might grin. The train slowed to a train stop in Vancouver, Washington, just across the river from Portland, Oregon. Voices and shouts erupted. The hoolies scrunched against the glass and furiously pounded on it.

As the doors slid open, the group poured out, just as similar groups of soccer fans erupted from the trailing subway cars. Outside, were the Portland hoolies. A sea of forest green shirts. An ambush. Hatchets in hands, though the sharp edges were turned in, probably part of a fair-fight rule. The glimmer of a knife changing palms. Sharp side out. Probably a small handful who broke rules.

Knowing they could not meet the Seattle gang in Portland without police action and UNSI interference, the Rose City Hatchet Club, Portland hooligans, had jumped the next town up for a surprise attack, or more accurately, a surprise invitation.

Diabliss urged her outside. *Defend new friends.*

Her eyes danced across the crowds as they clashed. The

high-speed train was about to leave. Two against one, outnumbered, and the Portland hooligans were better armed. The worse thing was that she wanted to join in. She imagined herself smashing faces, kicking knives out of hands. She saw a young boy, Chookey, a very young hooley she had just met, go down to the ground. A group of rabid Timbers supporters quickly encircled him and kicked at his head.

Join the group. Save the boy. Join the fight, a soothing voice whispered from the back of her head.

No. This is time I can spend searching for my dad. Her argument was firm, but she put her hands out to stop the door from sliding shut and, instead of whizzing away, she squeezed through. The thoughts of her missing father turned to anger, a smoldering hatred for everything wrong in this world.

Diabliss, I'm not kidding. They can't know we're a blackwing. Absolutely no flying, and no killing.

She felt a surge of extreme pleasure as she gave up control, and even more as Diabliss ripped open the crowd, saving the young boy first, and she felt elated as Diabliss pounded her fists into surprised faces, one after the other.

From inside the battle, Diabliss spied a pretty face following it and smirking. It laughed as Diabliss kicked and punched, but it was always watching Diabliss. Diabliss fought its way across the crowd to attack the man, but then it felt the small yet so familiar beat of another blackwing. How could it have missed the signals? It had gotten too carried away with the fight. It was so proud that the Mila-chick was enjoying her human bonding experience and finally appreciating the improvements to her physical shell.

Diabliss nodded as their eyes locked. They smiled at each other.

The other blackwing, in a stronger, larger human shell

tugged Diabliss out of the crowd. It could have resisted, but it did not.

The battle raged alongside the two blackwings, the gangs oblivious to their meeting.

The blackwing shared its human name, Anders. It had not picked a separate name as Diabliss had, and he called himself a *he*. He had truly become one with his host. *Anders and this human were equals.*

Anders had organized this small but growing army. He wanted Diabliss to join them. Mila needed to find her father.

It doesn't share the shell, Diabliss told him.

Anders laughed. *You don't share your body equally?*

It will in good time.

Demand it. Take it. We could be hunting the White Light, together, right now. We could be so much stronger together, stronger than the White Light even.

Yes, so much stronger, and it likes to hunt the White Light, but no, not yet.

Mila was fighting for control again. She was too confused and was losing trust.

It will see you again. It will think about our possibilities.

It jumped away and then ceded control to Mila. It wanted to keep control. It thought about keeping control, but not today. It liked hunting the White Light, but it also liked the Mila-chick.

Mila did not fully understand everything communicated between the two Blackwings.

"I'm letting you go," Anders called out to her across the still-heavy fight. "Your blackwing's weak and stubborn and it will get you killed!"

Anders then made some signals to some men who were nearby and shouted orders to the Hatchet Club, calling off the fight. He winked as he bowed to Mila.

There was something about Anders' eyes. The purple hue mesmerized her. Was it because he was a blackwing? Was Diabliss encouraging an attraction to him? That sounded like something he would do to increase her chances of survival.

The EC Elite declared victory and marched on as the small thug army jumped into various vehicles and raced away.

The fight had exhilarated Mila, and she had trouble breaking away from them as she followed the Seattle FC fans, marching over the railroad trestle into Portland. Though once she was across the Columbia River and stood on Portland soil, she walked away from them.

The group called after her, but she ignored their pleas. Mila hung her head. Even if she had only fought and marched for less than an hour, it was an hour she could have spent searching for her father. She made up for it through her running speed and endurance. Although she was initially mad at Diabliss for manipulating her chemically—jacking her up with adrenaline to draw out the violence and rage, and then feeding her dopamine so that she would not only enjoy it, she would crave it like a drug—she welcomed his alterations to her body that allowed her to cover ten times the amount of ground in a fraction of the time. She searched everywhere she could think of for her dad. He had not even lived in his apartment long enough for a single resident to recognize his picture. "Are you sure?" she asked each tenant in the building. The manager thought he had moved into a camp just south of Portland, but a transient said a police raid had cleared the camp, called in when some of the homeless began squatting in nearby neighborhoods.

"Nothing brings in UNSIs quicker than a squatter," said the leather-faced man. "Just ain't fair. Houses are empty anyway. These squatters is families. Kids and all. Just ain't fair."

He directed her to a wall with men resting against it, waiting for under-the-table day work. Her dad had stood at that wall some time back. One week ago? Two weeks ago? Three weeks ago? Longer than that, one man said. What Mila did know was that the longer she went without finding her father or hearing from him, it became less likely that he was even alive.

After three long days and nights of relentlessly searching, she found only more tears. Her feet and calves cramped. Even with Diabliss' modifications to her body and her increased stamina, he could only do so much. She had covered a lot of ground. She needed nourishment and rest.

Diabliss encouraged her to stay in Portland with Anders. *We can build an army and continue searching.*

"No. My dad would want me in school." Maybe not, though. At one point in high school he had suggested she drop out and work.

Mila understood Diabliss' motives. He incited her to riot, creating, altering, and re-routing her internal biochemistry, making Mila feel like she was going insane. But in a mad way, his survival instincts made sense. Diabliss was right. She had bonded with a group, even though they were raunchy thugs. Human survival was always easier in groups, and it fed an outlet for emotions buried deep within, while fostering an escape from thoughts of her lost father. Redirection. Another survival method. Move her thoughts away from something that was tearing her apart, something making each frantic search, each failed lead, end in something other than heaving sobs.

Diabliss, you don't understand how a daughter loves her father. I know it's a weakness, but it can't all be about my–– our survival.

Before returning to Seattle, she met with Anders again,

this time on a street in Northwest Portland. Mila was chasing a lead on a dishwashing job her father had applied for. She did not know which was worse, that her father had applied there and did not get the job, or that they forgot him and only found his application in a heap after she begged the manager to dig through it. As she stepped out of the restaurant, Anders stood there in jeans and a long black leather trench coat with a hoody underneath.

"How did you find me?"

But then she knew. He had been following her all along, and now she knew that Diabliss had kept this secret.

"I want to help you," Anders said.

Mila held up a picture. "Can you find my father?"

He shrugged. "The streets are pretty full, and they're always changing. There are a lot of drifters, homeless and lost souls."

"But you'll help me find him."

"Of course. I'll keep my eyes open," he said, "for a fellow blackwing, and a debt of gratitude."

A group walked by. Mila and Anders paused their conversation until the young men were several steps away.

"What if you're not helping a blackwing? What if it's just Mila?"

Diabliss stirred within. She considered his feelings, but she was still Mila Sadis, and Diabliss, though inside her, was still Diabliss.

"Then we're left with a debt of gratitude." He grinned. "And you're more than just a girl. Together, we're stronger than either of us can be on our own. I saw you fight, and that was probably your first one."

"I'm a student and not a fighter," said Mila.

"You looked pretty content throwing down a few days ago."

"What am I supposed to do, become a hooley punk and

give up being me?" she asked, her voice thick with sarcasm. "I just want to find my father," she said. "And then I want a normal life."

Anders shook his head and chuckled. "A normal life? That's not going to happen. And when it doesn't happen, you'll need me. When you need me, I'll demand my own favor."

She disliked his words, except he said them with more charm than arrogance. She wondered if his charisma was an added blackwing feature.

Anders held his hands out. "The favor won't be anything freaky. Probably just a coffee and a chance to make a pitch to a strong gal who deserves a good life. That said, the hooley life ain't so bad. These streets gave me my life back. I was lost before I was found. You like coffee?" he asked.

"I do. I like it hot. I like it bold, and I like it strong, but I like it in Seattle." *With Garrett.*

"If I ever go to Seattle, it will be with an army, and I don't need a university to teach me that you'll be back in Portland soon."

"You're dreaming." But Mila smiled. There were worse things than having someone on your side. And he was cute and confident, but there was another side to him that tempered a confidence she had mistaken for arrogance. He did have a sensitive side. If not for a stupid crush that would never be reciprocated, she would be slamming espressos or drinks with this bad boy.

"Yeah, maybe I am dreaming. I'm known for that," he said. "Anyway, I hope you'll come for me. I'd love it if you owed me that cup of coffee."

She squinted. Anders was doing his best to hide his teeth when he smiled. His teeth were pointed and sharp. Yes, of course, another weapon. Diabliss had suggested that change as well. And she did find that sexy. And his eyes! The purple hue with turquoise specks that looked as if he were wearing colored contact lenses. Enchanting. *Absolutely.* Yes, another weapon. Who wouldn't follow those eyes?

She had to get back to school or call her coach and beg for more time. She had to get away from Anders before he convinced her to stay any longer.

"Another time." Anders held back his jacket, revealing a can of spray paint tucked into his black leather belt. "This one is for you, and it's free of favors." He tapped on the side of the can. "Flammable aerosol and a lighter. I call it a White-Light surprise."

Anders had a mischievous look. Diabliss giggled. She nodded and took it, confused. She backstepped, turned, and jogged away.

She allowed Diabliss to take over and fly her back to Seattle. In the dark night clouds, filled with thunder, lightning, and rain, she sensed both Diabliss' yearning and fear. The blackwing, Anders, followed them halfway to Seattle, his silhouette flashing, illuminated by the electrical storm. Diabliss chased him off two different times, but it was unclear to Mila if it was a game, a defensive move, or if Anders was even really gone.

A few blocks from the University, Diabliss landed, ceding control.

Mila finally arrived back in her dorm room and crawled into bed without even changing her clothes Even if her dad was notoriously unreliable, he was all she had. She tried to remind herself that this was nothing new, and then swirling emotions battled over a dad who had run out on her before, her desire for a young man she could not stop thinking about, a new find who was interesting to say the least, and a desire to fly, to be strong, to take control of a life that was spiraling. It was a battle, but in the end the tears won. Jenna, her best friend, finger-combed Mila's bangs until Mila's eyes dried completely as she cried herself to sleep.

Mila was in her bed, her eyes closed, and her breathing and heart rate had slowed. Diabliss knew Mila was asleep and that her brain patterns were minimal. But it had to ask.

Mila, we need to go out and collect a few things. You said it could protect you. It will. You said not to make a dark sword, and it won't, though it needs something more than a human shell and a small metal pistol. You said not to hurt anyone unless it needs to save our life, and it will try its best. It promises. Now, it has to ask, Mila, can it go out and fly?

Mila stirred and rolled over.

Mila, can it go out?

Mila mumbled, "Tired. Just let me sleep."

It will keep you asleep. Yes?

"Yes. Sleep," moaned Mila.

Diabliss was thrilled. It loved flying in this world. It loved sharing a body with Mila, though it wished she would do more with it, as the physical shell was capable of so much more.

It will always try not to hurt anyone. It promises.

"Uh-huh," Mila mumbled.

Diabliss listened. Mila's roommate slept peacefully, her breathing and heartbeat slow. Without a sudden loud noise, she would remain in this state. Diabliss got out of bed, and through memory and by touch found the clothes it needed, including the scarf and hoody with the slits.

There will be a day when you don't need to hide who we are, Mila-chick.

Diabliss closed the door slowly, allowing a light click, and then crossed the hall, hopped down a flight of stairs, and then jogged outside. Within a second Diabliss had listened with the best of its senses and determined there was no one near. Before it hit the bottom cement step outside her dorm, it wrapped its face, and pushed out its wings. *It won't always have to hide,* it assured itself as it leapt into the air.

Diabliss knew it had to be quick. It had only borrowed Mila's body a few times. It always asked, though. It was easier to get her to agree when she was in this state of mind. It wanted to take her body and procreate with Anders. But Mila would not like that. She might like Anders someday. She was just shy. Maybe another time. Diabliss had to hurry.

Flap wings hard. Use full strength. Ahhhh. Diabliss loved the wind. If it was up to Diabliss, it would shed everything and have the cool wind running over the entire human shell. It would feel so good. Diabliss knew Mila would never allow this. Even at night. There was a word for that. Mila used it. Prude. Mila was a prude. Well, Diabliss would keep working on that. This body was soft in more ways than one. A soft side she was saving for someone like Garrett, and a soft side that made her defenseless. Diabliss could harden the physical shell from the inside. There were alterations to their body that Mila would approve of but were difficult to explain, so Diabliss did not always share. Mila knew she was changing and never told him to stop. She liked being stronger. She liked her new speed. She even liked flying. If only people were really free in this world, but they lived in their own lake of fire.

Diabliss had flown toward a mountainside a few nights earlier and found a red earth rich with minerals and microbes. Now it needed something darker. And her body could not handle rocks. *Not yet.*

Ah. There it was. A field. Piles of wood pieces. Piles of stones. And the rich warm black earth. There was so much here. Diabliss landed and cast its hand into the moist warm soil. Just a few handfuls. The body was difficult to feed without water to wash the soil down. *No. Just eat what you can and hurry.*

Then it heard the noise. *Pesky men. Grating flying machines. Everywhere.* The bigger machines had men inside. The smaller ones did not. They were tracking its movements in the sky. There were so many planes, manned and unmanned, and signals and waves bouncing here and there. How could he read them all? *Sorry, Mila. Self defense.*

A helicopter hovered overhead, and the side door opened. UNSIs dropped onto the piles of earth and stone and onto the ground between them. They had something wing-like hanging from their backs that slowed their descents and stopped them from breaking bones. The night sky filled with the human rain as nearly fifty men landed near him. They had metal pieces pointed at Mila. Not nice. And not fair. Not fair for them. One more handful of dirt. Now, Diabliss was ready. Yes. A metal piece was flying closer. Oh, not one. Hundreds. *Get low. Into the dirt. Out of the dirt. Jump. Fly. Yes. They won't shoot toward their helicopter.*

Diabliss changed course and flew straight at the black helicopter. It hovered, but as soon as Diabliss' direction was verified, it tilted and veered.

Fly with speed. Yes. Mila's shell flew faster than the machine, especially at short distances.

Diabliss gripped the landing skid and shoved the machine over. This sort of machine could not fly upside down. Yes. It would crash. The people inside, though. They would not die. Diabliss smiled. Mila would be happy.

But it had to make a point. Making a point was self-defense. Diabliss swooped down, grabbing a man by his helmet. Oops. The man unsnapped his helmet on his own. He flapped his arms and tried to fly. Diabliss felt laughter brewing.

The next one just fell to the ground. Not quite as amusing.

Diabliss veered, spun, swooped, grabbed men, flew up, and dropped them.

Just one or two more. They were trying to hurt the Mila-chick. *Self-defense. They are all trying to hurt its Mila-chick. Not nice.*

Most flapped their arms on the way down. They wished they could fly, too. Maybe they should be nicer to blackwings. Blackwings could show them how to do a lot of things.

After the men stopped shooting at Diabliss, and instead scattered and hid, Diabliss rewarded them by no longer flying the men into the air and then dropping them. And it had let all of them live. Mila would be proud, but Diabliss would practice humility and not tell her. Mila was fast asleep. Diabliss appreciated the Mila-chick, and it enjoyed this world so very much.

Chapter 9

Garrett's close friend Devon had gone missing and was most likely in a factory camp, or at least his phone was. Maybe his captors were jamming the signal. Maybe they had confiscated his phone when they brought him in. After keeping the coffee shop open an extra thirty minutes, hoping that Mila would come in and give him an excuse to delay his next action, Garrett hit the lights, locked the door, and hopped on his motorbike. Looking for blackwings was a good cover. Every person with a phone would be trying to record something they could show off or sell. The clouds were too low for drones to be effective, so this was a good night to roam. He could even say he was trying to help the UNSI effort to spot blackwings. He would tell them his vehicle transponder was maybe broken or had fallen off, and it had, even if helped by a hammer.

Garrett saw a black helicopter combing the sky like a dragon made of shadows with infrared eyes. The UNSI birds were easier to bear with the motorcycle helmet on. No noise. Just the road. But still, the helecopters reminded him of his urban enforcement duties in Syranistan. The skies there had raged like a hornets' nest, the rising smoke pushing the swarm into a frenzy. He broke a sweat. How could he not?

His friend, Devon, knew about the camps. He was out of work, his parents had kicked him out, and he owed money to a bank. He was a perfect candidate for a factory camp. Devon was aware of this, and that was why he had a GPS locator app on his phone and had given Garrett the code. Garrett had punched the number into the Internet and had written down the location when his friend had not made contact for five days. Devon was a caffeine addict, and Garrett's shop was the only place where he could afford the coffee—it was free to the poor. Garrett would be reported for sure if that kind of business model ever surfaced.

Why had he made the promise to Devon, the promise to break him out? Devon was an anarchist, and risking an entire operation, for one member, went against their code: The cause above all else. But Garrett was still addicted to chaos, and his addiction went as deep as their cause, a cause he was willing to die or go to prison for, and probably would someday. *Damn, this resistance shit is getting out of hand.* Why couldn't he just get up the nerve to ask that soccer player out, go back to school, and join her on her quest for higher learning? Live the drone life, just let someone else thumb the buttons for once. He hopped on his motorcycle, heading toward Devon's blip on the palm-sized screen, traversing slick streets on a cold, rainy fall night. Not only was Garrett taking chaos hits like it was crack, he had somehow regained his loyalty to humanity. What was going on in the United States was wrong. The Amera-fascist slip, even if the country was experiencing a downturn worse than the Great Depression, was wrong. The people and corporations benefiting from the economics of a police state and a suffering world were the worst kinds of people. When the nation's prison system became a number on Wall Street, when it became more profitable to imprison Americans than rehabilitate them—especially if you could put them to work—then good, ordinary citizens like Devon disappeared.

This mission was too high risk with too little to gain to involve his resistance network, so he would not have anyone watching his back or creating a diversion, and he did not even know if he could get near Devon, and if he could, whether he could break him out. Garrett's vehicle transponder had been disconnected earlier in the day. If he even went by a police officer or checkpoint, he would have to make a run for it and if caught would be jailed for tax evasion since the government-mandated beacon he had conveniently disabled measured and taxed the miles driven. The law had also been passed so that corporations and tracer armies could monitor human activity and use that data to market to them and predict them. *The corporations need every advantage they can get. It's the corporations who will lead us out of this downturn...* But more importantly, UNSIs would know where citizens were at any given moment, statistically where they were likely headed. If Garrett drove near a crime scene, critical infrastructure, or somewhere he did not need to be, if he became unpredictable, an UNSI team would be at his side within minutes.

Garrett stopped his bike at a stop sign even though it was night and the street was empty. For someone with so much disrespect for the government and laws, he obeyed the laws that made sense. Sure, the traffic light manufacturers paid kickbacks, along with the road construction and asphalt companies, but a stop sign still served a decent purpose. After the revolution, with everything in the world toppled, he would personally crawl out from beneath the rubble, put the knocked down stop signs back up, and sweep debris off the roads.

Side streets were less risky, but it would take longer to get there and to get away. His black helmet and clothes hid his identity, and his bike, though loud, was quick and cut through neighborhoods like a chainsaw through a dry log. He had a gallon of gasoline in his tank bag, allowing him an extra sixty miles without the need to make a stop at a gas station. He had customized his bike, and could flip off the lights if need be, making him more difficult to spot or to follow at night. He shivered. No matter how well he weatherproofed himself, cold wind and water droplets snaked their way in, biting at his skin. He liked it because the minor discomfort reminded him that he was still alive.

When he got within a mile of Devon, or at least Devon's phone, he would pull the pipe bomb from his pack and turn off the cycle's lights.

He would put a hole in their fence. He would put a hole in their psyches. He would put a hole in the system. And...

Boom.

Chapter 10

Mila stood on her toes in order to peer down and catch a good angle from her dorm window. Several students stood near two tables set end-to-end beneath a canopy in the courtyard. It was a "voluntary" checkpoint run by students, but the students were accompanied by armed UNSI officers, their black uniforms, bullet-proof padding, and helmets standing out in the myriad of student colors. There were similar stations outside each dorm, and library, and at the main entrance leading into the student pavilion. Each group was accompanied by a portable nurses' station as well. Students had lists and were checking off those who volunteered to have their backs inspected and give a cheek swab. Since the checkpoint was voluntary, it did not violate the law, but how long would "voluntary" last, and who really knew what would happen with the "did not volunteer" list, or more importantly, the actual students on that list?

She gulped. A biochemical cocktail from Diabliss steadied her hand, otherwise it would be shaking, especially after another rough night of sleep. Mila disliked the dreams that came with sharing her body with Diabliss. Eating dirt? Dropping people from the sky? Getting so much pleasure out of it that she could not stop, like a little kid dropping sticks off a bridge into a gurgling creek and then watching them bob and float away? Maybe Diabliss could help her sleep deeper. Forget her dreams.

Diabliss, I don't want to remember my dreams anymore.

Okay. It can manage that.

They are just random synapses and brain chemistry, right? Dreams don't mean anything, right?

Diabliss did not answer. Maybe dreams confused him as well.

Mila threw on her extra clothes. At least Diabliss kept her body temperature down. Normally, wearing a few layers under a baggy sweatshirt made her sweat piggishly, even on a cool, late-fall day like today. The bulky clothing covered the wings well enough to avoid looks, but when the spring and summer sun hit, school was out, and it was ninety degrees, layers, baggy clothes, and a backpack might not fly. What then?

After taking a deep breath, she stepped out of her dorm building. In a way she wanted to just turn herself in. At least she would not have to lie anymore or worry about being caught.

"Mila," someone called out.

She kept walking.

"Mila-chick, slow down, girl." The person was right behind her. Then she felt a punch on the side of the arm. *Kathy.* "I saw your name on the list. I wanted to check you off personally," she said, clipboard in hand.

"Yeah? What list?"

"You haven't heard?"

"No," said Mila. "But I can't sign up for anything right now. I'm running late." She quickly turned and walked away.

"It's a checkpoint. We're absolving ourselves. Proving that there aren't blackwings on campus. Sending a message to other schools, too. We're striving to be the first."

"First what?"

"First blackwing-free campus."

"That's great, Kathy. Check me off. I'm no blackwing. Do I get a free chalupa from Taco Bell?"

Not allowing Mila to brush her off, Kathy jumped in front of her, poking Mila with the clipboard. Mila glanced at the list. Most names were checked off, but not her name. A sea of blue checks—and hers, white like a bleached spot, a flaw, on new denim jeans.

Mila looked away from the list, wondering if Kathy would strike her with the clipboard next rather than her fist. "Yeah. Can you tell me about it later? I'm meeting Jenna."

Kathy's eyes widened. She grinned. "Jenna will totally understand if you're late. She had the early morning shift. Right here. Jenna created the whole program. It's started. Right here on *our* campus. Absolution checkpoints by people who want to fight Satan. People who follow God, the United States, and angels." Kathy puffed her chest out. "It's god's work."

God's work? Only, Mila understood what that meant. They know the "truth" and disregard contradictory evidence. Their side is right, so they can do no wrong. They will love anyone who is one of them, or at the very least has a chance of becoming one of them. It stops when they realize the conversion will never happen.

She needed to just hurry away. "Do I have to pay anything? I'm low on cash right now."

"No you—"

"I really can't afford to pay for a health inspection. You know I'm broke. I'm running late, too. Gotta go!" Mila spun around.

"Mila-chick," Kathy called out. "It's free."

"If it's free just sign me up."

"Talk to Jenna. She'll explain…" The voice faded until the distance finally muffled her out.

Mila jogged, deciding not to return to a walk, even when she was out of Kathy's sight. She needed something to smooth out her nerves and the running helped. She could not always rely on a calming biochemical infusion from Diabliss. She had to have some control, even if nothing she could do would lower her stress levels.

She was also still worried about her dad. If she went another week without hearing from him, she would have to go looking for him again. He could be working. Maybe he had to move far away. Maybe he was on the streets nearby. Would their phones get shut off soon? Hers still worked. She slowed as it buzzed in her pocket. It was a message from Jenna.

A few hours later, Mila opened the door to the coffee shop, passed Jenna, and then smiled at Garrett. She reached into her pocket and blushed. She panicked and groped at the other three pockets. "I'm so sorry. I thought I had money with me." How did she lose her last five? A thought inside her told her to just kiss him. It was Diabliss, nudging her. *No.* "I'm sorry," she said again as she turned to leave.

"Wait." Garrett's fingers dipped into his tip jar, extricating several quarters. He punched a few numbers into the till and put a few pennies of change back into the tip jar. "It's on me. Even the tip. Just tell your friend to quit glaring at me."

"Oh, Jenna?" Mila shrugged. "She thinks you're a terrorist."

"Great." Garrett winced. "Let's just hope she keeps that one to herself."

"She's harmless," said Mila. Her smile turned to a frown as another student entered and sat next to Jenna. *Harmless? Not really.* If they knew Mila was a blackwing, the authorities would be digging wings out of Mila's back with a scalpel in a heartbeat, without anesthetic.

Jenna smiled. They all scrunched closer to Jenna, pointing at her tablet screen.

"Mila," Jenna called out. "Get over here!"

"Moral Fellowship," muttered Mila.

"Nazi youth."

"Really, they're harmless," said Mila, glancing back at the chattering group. "I hope."

"Yeah. Young Nazis were harmless until they learned how to break glass and start fires."

Mila turned away, but the voice in her head was trying to steer her back. *Diabliss. No.*

You like him. It doesn't like them. Let's play with him instead.

It doesn't work that way. Mila turned around. Garrett smiled. "I owe you," she said.

"Really? Or are you just saying that because I bought you a drink."

"*Loaned* me a drink. I'm sorry. Yes. I really mean it."

"Maybe six then?"

"Six Ameros? Wow, a loan shark."

"Six o clock."

"Six o clock, what?"

"You can pay me back."

"Not if I lost my money. Like the rest of the world, lost might mean I don't currently have it."

"How about a walk?" he asked.

"A walk?"

"You know, on two legs? Walks are free, but today only, at six, after I close up."

"Mila, get over here!" shouted Jenna.

Mila turned back to Garrett and nodded, trying to cover her grin. She faked taking a sip from her coffee, but only because her smile prevented her from drinking.

Kathy arrived and burst through the door. She was out of breath. She hurried to Jenna's side.

The girls at the table hovered over the screen. Jenna said, "You've got to see this."

On the screen a man stood next to a wooden pulpit that had a gold cloth with a chalice stitched into it draped over the front.

"The picture's fuzzy," said Mila, setting her coffee down and squinting her eyes as she leaned closer.

"No," said Kathy. "It's not fuzzy."

"He's glowing," said Jenna.

Mila's stomach roiled. Her eyes went blurry with a red haze. The room spun and the table tilted.

"You okay?" asked Jenna.

Why was she so angry and afraid? She had to talk to Diabliss. Something was wrong.

It's them.

"It's another angel," said Jenna, voice quivering. "This one is going to speak to us, and he's in Seattle." Her grin bridged her ears. Tears pooled and then finally streamed onto her cheeks. Jenna and her friends hugged.

Mila, grabbing her gut, ran to the bathroom, found a stall, and shut herself inside. Then she got sick.

Let's leave and make a weapon, now, said Diabliss. *They're organizing. This one will rule.*

No. I have to learn more. What if you're wrong, and it's an angel?

If it is an angel, from your childhood myths, then angels are foul and evil.

I need to know more. I have to learn more.

They will manipulate the masses and use them to hunt blackwings. Diabliss makes you stronger, they will make humans weaker. People will not be free.

Mila wiped her mouth with a tissue. She did not remember drinking coffee earlier, and had not yet touched the "loaner" coffee, but the tissue turned black where she dabbed her lips anyway. *Gross.* She rinsed her mouth with water and spit in the sink.

Jenna came through the door.

"I was worried about you," said Jenna. "You don't look

good. Let's get you to the health room."

"I'm sorry. It just took me by surprise. Too much going on in this world. Too much."

"Do you need to see someone, a doctor or a counselor?" Jenna moved her face into Mila's line of sight, staring deep into Mila's eyes. Jenna's eyes were reddened from tears of joy, though now her smile had been replaced by a furrowed brow and a look of concern.

"Can I watch it now?" Mila asked.

"Of course, Mila-chick. The angels are here to save the world. The blackwings are demons. They are. They were sent by Satan. I knew it the first time I saw one. You didn't know, but, how could you? You don't go to church. You'll go to prayer circle now. I just know you will."

Garrett came up behind the group as they played the clip again. He stopped and tightened his black barista apron.

"He's beautiful," said Kathy.

"Uh-huh," said Mila, stealing a glance at Garrett.

"Mila hasn't seen the close-up yet," said Jenna. "The angel looks older, but he's still pretty hot."

Mila fumbled through her pack for a mint. She found a loose one at the bottom and popped it into her mouth, lint and all.

The clip started. The man's wings stretched out; they were beautiful and white, as if coated by thousands of fine feathers from a dove. A radiance made him difficult to look at. Even his skin glowed, but the wings, they were majestic and full of light.

"Holy Followers," said the White Light. "Come into the light." He spoke softly. His voice had a vibrato and harmony that made his words sound enchanting and musical. "The light is pure and good, and therefore good people will see and know in their hearts that this is true. There is a special place for Holy Followers, and they will rule over all on Earth one day, as the righteous already rule in Heaven. The White Light will guide Holy Followers in life, now and forever. We do this at God's command."

Jenna was going through her hysterical excitement again. Tears streamed down her flushed cheeks. "See? It's God's work."

Kathy rapidly jabbed Mila's shoulder with a stiff finger. Mila had to say something before Kathy broke skin.

Mila pointed at the screen. "He certainly looks like an angel," she said as her eyes adjusted. "The ones at the press conference with the president looked like angels too." At least what she thought angels should look like.

Don't stare at the White Light. There's no magic from God. It's brightening molecules. It's energy from a chemical compound that he's producing to stun and blind people. I see traces of a similar compound on his clothes. The White Light's inside this man. It's so horrible.

The wings stretched out, flapped, and then settled. He stared into the camera and spoke. "Do not be afraid of us," the angel said. "And just as importantly, do not be afraid to do God's work."

He's not an angel, said Diabliss.

Shhh. I need to hear him. I need to think. He looked like one, though. Maybe Diabliss did not know what an angel was. Diabliss was agnostic.

"We have been sent here to save you." The voice resonated musically, as if singing and speaking at the same time. "We will save you from Satan and his forces of evil. We will lead you to the light, and this light is from God. Most of you will see our light and recognize that it is good. You will see this because you are pure. Stay pure, worship at your holy places, and await our word. That is all for now." The wings stretched out again and flapped, lifting the man above the podium. The light radiated again.

A man in the background rushed to the awaiting choir, waved his hands, and they sang the religious hymn, *Hallelujah*. The angel flapped and hovered in front of a wall with a wooden cross hanging from it, his palms outstretched. The clip ended abruptly.

"What shut the signal off?" asked Jenna's friend.

"A blackwing attack," said Jenna. "They'll be sorry."

"Maybe it was just the government," said Garrett.

Jenna glared at him. "A government censorship conspiracy? You would say that. Those are dangerous words," she said. Her grin was gone, her eyes cold. She stood.

"Jenna," said Mila, "he's probably right."

"This is no time for your doubt, Mila," said Kathy.

"This, from you? Don't you have a guy to make out with?" Mila asked.

Kathy smiled and shook her head. "I've replaced earthly comfort with faith and prayer. For the most part," she said. "I am talking with a young man tonight, if that's what you mean."

Jenna was still glaring at Garrett.

"Stand back, Garrett," said Mila. "Jenna's glare can actually light people on fire."

Garrett shrugged.

"You don't recognize light and angels because you are not pure," said Jenna, still glaring at Garrett. "And don't think that I don't know this. You can't see the light." She looked to her friends. "Let's go. There's a church, a holy place of worship, and it has *free* coffee."

Jenna's remaining friends stood up. Jenna stopped and her lips parted as she realized that Mila was still in her seat.

"I might meet you there later," Mila said, looking up. "I love free coffee," she added.

"Holy Followers should worship at holy places," Kathy instructed, "and await their word."

Jenna looked at Mila and then Garrett. "Mila, we're going to the church. I know we'll see you there later, right? I just know we'll see you there. You see the light and know in your heart that the light's good. You'll be there."

Jenna, Kathy, and their friend left, all turning and eyeing Mila and Garrett before stepping outside where a strong fall wind tossed a few curled pale-orange maple leaves along the sidewalk. Jenna put her hands on her hips and glared, shaking her head.

Mila breathed rapidly, fearing she might have to run back into the bathroom again.

"You might want to go with," said Garrett. "This is heavy stuff. Real heavy."

"I'm all right," said Mila. "Jenna just doesn't know there's free coffee here, if you're nice to the right person."

"Free coffee at a church. And I thought I was the anti-capitalist. Maybe I should report her church for socialism."

"Uh-huh." Mila wanted to be alone. She needed to talk to Diabliss. But she looked up at Garrett.

No. Not now, said Diabliss.

You always say now.

Yes. But this now, we need to make a weapon and attack this angel. The tiny metal slinger, the gun, it won't be enough.

Right. Mila knew what would happen. Attack an angel and the people would fight back like fire ants guarding their queen. They would pull Mila's flesh off and pick it apart, and when that was all gone, they would take away the meat, and when you thought they could take no more, they would steal away the bones. If Diabliss thought they were only molecular clusters and bacteria now, just wait until they were that divided into millions of pieces.

Mila looked at Garrett.

"I understand if you don't want to go out with me. Your friend will report us if we don't see the light soon enough.

And just a warning, I've been known to cast a shadow."

"Shit. Let's hope it never comes to that. I did see a white light, though, didn't you? Is that what he meant, the bright glow?"

"He glowed, and it was white. That's all I know. I'm an emotional person, but knowing that about myself, I force myself to look for facts."

"Facts. Oh, don't let Jenna hear that. She'll report you as a terrorist for sure. Jenna loathes facts."

"Most people do," said Garrett. "Let's go take a look. See what the facts are now. You game?"

"I'm all game," said Mila. "All the time."

Now you play with him. Diabliss was upset.

Garrett pulled off his barista apron and disappeared through a door behind the counter. Mila stood. A walk would do her good. Garrett, however, returned with two helmets.

"Two helmets. Must be some walk."

"It's a short walk...to that," he said, pointing outside.

Mila looked out the front window. *That's his?* Of course. It was always out front against the curb. An all-black motorcycle. The paint was flat, as if it had been painted with a spray can. Where most motorcycles had chrome, it was also the same flat black, as if even the fenders had been sanded and then painted.

"Oh great," said Mila.

"Yeah. Great. That's our first fact." Garrett threw a scuffed red, white, and blue helmet at her.

Mila caught it like a ball and pulled it over her head as they stepped outside. Her heart fluttered. A motorcycle ride. Angels. Blackwings. Hugging Garrett Webb? This was getting to be too much. That was another fact.

Chapter 11

Mila wrapped her arms around Garrett's black leather jacket and squeezed as the motorcycle accelerated into traffic. She preferred control. She had fought to be captain of her soccer team in high school for that same reason. She liked autonomy more than power, and bad leaders always tried to take that away. Maybe her individuality stemmed from the relationship with her father. She knew what it meant to depend on someone, and what happened when that person let her down. Not that it was her dad's fault. Under improved economic conditions, he would have been a better father. She was worried—and angry—that he had not contacted her in two months. No phone calls. No text messages. No emails. Nothing. Was he even still alive? This final thought put a lump in her throat. Garrett's bike leaned and then jerked suddenly as they veered around a corner. If she hugged hard, she felt secure. A street-crosser with a cardboard sign jumped back after nearly stepping in front of them. She had better pay more attention—the ride was easier if she could predict when she needed to shift or squeeze his body tighter.

At a traffic light Garrett lifted his visor, then turned around and flipped up hers. "You doing okay?" he asked. He was a surprisingly safe driver. Almost too safe.

Mila nodded. This was what she had wanted for so long. To be close to Garrett, but as barren trees, unkempt bushes, and thick busy traffic whizzed by, she thought of Jenna and her friends, angels, her missing father, and, of course, Diabliss. Diabliss and his frantic calls for weapon-making. *We could make a weapon from that pole. Oooh. And inside that store. We need to get off. Maybe we should make a weapon now. By the way, you'll miss your life if you lose it. Are you so sure about this heaven? Is there proof? Perhaps we should make a weapon and try to prevent heaven just in case.*

He had to be a devil.

She could read many of his thoughts. They were in her head, after all. Only some thoughts were too complex or too fast, and she could sense he was hiding things. So much had changed without her even realizing it. He could direct cells and organisms, as well as manipulate atoms and molecules in her body, and he knew so much more than she could even comprehend. Microbes in the human body outnumbered human cells ten to one, and he somehow tamed or manipulated them to build, rebuild, take down, change. She tried to understand what he was doing, tried to slow his thoughts down, only he was not sharing everything, or she simply could not comprehend it all. But she did understand he desperately wanted to make a dark sword and had a growing fascination toward things that would burn or accelerate fire. Maybe demons liked heat. Maybe it had something to do with hell.

The White Light will find us. They're further along than you realize. Perhaps you can hump Garrett's back later, but if you die, you'll never get to hump his other side.

That's gross, Diabliss. I'm not humping his back.

It sure feels like it.

It's just a ride. Go away. I need my own thoughts. You're not being respectful.

I'll go away only if we can build something.

Like what, a dark sword?

Yes. A dark sword.

For what?

For cutting angels in two.

What if I don't want to do that?

You will.

What if I refuse?

Then they'll cut us in two.

I am not a killer. Now, leave me alone. I'm trying to enjoy myself!

Garrett sped up a hill past a wall lined with people waiting for odd jobs. He slowed and pointed. There was a different line of about a hundred people entering a small temple. Churches were never this busy on a quiet, late Monday afternoon. Jenna was at a different church, but Mila figured that all churches were packed to maximum occupancy after what they had seen and heard earlier. The helmet muffled all sounds, as if a mute button had been pressed, a relaxing silence. Mila leaned forward with Garrett as they accelerated away, and then eased up as they crested the top of Capitol Hill, a plateau bordering downtown Seattle where people with creative, dyed hair, tattoos, piercings, and various nonconformities went about their daily lives. It was one of the last stands of privately owned shops and restaurants—a falafel house, an El Salvadorian café, a Russian market, anatomically shaped baked goods—in other words nothing chain-like or mainstream. Garrett swerved suddenly and then slowed. He moved to the side of the street. Traffic stopped, and a man in a black UNSI outfit pointed to the shoulder where all the other vehicles had already moved.

After lifting his visor, Garrett turned and said, "We're not going anywhere anytime soon."

Mila looked down the road. Pulled-over cars were parked or idling as far as she could see. The center had been cleared, but then from behind them, an armored personnel carrier sped through the middle, followed by UNSI vehicles and a few UNSI motorcycles. Sirens wailed. Black helicopters floated in the sky. Mila had never seen this many helicopters in one location, and they were hovering much lower than she thought they should. They were eerily silent, not loud like the privately-owned helicopters that reported traffic and ferried rich people. A cluster of low-flying drones buzzed by, and then broke apart as each quickly went their own way.

Garrett grabbed her hands and put them on his waist and then grabbed the motorcycle handlebars again. He popped up onto the curb and rode down the sidewalk, against the swift stream-like motion of hurried people traveling in the opposite direction, which amused Mila until she recognized the single expression on each face. Panic. It came in various forms, but the eyes were always the same. Wide-eyed stare. Brain hijacked by fear. Groping and pushing to get to the front. By the time she had seen the fifteenth person with this look, she knew that her stare and her own thoughts were evolving toward this frenzied state as well. Like them, she wanted to go the other way. Like them, her pulse quickened, and her mind told her to turn around and run away.

What was Garrett doing? She wanted to know what the danger was before going too far.

When Garrett finally stopped, he pushed out the kickstand and eased the bike into place. Mila slid her leg over and jumped back as a gang of five or so people brushed by, sharp elbows and shoulders pushing her aside. Garrett put his forearm out and steered others away from the edge of the sidewalk, preventing them from knocking over the bike and Mila. Garrett was very strong, fending off a large overweight man in a suit. If Garrett only knew that she could easily lift him over her head...

"Everybody's leaving the area," said Mila, stating the obvious. She wanted to know why.

"Not everyone," said Garrett, nodding toward the street, filled with UNSI soldiers in black riot gear, stomping forward in unison. "We can go back." He said the words, but his body language intimated that he would rather stay.

Danger and commotion could be a good excuse to get away, but Mila's curiosity, the same internal voice that made her so different than Jenna, even before Diabliss, picked at her.

Were the people fleeing from hoolies or anarchists?

It's a blackwing. I feel his pulse. It floats through the currents in the air. It's about to be attacked.

On a nearby rooftop stood the blackwing, a man in his mid-twenties with short, spiked blond hair. His wings were hidden, but she knew what he was and could sense his presence. Through Diabliss, she could even discern the blackwing's emotional state, sensing electrical impulses in the brain of the blackwing's human body. The blackwing's defiance made her feel better. He looked down at her. He stared for a moment and then looked away, smiling. Their presence gave him courage.

Helicopters above him had him trapped, while UNSI forces on the ground had drawn weapons aimed at him. The blackwing stepped away from the edge, out of the rifles' sights.

"Let's watch for just a minute or two. See what happens," said Garrett. "If it gets dangerous, we'll leave."

Mila nodded, surprised to see him smiling. Couldn't Garrett see that this was a militarized zone, and with a blackwing nearby? Most men would act heroic and try to shuttle her off to safety. Most men *should* act heroic and try to shuttle her off to safety. *Great. Garrett's not heroic.* That figures. She knew he was too good to be true.

"Holy shit," said Garrett, pointing at the sky. The soldiers were already looking up, their assault rifles aimed. A dozen helicopters dropped from the clouds and hovered, evenly spaced into four rows of three. Out of the side of one, several paratroopers jumped, small black chutes opening behind them. They landed on the rooftop of the building next to the blackwing.

"Fast chutes," said Garrett. "A man can jump fifty feet and land like it's five."

"Stand back," said a city policeman armed with an assault rifle. He motioned with it for them to move.

"Are we not on a public sidewalk?" asked Garrett.

"No," said the officer. "It's been privatized." He laughed. "I can and will take you to a public jail, though. Maybe you'd rather speak with UNSI."

"No problem, sir. This just reminds me of my former life. I've worn a fast chute or two."

"Service?"

"Yeah." Garrett rolled up his sleeve to reveal his forearm and a tattoo of a Black Panther with a helmet on.

"How long?"

"Did my three, got injured, and got out."

"Wish I was onto a new life. Sometimes I wish I'd gone over." The officer eyed a nearby row of poised UNSIs. "Pay can't be any worse. Can't tell who's good and bad here."

"Good and bad? It's that way everywhere."

"You'll have to move away from this zone, or they'll have me guarding public restrooms. Bullets are gonna fly."

Garrett nodded, then placed his hand on Mila's back. They inched along the sidewalk, away from the motorcycle. In a way she wanted him to try to talk their way into staying longer, but who wanted to get shot or thrown in jail? Especially Garrett. He was not a student and probably did not have healthcare—not having healthcare alone could get him arrested. And he did three? Three what? What was that about?

"A city police officer," said Garrett. "That's a rare sighting. But then again, this is a civilian police activity. There's no war here. UNSI sure as hell shouldn't be here. The man on the roof isn't even armed."

"A state governor needs to declare Martial Law," said Mila. "Yep, this is an illegal occupation."

Garrett looked at her, again with a look of surprise. "I guess it is. I wouldn't know," he said. Then he nodded. "That's right. You read *Confessions*."

"You should, too. It's pretty good. I learn a lot."

A series of explosions rang out, causing Mila to instinctively jump back. Diabliss nearly shot her wings through her clothes.

Garrett stepped between Mila and the continuing blasts. "Gunshots," he said.

"Ya think?"

Garrett grinned. "Like I said, we can go any time."

"You don't look like you want to go," shouted Mila over the noise. "And maybe I want to see what's going on."

"Wow. You watch something besides what's prescribed, and with your eyes open. Are you sure you're a student?"

"Is this why I don't fit in?"

"Maybe," he said. Garrett jogged back the motorcycle, reached into a bag strapped to the tank, and quickly returned to her side. "Since we're here." He pulled out a small black lense slightly larger than his thumb, attached it to his phone case and stepped up on the back bumper of a blue, and white squad car, placing his foot on the trunk lid for balance. Standing on a police car, with bullets flying, phone in hand, he was braver than she had thought, and now, he even looked heroic. Mila did the same, climbing onto the hood of the next car down. They looked at each other, smiling nervously.

The blackwing on the rooftop ran to the edge. He had somehow acquired a weapon and fired a few shots toward the troops who had landed on the next building over. Then he fired into the air, a shot here and a shot there. When his clip emptied, he exchanged his assault rifle for a loaded one taken from a dead or wounded soldier. His wings shot out. He jumped, flapped, flew, fired, landed, ran, and jumped.

But Mila sensed he had been wounded. She could feel a pain that he was fighting through. She could sense the body pushing the bullet out. *Furious cells. Closing wounds. Binding torn flesh.*

Another group with fast chutes jumped onto the building across the street, and then on each surrounding building. Mila saw bullets searing through the sky from all directions. Each helicopter had a gunner as well. She could slow the bullets down so that she could see them, and so could this blackwing. What was only a matter of seconds, seemed like a minute. She wondered if time had slowed for her, or if she was just absorbing more details.

Diabliss could sense that the other blackwing was afraid of something. Diabliss was begging her to join the fight.

No. Why won't he just leave? asked Mila. *He can escape. Why should he?*

Blackwings are supposed to turn themselves in. Maybe he should turn himself in at this point.

Yes. When we are tired of living, we should turn ourselves in, too. We might need to help him.

No. Can't blow our cover.

Cover your face. No one will recognize you. It will fly fast.

Garrett will know. Everyone will find out. My life will be ruined.

It doesn't think that Garrett will tell anyone.

Mila looked at Garrett. Of course, he would notice if she disappeared and a blackwing wearing her clothes suddenly appeared. This was not a comic strip.

NO. WE STAY. WE DON'T JOIN IN THIS FIGHT.

The blackwing flew across the street, straight at some UNSIs. He flew into them and then up again with a person and something else in his free hand. A flailing human body dropped onto the street, a thud followed by a growing pool of blood. The Blackwing had the soldier's rifle, and soon was twisting, turning, and firing once again.

"He could escape," said Garrett. "He's fighting to fight."

"Why shouldn't he?" Mila asked, but then she wondered if those had been her own words.

Then, several bright lights erupted in the sky. Mila shielded her eyes. Garrett did the same. In several of the helicopters, lights shone out from the open side doors where the gunners had been.

"Oh, shit," said Garrett. "Angels. This could get interesting."

That was what the other blackwing was sensing. He was higher up and closer to them.

Fight. Fly, Diabliss demanded.

"Shit." She sensed more fear from the battling blackwing as he turned, landed, and acknowledged the presence of the White Light.

It's defenseless. Now, it's outnumbered. Not fair. Mila, it has to help.

Mila's thoughts raced. Diabliss flooded her mind with attack options. Diabliss wanted her body. He fought to commandeer it.

Mila, frozen and overwhelmed, still managed to hold Diabliss back. She felt anxious and dizzy. She keeled over. Whatever she had in her empty stomach erupted. It was black. She quickly wiped her mouth.

Garrett rushed over, placing his hands on her back as she quickly straightened, but she pushed him away before he could see. "We'll get out of here," he said.

Mila nodded.

NO! Diabliss shouted.

"No?" asked Garrett.

She had said it out loud. Mila nodded. "Yes," she said in

a weak voice that came with great effort.

Diabliss wanted her body so badly. He thought it was the only way to save the other blackwing. *We can still surprise the White Light with an attack.*

The blackwing landed on the street and sprinted away from the center of the action. The rows of UNSIs broke apart as they repositioned.

Garrett hurried Mila toward the motorcycle, though he repeatedly glanced over his shoulder. Mila could tell he was concerned for her, but also wanted to stay and record. If she remained here watching much longer, she would lose control. She not only felt Diabliss's strong emotional waves but the other blackwing's panic and despair. The blackwing pleaded for help. He stopped and quickly scanned the area, trying to find her eyes. He was telling Diabliss, and her, that the White Light would kill him without their help, without Mila ceding her body to Diabliss.

But if she did, she would lose everything.

No. *NO!*

Garrett looked at her again. He looked concerned.

I am not a fighter, Diabliss. I can't. We can't.

Diabliss fought harder. He was trying to hijack her brain, and somehow, she was stopping him.

Was she saying everything aloud? She failed to muster a smile.

Mila fought back a hatred for the White Light pouring into her mind and bones. She struggled to get on the back of the motorcycle and instead bent over and threw up on the street again. Her vomit was still black. She saw small black sticks and some pebbles. It was not coffee. It looked like dirt. The dreams. *Diabliss.* He had been eating dirt at night. The crazy thoughts she was having after waking up were not dreams. Diabliss had been taking her body out.

The angels are right. You're a demon. You're a killer.

You needed minerals and microbes. We needed nourishment. Bones are lighter and stronger.

Mila shook her head. *You make me so sad, and sick. I'm going to turn myself in. Not to Jenna. I'm going to have you medically extracted. I'm going to grab an angel right now. You can't stop me.*

"Oh crap," said Garrett. "I'm sorry, Mila. One second. I have to catch this."

Garrett jumped into the street as more soldiers poured around him.

The White Light swooped and then landed on either side of the blackwing, closing off his escape route. They radiated a brightness that burned Mila's eyes like a hot sun, but she watched anyway. A white flame shone. It was a sword.

"I will strike you down with the sword of light and justice unless you surrender," an angel bellowed.

"Never again," said the blackwing. He shot into the air and corkscrewed through the clouds.

Three angels took flight after him. All with wings flapping, emitting bright flashes like cameras at a Hollywood movie debut, their drawn and raised luminous swords pointed forward.

The figures disappeared into the clouds, dipping down and then back up again. Then two dark objects fell, close together, but far enough apart to tell that it was indeed two separate objects that had only moments earlier been one.

Mila felt pain, sadness, and remorse. Her breathing heaved in and out.

Diabliss?

Diabliss was emotionally crushed, as if a close family member had died. And Mila felt it, too. All those years the blackwings had suffered together, trapped in the burning sea, forging camaraderie as if they were one organism, and it had ended like this.

No. Not fair. Not fair at all. Three against one.

The amassing UNSI military did not count to Diabliss. They were a nuisance, but the angels were something else entirely.

I'm so sorry, Diabliss.

"What was that?" asked Garrett.

"The blackwing," said Mila, tears streaming down her cheeks. "They cleaved him in two."

"How can you see that far?" Garrett turned and stared up into the sky. "I totally missed it."

Three against one, with swords of light. Not fair. Oh, it will get them back. We can take at least one with us if they attack, but we shouldn't fight. We should flee.

The bright white lights sank down from the clouds, landing on the building above them.

They sense us, said Diabliss.

"I really need to leave," said Mila, looking down at her black vomit. "Too much coffee," she added, climbing onto the back of Garrett's motorcycle. *And Garrett will never want to see me or that again.*

He apologized profusely and started up the bike.

Mila held him tight, but she was just as ready to stand on the seat, jump up, and fly away, her wings testing the fabric on her back.

"Hold tight," he said as they slowly rolled off the curb.

Mila stared back at the mob of soldiers. A light brightened as an angel flapped its wings and lifted into the air, moving off the building toward Mila and Garrett.

Garrett picked up speed and turned a corner. The rest of the ride was a blur, with Mila checking over her shoulder three times before truly believing the White Light stayed behind. But even if the White Light followed them, she could not focus; her eyes were too filled with tears—tears she could no longer tell who they belonged to.

Chapter 12

Theo faced the camera, even though standing in front of a person pointing machinery at him went against his survival instincts. But this was not a weapon, or it was, but it would be his weapon. The temple of worship was full, and it could no longer safely fit more people inside. The humans demonstrated such enthusiasm for the White Light that if left unmanaged they would crush each other to death just to get closer to him. Theo loved the intense level of devotion, but he needed a military, not a morgue. He radiated his light toward the Holy Followers and faced the camera that was transmitting to billions of eager viewers. "Please, I encourage you to be patient, loyal, and loving to those who follow the true path of the White Light. Let us care for each other, for we are all bound under the same God. A God of many faces, but the one true God."

Theo disliked the spotlight. It was high risk, and he did not covet attention. He did it for the cause, the higher purpose. If only the blackwings would submit, life would be so pure, so simple. Theo smiled into the camera, opened his arms, and radiated his light. *Someday we will love you. But not today.*

"Every worship center, regardless of religion, must acquire and install a screen worthy of showing important broadcasts from angels," he said. "The White Light will unify this fragmented population, and together we will treat the blackwing infection." Translated broadcasts were already rapidly spreading throughout the world, but the United States, one of the two world superpowers, was already within his grips. Theo loved the zealousness so far. The growing legions of Holy Followers easily found the White Light path and believed with one hundred percent faith. Americans loved his broadcasts and of course the majority rightfully worshipped and served when asked to. Mesmerized crowds gasped and cried. When he floated into the air, it became a frenzy. *Amusing.* A lot of animals flew. Even bugs flew.

Theo glided, flapped, and hovered over the parishioners. He rose to the balcony, crossing along a row of glimmering stained glass and then swooped back down to the podium, where he landed not behind it but on top of it, wings flapping occasionally in order to maintain balance.

"The White Light is pure, sent by God, and the blackwings do not love you like we do. They work for the evil one you call Satan. They are agents of fear and destruction. They will leave your world in ruins and turn mankind into their slaves. You will not be able to defeat them on your own, so you must cooperate fully with the authorities recognized by the White Light, and you must rely on us, your guardian angels. The White Light will guide you through these dark weary times. We have taken you under our soft gentle wings. In the name of God and the White Light, everything is right."

In the name of God and the White Light, everything is right, crowds repeated across the world as they had been instructed. And again, the people repeated his message, this time louder, the thunderous unity vibrating the podium, tickling his feet, this time without instruction. *A wondrous feeling.*

As he hop-glided down in silence, he pondered the beautiful side to humans. The chanting subsided, and a hymn erupted behind him as thousands of Holy Worshippers burst into a glorious song. Music. Oh, how he loved these creative souls. They were already singing songs of White Light worship, using his own spoken words, and blending them with previously written ones.

Theo's eyes rested on the young student leader, Jenna. A model human. Uncompromising devotion. She was the exact opposite of a blackwing. Many answers could be found in youth. Impure visions of pink intertwined flesh fluttered in Theo's mind. Theo smiled, his heart warming, another human thing. *If only love worked as effectively as pain, and knowledge as well as fear.* Did that always have to be true? It was the young faithful like Jenna who made him fight so hard for human salvation. They both fought so hard. Shouldn't they share even shallow human rewards? Maybe when more humans like her embraced the White Light wholeheartedly, they could do what was right on their own. Loyal humans like Jenna would never fall into blackwing adulation. Theo flew to the aisle, walked to the fifth row, and then reached out, touching the young student's hand. He glided back to the stage, turned with outstretched arms, and walked away.

His backstage workers cleared out of his way and then busied themselves again as he passed. Two fellow angels joined him.

"The plane you requested is waiting for you," said John, his first original Holy Follower. "It will be a private meeting, as you requested."

Theo nodded. There would be less human ego if it was just the president without her advisors. She could pass messages to her puppeteers without posturing, without games.

Within an hour he was flying east toward Maryland on Air Force One. It was a faster method of travel and required less energy than flapping through the air like a common bird. Constantly analyzing risks and survival methods, he knew he could escape through the side of the plane if attacked and fly away, dooming the humans inside to their death. Yes.

Mankind was fragile, and they need the White Light. Theo had his sword of light. Humans could barely manipulate atoms and energy, but the blackwings could, and this meant danger. Those foul creatures. They will wish they had stayed suspended in plasma. The humans were extremely fortunate that the White Light found a way into their world.

Hours later, the plane shook as they touched down at Andrews Air Force Base. A long black car waited for him outside. The President of the United States was described by Theo's associates at the television station as the most powerful human. Of course, they rightly added that this was before the angels had arrived. Humans could be naïve though. Leaders were usually puppets. Real power usually disguised itself, a clever self-preservation technique.

Theo and two angels now with him flew down the stairs to a black limousine waiting on the tarmac. Theo waited for a moment longer than he wanted to when the door stayed shut. His human body coughed, its lungs tickled and annoyed by the pungent vapors. Yes, she would test his patience, and he would let her this time, maybe.

A fighter jet soared overhead, its exhaust screaming until it disappeared into bulbous white clouds. Yes. A show. A reminder that she had a military at her command. He would remind her that he disliked surprises.

The limousine door opened. Two men with flesh-colored wireless earpieces stepped out. They were armed with pistols on their belts. The simple devices would only inflict minimal and temporary damage anyway. The U.S. government knew were other ways to defeat the White Light. A few angels had already "disappeared", and that was why he was here.

Theo glanced around. *Must be ready to fly. Must be ready to fight.*

As the president started to climb out, Theo put his hand up, signaling for her to stay inside. He crawled in.

The president made eye contact. *Really? This close to me and direct eye contact? You really don't know any better?* She had to understand that his patience had limits. The White Light deserved much respect, but Theo was already learning that some humans could be…rebellious? Theo brightened his molecules quickly. She would see spots and halos for weeks.

"Theo. I'm pleased to meet you," she said, after averting her stare. "I hope your flight was to your satisfaction."

"It was."

She was quickly blinking her watering eyes, ignoring her pain well. "The plane is yours and is a token of our respect and admiration."

"I didn't bring it here to return it."

"Of course not." She chuckled. "I brought your favorite treat. I hope you don't mind. I personally asked John at your studio." The president picked up and held out a shiny silver serving platter with a single layer of jellybeans.

Ah. Theo's eyes widened. She understood that some pleasures were so pure and simple. "Your spying has served us both well."

He lifted one into his mouth.

The president spoke again. "Are we here to get to know one another? Are we here to discuss future possibilities with the world and this great nation?"

Her eyes still watered. Theo suspected it was taking every inch of fortitude she had not to rub them.

"Oh, of course," said Theo. "One thing first, Madam President."

"Anything."

"You've learned obedience, have you not?"

"I have."

"In every power system, there are those who pull strings, even with the White Light there are."

She arched her eyebrows, as if surprised.

"With angels, it is God pulling the strings," he continued. This time he chuckled.

"Yes, of course. There are those with influence and, of course, with us there is God as well," she said. "We too serve God. It's how things operate in America. It's how things have always operated here."

Theo picked up several jellybeans and one by one stuffed them into his mouth. After he finished chewing, he licked the sugary dye off his fingertips. "The center is good, but the outside, so much better. Eat with me and share your love for one of mankind's great accomplishments." Theo shoved the tray toward the president, who did not hesitate and, smiling, popped a bean into her mouth. "Cherry," she said with certainty.

"Yes. The red," said Theo, searching one out. "You have agents and intelligence, just as the White Light does."

"We are obligated to do so."

"They cannot harm any more angels, or you will suffer the wrath of angels, and God will no longer bless America. Yes, you can destroy one, two, or even a hundred of us, but not all, and more importantly, not millions upon millions of Holy Followers. Their loyalty has grown, grown to where you can no longer fight us. And you shouldn't want to. We are both on the side of God, are we not? Are you not on the side of God?"

"I am," she said. "We are."

"So, we have an understanding?"

"I won't lie to you and pretend I don't know what happened to a few of your fellow angels."

"Honesty with some is optional. With me it is a virtue."

"We were left with no choice. We are simple and only human. They asked for more than we could give. They asked for complete and immediate control of our militaries, of our nuclear arsenal. Some men acted."

120

"Yes. Young angels. They rushed for power too soon. That is why I have chosen a different path. Angels are now united behind me." Theo popped another jellybean into his mouth. "If our Holy Followers learn that after death, the tunnel of white light, the portal into heaven that they seek, has been turned off by angels because of actions by their own government, leaving them in emptiness, fire, or despair, after death, they will rise against you."

"They would."

"We can do that. We can make sure that humans cannot enter heaven through the portal of white light, for it is *our* white light. We are not only the guardians of human spirits, but we are their guides into the afterlife as well. And I will not hesitate to tell the humans that their governments have placed their ability to enter heaven at risk, if you do not cooperate." Theo knew the president was at a loss for words, looking for a way to respectfully ask him if what he said was true.

"We will cooperate fully," she said. "We have no plans to do otherwise."

"We all have plans to do otherwise. Let's just hope we don't have to resort to those plans. My agents have heard the whispers," said Theo. "There are a few, elite, who guide and shape mankind by controlling the world's wealth, as well as the militaries and media networks."

"Correct."

"I suggest we find our common love for God and that you all side with the angels, not blackwings and evil. Angels tried to save the blackwings once. We tried to preserve them for eternity. We will not make this same mistake. Together, we will teach them that embracing evil has eternal consequences."

"Yes, sir. We can work together. We will share this charge against evil with honor."

"You no longer have to fear your masters. If you are on the side of righteousness, we will bring you so much light, but if you falter, we will smite you and burn every human on this unholy ground who does not realize that the angel's light and God's light is pure, so pure."

"I understand fully and agree that an alliance would be healthy for us both."

Theo liked this woman. She did understand. Fully.

"You understand that loyalty has rewards. I like that about you," said Theo, smiling. He stuffed another bean into his mouth and chewed it, savoring the nourishment and taste. It was so good. "Continue your hunt of blackwings. Do not be soft. In the name of God and the White Light, everything is right."

"In the name of God and the White Light, everything is right."

"You are free to go."

"Wasn't I free all along?" she asked, smirking.

Theo smiled and tilted his head, finding her eyes. He flashed his brightness again, searing her gaze. Forget the halos and spots; she would only see a literal white light for weeks.

He had tried love, but alas, pain creates gain.

Theo shoveled another handful of jellybeans into his mouth, got out of the limousine, and shut the door. The president and her secret service agents drove off, most likely rushing to an eye specialist at a nearby hospital. Theo and his two angels flew to the top of the steps and again boarded the plane, their plane.

Chapter 13

Jenna put down her hot mug of herbal mint tea and placed her hands on her head. It was late. She had spent hours organizing for the White Light in addition to worship. She and her friends had finally stopped praying, and though she was disappointed that Mila was absent, she understood how Mila struggled. How could she not? Her dad would not work or could not work. *And what's his real story? What kind of a father, even in hard times, abandons his daughter?* But she wanted to help Mila. Mila had much to offer, and Jenna knew that beneath Mila's tough athletic shell, a shell without a mother, a shell with a missing father, that Mila was a brilliant girl with a good heart, waiting for the White Light.

There was much to accomplish, too. Theo was noticing her and helping implement her ideas—*her* ideas! His angels recognized the value of her blackwing-free campus absolution efforts and were now implementing similar efforts across the country. Her model program might be duplicated in all schools. It might spread worldwide! Jenna tried to focus, but it was difficult not to find Theo's eyes locked on hers at holy worship. It was only a glance. There were clear communications about not looking angels in the eyes, but somehow his eyes always found hers, or she just became too lost in her admiration. As she walked away from worships, though, she resolved to only be stronger in her faith and to fight evil harder. She had been blessed with the ability to recognize both faith and evil, and with that came responsibility.

When Jenna saw the empty dorm room, and at nine at night, only an hour before curfew, she frowned. Jenna had picked up the clipboard for her morning shift at the checkpoint, and she nearly cried upon seeing that Mila had not absolved herself with her newly formed White Light Infraguard—Jenna's own idea! The White Light Infraguard would even have uniforms, and power—with Jenna at its helm. There was a note in the book from Kathy. Mila thought she had to pay. But Jenna knew Mila was rebelling. Jenna had told Mila all about the school's mission to be the first blackwing-free campus. Mila knew the checkpoints were free. If she did not recognize how important this was to their school and country, she at least knew how important this was to Jenna. How would it look if the chief student organizer's own roommate had not absolved herself? That might encourage others to rebel—and at such a critical juncture.

What was Mila getting herself into? Jenna pondered ways to help Mila. Mila refused money, at least enough to really help; she was too proud. Mila did not need help with school. In fact, Mila could tutor advanced students. Mila had so many problems that were not only making her not see that the light was pure, but they caused her to resist and doubt the White Light as well. Jenna had to find a way to break through Mila's skepticism, her protective shell. Maybe she could help Mila literally. In turn, it might help her in other ways. Jenna made Mila's bed and then stepped back. The mediocre chore was too little to even be noticed. Jenna saw the laundry basket and shook her head.

What would Jesus do? Jesus had washed the feet of his disciples. If only Mila knew the light was good. So good. That the White Light washed the whole body, inside and out.

Jenna frowned. She did not have to enjoy this. Surely Jesus disliked the smell of feet. As Jenna hefted an armload of dirty clothes from the basket, a shirt fell with a thud.

Something was wrapped inside, heavy like a stone. She unfolded the shirt. A black metal object fell through the fabric, landing on the floor.

Jenna shrieked and jumped, and then picked the pistol up. Most of her tears lately had been tears of joy, but the streams breaking down her face and filling her eyes came from a deep sadness. *Oh, Mila-chick. What have you gotten yourself into?*

Chapter 14

Mila hugged Garrett's back as they veered in and out of traffic. She no longer watched the sky. She did not care. She felt Diabliss' pain, and it was so deep. How could he be evil and fall into an emotional chasm over a blackwing he did not even personally know?

Maybe there is a Heaven, and he went there, Diabliss. Her plea fell flat. No. The blackwing life was a biological experience. Through Diabliss, Mila could see the mechanisms, the atoms, molecules, how they worked together, how everything inside her was built, and how Diabliss had manipulated carbon atoms to make her stronger, how other changes made synapses faster. Cells and microbes worked together, manipulated into performing new tasks, and even DNA code had been modified. She could never replicate his maneuvers, but she knew it could all be explained. There was no soul in Diabliss, or her. No mysteries or magic. Every space, every particle could be accounted for. So, for Diabliss and the other blackwings, when they die, they die. It was a true end. That was sad and depressing, especially as it could be her story. If there was a God, he was likely not in her life, and maybe, not even in this world.

She called to Diabliss. *I'm so sorry for your loss.*

Garrett veered away from 45th Street, which would have taken them back to the coffee shop. She did not know where Garrett was taking her. Maybe he had figured her out. Who had black vomit? Maybe her head had spun in a circle. Would he turn her over to the White Light or UNSI? Either would suffice. The growing religious authority and the official military police authority were now on the same side.

After parking his cycle against a curb, he looked to Mila and said, "I know what you're thinking, but I swear I don't always do this."

"Where are we?" Mila asked. He had to be kicking her off the bike.

Garrett leaned forward. She still had her helmet on. He lifted her visor. "My place. You don't have to come inside," he said. "I can take you back to campus if you want."

Mila shook her head. Where was Diabliss now? Why wasn't he nudging her closer to procreation? She had always wanted to be physically intimate with Garrett. A month ago, she would have paid money to be at his apartment. A week ago, Diabliss would have urged her into a sexual frenzy if she had gotten this close. Now she felt alone.

Her eyes clouded again. She rubbed them.

Garrett put his arms around her and patted her back. "I can take you back to your dorm. I just think you need a break. I can see it in your eyes," he said. "Bourbon and a view. Nothing else. One short glass. Just enough to add a glowing haze and a slight blur."

Mila nodded. She could not go back to her dorm right now. Jenna's religiousness. Kathy crossing over to the White Light. The Infraguard's list. UNSI sweeps. Police checkpoints. So much confusion. So many enemies. Did she even have enemies before? No. She wished she had just turned herself in. She would be imprisoned, dissected, and killed, but at least she would know her end. *At least it would be the end.*

Garrett took her hand, which was no longer a small pool of sweat but dry, cold flesh. He had strong hands, and she had felt through his jacket on the ride a strong skeleton, solid and muscular. If there was much body fat, she did not feel it. But his touch was just right. Firm but soft, too. His chitchat went from coffee to the view. How could he discuss such superficial things after what they had seen? He had a pet fish, a beta, in a small bowl. Did she have pets back home? She shook her head. Of course not. Outside her crowded dorm, she was homeless.

Just take me away from my life.

The apartment building was made of cement blocks, beige-like sandstone with random protruding bricks at various points, like a climbing wall at a gym. Each apartment had a deck with black iron railings, and the view that Garrett must have been talking about was from the side of the apartment building that faced downtown Seattle.

They trudged up the steep stairwell over short, outdoor carpeting with a soiled high-traffic center. At the top, four levels up, there was a fire door. They were soon on a roof that had wooden decking and planter boxes. The plants were mostly brown and dead. Garrett pulled at a tarp covering an odd lump next to a banister. Beneath was an outdoor patio sofa. He pulled a few cushions out of a plastic storage bin and pushed them into place.

"Don't worry. It's safe. The termites pretty much stick to the building's support beams. They don't like the patio furniture."

Mila twitched a frail smile. How could he want to spend another second with her?

"We could fall through the building at any minute," he added, "but the patio furniture will hold."

At least she was away from campus, trying to personify a perfect sheltered life, while internally, she was not only falling apart, she was on the verge of exploding. Mila tried to speak. She was in no mood to seduce Garrett, or to be seduced. She just wanted enough time to pull the pieces of her life back together so she could make it through one more day—so her friends would not see her fall apart—see her lies spill out.

"Be right back," he said. "Don't fall through without me."

The skyline was beautiful, blue sky with fluffy white clouds. She would never enjoy them again, though. To her, the realm was a battlefield. Helicopters, drones, blackwings, and now angels. *Angels*. Maybe Diabliss was a demon. He took away her heaven and now was destroying what so many held dearly: a belief in angels. When she thought it through, though, it did not make sense. Is that what demons do? Take away your God and guardians, feed your doubt, steal your faith? *There must be more. This can't be it.*

Garrett returned and fluffed a blanket over her, tucking the edges beneath her. He had a bottle and two glasses with ice. Mila seldom drank. She was underage, but a glow and a blur? That was a sunray peeking through a horizon of dark clouds.

Garrett poured bourbon into the glass and took a cola can from his front pocket. He filled the glass, waiting until the foam crested and then receded before handing it over.

"You'll see Armageddon from here," said Mila, finally speaking.

"I hope I have my camera when I do," he said, winking. "It's a hobby, filming the end of the world."

She held up the cold wet glass, took a sip, and winced, shaking her head. Her whole body shivered.

"I can make it weaker," he said.

She shrugged.

"I can make it stronger."

Mila thought about it. She could use it as an excuse to kiss him, or more. "It's fine. Really. I'm not a big drinker. I'll stop when the glow hits—and the slight blur."

"Good idea. People who lose control are irresponsible."

"I'm certainly not that."

"I know. Soccer star. Scholarship. University—top

school in the Northwest at that."

Mila nodded, and then shivered as the autumn afternoon rooftop breeze hit. Garrett, sensing her discomfort, tucked in the blanket where he had missed a spot. Mila wondered why Diabliss ignored her body temperature. She reached for him. His emotions were withdrawn but still strong, perhaps even brewing. He was mourning. A helicopter flew across the skyline. A moment later, a fighter jet tore across the sky with a roar.

"You seem responsible," suggested Mila. "At least you work."

"Coffee barista?" Garrett shrugged. "That's another hobby."

"Yeah? What's work to you then?"

"That's where my lack of responsibility hits. I haven't figured that out yet."

"In this economy, who knows what a real job is. That's why I'm hoping to go to medical school. People will always get hurt, and will always die, but they'll pay to take away the pain and put off the inevitable."

"School's spendy," Garrett said. "Rich parents?"

"Yes, I was born from royalty. They threw me into poverty so I could learn valuable life lessons before returning to a home literally made from gold bullion."

"Each gold brick held together by the blood of poor people and children?"

Mila shook her head. "I wish. Not the blood part. The opposite. Mom died when I was ten. Dad's unemployed...I think." Mila burned her throat with some bourbon, trying to cauterize the lump forming in her throat. She coughed. "And your parents, your studies?"

Garrett looked into her eyes. He took the blanket and tucked a corner behind each shoulder. "Back up. The glow only comes if you give something up, and you're almost there. You need to give it room. So, make the trade a good one, and you'll make a lot of room."

I'm a blackwing and my dad's missing. Some days I don't get enough to eat, and I buy school supplies and books instead of food. And it's only going to get harder. Tell you that? A glow would be nice though. What to trade? What to trade?

"Let me guess. Jenna has a list of people who don't worship God often enough and you're on the list," said Garrett.

"You and me both." Mila sighed. "My dad's missing," she finally choked out.

"Oh, no." Garrett shook his head. "Unemployed?"

"Yeah. I'm afraid he might be dead, otherwise he would have contacted me."

"How long has he been missing?"

Mila told him how she had been waiting for a money transfer for several weeks but had not heard anything. "I don't know where he is."

"Do you think he's in a camp?"

"You mean the ones that don't really exist?"

Garrett frowned but nodded. He opened his mouth to say something, and then stopped and took a drink. He finally spoke. "I heard about someone who owed money to a bank. Unemployed. They plucked him off the street and put him to work, involuntarily. He got out of the factory camp, but he had to escape. If your father's capable of working but just can't find a job, that's likely where he is. If not, he could be in an UNSI relief station, but that's mostly where they have small children and elderly. A lot of the people in relief stations get trained and end up in factory camps eventually. Anything to pay off the national debt."

"And they can't leave either?"

"No. Not without help. That's what I've heard. Just

rumors. Can he work?"

"He can work; he just can't find a job." Mila disliked what she was hearing. Sure, it was just rumors, but she saw the article in *Confessions*. She saw the video clip. Factory camps were real. Garrett sat next to Mila with his arm innocently at his side. She lifted it over her shoulder, pulled it around her neck and leaned into him. She wanted to tell him so much more. He was a good listener. He sensed things that were unsaid, like she felt lost and did not want to go to her dorm. How her mind was full. Mila cried, the tears dribbling down her cheek and pooling on his long sleeve shirt.

"Your living allowance, even with a soccer scholarship, has to be tight," Garrett said.

"You might not ever see the money for the coffee, and definitely not any interest."

"Gave you. A cup of coffee costs me fifty cents. You're worth at least that much."

"Wow. I knew I could be bought but didn't know I was worth double digits. Fifty cents." Mila wiped a last tear and apologized. She wished Diabliss could moderate her feelings like he controlled her body temperature—or used to control her body temperature. Why couldn't he make her emotionally stronger and not just physically stronger? She wanted a numb switch. She took another sip. As her stomach warmed with the bourbon, she felt a little lighter "Ah. Finally. It's there."

"What's there?"

"The glow. It's faint, but it's there." Mila rubbed her eyes. They always itched after a good cry. "And the blur. Sorry about your shirt," she said, pointing to the wet spot. "And now it's your turn. I've let go of something. Something big. I feel better, and now it's your turn."

"My turn."

"University. You were in it."

"Studied communications—journalism. I had dreams of

news stories that weren't fed to us by our government and corporations."

"You should read *Confessions*." Mila nodded. "That's news. But that kind of stuff doesn't interest you."

"If somebody shouts a truth, but nobody hears it, did it really happen?"

Mila smiled. Garrett had just quoted a line from *Confessions*. Maybe he did like Confessions. He just refused to admit it. *A war hero who reads, feeds the poor, and gives them free coffee? Maybe he's Mr. Perfect after all.* "Liar. You do read it."

"You could say that," Garrett stood up. "Let's change the subject."

Mila shook her head. "Your turn."

Garrett nodded. "I guess I need a glow, too. This is kind of like truth or dare."

"Okay. I dare you to tell me something that will help you glow," said Mila.

"I got frustrated at so much hypocrisy. My parents supported war and torture, while taxing and indebting our generation until we would be their slaves. There was a time where I thought they were good people and the time came when I realized I was just different. A professor I studied under and who I admired wrote an article and got taken away. Nobody wanted to fight for him. I spoke out. I tried to fight the system, but then I was under scrutiny for being different. A troublemaker. My parents and guidance counselor thought I just needed the right medication. They just wanted to change me, even if it meant chemically. I knew that if I did a military tour the government and their world would leave me alone, I wouldn't have to be doped up, and I would disappear from their radar. The authorities won the battle, but I wanted to win the war. I went overseas, or Syranistan as we call that whole shit-bombed region. But it came at a price. I did three years in hell, right here on earth."

"And the price?"

"Oops. That's it." He stood up. "That was my trade. I got my glow." He walked to the ledge and leaned on the banister.

"Not fair," she said, burrowing deeper under the blanket, tugging the edges under further.

He pulled up his pantleg over his knee. A prosthetic lower, barely noticeable except at a close look, particularly at the seam above his ankle.

"A missing father's tough, but they aren't handing out gold bricks in Syranistan either. Well, maybe to military contractors, but not to boots like me."

"My god," she said. "And that happened in Syranistan?"

He nodded. "Yeah. You could say I didn't know what I was stepping into when I signed up."

"That's bad."

"I'm like Ghengis Kahn. We both spread our DNA in the same place."

"That's worse."

She had been thinking about herself while he was talking, but then had a flash to images of wounded soldiers, dead civilians, and refugees. Yeah. Garrett had more baggage that she did. "We're all travelers in this world, and baggage is a universal trait," she said.

Garrett smiled. "Wow. That's profound."

"It's from *Confessions*," said Mila. "I wish I were that eloquent."

The blanket thinned as an evening breeze kicked in and the sun set. The sky changed from a pink tangerine to dark gray, full of a looming night and pending rain. Mila folded the blanket as the first light sprinkles pattered on the deck. She gently took Garrett's hand and followed him into his apartment, the wind and wet spatters at their backs. They shut the door behind them.

Chapter 15

Theo walked past a cameraman who was tracing and lifting yellow and black cords and their corresponding electrical boxes. The cameraman nodded that he was ready. Theo eyed the anxious crowd, finding the blonde student who had again earned her spot at the front—not exactly an easy task. The Holy Followers of Theo and the White Light had well outgrown the original studio in an old Seattle cathedral. The professional soccer stadium would be his next venue. The world would be a better place without hooley gatherings anyway. People fought their way inside and crammed into the cathedral. Each pew was full, and people defended each seat and spot, as Theo agreed they should. Isn't salvation worth fighting for? He admired the young lady's commitment, found her eyes, and winked at her. *Yes, I've seen the updates. I've been keeping tabs on you. Such a worthy human. It's as if the White Light has crept into your shell.* Theo smiled, recognizing that a human tenderness was fighting for strength inside of him, while the righteousness of the White Light was taking control of her. He held out his arms and radiated his light.

Theo would start as a man, behind his pulpit, and then rise as the angel who would save mankind. Their God-sent being rises into the air and the worship blossoms and bursts like an exploding star. He could see in their desperate eyes that they needed him, and he could feel their empty desperate hearts yearning for salvation. Most followers already carried faith. Theo's visible, tangible proof only hastened their redemption and allegiance. They would promptly stamp out resistance and doubt, especially after forging alliances and bringing in help.

There would be a bloody battle, but blackwings would soon be defeated.

People who could not discern the Light as true, even those who were not hosting blackwings, harbored evil. They were wretched creatures. Why would they resist the White Light? Why would they disobey or question absolute authority? Worshipping and following the White Light only made a being stronger, and a White-Light allegiance guaranteed the survival of a species. They would soon learn that the White Light could kill every being upon this earth.

"Demons are oh so clever," Theo said to the camera. "They are much smarter than we give them credit for. First, they try to convince us that they don't exist. They blame evil and the many ills humanity suffers on poverty, circumstances, and unemployment, and even cast false blame on your own authority figures and government establishments. And when we see the demons rise before our very eyes, they try to convince us that they have not been sent by Satan, *and* that they are harmless *and* should be left alone. It is sad that they fool and damn so many souls. *Sad.* Blackwings and their followers do live under the spell of the dark master many of you call Satan. But the White Light will guide you to a righteous path, steering you clear of these evil forces. It is a path that won't always be there, for there is an end to every path. There is also a race to this end, a finish line, where angels are waiting to cheer for you as you cross the final divide between effort and triumph. The White Light is your portal to God and heaven. I implore you to seek and enter the Light, the only path, the true path, while you still can."

Theo brightened his light.

People wept. Those without seats dropped to their knees,

others held out their hands as Theo's wings stretched out, and with a few light soundless flaps he lifted himself into the air. It strained his back, but his human body was getting stronger and could resist a great amount of pain.

"There are demons among us, and you see them with your own eyes. Do not be fooled. 'Tis a battle between good and evil. You will feel it in your heart when you give yourself to God and his angels. There is also evil, and you will feel that too. If you give yourself to blackwings and darkness, and turn away from God, you will feel emptiness, exile, and eventually the burning, the wrath of angels. If you have a blackwing inside you, inside a friend, or inside a family member, the White Light will try to save the human soul. There is danger involved, but we love humans too much to waste their souls unnecessarily, for the time being."

Theo nodded to Jenna. She had already accomplished so much for his movement. He would grant her a genuine token of appreciation: *Power*.

"And now, Holy Followers. Join the fellowship of the White Light. Turn away from evil. There is a line, and Holy Followers must not only stand on one side or the other, Holy Followers must know what side of the line those who are near you stand on as well. Evil is smart. Demons are clever. And they are as real as this angel you see before you, an angel sent by God. Follow the White Light, feel our love for you, but heed our wrath, for we must banish evil and immerse this planet in God's army of the White Light. We must thwart evil at all costs, without mercy, without hesitation, and without remorse."

Chapter 16

The lights were always on in the dormitory hallways, even after curfew. The halls were peaceful and mostly empty as most students were sleeping or studying in their rooms. A few students respecting sleeping roommates by studying outside were propped awkwardly against the beige walls and only paused long enough to look up as Mila passed by. She wondered what they thought of a young woman with mussed-up hair and heavy eyes coming in after curfew. She wanted to tell them that her current hairstyle was a result of wearing a motorcycle helmet and not promiscuity.

Mila crept through the door. She had decided to jog home from Garrett's place a little after midnight, after he had innocently fallen asleep in her arms. She had wanted so much more than kisses and light conversation but fearing he might discover her wings, she somehow managed to hold herself off back. The light on the shared desk was on low. Mila squinted, but could see that Jenna's bed was empty. She thought that maybe Jenna was still worshipping at church, possibly one of many midnight vigils, until she saw that the bathroom light glowed from beneath the closed door and heard something rattle on the bathroom counter. The faucet shot on and off as Jenna brushed her teeth.

Mila jumped into bed, hoping that she would have enough time to fake falling asleep. There was a lump that tipped as she hopped onto the bed. A stack of clean, folded clothes. Mila smiled. *Jenna.* Jenna was spoiled. She hated doing chores, especially laundry. Jenna even paid to have her laundry done for her by a private service. What a day. First, a fabulous date with Garrett, and now, Jenna doing her laundry. A new friend made, and an old friend realized. She wished that Diabliss was sharing the emotions with her, but then she felt him. His fear. *What?*

And then she remembered. The dirty clothes in the laundry hamper. The gun wrapped in a shirt inside. Her heart nearly burst out of her chest.

Diabliss was awake and aware. Mila could sense his presence. *Yes, Diabliss. I know. If Jenna did the laundry, she knows about the pistol.*

Mila rushed to the hamper, but before she got there, the bathroom door opened, and Jenna came out in her robe. As Jenna got closer, the small desk light illuminated her puffy and red eyes. Neither girl said a word.

Mila straightened the knocked-over pile and began putting the laundry away.

"Thank you," said Mila, trying to read her friend.

"Thank you?" asked Jenna.

"For doing my laundry. Folding my clothes."

"Yes. You're welcome. I knew you were under a lot of pressure. I wanted to do something special. Jesus washed the feet of his disciples."

"I know how much you hate doing laundry. That really adds special meaning," said Mila. "I know you are a true friend. The best friend a person could ever ask for. Sometimes my dirty clothes smell like feet."

"You're a good friend, too," Jenna said. "That's what worries me."

"I'm not sure what you mean."

"You would be loyal to someone who doesn't deserve loyalty. It might lead you to do something you normally wouldn't do."

Mila tried not to show fear. Loyalty? Did Jenna know about Diabliss?

"I'm not sure I understand," said Mila. "I know things

aren't always as they appear."

"Yes. Things can be deceiving."

"They can be."

"Were you with Garrett Webb tonight?"

"Yeah," said Mila, surprised that Jenna knew his last name.

Mila really wanted to move toward the laundry hamper. To see if Jenna missed it. Maybe there was a piece of clothing still covering it. But Jenna was acting strange.

"Why didn't you tell me about Garrett and you?"

"I'm not sure what you mean. I'm not sure there is a me and Garrett. You know I like him."

"And you know I don't," said Jenna.

"I knew you disliked him. I figured it was just a personality thing, and you don't know him," said Mila. "He served in the military. I bet you didn't know that."

"Military? Oh, Mila. I don't trust him. You shouldn't trust him."

"He gave me a cup of coffee, some company, and a motorcycle ride. We hung out."

"You shouldn't accept anything from him. What have you done for him?"

"For Garrett?"

Jenna's voice cracked. "I found the gun."

Lie, Diabliss told her.

"I found it in a park when I was jogging. I needed money and I thought I could sell it. I don't think I broke any laws." Mila faked a laugh. "What? You don't really think I'm holding up banks, do you? That's real funny, Jenna. I'm still broke. No hold-ups. No cash."

Jenna stared. "I called UNSI," she said.

Mila looked to the door. Shit. How much time did she have? If they came, she would break through the window. Mila needed to grab a few things before her life officially ended. She grabbed a hoody and scarf.

"It's not what you think, Jenna."

"I know. You're confused. You'll see that the Light is pure. They are here to help us, and our country. There's more to this world than just you and Garrett."

"Jenna, I just met Garrett. We had one date, and it was unplanned. Is that what this is really about?"

"No, Mila. It's about an illegal object. It's about a gun."

"How much time do I have?" Mila grabbed her backpack but threw it down. What was she going to bring, a toothbrush? She just needed to get away quickly.

"Don't go, Mila. Stay. Let me help you find a better life."

"As a Holy Follower?" Mila grabbed Jenna and shook her. "Damn it, Jenna, how much time do I have left?"

"None. They're probably at his place already."

"Whose place?"

Jenna crinkled her nose. "Garrett Webb's."

"Why Garrett Webb's home?"

"Because he gave you that gun to hide. Because if Garrett Webb isn't a blackwing, he's a terrorist. I didn't report you, because you're only guilty of being naïve. I still believe that with all my heart."

Mila felt as if her entire world and life had crumbled. "Jenna, you are so wrong." Her voice shook.

"I've heard him sympathize with those dark vile creatures of Satan, in public. He needs to be taken away," Jenna shouted, bursting into tears. "He's corrupting you, Mila. You were so close to finding God, and I don't even think you know how close. I could see it in your eyes. There was light there. Now, you're so far away, far from the Light, and you need so much help. The darkness will swallow you."

Mila pushed Jenna back, burst out the door, and ran down the hallway, leaping the full flight of stairs. She rushed out the dorm into the night. She had to warn or save Garrett.

After wrapping her face with the scarf and securing her hood, her razor-sharp black wings sliced through the back of her shirt and hoody and flapped, lifting her high into the air.

Chapter 17

Garrett sat on an old leather sofa handed down to him by his dad after returning from active duty in Syranistan. Instead of facing the television, he sat sideways and stared out a window into the night sky and city lights, trying to straighten his grin. He had flipped the television off and back on several times already, mindlessly ignoring the channels and streaming options. He could not focus for more than two minutes, though. He tried to bring his smile down. Was this why people stopped rebelling? Love? Was that what made giving up the fight worth it? Garrett was already trying to determine what new major he could pick if he returned to school. A campus life with Mila? Right now, he would take that over anything.

In his lifetime, he had dodged bullets, IED's, enemy combatants, UNSIs, school officials, and city police, while fighting against what they stood for. Death, profit, and control. What did he love? Freedom. It was worth giving his life for, and that's what this had been always been about. Liberty. *Our country's engine is in disrepair. It needs to be rebuilt or replaced. The blueprint for a new engine was designed and honed over two centuries ago. Each generation denigrates and then saves this yellowed parchment, our Constitution.*

What did Mila think of the Amera-fascists? She read *Confessions*, but he was afraid to ask her true opinion. If she said she liked the government and the way things were, he would love her anyway, wouldn't he? He found himself grinning again. Tonight, his life had gained something. There was something about her. She was not like the other students.

She was an independent thinker. Open-minded. And he wanted to be with her now, tomorrow, and more. Before today, his life had value, but he had been willing to pay the price of his life for the cause of freedom.

But not now.

He would skip the meeting tonight. He could not shoot down drones and street cameras, or film UNSI beatings and assaults on civilians and their encampments. He would not blast holes in factory camp fences. Certainly not with a smile this big.

He got up, walked across the room and sat at his kitchen table. He opened his laptop and was about to turn on his computer when he heard a quiet step outside his apartment door. Something small, thin, and wormlike slid underneath the door. The wooden door rattled slightly as someone pressed on it. Most would not have noticed. Most would not have heard or sensed anything. But most had not spent three years in Syranistan sliding camera tubes under doors to see who and what was inside, pressing paper-thin C4 sheets onto the doors, blowing them into a thousand pieces, and then charging in to arrest the dissidents inside.

No.

Garrett dove to the floor, trying to land with the sofa between him and the door. He almost made it as wooden splinters, sparks and metal, and a wave of sound exploded into him. Sharp pain hit as fingernail-sized needles shot into his back. He rolled and stood up, ears ringing, and sprinted for the patio. As he rushed toward the back sliding-glass door, he saw movement and something on the glass over the lock. *That's right. They'd never come through just one door.* He rolled again, as the same flash of debris and noise exploded into him, this time piercing his back and legs with small cubes of shattered safety glass.

There was a glow at the back door. An angel. *Why would*

an angel be here?

Both escape routes were secured. The angel brightened to a point that Garrett had to squint and shield his eyes. A hand clutched his throat. He tried to press his thumbs under the fingers, but the grip was too strong. He tried to hack the arm away, but it was like chopping on a thick steel rod.

Spots from the bright light darkened as Garrett came to the verge of blacking out. He wondered if the angels were now working in tandem with UNSI across the land. If that was the case, he had underestimated the power of his enemies. His thoughts were fleeting as he fought to maintain consciousness. What did they have on him? He would be lucky to end up in a factory camp. But no, he knew he would be locked up or killed. Prison or death.

He had known this day would come, but why did it have to come today of all days, the day when he was no longer willing to pay the price?

Chapter 18

As Mila gained elevation, she stopped climbing just beneath the clouds. But she was ready to disappear into the dark gray blanket at the first sight or sound of a black helicopter. She raced toward Garrett, acknowledging that she possibly now had angels to contend with as the gun could be linked to a blackwing attack. She did not know how she would react if there was an angel present. Let Diabliss take over? He was clever. He would be better at battling an angel than she would be.

If we run into trouble, I'm turning my body over to you. So, be ready.

Diabliss was still quiet, but she had felt his fear, and he was ready to jump in. He was mad. He was depressed. But he still wanted to survive.

Streetlights and glowing storefront signs passed beneath her, and headlights and taillights scurried and veered in different directions below. There were layers of smog and exhaust that dissipated the higher she got. Her senses, more acute, attached to various scents, some good like trees and outdoor grilling, but most bad like the burning garbage that came with a city strike and delayed pickups and fried fast food. She saw movement among some trees and zeroed in on a bat flitting around in a city park. A stray alley cat crouched, ready to race forward and pounce on a dark gray rat.

Garrett's building was just a few miles away, and that was when Diabliss finally spoke.

It is ready to fight for you, but when will you be ready to fight for you, or me?

I promise, I will try.

It will teach you.

Mila did not answer right away, but finally nodded. *Deal.*

Do not enter right away.

Why not?

It's not safe. You need to circle and scout, either by air or foot, preferably both.

What about Garrett? They might be arresting him right now.

If they get you both, that will be worse. The name Jenna mentioned, UNSI, they were the ones fighting alongside the angels on the street today, right?

Right.

Approach with care.

Mila found Garrett's building. Diabliss helped, recognizing it quickly from their aerial view. She circled a few times, landed on the vacant roof, and ran to its edge. She was learning Diabliss's abilities, and she easily found which apartment patio was Garrett's. She half climbed, half flew, grabbing and standing on jutting bricks, holding on to and shimmying along deck railings, until she stood on a black iron handrail that was about two inches thick. It was much easier to balance herself on it with the occasional flap from her wings.

Mila gasped. The glass had been blown out.

Ready to go in, Diabliss?

No. Use your senses, Mila-chick. There are four men inside, and none of them are Garrett Webb. They have different heartbeats.

Mila stepped down onto Garrett's deck. The glass was gone from one side of the sliding glass door but intact on the other. She stepped to the side, listened, and then peered in. Diabliss was urging her to leave. He could see that an angel had been here, said that there were brightening molecules all over the place. He could also see molecules from an

147

explosion at the front door. She believed him but had to see the results with her own eyes.

The front door was missing and there was yellow crime-scene tape across the doorway. Garrett was gone. They had taken him away, but at least there were not any pools of blood.

Diabliss told her that turning herself in would just get everyone killed, including Garrett Webb, and she knew he was right. Of all days for her world to fall apart, it had to be the day she had finally gone out with Garrett.

An officer entered the living room from Garrett's bedroom. He saw her or at least saw something move. He would be at the door in a second. Even if Jenna did not give UNSI her name. Even if Jenna insisted that Mila was not involved, that Garrett Webb had undue influence over her, contact tracers would drag Mila in.

She thought about fighting them. They had no right to take Garrett. They had no right to be in his place. Instead, Mila jumped onto the banister and stepped back, falling straight down as the man's feet appeared at the shattered sliding glass door. Just before hitting the sidewalk, her wings pounded the air. She flew along the ground, tears streaming down her cheeks, and then shot up into the cold night sky, flying at a speed she did not even know she was capable of achieving, to a height she did not know she was capable of attaining.

Chapter 19

The room was black, and Garrett wondered if this was due to darkness or an injury, as he groped along the room's perimeter. A dim light stung as a switch flipped outside, illuminating a hallway beyond a metal door with a food-tray-sized gap at the bottom. *Solitary confinement.*

Cinder blocks with a smooth latex paint. A cold smooth stainless-steel slab the size of a single bed anchored to the wall. No sheets. No pillow. Nothing that a prisoner could use to hang himself. Not that he wanted to. Not yet. He found the metal sink and drank from the faucet. He knew there would be a single toilet and that they would remove it if he resisted.

Most soldiers serving overseas witnessed the various methods of enhanced interrogation. In fact, it was the chill that had awoken him. Perhaps fifty degrees? Garrett shivered. Textbook. They would freeze him out for twelve to twenty-four hours. Spray him down. Wet and cold. Then a dry blanket for answers. Then hot coffee or warm food for more. If that did not work, if they did not believe him, or if they wanted him to confess to doing something he had not done or to seeing something he had not seen, then the water boarding. Add confined spaces, insects, darkness. Garrett knew the playbook, but did that change anything? Did they have a protocol for a prisoner who knew the rules of engagement?

The door opened. He winced as a noise erupted and water on cold skin stung like a thousand needles. Yes. Fifty degrees and sprayed wet. In paper-thin hospital pajamas. Yes. They would even take those away, only it would not work; Garrett lacked modesty.

If he cooperated too soon, how would they ever believe

he had disclosed everything? Garrett tried to block out the list of things they would do to him. He tried not to think of new things they might try.

"Three years active duty. You know what you're fighting for. You know what you're fighting against. And you still turned on the United States of America," said a man's voice. "You're a traitor."

How much did they know? Who had turned him in? *Admit nothing for as long as possible.* How many of his friends did they have? Shit. *What if they arrest Mila?* No! She is innocent! But will that matter? They will use her against him if or when they find out he cares. He wished he had asked her out months ago and then had walked away from it all.

The door slammed shut.

Mila, you have to land eventually. We need to find shelter and energy. It can take over. You are weary and your emotions have shut down a part of your brain that is involved with reason. An air machine has detected you with electronic signals. It's following but at a distance.

Mila turned. She still had her face wrapped but was tempted to throw the scarf to the ground. At this moment, she hardly cared who knew. Diabliss was telling her to find a safe place to rest and eat, that her body felt weak. Diabliss felt her emotions. He said it was similar to when UNSIs and the angels killed the blackwing.

I'm fine, she told Diabliss. *It's time for you to see what anger combined with adrenaline and not giving a crap does.*

Mila flapped toward the helicopter. She sensed that it was turning away. *Run away, UNSI bastards. Let's see how you like it.* And the chase was on.

After several minutes of playing the crow chasing the sparrow, she let the helicopter escape.

But then two more arrived accompanied by several

drones.

I can't go on, Diabliss. Take my body. I don't care anymore. Exhausted, Mila relaxed as she ceded control of her body and mind.

Yes. It will teach them not to side with angels. Not to chase us, Diabliss assured her.

Diabliss flew away from another fireball. Black smoke snaked into the sky. Revenge felt good. Sure, the men crawling out, narrowly escaping the flames, were only following orders, but they were sent to kill blackwings. That was an order that when followed would come with consequences.

It had tried to mind its own business. Blackwings came in peace. Diabliss had to find other blackwings, like Anders in Portland, so that the system against them would change.

And the Mila-chick. Poor Mila-chick. She had lost everything. They understood each other now. They had finally connected. She understood how it felt when they snuffed the fellow blackwing. When the blackwing died, a human had died as well. Death was so certain, killing so common, that it only hurt when it happened to those you knew. For a species still in group-survival stage, humans were so fragmented and valued life so little.

Mila wanted her body back. She had unfinished business at school. Diabliss knew that this was not a wise strategic move. She finally agreed to wait. Mila recognized now that there was a war. If they avoided angels, defended themselves and occasionally attacked, they would have a chance. And just as important, she wanted to win. She had a gene that made her want to compete to win, and it was now directed toward her life, her survival. That was good.

Yes. She would consider an alliance with Anders. Yes. She agreed to let Diabliss make a dark sword. Yes. Mila was nearly treating Diabliss as an equal. It would do the same. No eating dirt without permission. No attempts to procreate with or create an attraction to Anders. If it was going to hurt someone, it'd make sure she knew about it first.

As Diabliss landed on the rooftop of her neighboring dorm back on campus, it told her again that she should get as far away from this place as possible.

We agreed, she said.

It had, but still.

Diabliss convinced Mila to sit still and observe for at least one hour. Yes. There was an undercover officer. A man too old to be a student. A stranger, walking a pattern. Around the library, through campus commons, between each dorm. It took him twenty minutes to make his loop.

The mysterious man made another pass. After Diabliss confirmed that any UNSI officers or nosy students were gone, it leapt into a tree, tucked in its wings, and climbed down. It stood at the tree's base for several minutes and then casually turned and walked, ceding control to Mila.

Once inside the dormitory, Mila removed her face scarf and ran up the stairs to the second level. It was after curfew, but there were plenty of students up and about. She smiled at a few students in the hall. She sidestepped two freshmen boys who were wrestling outside their door. A resident advisor told them to go to bed and that if they refused, he would call campus security. Their huffs and uhmps stopped.

Mila leaned back against the wall next to her room. Maybe she could just leave a note. No, life could not be that easy. She unlocked the door and stepped inside. It was dark, and Mila's instincts told her not to turn the light on. Never wake a roommate up late on a school night. Mila reminded herself that these were times where she had to ignore instincts and instead do what was necessary and right.

She flipped the light on.

Jenna was on the floor next to her bed. She was on her knees, praying. She opened her eyes and stood. She wore a short nightgown. Her knees were red. Jenna's eyes were puffy and raw as well. She had probably been praying for hours.

"You have to sleep sometime," said Mila.

"I'm praying for forgiveness. That's what Theo wants. I aided a terrorist by not reporting Garrett earlier."

"You're wrong about Garrett," said Mila. "That's why I came back."

"To protect him?" asked Jenna.

"Yes. To protect him, because he's innocent, and to grab some things, so I can leave."

"Leave?" Jenna shook her head. "Garrett, innocent?"

"Jenna, you had an innocent man taken away. I need you to set things right. I wasn't protecting him."

"It's human nature to lie to others, but especially to ourselves. That's why we trust in the White Light. It's a fight for truth and a fight for what's right."

"Says who?"

"Theo."

"Theo."

"Theo can save you. The White Light will save you. You can be on the side of angels. The right side."

"That," said Mila, "would be a lie. We don't know what or who they are, or why they are any different from blackwings."

And the White Light is cruel and vile, added Diabliss.

Thanks. Don't need your help, Diabliss.

Jenna huffed and her mouth opened in awe at words she obviously deemed blasphemous. "I could have you taken away just for speaking those words."

"Tempting. I could use the all-inclusive vacation, but I

didn't come here to argue with you. I came to set things right. Garrett is innocent, and you will call them and tell them that much."

"I will not."

"You will," said Mila. She stood with her chest out. Diabliss whispered that outstretched wings would scare Jenna to a near heart attack.

"I might hurt you," Mila added.

"I'd still love you," said Jenna. "That's what the Light does, but only a fool aids Satan, that's what the Light says. I have no use for fools. Please, don't be a fool, Mila."

Jenna held her hands out. Mila cradled them in hers as Jenna began to pray. Mila closed her eyes. Did she feel anything—a tickle, a light, a glimmer of hope, anything? Nope. Nothing. Mila let go. Jenna had been a true friend, but she was a Holy Follower now. A Holy Follower who turned in innocent people.

"You had no proof against Garrett. You have reported an innocent man," said Mila. "I'm going to tell them how you didn't report me and how you lied. They'll never trust you again. And worse than that, after we're both picked up, I'll kick your ass in our prison cell."

Jenna opened her mouth to speak, but Mila held up her finger and shook her head.

"You'll be checking names off your patriot list from a wheelchair," Mila said. "If they'll even let you be in a position of authority."

Jenna glared.

"Anyway, thanks for doing my laundry," said Mila, turning and opening the door. "I know you'll do the right thing. I love you, Jenna. You're not horrible on purpose."

"It's the devil fooling you," Jenna shouted as Mila briskly walked down the hall. "You've let it inside you."

"That's right," Mila said. "I'm worse than you think.

Worse than even you can imagine."

Once outside Mila found a dark gap between buildings. She hopped into the air and flapped slowly up.

Bring the helicopters. Show me an angel. Yes, I'll show you the devil inside.

Chapter 20

"Tell us about the girl," said a deep electronically altered voice over the speaker.

Garrett knew they did not need to disguise the voice and that it was an intimidation technique. Garrett was inside a box not much larger than his own body. It was on its end, making it twice as uncomfortable. He had been standing for hours. Days? No. Not that long. Not yet. But it was intimidating.

He thought hard. What did they know? Which girl got caught? He thought about the loosely connected organization, their many various missions, and his fellow anarchists, some anonymous, some close friends. Did he even know the names? Probably. Which were the ones most likely to get caught? Which ones were high-risk? Stupid? There was a tough aggressive girl named Brianna. Her hatred had consumed her after her younger brother was taken. There was talk about a rescue. Did they try it and get caught?

"We found the evidence. It was written down in plain sight."

Garrett closed his eyes. They knew about his writing. Tears streamed down his face. He would never feel the soft warming touch of daylight, walk more than fifty yards in the same direction, or tap the keys on his laptop while deep in a writer's trance. He would never string words together unless it was graffiti on a prison wall.

"His heart rate is going up," said a different voice, also altered. "Why are you so scared, Mr. Webb?"

No. It's a trick. A confession. That's what they want.

But that's what will make them stop.

No. If the request for information is vague, it's a trick.

Don't say anything. Don't confess. Don't tell them you're the Agorist.

Garrett shuddered and tried to slow his racing thoughts and breathing, but the heart rate increase was beyond his control. Scanners somewhere in the cell would be monitoring his stats in order to detect lies, maybe even reading brain activity. Had they gotten that far yet?

Don't think. Don't speak. Shit. He clenched his jaw, trying not to scream.

"We know what you're thinking. We know we're on the right track because of your internal statistics as well as your peculiar behavior," said the mystery voice through the ceiling speaker.

"He already confessed. We might as well throw his useless corpse away," said the second voice.

The first man spoke again. "We've got him. It's a wrap. Time to cooperate and save yourself, Mr. Webb. That's what your accomplices are doing. Tell us more."

No. Garrett had heard that one before. *Time to save yourself.* That was textbook. They were bluffing. But why would they use textbook? They had to know his history. He was a veteran. Sometimes that carried weight. But a lot of veterans were anti-gov. U.S. servicemen loved their fellow citizens and America too much to give up on freedom. That was a primary reason the federal government used privatized foreign UNSIs domestically. It was not all about free trade and debt. It was about following orders that were illegal and immoral. Garrett held back a scream crawling out of his belly and breathed deeply. If they had him, they had him. He would bite his tongue off before saying something. His calves twitched and then the muscle movement was followed by a sudden sharp pain, in one calf and then the other. Cramps. He hopped like he was on hot coals, but his knees could not bend in the tight space. His chin quivered; a yelp ready to erupt.

The desire to talk was stronger than before. His breathing quickened again.

"What would you like to tell us, Mr. Webb?"

The previous room had been black and dark. Garrett was unsure what had happened because now the room was bright white. He was on a firm bed with clean sheets. His arms, chest, and shins were not even strapped down. He thought that maybe he was in an institution and his horrible life had been a hallucinatory nightmare. He sat up and wiped sweat off his brow. A blanket, too? His eyes went to the ceiling and his heart sank. No hanging light fixture. His fragile mind tore thin strips from the sheet, making a rope he could hang himself with on the imaginary protruding light fixture.

Where has our democracy gone, Madam President? This world, this shift to fascism, detention without due process, torture, and to U.S. citizens? She would be easy to blame, but it was not her doing. There had been a gradual induction into establishment thinking that had occurred over the course of two decades. Make the people afraid and they will let you do anything, especially when it is done to someone else. Exploit every crisis. Fascism always feeds a panicked population.

The door was painted hospital white and made of prison steel. There was a gap of three inches by ten inches, where a food tray slid quickly through. He wanted to peek out but feared what he might see. A similar gap across the hall? The small room that was standing room only, the one he had been forced to stay in with cramping legs for hours and hours? If he saw that room again, he might scream. No. He could not look. He hopped off the bed and collapsed to the floor as his tender calves cramped up again. His muscles felt ripped open. He had pushed the memory of his foot out of his mind. This was bringing the memories back. The muscle spasms subsided, and he crawled across the room and sniffed at the plate. Sometimes you could smell the medicine, the hallucinogens they would try to feed him, hoping to loosen him up. Did they do that here, or were drugs only administered to Pakistanis and Iranians? Starve a man and then feed him food laced with truth serum. All Garrett smelled was food. He would chance it. He probably confessed already anyway. Maybe he was already serving his prison term.

Garrett ravenously scarfed down a cold hamburger with pale green beans, then stood and limped toward the bed. If the room started to spin, he would make himself throw up, only he could not tell whether the room was spinning or not. Nothing seemed real. Was that part of his interrogation, or was it a toll from the past several days?

As Garrett crawled into bed, he found the small pen-dot in the corner of the ceiling. A camera with a small wire going into the wall. Garrett smiled into it, and as he did so, the door clicked open. A man in a long white medical jacket entered, pushing a stool with wheels. He sat on it next to Garrett's bed. He was a brave man. Garrett could easily jump him. Hands on the neck. Thumbs into the eye sockets. A push here and a push there. Yes. The stranger could be dead or blind in under a minute. Did Garrett have the strength? No. Too late anyway. Two armed men followed and stood by the door. Each had their hands on their Tasers. Each wore Beretta M9 pistols as well.

"Mr. Webb," said the doctor, "thank you for finally speaking. That's why we promoted you to better accommodations. You finally gave up the girl." The man took out a small pad of paper and a pen from a side pocket.

The man smiled and nodded to Garrett and the pad. Garrett was supposed to say more. What woman did he give up? Or did he?

"I gave up a woman?"

"Yes," said the man.

"You're not a doctor, are you?"

The man shrugged. "If you need a medical doctor, maybe we can finish early today." The man nodded toward his notepad. He was going to wait. The power of the pause.

Garrett nodded. "You have the woman? She's the mastermind of the entire organization. In fact, she planned the entire heist. The jewels, though, she ran off with them. All that cubic zirconia." Garrett knew he should keep his mouth shut.

The man frowned, his face and eyes showing pity. "Terrorism must be so lonely."

"It is," said Garrett. "In fact, it's so lonely, I don't even know I'm a part of it. I don't even know what I've told you, if I've told you anything."

"So, that's your only confession today? That you're a lonely terrorist?" The man shook his head. "That, Mr. Webb, was not part of the deal."

"What deal?"

"The deal for the room. We'll have to move you back to the smaller room, where you can give the girl's name again. That might get you one more night of comfort. Give you time to think about your loyalties. You know how it works. We ask for names and answers. If you tell them more than once, we know you might be telling the truth. Isn't that the way it worked in Syranistan?"

Garrett straightened his shoulders. "I am a veteran."

"Most kids are."

"Doesn't that mean anything anymore? I've killed for the Amera-fas...Union. I did three years."

"You say that like it was a prison sentence, when it is an honor to serve your country and its allies."

"What would you know? Have you ever spent time on a front line? Have you ever stepped away from a desk? Have you ever seen a friend's head explode and wiped parts of his brain off your uniform, and then wear him and smell him for days?"

"And carry his ghost in your bones?"

Garrett stared at the floor, but he nodded.

"Is that why you refused to re-enlist? We know you're a veteran, and we respect that. You're getting preferential treatment even though what you've done is despicable." The man frowned again. The look of pity returned. "Your mother. She cried when we told her what you're involved in. When she found out what you're under investigation for."

Garrett smirked. "Now, I know you're lying. You obviously haven't met my mother. My mom doesn't cry. She makes men cry."

"Your mom isn't a patriot?"

"She is. Like me."

"She cried when we told her about the girl. The girl whose name you have to give to us again."

"For verification."

"Yes. To verify that you told us the truth."

Garrett did not know what to say. Had he really confessed? Did he give up Brianna? Who else had they caught? Why hadn't they said anything about agorism, or anarchy, and his writing? They called them terrorists and the writing terrorism. He forgot that was how they defined it. What girl did he give up? They were bluffing. But why did they say "girl"?

"I'm not talking. I want to cooperate, but I do have the right to an attorney. We're not in Syranistan."

The man's eyes narrowed, turning cold. "How would you know where you are?"

Garrett thought about it. He did not know, and they would not tell him. He could never prove he was in the states. No. They were bluffing again. If he were imprisoned outside the states, wires would clipped to his balls, attached to a car battery in the corner.

The man stood, turned his back on Garrett, and pushed his wheeled stool toward the door. "Too bad. I guess you lose the accommodation. Maybe next we take that high-tech foot back. Would you like that?"

Garrett shook his head, too weak to argue. But not the box. Go ahead. Take the foot. But not the box. His legs were already cramping. Even his prosthetic lower seemed to cramp. If it was in his head, was it still real? The doctor signaled and four men came in and the straps were over him. He tried to sit up and struggle but could not escape their hold. He saw a needle, felt the sharp jab and the room spun.

"Mila," the man said from the doorway. "Mila was the name you were supposed to give us."

"No!" Garrett tried to scream but his throat was too dry. "No. Not Mila. I just met her. She's innocent." He wanted to say more, but the room was rotating too fast, and the blackness had already begun erasing bits and pieces of his consciousness.

Not Mila. No, not Mila.

Chapter 21

Theo swallowed a red jellybean. How could they be so good? He sat across from the president, inside her former jet.

"Madam President," said Theo, "I know you won't like the beasts. Your Congress would never approve, at least not without compensation, but your banker friends?" He leaned forward, inches from her face. "I am nearly telling a lie when I say friends, and I abhor lies. Your financial supporters don't care. They care about people in the same way a shepherd cares about his sheep. And we are shepherds here as well, only now we are raising Holy Followers. The White Light is the only thing this government should care about."

"And those creatures serve the White Light's divine purpose."

"Yes." Theo stood. He liked standing over this president. She was strong, cold, and smarter than most humans, and she was not easily intimidated. That could be dangerous, but if she believed her end was being served, she would follow orders. "Holy Followers, those who have sworn an oath and wear the white loyalty band on their arm, shall have special privileges and powers that allow them to face and seek out the terrors before them."

Millions upon millions had turned their lives over to the White Light, in the name of God, yet a small but growing percentage had not. That annoyed Theo. He had no patience for doubt and debate, not with blackwings on the loose. *There might be a day when we will bring you glory, through love.* But not with blackwings here. *Today, we will bring you glory through pain.*

Theo radiated light and added a musical note to his

words. People became enchanted when he did that, even the president. Theo spoke, "We open the portal one more time. We let new beings through. They will adapt to our world, and then they will do our bidding. They will hunt the blackwings down. Yes, they are demons and minions of Satan, just like the blackwings, and yes, they are from the place you call hell, but you need not worry. God created these simple beasts for a purpose, and like beasts of burden, they will serve us. They will merely add to the effectiveness of your UNSI agents. Also, I am not asking, I am telling so you can prepare, so you can assist."

The president nodded. Theo could see her thoughts as if they were floating in the room between them, and so Theo spoke again. "I know. You think you should share power. Your pride tells you to exert some power, only you and your ruling class don't have as much power as you all think you do. You print paper, call it money, and use it to buy power. Why couldn't the White Light print paper and tell your subjects to use it instead?" Theo thumped her with a stiffened index finger on her breastplate. "It's best you and your elites never forget that the White Light was sent by God and wields God's swords."

"People are simple in some ways, and complex in others, but we are trying. *I* am trying."

Her face drained of color. She was truly frightened for her life, or she was good actor. The fact she was not begging for her life and was negotiating at all indicated she was courageous, and perhaps this was the first time she had felt this much fear. Theo patted the president on her forehead like he had seen so many people pet small dogs. She closed her eyes. "Your men are simply not capturing blackwings quickly enough. Four angels were burned in Portland, Oregon. *Burned.*"

"And this killed them?"

Theo glared at the president. "I know that your secret police capture angels and explore weaknesses. Just don't ever think that we don't have legions of angels ready to enter this world and commandeer every soul in it by force. But most important, don't think that we will ever need to enlist more angels."

"Our law enforcement agencies are classified as government agencies, but these are semantics. They follow their own rules. We lost control of them a long time ago. We are usually aligned but not always. That will change. I can have the agents who offended you and those who ordered this dealt with in any way you deem appropriate."

"Yes, do unto them as they have done unto us. We are God's servants, and we are here to save humanity from the forces of Satan. When they do these vile, evil things, it's because they have secretly turned their souls over to an evil master."

"Yes, Theo. I will take care of them right away. Every person who participated. Those who gave the orders, will burn. For the White Light is Right."

"The White Light is Right," said Theo. "And you know how I know about my fellow angels?"

Without hesitating, the president said, "You have nearly one hundred million Holy Followers around the world, and the numbers are growing. Even though the majority are on the bottom of the economic pyramid, many of the Holy Followers are uniformed, your growing White Light Infraguard, and many Holy Followers are secretly in critical, strategic, military, financial, and political positions. And we do not know who they all are. In fact, when there's no white arm band or white Infraguard body armor, there is no way of ever knowing who follows the White Light."

"And you? Why do you not wear the white arm band? Are you not an official Holy Follower?"

"I serve the country first. I hope you believe me when I say that I am as loyal to you as any Holy Follower."

"Because it serves your country," said Theo. "Profess your devotion to the White Light on camera." Theo knew she would say yes, but it bothered him that he had to order this. Why couldn't they all be like the young devotee, Jenna? Why did he always find himself thinking about her? The White Light would find a way to emulate Jenna's devotion and reward that kind of loyalty with power.

The president looked down, away, and then spoke, "Of course. And your beasts. The siccums, or dirt hounds, still worry me. I wish I could convince you that other methods will prevail."

"Sometimes we must make sacrifices. The siccums are not to be killed. I will bring in only ten legions and sprinkle them throughout the world. They will chase the blackwings into the sky, where they will be easier to find. They will kill some blackwings on the ground as well."

"And the collateral damage?" she asked.

"The collateral damage. Yes. They can only travel by night, so few people will see them. Your sun will burn them after it rises if they are in the open, so they will hide through the daylight hours. There will be many humans damaged in the hunt. This is the fault of the blackwings, and they are responsible for any deaths."

"I can make sure the press responds accordingly."

"You are a good ally," said Theo. "They will feed on blood until they find their blackwings. They will need to eat nightly."

"So, ten thousand. Not all in the Amero Union?"

"Correct."

"So, ten thousand dead per day around the world. Less blackwings. Three to four million per year."

"If it takes that long."

She nodded. "Most of the people out at night are terrorists or have low moral character," she said matter-of-factly.

"And they won't *always* feed on humans."

"The cost is fair. And you'll help us rid the world of them when they're done?"

"I will. But understand that I'm not asking your permission. I'm glad that you agree though."

"Thank you for working with us on this blackwing problem. The Amero Union, particularly the United States, has led the world for over a century. With the guidance and mercy of the White Light and God, we will all flourish."

"Oh, we will."

The red beast in the sprawling suburb took form and crawled from the earth. It sensed movement and pounced. There was a yelp as a four-legged creature, not much different from the siccum, only much smaller, met its end. Its two-legged master screeched and ran away, still holding a small rope that had been wrapped around its writhing four-legged slave. The siccum would chase that being down later.

A warm syrup filled the siccum's maw. Oh. It was so good. It lapped at the pool and then traced its source to the dead creature and placed its maw over the open wound.

The cold dark space was gone. The White Light had finally set them free. They had to earn their freedom, though. The beast wanted to feast on the White Light, but no, that would put them back in the cold dark space where they could not move and could not die. And the light. The White Light always hurt. This world, though, plenty of dark, but the burning star would rise. It would need to feed frequently. At least there was plenty to feast upon. It could smell the trail of flesh, the sweet wafting molecules. The siccum could tell that this world was soft. Syrup would be easy. It had to find a bit more before dawn.

Another odor drifted by. Ah…blackwings. It sensed that one had been near. That's why the White Lights released siccums on this planet, for the hunt.

The siccum grunted and rolled over, sawing its back in the course earth, trying to get its wings to come out quicker. The siccum liked blackwings—in fact the siccums liked anything with rich syrup inside.

Chapter 22

The room Garrett sat in was different than any of the previous rooms. All the other rooms were tight confined spaces, and always white. This room had been painted beige. His chair even had a thin cloth padding rather than cold steel or hard plastic. A guard had told him he was being released, but Garrett figured this was a part of the interrogation. Show him what release looked like, let him feel the emotions, and then jerk him back in. Ask one more question. Demand more to his story. If he confessed, and argued Mila's innocence, they would only pluck her off the street and try to find a link. If he said nothing and maintained his own innocence, they would not be able to tie her to anything. If they did have Mila, it meant there was no real evidence. She was as pure as a girl could get. They probably caught her on surveillance. They had probably raided his place on a lead but did not count on him covering his tracks so well and now wondered if they had anything but a confused veteran.

A man entered, the same man who had interrogated him previously. He had changed from his white lab coat and was wearing a black suit and red and blue tie. His polished black dress shoes reflected the overhead lights.

"The girl, Mila, is on the run. She is now wanted by UNSI officers for routine questioning. You can save us time. Tell us her whereabouts."

"You'll probably get promoted when you find her. She's a criminal mastermind. She's in charge of every evil organization known to mankind," said Garrett. He shook his head. "Is everyone working for the government an idiot? Sorry if I'm losing faith here, I only just met her. She came into my coffee shop a few times. She came back to my place one time and only stayed for a few hours. I kissed her and nothing more. She's as pure as a girl can get."

"A source above reproach, a Holy Follower, turned you in as a terrorist," said the man. "After we picked you up, Mila conveniently disappeared."

"She's probably looking for her father. He's missing. Maybe the person who turned me in is your terrorist," Garrett said. "I'm a veteran. I'm loyal to our country. I'm just trying to get by. Nothing more. Nothing less."

"The source was a devout Holy Follower. Maybe she was misled?" He shrugged his shoulders, leafed through his paperwork, and then stared at Garrett, squinting his eyes. "Maybe she wasn't, and you just got away with something. We'll find out if she's missing a father."

"It's just games between college girls. That's why I usually stay away from them. I broke my own rule, and I've paid the price."

"We do not believe yet that your involvement was entirely innocent, but all else appears to be in order. Since this is part of an ongoing investigation pertaining to domestic terrorism, these events can never be discussed outside these walls." The man closed his folder and hugged it against his chest. He raised one finger to his lips.

"Not even with an attorney?"

The man shook his head and again held his fingers in front of his lips.

"We used to have rights in this country," said Garrett.

The man chuckled. "When?" He balked.

Garrett nodded. "Good point. Back when there were only plants?"

"Not even then. Let's put it this way, it's better than what was dished out in Syranistan."

"I followed orders."

"You're a killing machine. Over sixty confirmed kills in three years. We could still use a soldier like you."

"I'm not all that impressive. They were fighting us with sticks and stones."

"Figuratively true, but not literally."

"And I got wounded."

"Hardly noticeable. Thank you, technology."

"Are you a field veteran?" Garrett asked.

"No, not of the battlefield."

"Figures."

"We can't all sling bullets. Some of us have to sling thoughts."

"Well, it's working great. Economy. Shot. Freedom. Shot. Justice. Shot."

"Would you like to be returned to Syranistan? I could make that part of your release. We could discuss this again in say, three years?" He stared at Garrett, who shifted uncomfortably.

Yes, this man had him.

"Tell me how their economy, their freedom, and their justice, compares to ours." The man looked at Garrett with a frightening cold-hearted glare, knowing he had the upper hand. "You could be under the earth, like so many who came across you during your tour."

Garrett shook his head.

"I thought you might see things our way," the chief interrogator said.

They finished another short interview, and then Garrett was left in silence for what seemed like hours. A guard brought in Garrett's street clothes and told him to change right there. Was this a trick, to get his hopes up? It was not working. As Garrett put his clothes on, he knew he had no hope. Not only was he in custody, if he got out, he would be under strict surveillance. If he got out, he would likely have no chance with Mila. Why would she ever want to date someone who came with his kind of baggage? And how could he ever put someone as sweet as her in harm's way again?

The door opened. A man placed Garrett's hands behind his back and cuffed them. He placed another set of shackles around Garrett's ankles and connected the ankle lock to the wrist behind his back. "Mr. Webb, follow me," said a tall, square-shouldered guard.

Garrett shuffled out of the room, down a hallway, and into a large foyer, where the man in the suit was waiting, along with two other men. Garrett could see outside, but there were guards inside and out. Two secure locked doors led to the outside. If it opened, he would run for it. Bullets or no, a death for a breath? He might take that trade. There had to be more to his release, otherwise they would be wearing smiles, even fake ones. Instead, they motioned for him to approach.

"Mr. Webb," said his interrogator, "we would prefer to release you. We had a judge's order allowing us to take you into custody, as well as the congressional panels' approval of our interrogation techniques. We could hold you and interrogate you for another sixty days."

"But let me guess. Today's my lucky day."

"It is."

"When I get out, I'll buy a lottery ticket. My lawyer?" Garrett asked, nodding toward a stranger in the room.

"Yes."

A squat balding man spoke up. "You can leave now, but you can never claim that the interrogation methods used were cruel or unusual. You will not have the right to compensation, but you will be reimbursed for your days here comparable to your average earnings based on last year's tax returns. You have also waived your right to appeal to your elected representatives or any other government entities. This is a terrorist investigation, and silence is necessary to preserve this institution during a time of war. State's secrets."

"I'd lose anyway," said Garrett.

The two men nodded.

"Where do I sign?" Garrett asked. "Or do we need a knife? Is it signed in blood?" There was a time where he would have refused on the grounds of principle, or at least he thought he would have. But no. Whether they realized it or not, they had discovered his limitation. The intimidation, the interrogation, and the torture worked, but Mila was the key. They found one thing he cared about besides law and country. He would have died for law and country. All those months of shielding himself from care. All those months of keeping a wall around himself. And one motorcycle ride, a night of hand holding, and a few soft gentle kisses had brought it all down. And she would never see him again, as she shouldn't.

"Just give me the damn paper. It's not a confession, right?" Garrett asked, skimming through the black and white blur, trying to tell himself to slow down and read the actual words.

"It's not, Mr. Webb. The informant recanted her story. Under normal circumstances, we'd keep you here longer, much longer, but seeing you're a veteran and you've cooperated, you're getting a break," said Garrett's interrogator. "The agreement simply says your incarceration and questioning never happened. If you ever say it did, you can be arrested for treason."

"I won't get junk mail now, will I?" Garrett asked, looking up. "Do I put down my email address for coupons and special offers?"

"Not one piece of mail and no coupons, at least not from us."

"This never happened," said Garrett, shaking his head and shifting his feet. "Tell that to my calves."

Chapter 23

Mila flew through thick droplets of frigid rain and a fall temperature drop that was all too common in Seattle. Her sopping-wet clothes were heavy and clung to her skin. The generous soaking allowed the cold to stick and seep toward her bones. She had been flying and rooftop hopping for two days, returning to Garrett's place each night, and each night he was still gone. Diabliss finally moderated her body temperature so that she felt as if she were under sun's rays and the wetness was only a summer splash from a heated pool, and this annoyed her. Good feelings were undeserved and unwanted.

He called the temperature elevation energy conservation. She called it meddling. In the University district, through Diabliss' guidance and research, they had found a research facility specializing in nanotechnology, amongst many things, with the necessary tools and elements for building a dark sword, a lightweight weapon that Diabliss said could cut metal or stone. They needed three days inside the facility— the next long weekend they would find a way in. Diabliss would figure out everything once inside.

Flying near her school only increased Mila's loneliness. She wanted to find Jenna, confess, and beg for forgiveness and her old life back. Why did this world have to be so difficult and complicated? The raindrops blurred her vision, but she still spied a family pushing a grocery cart below. They disappeared under an overpass. Mila circled back as another small group entered the cement structure from the other side. It caught her attention because the area was uninhabited and mostly abandoned industrial buildings. Mila landed around a corner and followed them into the darkness. No human contact for two days was driving her a little crazy.

Mila passed a small crackling campfire surrounded by two parents with a young girl and a baby. The dead-end street beneath an overpass with heaping junk piles, sprawling tarps and tents was unhealthy for kids, but what choice did they really have? Mila could see the sadness in the parents' eyes. They had likely been foreclosed on and had two choices, a factory camp, where eventually the kids would be adopted out or sent away to government school, or this small but growing tent city. Life in the shadows revealed a new world to Mila. She had expected and hoped to find blackwings like herself. Others on the run. But the nighttime streets hid more than blackwings, something much darker, much more sinister. Street people lived like rats, scurrying, scavenging, digging burrows under musty bridges, popping in and out of sewers like moles, desperate to avoid the next UNSI sweep. These people did not care about blackwings. They certainly ignored a quiet girl like Mila who minded her own business. They smiled and nodded, but never questioned. Nobody asked anyone anything.

Although most ignored strangers, a young girl, bored or curious, approached Mila and sat alongside her. "My mom said I shouldn't talk to you," said the little girl.

"You should obey your mama," said Mila.

"She said shouldn't, not don't. Where's your mama?"

"She passed away a long time ago—when I was a few years older than you."

"Where's your daddy?"

"He disappeared," said Mila. After sensing concern, Mila added, "I'm sure he's okay, though."

The girl, about five years old, had a sick baby brother. She explained her parents' dilemma without emotion, as if she could repeat it but not understand it. Do they turn the baby in so it can get the medicine it needs, and risk having the family placed in a camp and separated, or do they hope and pray the baby heals on its own?

Mila smiled at the girl as she shared her toy stuffed rabbit, bouncing it along Mila's crossed leg. She eventually left to be with her mom, dad, and her baby brother. Mila's problems shriveled a bit. This young girl was in for a much harder life than Mila. At least if Mila needed something, she could likely just take it. Mila stood and walked over to the family. She asked if she could hold their baby. Although its nose ran and the outside air was cold, the baby warmed Mila's arms. The mom and dad seemed grateful that anybody cared enough to ask. They talked about the cold, wet, polluted air and how the baby cried most of the time. It coughed and rasped as if hearing their words. When Mila understood its condition better, she handed the baby back and left.

After turning a corner, Mila ran until she found a drugstore five blocks away. The street next to it was busy with evening traffic, but the parking lot, like most retail parking lots, was empty except for two vehicles.

Diabliss understood what she was doing, and Mila sensed he was laughing. *Take what you want, it says. Why pay?*

"Diabliss, you're encouraging me to steal," she said. "You probably shouldn't encourage me to break the law."

Encouragement. Is that what you call it?

Mila threw her scarf across her face and flipped her hoody up. She walked quickly through the front door and hastily made for the back of the store. A customer, seeing her wrapped face, stepped out of the way, dropped the shampoo bottle she was holding, and then dashed toward the front exit. Mila had been too young and barely remembered the days when everyone wore masks, but now, a person walking into a store with a covered face meant a robbery.

Mila had to be quick.

After hopping the counter, Mila did not waste time and went straight for the pharmacist. He reached under the counter with his right hand. She peeked under it. Sure enough. He had sounded an alarm. She grabbed the elderly pharmacist by his throat with one hand and then grabbed his belt by the other. Utilizing Diabliss' alterations to her strength, she lifted the frightened man six inches off the ground, pushed him against the wall, and then set him down.

She patted out the wrinkles in the shoulders of his white coat. "You understand that I can break every bone in your body?"

He scowled but nodded.

"Amoxicillin," she said.

He went to a stainless-steel refrigerator and pulled out a small bottle. Mila looked over her shoulder. The store manager had run back and now held a cell phone to his ear. Upon seeing Mila, he ran back toward the front, disappearing behind a large candy display.

Mila pushed a small notepad from the counter toward the pharmacist, who held the bottle hesitantly.

"Don't be a hero. In this world, heroes die at the beginning of a story," Mila said. "On the paper. Baby dose. Six months old."

The man nodded and scrawled the dosage. He even retraced a number, making it more legible.

"Thanks," she said.

"It needs to be refrigerated."

"I'll find a way," said Mila. "Or come back for more."

The man glowered, obviously disgusted.

"Don't be a jerk," Mila said. "What's the right amount of profit for a dying baby?"

The pharmacist's face relaxed, and he nodded. "We're open until ten," he said. He pointed to a back door as they

177

both heard shuffling and approaching footsteps coming from the front of the store.

Mila ran, kicked the door open, and shot her wings through the back of her hoody. A police car was parked at the front, and another was rounding the corner, careening toward the back of the store, but Mila was already flying into the night.

Diabliss told her he could sense ripples through the air, and that on a clear night they would somehow sense her flying, so she traveled by rooftops, running and leaping, with short flights across the gaps, and for an extra measure, she cut through alleys by foot. She lifted a loaf of bread and a box of donuts off a bakery truck. Yes. She was now, officially, a thief, so why not grab a bite and some comfort food as well.

The lone dark corner under the small highway overpass beckoned. Cars rolled overhead like crashing waves. Conversations subsided as Mila wandered into the cavern-like area, but as each group either recognized her as having been there before, or saw that she was a woman alone, their voices returned. There was laughter, weeping, and whispers, interrupted by the occasional belligerence or scuffle.

She found the little girl and their family. The father had left to find formula and water. Mila was thirsty, too. Here she was in the rainiest city on earth, but without running water, her voice was coarse, and her throat parched.

"Take this. It needs to be refrigerated soon," said Mila. "Find a coffee shop nearby and just be honest. Tell them you don't have a functioning fridge, that times are hard, and it's for the baby. I'm sure they'll keep it there for you. Follow this dose." Mila handed over the crumpled piece of paper.

"I don't know what to say." The woman's voice turned to a whisper, her tears forming and about to spill. "I don't know how you did this."

Mila broke open the donut box and pulled one out. She

stared and then took a bite. "I'm a cop," she said, mouth full, pointing to the pilfered box.

"Whatever you are, thanks."

"Don't stop giving this to the baby until it's gone. If you do, you might make the chest infection worse. Can you do that?"

The woman nodded, the tears now streaming down her face.

Later, the father returned. Mila had already moved to her own personal spot in the dark shadows and had just nearly fallen asleep. His dark outline loomed before her. He tugged her up and off the ground and then hugged her until Mila finally pushed him away, insisting she needed sleep. But she felt good for the first time since her quiet night with Garrett.

After a few nights of sleeping pressed against a hard cement pillar on a sidewalk that seemed even harder and less forgiving, Mila was approached by a mother in soiled clothes with daughter of fifteen or so. Whenever a new person appeared, Mila hoped it would be her father. She shuddered at what he must be going through. She felt the crick in her neck, and even with the ability to regulate her body heat, the cement emanated more than just temperature. It stated that life itself was cold and bleak. Unless he was also a blackwing, her father's experience would be worse than hers.

"She's diabetic," said the mother, her jaw quivering. She handed Mila a small script.

Mila nodded. "I'll take care of it." There were more people coming to her each night. At least her blackwing empowerment allowed her to care for those in need. Now if only superhuman abilities could help her achieve a normal life.

The pharmacies within a ten-mile radius soon had armed guards stationed out front. Didn't they know by now that blackwings could fly much farther than that? UNSI patrols increased as well. Sure, Mila wanted to keep a low profile, but many of those in need were children or seniors. All were unemployed or with unemployed parents. In this world it was not that people had not planned or saved, there was no work, or no living-wage work—at best, high-tax low-wage slave jobs. Basic health care plans, even subsidized ones, were a waste of money people did not have. Most people were on a treadmill that churned faster than they could run.

The mom turned away. The fifteen-year-old girl stood for a moment, as if wanting to hang with Mila. Mila had nearly forgotten that she was not much older. Mila kept to herself as much as she could, but she craved companionship as much as anybody. In the last week, she had already called her coach two times, finally leaving a message that she was searching for her dad. Mila had also called Kathy, leaving a message to email the same story to her professors. Mila had indeed flown to Portland and combed the streets once again looking for her dad. Mila understood young and lonely.

The girl said, "I don't know how you do it, but thank you for helping us and being so kind. My mom cares more about me than I do. I'd just as soon end it all."

"You're worth more than that," said Mila. "Don't ever forget it. The world will change. Maybe you'll be the one who changes it."

"When I grow up, I want to be just like you."

"I hope not," said Mila.

"You help people who can't help themselves."

Mila scooted over. "Here, sit. We'll talk about school, love, life, makeup, and soccer—things that don't exist right now in our world." Only they talked as if it all did. As if it was just around the corner and they were only taking a momentary break. After a few hours of giggles and conversation, the teenager's mom eventually called over that it was time to sleep.

"Thanks." The girl smiled, turned, and walked away to a small lean-to she lived in with her mom that was barely under the crowded overpass and just out of the rain.

Mila's thoughts turned to Garrett. She planned on flying by Garrett's place one more time. She had flown by the coffee shop a few times recently, but strangers now worked there. A sit-down coffee appealed to Mila, but she feared running into Jenna and Kathy, so she never stayed.

Shortly after dark, she dropped off a full diabetic monitoring kit with insulin for her new teenaged fan. Then she found an empty alley, and after covering her face as she had so many times, she worked her way into the cloud-filled night sky.

Mila returned to the growing under-bridge tent city. She nearly flew to Portland, to again look for her father, but realized the futility. Her father could be in any city or even any state, if he were even still alive.

She knew she could not help everyone, but it seemed every homeless person with a medical condition had arrived at the under-bridge compound. The growing lean-to village now spilled out from under the freeway. This would attract trouble. A similar encampment nearby had been raided. It was an ugly scene. People flushed out and then beaten down by the UNSIs.

The increase in numbers also meant more crazies.

Five miscreants had made a brief appearance the night before. They drank all night, made too much noise, and then left. The campers, especially Mila, hoped it was for good. But they only returned the next night with more to drink. When dawn hit, they were still partying strong. Smoking meth, too. They had two skinny unkempt teenage girls with them. At first it appeared that the girls kept to themselves, but a closer look revealed that they were joined at the wrist by a cable with a lock. She flashed back to when they had arrived the night before, and then Mila's eyes went to where the girls had sat all night. Another cable was latched to a cement block. These girls were slaves on a leash, most likely sex slaves.

It was one of many dark cold realities that came with a collapsed economy and excessive homelessness.

Mila watched as the street thugs surrounded two young men. Bystanders scattered—fearful and intimidated, looking only at their own feet. With a hard shove, the skinnier of the two young men went down to the ground. A kick followed.

Mila stood.

"Leave them alone," she said. "And get out of here. That means, you can leave this place in peace or in pieces."

The men turned away from Mila, a few of them laughing outright. Another kick went into the man on the ground. His partner crouched down and shielded him with his arms.

"Oh, this should be good," said one thug. His friend nodded. All five men approached Mila.

Mila knelt and stuffed a few personal things into her backpack. She wanted to be ready in case she revealed her blackwing status and had to rush away. She did not have the patience or tolerance for bigots and bullies and knew that if blood flowed, it would not be hers. In a strange way, she was beginning to like that. To Mila's surprise, a few more people approached when the hooligans confronted her. They were people she had helped, even an old man with new prescription glasses whom she had saved from near blindness after he had lost his only pair. But the gang was better prepared. A knife came out, and then another. The third man broke his bottle. A steel pipe slid down the sleeve of a fourth gang member, and Mila could tell by the movement that it was packed with sand. The final man stood still, and Mila guessed by the way his long jacket was undone that he had something hidden. He turned and laughed, and Mila saw the pistol on a belt holster on his left hip.

"We're not afraid of women, children, fags, and, particularly, broken-down men," said the tallest man.

Oh, can it have this, please? asked Diabliss.

No. I can… Mila shook her head.

"Having doubts now?" asked the man with the gun.

"Yes," said Mila. "But not the doubts you're thinking. I'm giving you one chance to leave."

"No. You won't ever see us leave," said the man with the gun. He looked to the young girls and then back to Mila and smiled. "You'll be a nice souvenir."

"You won't leave?" Mila asked.

"No," he said.

Mila pointed. "The girls stay. The cable comes off. If I ever see you collecting teenage runaways again—in fact, if I see you with *any* girls—I'll rip your fucking arms off. This is your one chance to walk away."

The men looked at each other and laughed. They passed around their vodka bottle, talking about how fun this was going to be and telling the people who had amassed around Mila that they could not fight a blind two-legged dog and win.

"I'm really a considerate person," said Mila, looking at the girls, girls staring at the pavement, girls without even a glimmer of hope. "But you're being extremely rude, and I warned you. I gave you a chance to leave. And you will regret your god-awful poor decision-making abilities for the rest of your short lives."

Yes, Diabliss. You can have them. But no wings. And don't make a bloody mess in front of the crowd. Try to keep it PG-13, if you know what I mean.

Diabliss really wanted to fly. It had developed a fondness for carrying nuisances into the air and dropping them. But only five men? It did not need the wings. Diabliss looked at the two girls. *Slaves.* It knew *exactly* how the girls felt.

Diabliss moved Mila's mouth into a smile, then bared her teeth and hissed.

The men disliked that. They moved in. Diabliss couldn't even make a mess? Not fair. Oh, it wanted to pull the arms off and chase them away while they bled. No. That's likely what Mila had meant by no mess, particularly not a bloody one, *in front of the crowd.*

Diabliss knew the best ways to strike and figured that the one watching from the back was most likely their leader. Of course. The man with the gun.

Diabliss ran forward, jumped, and wrapped its legs around a man's waist, its forearm and elbow slamming into the throat. The man's Adam's apple collapsed.

Diabliss hopped up. It was not afraid of the pistol. This man would only have time to gasp for air, and fail, all without blood, *in front of the crowd.* As the other men moved in quickly, Diabliss threw them aside. No mess.

Diabliss looked at the young female prisoners and shook Mila's head.

There should be a mess, it said.

Diabliss broke one pair of arms and then another.

These men would never grab girls again. Diabliss chased them out from under the bridge, and as the men turned into an alley and out of sight from the tent city a few blocks away, Diabliss rounded them up and then started with the legs.

Soon, all the men could do was crawl, wriggle, and writhe like worms on a sidewalk. *Slaves?* They would be pavement slaves forever. It knew Mila preferred the bloody mess away from the families, but she did not say do not to kill them. Diabliss closed their throats, taking away their breaths. It looked into their eyes each time and watched them go away. After the flurry of cells diminished, it stacked them inside a dumpster. Diabliss thought again about flying them into the air and dropping them, but that would bring attention. And they might bleed. No bloody mess Mila had said.

Then again, maybe a small trail of clues could be a good thing, and hardly messy at all. *Yes. With bait, it could hunt the White Light before it hunts us.*

Mila wanted the wings hidden, only no one was looking. Mila disliked it when the bodies were dropped while alive, but Mila should not care if they were dropped while they were dead.

Diabliss, what are you doing?

It didn't fly in front of the crowd. No mess. No blood. But it's a war, and someday you'll understand.

Diabliss picked up a body and flew. It dropped the corpse on a police vehicle several blocks away. Diabliss lifted another dead limp man and flew with him, dropping him on an empty commercial building's rooftop.

Mila, this is war.

This will bring the White Light closer, said Mila.

Yes. It will. This is self defense. Trust it.

Chapter 24

People no longer fit inside the church, so Theo had cancelled all professional soccer games in Seattle and Portland. He now occupied the soccer stadium. A hundred thousand plus had arrived, and more amassed in the streets outside the stadium. This was now the largest permanent religious venue in world history. And he could still fill a larger one. Theo thought about sending the masses home. Didn't they realize they could see his message from anywhere? Whenever he spoke, he was livestreamed and on every station. Not just one or two, or even the major networks and streams; he was on all of them, as well he should be. Soon, there would be an angel and a million Holy Followers in and around every stadium throughout the world. People could watch from home, but they used feelings and not logic when it came to the White Light. This was good. This would make the battle easier. This same emotional wiring made them hate and fear the blackwings.

Theo sighed at the knock on the door of the small makeshift broadcast station inside the stadium. He knew what it would be. A question. People can't think on their own, can they? How hard was this? Broadcast a message. Hunt down the blackwings. Turn them over to the White Light.

"Enter," said Theo.

"Sir," said a man, his eyes staring at the floor, "there is another report of a creature from hell feeding on humans. There are pictures on the Internet. What should we do? More of Satan's minions, obviously."

"And you assume that I do not know of these creatures?" asked Theo accusingly.

"You hadn't said anything. There are reports on the Internet. A video. It attacked the man holding the camera."

"Ah, more creatures from hell. The end must be near."

"Yes."

"People should always be aware that salvation and the final battle are always around the corner."

"Should we prepare an alert?"

"An alert?" Theo asked.

"An alert, so that people, or even the White Light Infraguard, can be on the lookout for these creatures and turn over leads to angels—the White Light."

"You can say angels. It is right and good to call us by familiar names. Unless you doubt that we are angels?"

"I promise I do not," said the man, leaving his mouth open, his face a blistery red. He looked shocked that Theo would even ask him this.

"These creatures have red skin, more eyes than usual, and crawl on the ground like a common earth hound, though they try to fly with wings too small to lift and support them in the air?" Theo asked.

"Yes, and they are much larger than a common hound." The man looked up and smiled. Upon making eye contact with Theo, he quickly looked down, but not before Theo flashed his light, stunning the man.

"Men should never look angels in the eyes, especially at close range." If they could not look angels in the eyes, they could not easily attack them. The blindness would be temporary, but only because Theo wanted it this way, not because his servant did not deserve permanent blindness.

"I'm so sorry," the man sobbed. "I looked by accident."

"Still wrong," said Theo. "And again, the pictures?"

"Yes. That's what the pictures show. A monstrous hound, obviously in league with blackwings. You are familiar with these creatures?"

187

"Of course. The blackwings are evil, as are these creatures. They are from hell, and they are foul and evil, but we will leave them alone for now, for they will lead us to blackwings."

"We leave them alone?"

"Yes, and then we fight them when I command. We will always fight evil in the end."

"So much evil," the man said. "Thank God for angels."

"Yes," said Theo. "Thank God. Now, we have been too nice to traitors. Terrorists are working with blackwings, and we need to arm more Holy Followers. The final battle is near. Your Satan is growing afraid, but Satan commands an army that is growing too strong to deny any longer."

"I feared this was so. Many of us have feared this is so. There were reports. Armed rebellion. Against the government. People are taking sides."

"Yes. We all knew this would happen."

"Is Satan near?"

"Satan is here," said Theo, "and he is a blackwing."

Chapter 25

It snorted and crawled out into the darkness. It smelled the air. *Yesss.* A blackwing was nearby. The beast watched with its three eyes, forward, up, and behind. Next to the siccums, it seemed that only the tiniest creatures in this realm had more than two eyes. The siccum jumped into the air, flapped, and landed several yards away. Oh, if only it could go higher, like a blackwing, like the White Light. No. The White Light made it this way. It would have too much power if it flew. Yes, too much, and then it would eat too much.

The siccum saw movement. *Two humans.* No. It had time to find more. *But these are so close. Yum. Warm syrup.* No, find the blackwing smell. With difficulty, it veered away, scuttling between two dwellings into a narrow roadway with reeking heaps of garbage.

Ah, a group of young humans against a metal fence. They sucked from glass bottles. The siccum would suck from them. It picked up speed. Molecules floated through the air, drawing it to the right body like a string. Breath, floating cells and microbes, all given off by a blackwing. The siccum followed the trail of floating particles and leapt.

The air was smoky and pungent. The blackwing, in its human host, swayed in a stupor. Upon discovering the siccum, the blackwing's hidden wings shot out. The other humans screamed, though they stared at the blackwing. Hah. They did not know.

The blackwing rose into the air, but it was too late. The siccum's vicious razor-sharp teeth dug into its throat, ripping half the neck off. The blackwing managed to gain altitude, but the human head was barely attached, and its body lost fluids faster than it could replace them. The siccum fell to the ground with a mouthful of flesh. Not even a blackwing could repair the tear in such a short time.

The blackwing fluttered and dipped. The siccum leapt into the air, beating its tiny wings as hard and as fast as it could, nearly catching the blackwing's foot.

The frantic wailing humans scattered.

The blackwing gained altitude and then lost it again. Before hitting the ground, the blackwing reached up with its human hands, trying to place the dangling head back in place, trying to slow the blood loss, trying to get blood to its brain. Yes. Even a blackwing needed that. The blackwing flapped its wings but crashed to the black asphalt.

The siccum again tore into its mark. This time it had it by the leg, pulling against the blackwing, using its front claws to reel it in. The blackwing let go of the head in an attempt to to fight the siccum. The siccum flapped, crawled up the body, and again found the neck.

The blackwing kicked its legs as the siccum's maw found its way through the neck, snapping through the spinal column, severing the head from the body. The siccum lapped at the warm fluid and nibbled at the gaping hole like a teat.

The siccum heard noises. Shouts. But it was so good. Through its hind eye, it saw another human. Not a blackwing. The siccum lapped and suckled.

There was a loud blast, and then it felt a sharp pain. A hard piece of metal landed on the ground next to him.

This human had hurled something at him. The siccum was hungry enough for two. It turned around.

Nope. Three.

It leapt onto the human as it shot more metal at him. Each fired piece sank into its hard flesh but then bounced to the ground. The blackwing blood tasted better. It contributed to the deal, too. Kill blackwings, and maybe the White Light will forgive. No. Not likely. Kill. Enjoy the blood while it ran in their streets.

One human down. One in the car. The siccum jumped onto a vehicle, bit into the windshield, and broke through. It tore the human to shreds, lapped at the blood on the floor, and then returned to the blackwing.

No. Blackwing human can't put head back on. The thirsting siccum thrust its face into the red gaping hole once again and finished its job.

Chapter 26

The crowd under the overpass, including the people who had defended Mila, now looked at her differently. Fewer requests for medicine simplified her life, though she sensed the need had not decreased. She missed helping people, but she also realized she wanted people to like her again and not be scared. She had hoped it would allow her to despise herself less. The jury was still out on that one.

A skinny old man wearing baggy jeans and a dusty sports coat, approached.

"Thanks for the medication the other day," he said, scratching his unkempt beard.

Mila had picked up a year's supply of unaffordable pain medication for his arthritis.

"No problem," she said, watching the people watch her. "Did it help?"

"Some. I'm standing straight. Haven't done that in six months. The only problem is it says to take with a full stomach. Don't have one of those. Don't know many who do."

"Try the bakery down the street. Day-old bread and store returns are free. Tell them I sent you."

"They know you by name?"

"Nobody does. Just tell them a tough young lady sent you. They'll know what that implies."

A cacophony of cheer and groans erupted from a group of card players in front of a hissing bright white lantern.

"I suppose they will," said the man. "Thank you. You've done a lot to help around here. You need to watch your back though." He looked over his shoulder and eyed the various campsites. "Maybe you don't need to. Yer pretty tough. There's whispers though." He coughed and patted his empty front pocket, searching for cigarettes. He lowered his own voice to a whisper. It was more like a rasp. "A reward. A reward for people who are different," he said, spreading his arms out wide. He flapped them two times and then winked.

Mila nodded and smiled. This man, although always thoughtful and caring, usually kept quiet. She appreciated the warning. The kindness raised her spirits.

He hobbled away, and then stopped and faced her again. He held up his index finger. "You know one thing I could use is a carton of cigs, or even just a pack."

Mila shook her head. "I can't be a vending machine."

He grinned a yellow toothy smile and limped away. "I'd hug you if I wasn't so stinky," he said with his back turned. "More than that, if I weren't broken and old."

Mila smiled, but she knew what he was saying. There was a lot of soft chatter and arguments about money and needs. Desperate people did desperate things, and as shadows shifted or a new people arrived, Mila tensed and readied for fight or flight. Hopefully, she would be leaving this place real soon, without drawing UNSIs and angels who might dislodge this growing tent city. She missed the college life and wept over it just like she did her father. Diabliss refused to moderate her emotions.

You wouldn't know Mila without emotions, without thought, said Diabliss.

You'd like this person better. She'd be hardened and battle-ready, Mila countered.

Mila stood up quickly as a new group arrived and then settled. Crouching on her feet, she readied to jump up and break out the wings. Over her back, in between her wing lines, she finally had a dark sword. Diabliss had built it in three nights and a day. It was fascinating how he worked, like a blacksmith, only on a sub-atomic level. Diabliss explained how even a stone was mostly space, a mass of spinning sub-atomic particles, and he only brought them closer together, creating a masterpiece in metallurgy. A thin sword so light, yet as hard as diamonds. A sword that could slice through stone but felt as light as a feather. She could cut an exit through a brick wall if she needed to. Beyond the sight of others, Mila had practiced with the sword, with and without Diabliss' guidance.

The scariest thing was that she enjoyed it. Diabliss was wearing off on her, but there were things that confused her.

Diabliss, explain one more time why we are storing gasoline.

Diabliss had insisted that they stockpile gasoline in an abandoned office building a few blocks away. They had siphoned gasoline from government vehicles in a lot at night.

We will use fire to expose angels.

What will fire do?

Expose them, Diabliss said.

And it won't burn us? Even my hair? I don't want to be bald and beautiful. Just beautiful.

Okay.

Diabliss? I was being sarcastic.

Yes.

I want to keep my hair. I need all the beauty help I can get.

You are beautiful. Men want to procreate with you. It can see it in their eyes. Even the male pharmacists when we're taking medicine from them. As soon as they realize we're not going to kill them, their eyes sweep over you, and they want more than a robbery.

Right. I want to do another fly by.

Maybe we could find Garrett and free him. They couldn't keep him inside of anything we couldn't cut our way into.

I wouldn't know where to look. He could be anywhere.

Mila walked out into the darkness, around a corner and into an alley, where she pulled off a sweatshirt that covered the pre-slitted hoody and wrapped the sweatshirt around her waist. She flew up and circled outward.

Two blocks away she found a UNSI investigation underway. It had taken nearly a week for someone to report the bodies on various rooftops. The same bodies that Diabliss had dropped. Yes. Part of the plan, Diabliss' plan.

I know. I see them. I don't like this, said Mila.

Angels will come next, said Diabliss.

Are you sure?

Yes.

I don't like this.

Exposing angels, sending a message, it's self defense.

Exposing? Don't call them angels if you plan on hurting one.

That's what you call them.

It just doesn't sound right. Hurting angels.

It sounds right to me, he said.

Call them the White Light, the enemy, but not angels. Oh, Diabliss, is this the only way? I really don't care. They can have Seattle. Maybe we should join Anders in Portland.

Without listening for an answer, Mila turned over control of her body to Diabliss.

Diabliss circled, then landed in the dark next to several UNSI officers. They were combing through and recording the crime scene where the dead body had been replaced by a spray-paint outline.

Diabliss sprinted to the garbage can. *Self-defense. Yes. And only self-defense.* Run out. Scare. *And then self-defense.*

The first UNSI officer screamed and quickly groped for his side arm, but the pistol had not even lifted out of the holster before Diabliss had knocked the gun to the ground. It wanted to hurt the man more. Maybe later. Another man had his pistol out and had already fired. Diabliss swung the first man around. Oops. It was just his arm. It would heal.

Diabliss crouched and ran low, crashing into the officer who had just fired, punching him in the chest. The force sent the officer into the alley brick, knocking him out even with his riot helmet on. The pistol. Diabliss grabbed it. Bullets flew in his direction. These pistols were inaccurate from a distance. Diabliss crouched on the rooftop, analyzing the piece. It leaned over the edge and pulled the trigger several times until the clip was empty. It made the men run and hide.

Mila tugged for control. *Damn. Mila has a temper.* Diabliss was calm.

It didn't kill a single man.

Give me my body. What did those men do to us?

Didn't kill. Just hurt. But Diabliss wanted to. It did not want to give Mila her—*their* body back. It wanted to finish the men. No. There was a greater cause here. It did not want to fight the Mila-chick over the use of her body. But fighting these men would bring angels closer.

Diabliss flew up into the clouds.

Diabliss did not understand how Mila could not want them dead. How she could not savor their suffering and defeat.

If she only knew. If she only knew how happy these men would be to shoot her out of the sky. How they would take turns standing over her body, snapping pictures. How they would brag about killing a blackwing to their children. How they would step on her and pull her wings off and save pieces for their grandkids.

Oh, if only Mila understood that this was happening already.

Mila circled over Garrett's building, dropping out of a thick mist. A coat of moisture gripped her. Sometimes, Diabliss adjusted her temperature, but not this time. She enjoyed the chill, how it made her teeth chatter, and even how it made her hurt. She dropped and the air warmed, and then her heart skipped a beat. She hastened in a full breath. Garrett's black motorcycle was parked on the street below. She had been checking in almost daily, and it had been parked in a different spot. She was a dark speck in a night sky, and although she wanted to swoop down immediately, she refrained, knowing that she should not endanger Garrett, and fearing the worst, that Garrett now hated her and would avoid her.

She landed on a rooftop of a taller building two blocks away and watched the streets and the sky. The last thing she wanted was to draw more attention and additional UNSI forces to Garrett's place.

She had pondered her motives for days. It was not Diabliss' desire to procreate that was driving her toward Garrett Webb's home. It was chemistry, and she hoped, love. She had dated several boys over the years, had many crushes, and felt enamored for short periods, but nothing felt the way she did when she was with Garrett, especially after their evening on the roof deck.

A sex-drive that had been wiped out by exhaustion from sports, studies, worries, and stress had a chance at revival. Even though Diabliss incessantly urged her to procreate with Anders or Garrett, she would not need Diabliss' help with Garrett. But what could she ever do? How would ridges on her back feel to a man? What if she screamed in pleasure and her wings burst out? What if Garrett rejected her? She could only be a tornado in his life, and who would willingly choose a tornado?

A person was sitting on the patio sofa.

It's him, said Diabliss.

How can you tell? she asked, though she knew the answer.

By his heartbeat.

Mila landed on a nearby building.

Diabliss, sweep the area for electronic surveillance. See if they're watching us.

There are two cameras on the poles, watching the doors. The clouds overhead are blocking signals from eyes in the sky.

Mila listened as Diabliss rattled off various observations and dangers. He could detect so many things, even with her heart pounding so uncontrollably. He could pick out most signals and trace them to their sources, but Mila gasped for breath as tears readied to erupt. Garrett Webb. One building. Fifty feet over. Ten feet down. That was how close he was. She wanted to see him. Touch him. Hold him. Just one time. Then she would leave forever.

No.

The clouds are parting, Mila-chick. The eye in the sky will find you watching him. Go to him now or fly and hide.

Mila wiped at her tears, but they were coming too fast. It was like trying to catch all the raindrops. She wanted to explain everything to Garrett. He seemed so true, but as much as she knew she loved him, she shuddered at the thought that he might not feel the same way. As the clouds parted, she turned away, swooping up into the drifting gray veil.

Garrett pulled the cover off the patio chair. His eyes blurred from the cold wind.

He grabbed a bottle of bourbon and poured it onto ice. He had left out the coke. No glow. Nothing sweet. He wanted straight heartburn, a quick numbness, and to fall asleep without thinking his calves were going to cramp, without thinking the front door to his condominium would shatter into a thousand pieces followed by a thunder of shouts and a storm of boots and black weapons aimed at his face and heart.

Go ahead, just shoot my heart.

Garrett gulped down his bourbon. He had not heard from Mila. She would be long gone, either finding her dad or changing schools, likely anything to escape from the wrath he must have brought down upon her. Could he blame her? *But she had felt so right.* There had been many others, but they were nothing like Mila. Mila, when she walked into his coffee shop and approached his counter with confidence and sarcasm, when she said yes to a ride, when she wrapped her arms around him, and her fingers had dug into his waist to steady herself. All he wanted now was a chance to open up to her and explain. Only, what did they do to her? What lies did they tell her, or even worse, what truths, and what would they mean to her? It had been flattering that she had even read *Confessions*, much less enjoyed it and could quote from it. Maybe she was a Holy Follower now. Garrett thought he even loved Mila, but enough to become a Holy Follower himself? No.

Garrett cursed at himself. Crazy thoughts. He poured more bourbon into the glass and gulped it down. The sky was blurring. A gnawing sound, better than white noise, an internal static in his head drowned out even the heavy street traffic below. A black shadow moved overhead. A blackwing or a black helicopter. He hoped it was a blackwing, and he secretly hoped blackwings would stop the madness in this country.

Garrett grabbed the plastic and covered the sofa. Another night down. How many to go before he would be over her? He might as well drink the water. Fill up on Flo-Rite. At least he would forget what was important to him.

Seeing Garrett hurt. It not only broke her heart, it reminded her of what she used to be. Proud. Popular. A student. An athlete. Now she lived under a bridge—not that there was so much wrong with the people there. Most of the homeless were families down on their luck just like she and her dad were.

Mila returned to the bridge to find the people gone and UNSI forces with dogs combing the area. A riot truck was pulling away, likely full of people. Mila watched from a nearby building. She could see several pools of blood. She shivered, thinking of the women and children. She hoped they were unhurt and safe, and would at least be fed or cared for. As the men cleared the area of stragglers, arresting a man who had escaped into some bushes, a van backed up. The rear door opened, and a red dog jumped out, only it was not quite a dog. It was red and it had small wings.

She felt Diabliss stir inside. He had been unusually quiet. He had been trying to avoid or understand the emotions she was feeling after seeing Garrett. But not now.

Three eyes. Red polymer skin. Not from this world. A killer. A siccum.

Let me guess. It's here to hunt us down and kill us?

Yes.

Can you escape it?

The siccum can fly, but not very high. We'll escape. We just have to be ready. They are quick, and they are relentless. It will track us until one of us dies. It's pretending it doesn't see us. The eyes shift, but one stays locked in.

Mila could see two of the three scrambling black dots on the top of the head, but one was locked in her direction. Mila turned her body over to Diabliss, she jumped into the air and Diabliss knew what to do. He took control and fluttered away, the creature bounding down the darkened street after them.

Diabliss circled and watched. The red brute followed its trail. Followed his scent. Exactly. Circling where Diabliss circled and stalling and staring up when Diabliss gained altitude. The siccum jumped up, snapping its jaws at the air, tasting solitary molecules floating down that gave Diabliss away. The siccum, even flapping madly, could not raise himself very high or stay up for long, but Diabliss knew the White Light's tactic. Drive blackwings into the sky. Keep them off the ground. The human shells will waste energy flying about, and the waves floating through every inch of sky, would tell the men and the White Light about anything moving that was larger than a bird.

Worst of all, this siccum was about to ruin the angel trap it had been working on. Sure, Diabliss could attack by other means, but sometimes Mila was so soft. She might make Diabliss stop preparing for the White Light. It was self-defense. She did say that self-defense was okay. No more killing for fun, though. It had promised, but fun was a vague word. Just because it enjoyed something, did not mean it was fun. Diabliss liked defending Mila's shell. Diabliss liked the Mila-chick, and Diabliss knew she liked Diabliss more than she realized. Diabliss flew away from its trap, leading the siccum along, dropping to the ground and running at safe distances in order to throw the drones off.

It was nearly morning, and the siccum slowed, then entered a house.

Diabliss smiled. Yes. Siccum must feed. Siccum must hide from light. Diabliss disliked light, but it did not burn. Siccums' skin would burn. Diabliss flew away, hearing screams below as the siccum prepared for a bed-time snack.

Mila was furious. The people in the house were about to die, and Diabliss was leaving. There were probably women and children in there.

You say don't kill. Self defense only.
I shouldn't have to say, save women and children.
It shouldn't have to say, save blackwing on building.

Mila got even madder. I won't share my body for weeks, if ever.

Could Diabliss tell when she was lying? He could tell when she was upset. How could he not see the difference between killing a siccum while defending the innocent, and risking exposure and throwing away life as she knew it to fight her government, even if it meant saving a blackwing? This was different than killing UNSI forces to defend an innocent blackwing. And killing angels? Most people believed angels were good and sent by God. Even Mila's childhood prayers taught her about angels. Guardian angels. Shit. If Diabliss killed an angel, the whole world would turn against them.

Okay. Give it the body back. Hurry.

Mila ceded control.

Fortunately, the siccum was playing with its food. The family of three hovered in a back corner behind a flipped-over table. They were screaming hysterically but somehow grew even louder as Diabliss entered, its wings still extended. The siccum was surprised but unafraid. It turned on Diabliss. The siccum tried to slow its attack when it saw the dark sword, but by then it was too late.

The skin was thick and strong, but eventually the sword cut through, and the head rolled onto the wooden floor toward a terrified shrieking family, whose evening dinner experience would never be the same.

Here you go, Mila. It hopes you're finally happy with it.

She was.

Mila flew to a long-abandoned cement office tower with

tinted windows, Diabliss steering the way. They entered through a door on the roof and went down a few levels to one of the few offices that still had carpet.

And Diabliss? I don't know what you like about this building. It stinks like gasoline. This human body is going to get sick. This human body is going to find a new home.

It's for angels. In case they show up. Self defense.

They don't like gasoline?

They shouldn't.

That was the other thing. Diabliss was taking liberties and keeping secrets. She realized he was collecting gasoline, gallons upon gallons—too many to count. It reminded her of when he had been eating dirt.

Are you opening a gas station? Mila had asked. *Because the future is electric.*

No.

I'm being sarcastic. You need to learn sarcasm.

It will take a class.

Clever, Diabliss.

Diabliss was catching on to and acquiring many human attributes, but the sense of humor was difficult. Sarcasm went right by him most of the time.

Mila finally stretched out on the hard floor's thin carpet with her jacket under her head. She did not want to sleep, if she even needed to anymore. It would be just like Diabliss to adjust her body. A body without sleep would be so much more efficient, at least that is what he would tell her.

Mila loved sleep, though not as much as she missed a warm room and a comfortable bed. She tried not to think about Garrett. She tried not to think about her father. She tried not to think about school and Jenna, and she tried not to think about the missing people, the families who had been swept off the streets like debris. She dozed off finally.

Diabliss did not sleep and did not understand why Mila wanted to. Sleep was a world of nightmares, random synapses, and impossibly illogical thoughts. She was a little girl running from something monstrous. Mila was terrified. Her father was there. Mila ran to him, but he was running as well. His legs were longer, and Mila's were childlike, short, pudgy, and clumsy. It could tell the tears were welling up. It could feel the terror rise within her. Her father was too fast. He would escape the monster, but poor Mila-chick.

It tried to whisper to her. *'Tis a dream.* But Diabliss could not reach her in this world.

But then it realized it had to wake the Mila-chick. The dream splintered.

Mila woke to the soft swish of helicopters rattling the windows. When the UNSI soldiers landed on the roof, their footsteps tapped lightly like the quiet patter of rain.

Mila, we are about to be attacked. Self defense for sure.

Mila was still groggy. There were chemicals in her brain, challenging her, telling her to lie back down and go back to sleep, even in the face of danger. It was times like this that Diabliss wished to take complete control and change the body for good. Mila needed so many improvements. Harder, sharper, longer nails. The teeth were too flat and dull, especially the front ones. They should be sharp.

Mila, there are UNSIs moving up the stairs, more on the roof, and two angels nearby.

Mila finally snapped to at the mention of angels. At least the word angel no longer had the soothing effect it once had.

Diabliss wanted her body. It wanted a fight. She wanted to escape.

No. You kill too many innocent people. Let's just go.

It has a plan.

No. If you don't want to find out about heaven, we should

escape. I'm scared.

Even though it was dark outside, Mila could see UNSIs on the building across the street. She ran to the window and saw a flash of lights erupt on the third floor, and through Diabliss-enhanced ears, heard the screams. A child's face appeared in the window. The child collapsed.

Diabliss, the squatters across the street need our help. We have to get to them.

When she looked up, she made eye contact with the angel on the rooftop, even from a hundred feet away. Mila shrieked and jumped back.

It's coming, and it knows you're afraid.

Mila was indeed afraid. She pulled the mask over her head and threw her hoody on. After unsheathing the sword, she slung the hilt over her back. Her wings popped out and stretched. She fluttered a bit, readying herself for flight, and then pulled the wings in close.

"This thing better work," she said, slicing through the air.

Mila, you need to do something. Now.

Mila sensed by Diabliss's urgency that he meant it.

"Okay," she whispered. "We hop to the building across the street, and then fight." They were in what had to have been a large conference room before the building had been abandoned.

Pour the gasoline on the floor.

Mila shook her head. "Too dangerous."

The squatters across the street. Men, women, and children, they are dead. The heartbeats stopped. The angels will do even worse to us. We can't save everyone. We were too late.

They were dead. The child's face, too dirty and too far away to tell if it was a boy or girl, had been killed, along with the others. "God-damned UNSI bastards," she said.

And god-damned angels. Pour the gasoline. It will scare

them away.

She grabbed the first can. The fumes smelled harsh. With enhanced senses, it was much worse than usual. She could detect the toxins and taste them on her tongue.

As the door burst apart, blown to pieces by small explosive, Diabliss slowed things down for her; she jumped aside as a spray of bullets filled the side of the room where she had just been standing. Mila realized she needed to fight and kill. After a blast to her left, she crouched down. Another slew of bullets crossed the room like a swarm of bees. UNSI soldiers poured through the hole, and just as a man was about to land on top of her, her arm moved, and the feather-light dark sword sliced through the air, slicing the first mercenary all the way through.

Mila froze. Diabliss implored her to fight as another stinging bullet entered her body. Too many more and they would be finished. Too many more and they would have Mila.

Mila, Diabliss begged.

Mila dropped the sword to the ground and crouched down.

Diabliss could sense that there were a hundred bullets coming toward her. Another hit. Diabliss allowed the pain. Mila screamed, and finally, finally, she picked up the sword and slashed out at another soldier-for-hire, cutting his belly open. She looked in horror and threw the sword down again. She knew they were here to kill her, only they were following orders. Those same orders, though, had led to the massacre across the street.

Please, Mila.

And then, she ceded control to Diabliss.

Diabliss snatched up the sword and hacked at the legs near him until a path had cleared. It saw the bullets coming, and now was able to avoid them, it bent forward and backward, popped out the wings and flew to the other side of the room. It rolled Mila's body and ran behind them. The men panicked and fired into themselves. Then Diabliss saw the glow in the hall and then in the doorway as the White Light entered. The two beings had their white swords of light, and they had smiles that hid their true intent. Diabliss was happy, wanting nothing more than to cleave White Light in two.

As they entered, Diabliss found the closest metal gasoline can and struck it with the sword, sending a spray of gasoline across the room.

Panic-stricken men saw the cans of fuel, smelled the fumes, and ran for the door. Only, the angels blocked the men, turning them back. The UNSI's made their way to the side of the room, finally escaping behind the angels.

It struck another canister. This time a shower of sparks sprayed across the room, and then, as the flames from the pooling gasoline erupted, Diabliss dove out the window, popping its wings out just before hitting the ground.

Diabliss fluttered for a soft landing and some balance. It turned around and faced the brick building with flames lapping out a window like a serpent's tongue. The White Light would be coming any second. It patted Mila's hair, making sure the human shell was not burning. It had promised to protect the hair. It smiled because it had.

A blackened being, smoldering and engulfed in flames, jumped through the window, following in Diabliss's path. Its blazing wings flapped, but it struggled, spun in a circle, and landed on the street near Diabliss. The scorched creature screamed and bawled. Diabliss should have known the White Light would keep the pain.

Another winged being, in a similar scorched condition, flew out the window, fluttered, and unable to gain altitude, also landed nearby.

Diabliss sliced the head off the first creature and kicked the head away from the body as its arms reached forward. It bared its teeth and its eyes followed Diabliss with each roll until the head went still, eyes still searching frantically until finally finding Diabliss. The eyes glared. It would be the last thing they did.

The other creature, a charred shell of the White Light, ran down the street away from Diabliss, who gave chase. The burnt creature leapt into the air, only its wings were damaged. As it realized Diabliss would catch it, it turned.

"And we let you live," the smoldering angel hissed through sharp teeth. "This time, your species will die." Its chemical-permeated human skin and external layers of muscle tissue had burned away, and it was struggling to even stand on an internal white polymer frame. The brightening molecules awed humans, but as Diabliss had suspected, and Anders had already figured out, the White Light on the outside were extremely flammable. The air was full of pheromones crying for help, another communication method the angels utilized besides human sound, physical signals, and speech.

"Maybe so," said Diabliss. "But you'll never see us end." It seldom spoke through Mila. The voice sounded different. "On this world, the angels will burn, not us."

NO! Mila screamed. *The angel's unarmed.*

Unarmed? No such thing. Diabliss hacked off each wing. Then it removed the head and kicked it away from the charred creature. Smoke rose and Mila tried to commandeer control so she could spit and cough and expel the harsh acrid chemicals.

You said you'd expose them.

It did. Angels' magic went up in flames.

Diabliss shot up into a helicopter overhead, despite more of Mila's internal screams and pleadings. As soon as the military bird went down into an abandoned building a block away, the other black helicopters retreated into the distant sky. The armed UNSIs on the ground scattered, finding cover.

Exasperated and resting against a tree in the thick of a wooded Seattle park, Mila worried about the bullets lodged inside of her, even though she could feel that Diabliss was manipulating proteins, enzymes, and cells, and pushing the metal slugs out as if they were small wooden slivers being pulled out by tweezers. One fell to the dirt. Mila pulled a sleeve back and looked at the area where the bullet had entered. The circular area was pallid like a scar. There was a light tingle, and then Mila rubbed the skin with her thumb, unable to detect the area where she had been shot.

Mila dry-heaved again. She had breathed in the smoke from the burning angels, and although Diabliss insisted there was no internal damage, she could not expel the god-awful foul smell and taste of burning flesh.

No. This is not good, Diabliss. You're horrible. I'm horrible because I have you inside. We burned angels.

Yes, Diabliss said. *The brightening molecules. Clever, enchanting. Tricky to humans, but preliminary studies indicate they are extremely flammable, and those heads, they come off easily.*

You shouldn't enjoy this. I hate this, and us. On earth, a lot of people believe in angels, and think that they are good. People love angels.

This isn't a child's fantasy or an ancient myth, and I haven't seen magic in this world yet, only trickery. Everything can be explained so far. Everything. The rest are opinions, wishes, and perceptions, that's all. Imagine a fire that never ends. A burn that never heals. Our damnation and suffering was meant to be eternal. And its only sin? It didn't grovel before the ruling class, the White Light. All angels can burn.

Diabliss, what good is survival if I end up hating myself and my life?

Chapter 27

Garrett set his water glass on the kitchen table. Crackling wood as the door jamb settled after a temperature swing, a creaking hallway floorboard, or wind whistling through the screen door—and Garrett not only jumped, he sometimes rolled, cradling his head. The knock at the door not only startled him, it jolted his heart like an electric shock. The PTSD from his abduction was as bad as the PTSD he had experienced in his first year home after returning from Syranistan, when he could not cross a street without checking for snipers or enter a building without circling it first and checking the upper windows from a block away. And what had brought him out of this state? Writing. And his writing had turned to *Confessions of an Agorist*. Although seditious, *Confessions* calmed him better than meds, better than exercise, better than booze.

This knock was real though, wasn't it?

It was likely a follow-up interview by UNSIs.

"Who is it?" Garrett asked.

"A friend who wants to watch Fax News with you," said a familiar voice.

Devon. He should not be here. They should not talk. His place was likely bugged. Garrett opened the door. Neither friend spoke. Devon nodded, acknowledging he knew something had changed. How could he not know? Garrett had disappeared for over a week and someone in the neighborhood would have seen that this was an UNSI and angel action. They knew what that meant. Unlike Devon, Garrett had not been taken to a poverty camp. Angels were not hauling people away because of unemployment and debt.

Devon was risking his personal freedom and breaking a rule. Devon, like Garrett, knew that most people who were taken away bowed to threats, intimidation, and blackmail. They were flipped and turned into informants. Garrett had returned to his coffee shop as if nothing had happened, but many of his usual customers, faces from the night, hooded anarchists who usually came in and said nothing anyway, had shied away.

After closing the apartment door, Garrett, maintaining his silence, led Devon to the living room, where he turned on the television, setting the volume unusually high. Sure, if they really wanted to listen in, they could unscramble the soundwaves. They could even determine the channel and delete the exact words and sounds. He hardly cared anymore, but he would still make them earn his next period of incarceration. At least the government data collectors would add Garrett's time watching Fax News to his personality profile. That was why he regularly websurfed hard-line government-support propaganda websites. Government agencies looked for people searching and watching subversive sites and channels. Doing the opposite neutralized Garrett's profile and made him look passive and patriotic.

Devon winced. Garrett knew Devon well enough to know it was sympathy. Was Garrett's pain that obvious? They had known each other for some time and had been through a lot together. Devon obviously recognized that a light in Garrett's eyes had been snuffed.

After turning a radio on in the bedroom, Garrett returned and whispered in Devon's ear, "You shouldn't be here. I'm being watched."

"I know."

"You're risking too much by coming here."

"We've been watching you, too," said Devon. "You have friends who care. UNSI stakeout? Yes. We know. One, maybe two, blackwings are keeping an eye on you as well."

Garrett placed his hands on his forehead. "Black*wings*? I can't just have one? Are they with UNSI now?" This would be too much. Too much darkness. If this was the case, then the fight was nearly over and it was time to give up.

"We don't think so. Blackwings are fighting angels. Angels are killing blackwings. Angels are working with UNSI. An enemy's enemy."

A commercial ended and a news segment was back on. Devon and Garrett watched for a few minutes making a few superficial pro-government comments. Garrett wanted to tell Devon about the room, the torture, the incarceration, but he could not. His words were stuck.

Garrett shook his head at Devon and then playfully raised his middle finger at him.

Devon grinned and shrugged. Devon was indeed a good friend. Sure, Devon owed Garrett. Garrett had busted him out of the factory camp, but Devon had to understand that this was different, that he was putting himself at risk by even associating himself with Garrett.

"How do you know I didn't flip?" Garrett whispered with a cupped hand.

Devon grinned, pointed at Garrett, and then shook his head, laughing. "When you flip, it's all over anyway."

Garrett wished the idea sounded preposterous to him as well. If only Devon knew how close Garrett had come to giving up names, even Devon's. If only Devon knew that Garrett was not one hundred percent sure he had witheld names. That is what verbal threats, drug-laced food or drink, sleep deprivation, and confined spaces did to a person—true or false—say anything to get out.

Devon leaned into Garrett's ear and whispered, "We're losing people. We're losing the fight. If you're still in, we need you. Young people need to hear your voice. They need to be led."

Garrett understood. *Confessions*. It terrified him to even look at a laptop. Every creak, wind gust, neighbor noise, or bird's shadow shooting across a window, placed him on the verge of falling apart. Garrett wondered if there was such a thing as karma. This was how his enemies in Syranistan must have felt. And yes, some of them had to have been innocent as well. Nothing was one hundred percent accurate. But Devon was right. He needed to get at least one issue out quickly. Garrett nodded, letting Devon know he would at least try—even if it was risky. If it meant certain death, it would be an easy decision to go forward, but torture and incarceration? And all for a jumble of words? That was an intimidating trade. Garrett turned off the radio in the bedroom and turned the news to a basketball game replay. They enjoyed a drink and talked about ordinary things. The sport channel was the last bastion, even it was all replays. All other channels either played Theo's daily messages, celebrities and Holy Followers who had gone public with their devotion to the White Light, or news specials on turning in or not turning in blackwings.

Jenna and her friends, all Holy Followers, had come into his coffee shop, scaring off his customers. They were wearing new uniforms, the white stormtrooper riot gear. It was a youth movement led by students. The White Light Infraguard. *Where's Mila? Is she a Holy Follower now? Was she an unrecognizable initiate marching in the White Light Infraguard?*

A separate news blast announced that blackwings thirsted for blood and were the equivalent of a modern vampire. Another report said they were after souls. Garrett laughed. News blasts were rarely true, and most often a twisted opposite. Blackwings were a mystery.

Devon left, but not without letting Garrett know one

more thing; anarchists were upping their game. An unknown faction, possibly rogue hoolies or a separate group of dissidents, was breaking open more poverty and factory camps. Someone was arming the homeless as well. The time to rise might come sooner and cut deeper than they had hoped. They would have to act fast. The Holy Followers were growing at a much faster rate, and the student White Light Infraguard was organized, deputized, and armed with tazers. They were searching persons and property looking for blackwings.

Garrett wanted to write but struggled. A motorcycle ride often cleared his head, and so he left his apartment and hit the street. He had turned the locator beacon back on. If he were under surveillance, as he had to be, they would notice the absence of a mandatory vehicle beacon and he would be back in the can. Wow. He was nearly on his way to becoming a law-abiding citizen.

Garrett found himself cruising the perimeter of the University campus fence, perhaps hoping to catch a glimpse of Mila wandering within, or even better, just outside. Why else would he be here? Instead of finding his crush though, he found his first new story. Holy Followers, not UNSI, now controlled the campus, and some even patrolled the surrounding neighborhoods. Dressed in white, high-density plastic riot gear suits, they stood out like angels in the night sky. He faked a motorcycle repair until he understood their agenda: Knock, search, and absolve. A new executive order allowed it. *Any area within one mile of a school campus or any other critical infrastructure can be absolved of blackwings at any time for any reason by any trained Homeland Authority Official.*

Yes, the homeowners could refuse, but what would happen then? The only thing the sheep did not say as they let the white-clad wolves within was *ba-a-a-ah.*

After watching lights move from room to room, bodies crossing curtains, and hearing muffled dialogue during another search, he started his motorcycle up and sped away from campus, seeking out another story. He slowed through dark alleys, and that was where he found the first body. Decapitated, but there was no puddle of blood. There should have been two gallons spilling out of the neck onto the pavement, but it was dry. He hopped off and looked around. Blackwings? The news reports suggested blackwings were vampires. Garrett analyzed the body. In a different alley, he discovered another beheaded, bloodless corpse. He touched the skin on the wrist. The body was still warm but there was barely a trickle of blood spilled and no blood pouring out, even with visibly open wounds. It was as if it had been drained. Had something just fed on this corpse? There was certainly a story here. *Confessions* was about more than injustice and anarchy. It was about arming people with knowledge. Garrett pulled out his phone and snapped a few photos.

Something moved away. A dog? It was on all fours. It looked bigger than a dog and moved too fast. Blackwing? Garrett hopped onto his bike and raced away, watching over his shoulder, wondering if a blackwing would swoop out of the sky and carry him to his death.

It used to be a twenty-four seven world, and still was for many, but these days twenty-four seven went to a rougher bunch. Hoolies. Homeless. UNSI. It was late. People rarely strolled after dark. There was an unofficial six-to-six rule practiced by most civilians. Six AM to six PM. Off the streets after dark and inside until daybreak.

As he rode on, Garrett saw a small symbol spray-painted on a stop sign. It was a paint that would wash off in the next rain. That was how they communicated with each other in Seattle, knowing their regional weather patterns in short time would erase any trails. He stopped his bike in the middle of the road, watching his side mirrors for approaching cars.

What would happen if he showed up to a meeting of anarchists? If he were recognized, would they trust him or cast him out? They should toss him out. Garrett thought about how he had wanted out after meeting Mila, but that was when Mila was a possibility. Shit. He flipped off the transponder and hit the turn signal. Yes. He was going. Garrett read the signals, though it got tricky, some codes had been changed. He eventually found the meeting place in a darkened park. He rode his cycle about a block away and parked it. He found a brown paper bag in the gutter. He emptied it and crumpled it up until it was soft like fabric, and then made eye and mouth slits. He looked around until he found a plastic bag. He tore a strip off and looped it around the neck, tying it off, and jogged into the park toward a clump of dark shadows. He crouched next to the base of a large fir tree. He recognized some of the jackets, some of the masks, a few whispers, and even knew some names.

After about five minutes, an unmasked man stood up. This was against protocol, but nobody was complaining. He was a young handsome man. There was something about his eyes. They glowed, like two swimming pools lit up at night. He looked familiar, too, but Garrett could not place him. He even walked right up to Garrett and patted him on the shoulders like he knew Garrett. "Tonight, we continue our war against an illegal, oppressive government. The United States Constitution has been dismantled, politicians bought and paid for, elections manipulated, and until democracy is restored or the current structure torn down, we consider this regime to be a forced enemy state that we are at war with. Since we are unable to peaceably assemble, it's up to us to un-peaceably dis-assemble. They've stepped up their game, and we're stepping up ours. If there are any cowards, anyone who is not ready to trade your life for freedom, you best leave now." The man crouched down again.

This was the meeting's general format. Stand up and speak and then get down. Anyone could talk, but anarchists knew the difference between a poser and true dedication.

Risking your life? That had always been the case, but this was different than taking out surveillance cameras, breaking into empty office buildings, and blowing holes in factory camp fences. Different than filming police roundups, prison camps, and telling anyone who would listen about Flo-Rite. Wasn't it? Or was it different because only three weeks ago, the actions were his ideas? Were his acts just as treasonous? "Un-peaceably dis-assemble." Wasn't that from *Confessions*?

The group gathered around a paper map as a man with a red laser pointer traced over dotted lines leading to a building. Another man wore a small backpack. Garrett guessed it held explosives. Garrett thought about leaving. There were those who could ignore injustice and then there was this group, 3A, *Anarchy Action Always*. When pinned against the wall, some threw their hands up into the air in surrender while others launched fists and arrows.

"The country is so broken that parts of it have to be destroyed so it will be forced to start over. A corrupt system without justice and law cannot be fixed by legal and just means."

Garrett laughed to himself as someone in the group quoted words he had written. He thought he could walk away from all this, for fear or for Mila, but no, when it came right down to it, there were two powers gripping his heart, Mila and antifascism.

An hour later, Garrett found himself running from a smoldering building, his lungs and leg muscles burning. The UNSI torture cell, similar to the one he had been sequestered in, had been blown wide open. Eleven men and women inside were freed. Two members of the group broke away, and Garrett nearly stumbled as dark shadows grew out of the two men. He slowed and watched as the ebony shapes morphed into wings, and then the same thing happened with one of the escaped prisoners. The three men, including the man who had spoken during the anarchy forum, were blackwings! The two blackwings with their blackwing escapee shot into the air. Now, he understood why the man without the mask looked so familiar. He was the blackwing from the Portland press conference—the one who had gotten shot.

Without thinking, Garrett pulled out his camera and filmed the trio's departure. Garrett also had taken a picture from inside the jail. In a cell, there was an animal. Red. Leathery. Garrett stopped running for a second, unable to wait, he had to look at the picture closer. It looked like an extremely large dog. But a giant red dog with three eyes? These were different times. It had moved. It had growled. It was hideous, chest-high, and it was real. And one of the men who turned out to be a blackwing said this beast was no prisoner.

A siren wailed behind him. Garrett was nearly to his bike and would be off before they reached him. In the air, the three blackwings chased by drones flew toward a trio of UNSI helicopters, dark specks barely visible in the charcoal sky.

An orange mushroom cloud stamped the night sky. One of the helicopters crashed. Now, the anarchists could run free.

Chapter 28

Theo left the stadium, pausing at the top of a long flight of steps as he did every morning. The people roared and pounded their hands together. As he looked at them, he realized something was wrong. They were getting louder because the numbers were growing, but they appeared frailer than when they had arrived. Thousands slept on the street, under tents and tarps, and in the nearby vacant warehouses and office buildings that had been donated to his cause. As far as his human eyes could see, people were waiting, and yet more arrived continuously. Theo loved humanity. They knew their place. They knew to worship the White Light, though there were some who might lead them astray. He would save them from themselves and guide them toward the White Light, but in addition to guidance, they needed food and arms. Human flesh was so fragile.

Theo called the president. Yes. Another order. Yes. You need to obey. Theo could sense what the president was contemplating: If she feeds an army of Holy Followers, they will grow in numbers and strength. If she does not, the White Light might just take what they need. Armed Holy Followers around the world would create the largest mass infantry in human history. She could not risk open war with angels and Holy Followers, both of whom had already infiltrated the law-making and enforcement branches of government, but more importantly, the ever-hungry military industrial complex who would be quite anxious to arm, well, anyone.

Yes. Madam President would help make them stronger. And yes, it was still in her best interest. But who would pay for the food? *How dare she even ask him that.* Holy Followers should eat, and not only that, they should eat the most and the best. Yes. This was a power change, and a class change. Yes. Hire only Holy Followers in government or authoritative positions from this point on. Print as much paper money as you need to. Angels will enforce its value. She tried to think of a way to avoid ceding more power to the White Light. *Don't even try, Madam President. Just obey.* Theo knew what scampered through her predictable brain. She was thinking that the U.S. government and its controllers would have even less control. Why could some humans—Holy Followers like Jenna—maintain one hundred percent faith in their authority figures while others speculated, plotted, and doubted what was obviously righteous, true, and necessary?

Holy Followers were ready to truly serve the cause, the White Light. Those who delayed might not conform in time.

Theo felt so good. He could manipulate the molecules within his human body to feel pleasure, sure, but he really was enjoying this world, even without biological manipulation. He loved the people who served the White Light. They were eager and willing to do anything to serve the purpose, and others were predictable, greedy, or complacent enough to manipulate or move aside. Oh, why did the cursed blackwings have to turn away from the White Light? Why don't they know their place and just obey? Theo would have loved them just like he loved humans. He would have brought them into the White Light embrace. Only, Blackwings had to question. Blackwings had to know why the White Light was in charge, and more disgustingly, why not them. They just could not understand how simple it was. Serve the White Light and you have control. Serve the White Light and you have freedom. Theo's millions of followers understood this simple principle without the need for proof or reason.

Theo flew back down to the stage on the field. People

raised and alerted others upon realizing that Theo was before them again. Many of them began to sing. Even strengthened, Theo's body still had many sensitivities. These untrained singers hurt his human ears, but the worship made Theo glow inside. Theo radiated the light. He spread his wings and flew out over the crowd. They knew to avert their eyes when he got close. Touch a few. Yes, these soft fleshy beings had given up their minds and bodies and would worship the White Light for the rest of their lives, as they should. A feeling crept into his heart. He could feel it in his chest. Yes. The racing biochemistry. The men and women serving before him deserved to be stronger.

He would teach the loyalty oath to them all. Then he would feed them. And as they strengthened, he would arm them and train them.

He flew to the epicenter and radiated his light to the point that white sparkles fell like snowflakes. Using his harmonic voice, Theo spoke, sending waves of music and sound into all beings within, as well as through the amplification and streaming systems that carried his message to those far away.

I will follow God,

And do what is right,

I will follow God, and God's White Light.

Theo repeated his words, and then, so did his crowd. People with tears in their eyes scrambled to scribble the words on notepads, their arms. Others held up wrist-pads, phones, and other electronic recording devices.

God's White Light. God's White Light. The crowd chanted. Yes. Simplicity. The people roared. Hundreds of thousands of voices erupted, shaking the earth.

The first helicopters appeared on the horizon and soon hovered over the crowd, the sunset burning the Olympic Mountain Range orange and purple across the Puget Sound behind them. The spinning rotors of the machines were easily drowned out by a renewed chanting crowd as the first helicopter lowered a crate of food.

The president had proved she was an obedient Holy Follower; she had understood what she needed to do and how quickly she needed to do it.

Humans were simple, and Theo loved that. *Feed them. Arm them. Guide them.*

Chapter 29

Garrett wrote through the night. The government puts Flo-rite in the water as part of its pacification and birth control programs. It is an active ingredient in most antidepressants, and it reduces sperm counts. Do you really believe that they mass-medicate the entire population, including adults, in order to prevent tooth decay in poor children, with a topical solution? We are a sleeping, medicated nation, and we do not really care about much. We compulsively follow our celebrities while ignoring our wars.... The new White Light Infraguard, a growing legion of overzealous armed Holy Follower thugs, performs illegal searches, and if we say "no" to their absolution efforts, an illegal incarceration follows...There is a war on freedom and liberty, and the primary weapon used against us is mass hypnosis...

At five AM he stood, ready to ride off to work.

Garrett's hand shook as he downloaded the new issue onto a memory stick. It was not his best writing. It even had reprint articles from previous issues, but he had done it. It was hard not to write about torture, only that might give him away. He scrambled the files on his hard drive, erasing any trace that he had authored the piece.

He rode his motorcycle through early-morning traffic. He hated UNSI. He hated angels. He hated Holy Followers. He hated everything and everyone.

At Sweet Perk he plugged a memory stick into a reader and handed off a copy, and then another. Garrett told each recipient to be extra cautious. They looked nervous. He could see in their eyes that they did not trust him entirely. Some just took their coffee and shook their heads. There were some that would never trust him again. There would be more instances of turning in the names of whomever they got the file from. Would this be the issue the authorities finally traced back to him?

Since he had been taken away, his business had fallen behind. His friends had attempted to open and operate the shop, but the landlord would not give them a key to the backrooms. When they forced their way inside, they could not open the safe, and they knew that a bank would never allow them access to what they needed. They chipped in, put together a working till, and made some sales, but things operated sporadically at best. So, Garrett was already a few weeks behind in revenue and would likely never catch up. He had thought about selling his motorcycle to pay the electricity or his quarterly tax estimate, but he just could not do that. If he were to end up on the street, he would rather be able to move quickly on it. His motorcycle was not only a mental means of escape, but a literal one as well.

Garrett was about to close shop when a customer arrived. He jumped to defense mode, thinking there was something unusual about the person with a hoody pulled up, wearing face scarf, a backpack, and dark glasses, until he realized that this was a woman. The glasses came off, the hoody and scarf dropped down, and Garrett's heart rumbled to life and then crackled like thunder in his chest. This girl had coal-black hair, but it had been dyed; it was Mila.

Chapter 30

The University clock chimed its ninth chime. The dormitory hallway outside Jenna's room would normally be filled with frantic weekend hoots and hollers but instead it was unusually serene. Kathy hopped off Mila's bed, made herself another screwdriver, and then slurped away at her nearly clear vodka and orange juice with ice in a bright red plastic tumbler. She staggered back a step.

"We have to help her," said Kathy. "Mila doesn't just drop out of school, quit soccer, and shack up with some anarchist. I don't care if it's winter break soon. She might not make it back before flunking out entirely. We have to find her."

Jenna cringed as Kathy rested her hand on Jenna's white Infraguard helmet sitting on the desk. The fingerprints left on the clear faceplate after Kathy moved away bored into her. Jenna rolled off the bed and immediately rubbed out the blemishes with her pajama forearm.

"She's not answering her texts," said Jenna. "I've tried to reach her. I love Mila-chick. She's our sis."

"I had my new boyfriend follow Garrett Webb from the coffee shop and spy on him. Nothing. Garrett goes to his apartment and gets on his computer. Nobody else is there."

"Probably looking at porn."

"Probably," said Kathy. Her eyes changed and opened wide. She slapped Jenna on the arm with the back of her hand. It made a loud noise and a red mark. "Maybe he's a perv and he killed her! Oh, God." Kathy's eyes glistened.

Jenna shook her head. "Put the juice down. I don't think it's like that at all. She just ran away."

"From what?"

"She's under a lot of pressure. Her dad has been missing for months. He probably drinks his income. Who knows? Met him once, shortly after we moved into the dorm. He's real skinny—like unhealthy skinny. Shifty eyes, too. Maybe he's a druggy."

"I can't believe she did this to us. Damn it, Mila-chick. She knows how much we care." Kathy held up her drink and nearly lost her balance. "The three amoebas," she slurred.

"The three amoebas," said Jenna.

That was the name they had given themselves after celebrating a soccer win too hard one night when it took all three of them locking arms just to make it down the dorm room hall. They staggered, shifting and bouncing like an amoeba, even sucking in and capturing a few wandering students. Kathy's eyes widened. She smacked Jenna on the arm. "Hey. Maybe we can find her dad."

"How? Mila could not even find him."

"Look him up. You have access. You're a big-shot White Light Infraguard leader." Too many of Kathy's words ran together. She was definitely buzzed.

Jenna did have access and full run of campus security, which had been expanded to include nearby neighborhoods. She could literally walk into any UNSI tent and sit down at one of their computer stations, but would this be a betrayal to Theo? He was taking notice of her. He had even called her personally to commend her on her Holy Follower initiatives, particularly her ideas for the White Light Infraguard. Jenna thought long and hard as Kathy impatiently rapped her fingers on the desk like a ticking clock. Theo would want to guide Mila to the White Light. The White Light Infraguard could use someone like Mila.

"Mila's thinking isn't right," said Kathy, hitting Jenna on the arm. "If her thoughts were in order, what would Mila do for us?"

"Anything," said Jenna. "If we truly know Mila."

"We do!"

Jenna shook her head. "What if we don't know her anymore?"

"We do."

"What if we never really knew her?" asked Jenna.

"We did."

"She might never be a Holy Follower." Jenna again shook her head, as if shaking away her doubt. "No, she will."

Jenna stayed behind after her White Light Infraguard meeting. A hall had been turned over by UNSI and was now the official headquarters for the White Light Infraguard, University of Washington Chapter. Her hands shook, but she smiled—not because she would be jumping on a UNSI network and searching for Mila's father, but because an angel, a personal servant of Theo, had conveyed Theo's message that the White Light Infraguard would be trained and armed, and she would be in charge of it all. Right now, they were only armed with warrants and laws allowing them to search, seize, and report. *'Tis a battle betwixt good and evil*, he had said. Tasers. Side arms. Eventually, particle wave guns. All necessary weapons to enforce blackwing-free ideals of the White Light. They would be charged with national security, working alongside UNSI, and in some cases the U.S. Military. Infraguard would be charged with absolving residences and businesses of blackwings, utilizing any method necessary. Civilians would help by showing loyalty with their white arm bands. Finally, some serious action. Blackwings could not hide for long. The new Infraguard uniform was white and bullet proof, with a matching riot helmet, and combat boots. It did not officially glow, like a real angel, but outside of a tinted face plate and grey urban-camouflage boots, the uniform was certainly white and pure.

Most of all, Theo had personally praised her efforts. And she was entirely, wholeheartedly devoted to God and Theo. He noticed her, and she liked that.

If the war was over or unnecessary, there might be the possibility of romance between angels and humans, but no, the country and the world had been invaded by a soul-jacking force that hated God and personal freedom, and Jenna, under the guidance of angels, would drive these beasts to Holy Hell. She had taken the oath—the oath of allegiance to God, his angels, the United States of America, and their allies. Her duty? Find blackwings and anarchists. Detain. Search bodies, homes, offices, and report findings to UNSI. And this all made her plan even more disconcerting. She had to be certain she was not betraying the White Light.

She prayed to the White Light until she felt relaxed. Yes. She could still find Mila's father. The war effort needed athletes like Mila. She was strong, disciplined, and already understood purposeful group dynamics.

Jenna pulled up Mila's records in order to find her father's name. *Bradley Sadis. Please report whereabouts to Jenna Voit, White Infraguard Captain. Using information to recruit qualified athlete to cause.* She pressed enter, sending the message to UNSI headquarters.

Chapter 31

Mila shuffled her feet and paused one last time outside of Garrett's coffee shop, still unsure of what she would say. Even with Diabliss lowering her blood pressure, impeding an adrenaline flow, and shooting down butterflies fluttering in her stomach as if they were swirling targets in a video game, she was nowhere close to serene. But what was serenity anymore? As she stepped inside, she wondered if Garrett would kick her out. She would not blame him if he did. Did he recognize her with black hair? It was straighter, too, and probably oily. She wanted to speak but feared she might only hiss and squeak like a leaking balloon.

Garrett had not ushered her to the door, demanding a departure. Instead, Garrett locked it and flipped over a sign. It was near closing time anyway. He twisted a few blinds, dimming the external light, allowing the electric lights to take over.

Mila had rehearsed what she was going to say, at least three different versions, along with extensions of each speech. But she drew a blank now. Even Diabliss was scurrying within her, trying to bridge synapses, trying to build and rebuild word networks. Communications, down.

Maybe it is better you do not speak. Just procreate.

After seriously considering Diabliss' advice, she wondered if Diabliss was making Garrett look this handsome. *No, Garrett's hot. He always has been.* Her heart thumped and pounded. As Garrett approached her, Mila had trouble reading his face, but instead of pushing her away or out, and instead of words, he embraced her. Mila did not care if he felt her back. She did have a backpack on, but he did not seem to notice anything, he only held her close. And pressing against him, looking up into his deep eyes, felt so right.

Diabliss wanted to hold back her tears. They were a sign of weakness, but Mila knew by now that it meant his doing so would also stifle her emotion. Diabliss was learning. He just wanted her stronger—he always wanted her stronger.

Garrett looked into her eyes, and Mila gazed back into his unblinking emerald green orbs. Something looked different. Perhaps a spark of arrogance that was there previously was now gone? His hair was longer, too.

"Don't cry. You'll make me cry," he said, grinning.

"Yeah, right," said Mila. "You're too tough."

He put his hands on his temples, and then shook his head. "There was a day where that was true, but it passed some time ago."

Did Garrett know that he had been arrested because of his association with her? Did he even know that it was Jenna who had turned him in? If not, what would he think when he found out? She would need to tell him everything.

No, said Diabliss.

I want to be honest.

No, lie.

I know you want to guard my emotions and my life.

Our emotions. Our life.

This was the first time Diabliss had confessed to sharing her emotions. Neither one of them knew whether it was best to alter or extinguish them. Who or what in their right mind would want a young woman's emotions?

Right. Our emotions. Our life…but this needs to be done right. If I'm wrong, I'll give you more control and not less.

Yes. That way might be better anyway.

Mila wrapped her arms around Garrett, drawing him closer, her head resting on his shoulder. The tears were coming back again. She had been a long time without friends, and maybe if he was not kicking her out, it meant she still had one left.

"You don't know how badly I need a friend," Mila said.

"You've got one here. I'm sure you have more than that. Jenna and Kathy?"

Mila shook her head.

"You'll make up."

"No. We won't. We can't. Something happened, and things went too far. Jenna and I can't be friends again. I'm alone."

"I went away," said Garrett, looking down, hiding from Mila's curious eyes. "I didn't know if I'd ever hear from or see you again."

"We need to talk," Mila said, "seriously talk, but I don't know where to begin."

"Begin in the middle, the end, or you can do like most people, and start at the actual beginning."

Mila opened her mouth to speak, but Garrett put his finger to his lip. "We should make another trade. I've got secrets, too," he said.

"Don't we all?"

"I'm also not sure this is the best place to talk."

"Mine is a big trade, but I don't expect anything back," said Mila. "I just hope you'll stay with me."

After Garrett removed a small basket strapped to the back half of his motorcycle seat, Mila and Garrett climbed on and the two zipped out onto the street. Traffic was gridlocked as usual, due to breakdowns, stalls, detours, roadblocks, and construction, not due to a large amount of people going to work at various places. They were riding to Mila's chosen location first. She guided Garrett by tugging on a left sleeve for a left turn, a right sleeve for a right. Occasionally, Garrett took an alternate route, circumventing checkpoints and closed sections. She was uncomfortable speaking freely inside his coffee shop. She felt as if she were placing him in enough danger. Garrett did not want to speak there either but also wanted to avoid his place for some reason. He still had not said anything about Jenna falsely accusing him and turning him in to UNSI, but what Mila was about to tell him would likely make Jenna's false report seem like a birthday present.

"We've got about fifty miles before we need to fuel up."

Mila nodded, but they would not be traveling that far. Another gasoline shortage had been announced on the news, and not only were the prices abnormally high, again, the wait lines were over four hours, and that was if a driver could find a place that had not run out. The chain reaction this created was routine. Restaurants no longer received fresh food, grocery store shelves went barren, and prices shot up. They passed a bootlegger selling a gallon of biofuel for twenty Ameros. Not a bad deal, especially with a motorbike, only you never knew what you were getting until you ran the fuel through the vehicle. At least that is what the University literature always said. Maybe it was to keep students from buying outside the cartels.

They worked their way into the Shambles, an area centered around several abandoned factories and office buildings filled with squatters, black-market activities, and hoolies. She wondered again if she was putting Garrett at risk by coming here. It was after sunset, but the light would hold for at least another hour. The EC Elite, the group of hooligans who at one time had centered around 45th Street but had since been pushed fifty blocks away, lived here. They had learned on the Portland train not to harass Mila, but a few had to be reminded. Now, all she had to do was take off her helmet if any members approached. Even with numbers, they would walk away. Mila jerked on Garrett's arm and he pulled into an abandoned lot. There was a small parking garage with spray-paint streaks and gang messages. Mila was even getting so she could recognize and read some of them. There was Chookey's mark, the teenager she had saved from Portland hoolies. She hoped he would survive until the nation's economy recovered—if it ever would. Mila led Garrett into the abandoned parking garage.

"I've never been in this classroom before," Garrett said. "Is this the new University complex?"

"Funny, but no. And I promise I'm not a crazy ex-girlfriend bringing you here to kill you." Mila quickly shook her head. Her face reddened. "Not that I was ever your girlfriend or anything."

"Hadn't thought of that, but then again, if you were a crazy ex trying to kill me, you'd probably lie so I'd let down my guard."

"I guess so," said Mila. "I'm not lying. Though if I was a murderer. I'd likely also be a liar, and I'd be lying to you right now about not lying."

"You're not bringing me here to knock me off. If you're working for the competition and planning a hostile takeover of the coffee shop, it's nearly under anyway."

Mila took Garrett's hand. He was smiling. Mila's only hope was that Garrett was feeling what she felt when she held his hand, how her heart melted, and how she felt owned by him. Even Diabliss sensed the loss of control and struggled with it. Though he mostly pawned it off as a desire to procreate, which he favored.

A skinny cat darted away, and Mila, having been in this garage before and having befriended and fed this cat, knew that it was feral. If it was scurrying away, they were not alone.

"Step out now, and I'll let you walk out of here," Mila shouted into the darkness of abandoned shanties, cement beams, and deep shadows. The last thing they needed was a sneak bullet. A hooley might shoot first and then ask, "who goes there?"

Garrett chuckled and then looked at Mila. "I didn't hear anyone, did you?" he asked.

Nodding, Mila tried to smile and be cute, but she knew that from this point on, cute was not a likely picture.

Three men emerged from behind a wall. They wore black shirts and pants, as did everyone in their firm. One man flashed his hands, showing his signs. The other two had a knife out and a pistol already drawn between them. Standing tall, Mila stepped forward.

"Mila-chick, that you?" asked the man who had made the signs.

"Yeah," she answered.

"We're just sweeping. Keeping people out. Keeping it clean."

"Clean of people like me?" Mila asked.

"You're as clean as a girl gets. You're welcome here any time." The three men wandered to the edge of the parking garage. Two of the men hopped over the edge. One paused before exiting. "I'd ask if you're safe with him, but I guess I should ask instead if he's safe with you."

The two other men laughed, and the third followed them into the street.

"Am I safe with you?" Garrett asked.

Mila could see he was smiling, even in the dark. "That's the million Amero question," she said, relaxing her back muscles, preparing to slowly release her wings.

Chapter 32

Garrett looked around nervously as footsteps thundered like a sudden sheet of pounding Pacific Northwest rain. "If you have something to say, you'd better get it out." Garrett shifted his feet and clenched his fists. "We've got company."

Mila's wings tensed but stayed inside the fabric. She opened her mouth to speak, but the words did not come out.

Fifty or so gang members hopped into the garage and sprinted toward Mila and Garrett. On the other side of the parking garage, engines revved, echoed, and roared, and then tires screeched down a ramp. A small band of men ran into the section where Garrett and Mila were. Garrett stood in front of Mila, likely a protective instinct, but then he looked at her and shrugged. "Your gang, I guess. You're a hooley now. Is that your secret?"

Mila shook her head, but again she was distracted. Chookey, her young friend, had broken from his pack. He had a shaved head and a tattoo of a star next to his left eye and more tattoos on his arms that told of battles he had been in. He was a skinny little kid, not more than fifteen years old, but had probably seen more fights than the oldest university student she knew. More than anyone she knew, really. The hooley life was one of gangs, protection, and brute force. Throwing down was more than a hobby, it was their occupation.

"Raid. UNSI," Chookey called. "They're clearing us out."

"I thought they left you guys alone," Mila wondered out loud.

"They want us to join the White Light Infraguard.

Captain said to piss off because they cancelled soccer, so they sent in the UNSI's." Chookey looked over his shoulder and then backed away. "They're coming in hard. They popped three already." He looked to his friends, now hopping the short cement wall. "Gotta scat'. Even you gotta scat', Mila-chick." Chookey sprinted after his friends.

"Even you gotta scat?" asked Garrett as he and Mila jogged toward his cycle and climbed on.

"I guess so," she said. Once again, the authorities were causing problems for her and Garrett.

"That's not what I meant," he said.

Yes. More dishonesty, but how could she tell him just before fleeing on a motorcycle that she was a blackwing. He would probably flee from her. Maybe he would head straight for UNSI. He had nothing to hide.

Garrett rode in the direction that Chookey and his friends had run. Some cars and a few motorcycles in the garage came down from an upper level and raced away. In the sky, black helicopters hovered, dipped and then moved slowly forward as men dropped from the open sides. Fast chutes opened. The men landed, unclipped their fast chutes, and charged with raised weapons.

"Maybe you should surrender so nothing happens to you," said Mila. "I'm sorry I got you into this. I just wanted a quiet place to talk."

"Not your fault. Especially the noise." Garrett shook his head. "Too many bullets flying. You should get off the motorcycle. They might not hurt you if lie on your stomach and put your hands behind your head." He stopped the bike.

"You'll be safe with UNSI. I won't," said Mila, securing the scarf across her face, raising her hoody.

"If we make it out of this mess, we definitely need to talk."

"Agreed," said Mila.

"Look," Garrett said, flipping up his helmet's visor. The vehicles that had exited the parking garage, motorcycles and cars, had turned around and now raced back toward Mila and Garrett.

But that was not what had Mila concerned. The asphalt chipped apart right at their feet, and then Mila felt the pain in her leg. As Diabliss shut down the nerve centers that would have had Mila jumping off and rolling to the ground in pain, and began pushing the bullet from her flesh, he also increased her awareness. UNSI had guns on all rooftops and men on the streets trotting down empty alleys. Mila watched as a group of hoolies running from the cover of one building to another got mowed down. Bullets flew into them as if UNSIs were intent on making corpses and not arrests. UNSI had commandeered the building's rooftop perimeters and were not only firing down on anything that moved, but anything that stopped as well. She heard popping noises inside the buildings and a smoky gas seeped out of a few cracked windows. UNSI was inside, sweeping abandoned offices, popping gas canisters, smoking everyone out, and shooting down stragglers whether they were armed or not. Any second another bullet would tear into her, but she could take a few bullets. Any second, though, bullets would tear into Garrett, and he would be dead or critically wounded.

At an outdoor lot, the hoolies parked their vehicles in a circle and hopped out. The men and boys, along with a few women, leaned against the metal within, determining which angles protected them, and then signaling the position to the rest of the gang. A white shirt waved, but the arm that held the surrender signal wavered as a circle of red blood appeared on the white skin. The UNSIs did not want a surrender. Why would they? Jails were full. These troubled gang members would not work in a factory camp or serve in the military. A man popped a trunk and within seconds, they were well-armed. Mila and Garrett joined them.

The late-fall sun dropped, and clouds rolled above, but as fast as darkness came at this time of year, it was too slow to save them. Time would only give the invading force another advantage.

The hoolies fired back, but the shots, sparing and random, did little to dissuade the UNSI raid. The hoolies were surprised and on foot; it only took about five minutes before they whispered about running low or out of ammunition. The UNSIs would not run out.

The bullets stopped flying for a moment as a helicopter moved in. The military bird was different from the rest. It was a cargo transport helicopter and had a box beneath it. Someone guessed acid, another shouted that it would be a gas, while yet another yelled that it was a bomb. When the steel door slid open, something dropped out, and it was alive.

A blood-red beast about the size of a lion flipped through the air, reeling, but landing on its feet like a cat. It sniffed the air, three black eyes on its head blinked as it took in its surroundings. A man near Mila stood and fired a bullet into it. The bullet hit the thick skin, but the slug popped out, rolling to a stop on the ground beneath it. A short stubby tail about four inches long wagged excitedly. The animal looked like a large dog, but it clearly was not, or it clearly was not a dog any longer.

Mila knew what it was doing. It was looking through the air, distinguishing molecules, looking to the ground, seeing the trail, and locking in on her. In the two seconds it took for Mila to realize this, it was trotting and then bounding toward her, bearing sharp teeth in its ovular mouth, batting tiny red wings on its back.

Mila stepped onto the trunk of the car. Garrett's arms reached out to hold her back, but she moved away from his grasp. She reached over her shoulder and drew a short dark sword. After slicing it through the air a few times, the thin black metal sliver lengthened to about four feet long. She jumped from the car and ran in the direction of the siccum.

The UNSI troops reared back as if they had lit a fuse and were now wary of an impending explosion.

Let me take over.

No. Not with Garrett here.

The siccum flapped into the air, lifting to shoulder level. Its claws on all four paws sprung out.

The hind legs will be the most dangerous.

Mila dropped and rolled beneath the creature, standing while stooped over and slicing at the rear legs as she passed under. The sword struck, but it did not do any damage—at least none that she could see. The legs suddenly kicked down with a force that pushed her into the asphalt, knocking the wind from her. The claws punctured her jacket and shirt.

Before she could get up, she saw Garrett hopping over the car. She shook her head. "No, stay back," she shouted.

The hound-beast squealed a deafening high-pitched roar and rolled onto its back, waiting for Mila to close in. When she did not, it flipped onto its feet.

The rear legs.

I tried.

You'll have to hit them more than once.

As the siccum leapt into the air, Mila sprinted and rolled, and then stood with her sword raised. It soared over her, and she hacked at a hind leg once more and then again. She saw the tear, and as the siccum stopped flapping its wings, bringing it abruptly to the ground, Mila swung again, putting all her strength into it, and the sword finally cut through.

With a mangled back leg, the siccum limped and circled. Mila looked at the creature's eyes. Probably the most exposed portion. The siccum still pounced, even with three legs. Mila batted at the forearm and then struck the neck. She threw her

240

weapon into the neck, over and over, until the skin at the beast's forearm and neck began to weaken. She finally broke through and the head fell to one side. With one strong swing, she severed it.

She looked at Garrett apologetically from fifty paces away. "I was trying to tell you," she said. She ran to him and jumped, landing next to him on the hood of a car. "I didn't want it to come out this way."

Explosions rang out again as gunfire erupted. Mila and Garrett jumped behind the car with the crouching hoolies just as bullets tore apart the metal where they had had been standing.

"I'm not sure I understand. Who are you?" he yelled. His eyes looked so different than they did when they were enjoying their rooftop bliss. So different from when she saw him at the coffee shop after being apart for so long. He looked confused, as if he did not know Mila at all. What worried Mila the most was that he did not truly know her. No one did anymore. She barely knew herself.

Bullets fell from the sky. Another helicopter with a metal storage container maneuvered into place. The helicopter that had already dumped its siccum, swung to a different angle, spraying bullets from a side-mount machine gun.

Mila had not wanted to turn her body over to Diabliss. She did not want Garrett to see what she had become without explaining more to him. She certainly did not want Garrett to see what Diabliss would do when attacked, but Mila had no choice. Too many helicopters. Too many soldiers. And she could hear the grunts of another anxious siccum about to be released. Angels would be here soon as well.

"I'm so sorry, Garrett. I'm so sorry you're going to see me like this. It isn't me." Turning to the hoolies, she said, "I'll distract them. Take Garrett away." Mila looked up at the sky and headed back towards the UNSIs. "Take care of him, or

I'll hunt you all down one by one." She adjusted the scarf over her face.

Mila's wings shot out of her back, tearing through the hoody she was wearing. *Here you go, Diabliss. Anything to save Garrett.*

Anything? he asked.

Anything, she said.

Chapter 33

Chookey grabbed Garrett's shoulder and pulled. Garrett resisted. Instead, he stared at the chaotic sky in disbelief. Mila, *a blackwing*.

Another horrific scream preceded another UNSI falling from the sky. Bullets no longer flew toward the hoolies. Garrett knew what Mila was doing. She was drawing the fight and the fire, granting them an escape. She had given up her secret for that, but that was also what she had been keeping from him, and why she had brought him here, to tell him.

The UNSIs on the ground took up defensive positions, but Garrett could tell they were retreating. Were blackwings immune to bullets? She had to have been shot multiple times.

"My God," he said out loud as Mila drove a helicopter into a building. She fought as if possessed, showing no mercy, perhaps even enjoying it. *She's not smiling, is she?* he wondered as she scattered some nearby UNSIs. Mila now soared with not one, but two men, one dangling in each hand. She dropped them on top of an UNSI squad like they were water balloons. Garrett thought he had seen it all in Syranistan. He had not.

Chookey spoke up. "Dude, you're girlfriend's pretty bad-ass."

Garrett nodded.

Mila again drew her sword, black like coal, and hacked away. A bloody battle ensued. Red sprayed like rain. None of the crimson pools belonged to Mila.

"That's why you got to come with us. You're one of us until she says so."

She had said she would hunt the EC Elite down if they

did not take care of him—if they did not save him. Garrett looked over his shoulder again. Mila was chasing a group of men down an alley. She was flying over them and had anticipated their direction. Bombs away. Another soldier dropped from the sky. Yes. There was no doubt in Garrett's mind, or the minds of the hoolies. If they did not save him, she would hunt them relentlessly and slice them to bits.

Chookey placed a small pistol in Garrett's hand. Garrett acknowledged he knew how to handle a piece by verifying that the small .380 was loaded. There was no safety, so Garrett was careful not to place his finger on the trigger. It would only be good up close. Not a lot of accuracy or stopping power.

"You a killer, too?" Chookey asked as they ran away with the group.

"Syranistan. I've learned a thing or two."

"Shit," said Chookey, struggling to catch his breath. "You should be saving *us*."

They sprinted through a section that Mila had cleared for them. UNSI troopers in the southern portion of the decrepit industrial section were either hiding or had retreated. The least of their worries though were fifty or so ragged hoolies. Mila threatened UNSI lives, the hoolies did not.

As they neared a chain-link fence emcompassing the closed-off hooley-run district, a gang member pulled out wire cutters and snipped away until a human-sized flap could be folded back. There was a drainage channel with murky water leading into Lake Union, and a road up the embankment on the other side of the water.

"Down," a man yelled. He spoke with authority and his group immediately dropped to the ground.

Garrett squatted and froze as the crackled pavement with weeds growing through it and his fellow escapees lit up around him. Garrett looked up, expecting a black helicopter with a sweeping spotlight, but instead, three angels flew overhead in the direction of where Mila had been fighting, the combined intensity of their light radiating a moon-like glow over the ground below. The glow passed over the crouched hoolies, leaving them again in near darkness.

Mila. As confused as he was, and as much as his survival instincts from three years on a battlefield warned him not to, he began to turn back. He had to warn Mila or help her.

A gun pressed to the back of his head, and the man who had commanded everyone to drop when the angels passed overhead whispered threateningly in Garrett's ear. "Stay close. Until we figure out what to do with your ass, you're one of us."

"Or?" asked Garrett, staring off into the distance.

"Or you're more like one of us who's back there bleeding and dead, shithead."

"Understood," said Garrett, turning to face a grinning bald man with a handlebar mustache and faded multi-colored tattoos running up his muscular arms and short thick neck.

The group ran across the drainage ditch, crossing the water as soon as the first man waded in and waved, showing that it was beneath his kneecaps. Garrett breathed through his mouth, covering it with the top of his shirt, trying not to smell the industrial waste combined with anything else that had been dumped into the channel. But he was alive, they were no longer being shot at, and as far as he knew, they were not being chased, though that would not last. They climbed up the other side of the embankment, and again the man with the wire cutter moved to the front. Another portal in another fence was cut open and several men pushed their way through. The bald man who had coerced Garrett into leaving with a pointed pistol held up his hand. They waited on his command.

Garrett could tell by the sounds of passing engines that

the road was busy. A small group stepped out while the others stayed on the sloping cement of the drainage ditch. Chookey lay next to him on his back, hands folded behind his head, watching the sky. A new helicopter and a dozen drones raced toward Mila.

The bald man, the leader, leaned through the chain-link fence and barked, "Get your lazy asses through, now."

As soon as Garrett stepped out, he realized their plan. The hoolies, weapons drawn, stood spread out across the road. As cars slowed, they ushered the civilians from their cars. A laughing gangster knocked a man down who had resisted slightly, by moving slowly. And that made all the civilians move faster. Several hands pushed and shoved Garrett and Chookey into a car-jacked vehicle with six foul-smelling men already stuffed inside.

The driver did not say anything until Garrett looked over his shoulder and the driver told him to look straight ahead and act normal. Garrett agreed with him when he said they were lucky to be alive. Yes, Indeed.

But Mila, could Mila be so lucky? *No.* He had seen a blackwing killed by angels before, and so had Mila, yet she stayed anyway. His mind screamed in agony, *MILA!!! NO!!!*

Diabliss had brought the soldiers, helicopters, and siccum to their knees. Any soldiers left were cowering in the dark and scurrying under anything that would give them cover. Diabliss listened for radio crackle, and then it found it and ended the noise.

The more it fought, the further Garrett could get away, and the less likely there would even be a chase.

Then it felt the pulsating ripples of heat. The approaching radiance. The White Light. The strength of the glow terrified Diabliss, especially as it realized that the brightness and strength came from not one strong White Light but three together. It thought about flight, but there was one siccum left, tracing its path, running through alleys, fluttering in the lower altitudes, and it would continue to do so throughout the night, eventually wearing Diabliss down.

The angel's weakness—that the brightening molecules on their skin were much more flammable than regular human skin cells, especially Mila's human skin that had been infused with toughening polymers—had given Diabliss confidence. Only finding fire to attack with was not always that simple. Creating a trap took time, and Diabliss did not have time.

There were vehicles filled with flammable fuel, but Diabliss could not stay on the ground long enough to access them. The siccum stirred below, circling, fluttering, following.

Mila wanted Diabliss to fly away and hide. She thought she disliked it killing angels, but what she really did not want was to be caught killing angels. She feared being labeled by her society. Why couldn't she understand that the label already attached to her by society placed her on an equal level with insects? Her society would do anything to squish her with its foot.

Diabliss flew in a circle. Below were many dead hoolies, but there were more dead UNSI mercenaries. Mila wanted to survive. Her heart mourned the dead and wounded even when they were trying to kill her.

Why does this have to happen?

Because they hunt those who do not worship the White Light, anyone who doubts their authority. It's not just us. This happens even when you're not a blackwing. It's their way of survival.

The angels lingered patiently on a nearby building, likely waiting for Diabliss to tire. Diabliss drew the sword. Time to get busy. *Need more ground.* Diabliss swooped down at the siccum, hacking and withdrawing, and attacking again, until a wing was wounded, and the siccum was fully grounded. The angels made their move, spreading out but still gliding cautiously toward Diabliss. Then Diabliss flew away. The siccum would be following by ground, but it would not be able to leap some walls and would have to go around buildings.

As the angels surrounded Diabliss, their triangulation limited how much it could turn. There were three, and what they wanted was to pen it in, channel it into a direction. They knew eventually it would tire, but so would they. Brightening took energy, though they had not fought two siccums and a hundred men. They had not just pushed out seven bullets, and they did not still have one lodged within. And it was three beings against one. *Not fair.*

Diabliss swooped down, ran into a small drug store. Mila struggled against Diabliss as it found hair spray and a lighter, and then it exited through the rear.

Yes. It stole. And then it was up in the air again, worrying more about whether the angels saw what had happened than Mila-chick's concern over stealing.

Thief, said Mila-chick. But that was not what she was mad about.

Yes, it is a thief, said Diabliss. No. Mila-chick disliked being mocked in her own body, but it was its turn, and it was saving the Mila-chick.

I know what you're doing, the Mila-chick said.

I know what you're doing, mocked Diabliss. It was ready to turn the Mila-chick off. She would never get control of her shell back if the angels destroyed it. Diabliss had to teach Mila-chick about energy and life. She might take survival more seriously.

Mila simmered inside. *No. I know what you're doing. Stop. Don't.*

Stop. I know what you're doing. I know what you're

doing. Stop, said Diabliss.

It saw the metal rooftop with the ventilation shaft sticking out of it. Diabliss crouched next to the shaft. It had a chocolate bar encompassing nutrients in the pocket, and so it crouched and ate, saving its energy.

At least it fed us chocolate and not dirt.

The angels circled above in the night sky. They were too afraid to come close. That was good, too. Let them burn energy, while Diabliss stored and saved energy. Diabliss had their surprise, though.

It ran for a door on the roof. Inside, at the top of a dark stairwell, Diabliss took the dark sword, poked a hole at the bottom of the door, and then waited until the feet showed outside, and another pair. Yes. Then it held the lighter out and lit it. *Burn, White Light. Burn.* It pressed the red plastic button, and as the hairspray touched the small flame, the chemicals burst into a three-foot wave of fire.

No, Mila screamed.

It kicked the door open. The angels had their swords raised. They tried to cover their faces in time, but the fire spread too quickly.

She hated what Diabliss loved, burning the White Light, burning angels. How they screamed, how they cried, and how their wings flapped, and the beings transformed from her childhood guardian to a tortured blackened soul that suffered and would die. Mila did not understand that this was justice. It was the White Light who had burned blackwings first. The prison? The pain? The blackwings had trusted these monsters because blackwings did not know there was another way, at least not until it was too late.

Out the door. Cover body with wings. Through the flames. Check hair. Diabliss cleaved the White Light in two and beheaded the other. These bodies would be done. Now, with only one versus one, it was a fair match. Diabliss chased the glowing creature away. It would hack the wings off and then watch it drop from the clouds like a dead rat tossed off a bridge.

Yes, the blackwing Anders had shown Mila the aerosol spray can in Portland. Anders had said this tip, a way to burn angels, was free, but it owed him one.

Chapter 34

Four columns of ten students marched into Red Square, a brick open space on the University of Washington campus. Each member of the White Light Infraguard wore a suit of high-density white-plastic bullet-proof armor and a helmet with a tinted face shield. The uniforms were unisex, but it was still possible up close to discern between some men and women. Students without Infraguard uniforms stood and watched, their hands down to their sides, none moving, even though there had to be several students who would be late for class if they remained.

Jenna stepped out front. She eyed the crowd. A young bearded man inched along a brick wall behind a frozen cluster of students. She pointed and whispered the location into the mouthpiece on the rim of her face plate, transmitting to her fellow White Light Infraguards. At her command, each row broke off, forming a square with the four rows, facing outward. The row closest to the bearded man marched forward. They pushed their way into the crowd, and the first Infraguard to arrive whipped his Taser out and stunned the young male target. Several other students near him stepped back, hands up. Each student wore a white armband with their RFID inside, but the man writhing on the ground had a bare arm. If he had just faked the white arm band and had not moved like the other students, Jenna might have missed him. She again spoke into her mouthpiece. She crossed the large brick courtyard and stood over the tasered man and waited patiently until his muscle spasms and groaning stopped, and the man was done urinating in his pants. She pulled her own electroshock weapon from her side holster and placed it on his left cheek.

"Check his back," she said, nudging the near side butt cheek with her foot.

An Infraguard leaned over and jerked the shirt up until it was over the writhing man's shoulders.

"Move a muscle and you'll be pissing your pants for a week," said Jenna. She squatted and then patted, poked, and rubbed the skin, paying special attention to the area around the shoulder blades. "He's clear."

Jenna eyed the nearby students suspiciously and then pointed at a student.

The girl stepped forward from the crowd. Her shaking hands went slowly into the air. "Permission to speak," she said, her voice so broken it was nearly a whisper.

Jenna nodded.

"He's my boyfriend." Her voice shook more than her hands did. "He's not a student. He climbed Campus Wall last night so he could visit me. We're in love."

"Is he a hooley or an anarchist?" asked Jenna.

The nervous girlfriend shook her head.

"Terrorist," Jenna said assuredly.

"No," the girl said. "He did something stupid."

"And illegal," said Jenna. "Entering a critical infrastructure without credentials, without the proper registration procedure, *during a time of war*," Jenna said.

The student nodded. Her jaw quivered. Her boyfriend on the ground closed his eyes as if praying, a tear spilled and pooled in his temple. As his girlfriend saw this, she broke down and bawled, her breath heaving.

Jenna stood patiently and waited until the girl was done and had calmed a bit. "They're likely innocent of greater crimes," she said. "Embrace the White Light, don't challenge it."

Be swift to dispense judgment and justice. That is what

Theo himself had said in his directive.

"No charges." The student's eyes widened as Jenna said this. "Yet," Jenna added, smiling. "Interrogate the boy. Forty-eight hours confinement for both. Anything explodes during that time and we'll burn both lawbreakers right here in the courtyard."

A White Light Infraguard stepped forward and shot the girlfriend squarely in the chest with his Taser. Her legs buckled. She convulsed before hitting the ground, shaking uncontrollably as Jenna walked away. Jenna called back the fourth row and waited until they rejoined the four-wall formation, less four who remained behind with the prisoners.

Jenna punched a number into her wrist pad. "Students standing in the courtyard outside of Suzallo Library step forward into the courtyard." Her voice, patched into the school intercom system, echoed between the buildings. "I want to see feet on red brick. Down from the steps."

Several people in the crowd groaned as they ambled forward. A delay. Poor them. She was only trying to save their lives and their souls. *Blackwings. Terrorists. A war? Don't they realize this is not an elementary school fire drill?* She tried to remind herself that they were students. Sheltered students. Many of whom still had not found the White Light. The same White Light faith that now emboldened Jenna with each step and breath she took. The White Light was with her always. She was always caught in its radiance, a radiance that felt like the warming endorphins after a long run. Performing her patriotic duties only enhanced these feelings.

Jenna spotted a woman. The crowd continued to assemble in the courtyard, leaving her in the back. *Suspicious indeed.* Jenna turned away from her in case she was watching.

"In the back. Suzallo Library. To the right of the main entrance. A woman in a gray Washington hoody. Blue jeans. White shoes. Auburn hair. Close in on my order."

There was a commotion as a person stepped away from the crowd and walked directly toward the White Light Infraguard. A student, wearing glasses, a wool ski cap, and carrying a leather tablet-bag around his side had his hands up.

"Excuse me. I hate to interrupt," he said. "But this is an illegal search and seizure, according to the United States Constitution."

Jenna again punched in her code, accessing the University PA system. "Executive Order 130011 issued by the President of the United States allows any member of the White Light Infraguard to perform search and *clearance* inquiries, as necessary, in order to pursue and absolve people and areas of blackwing and/or terrorist activities. There has been an illegal activity. A trespass. More than enough due cause for suspicion."

Jenna punched another button, changing frequencies so that only the Infraguard would hear her orders. "On my command, move in on the female student with the gray hoody. The hoody was just pulled up, possibly to hide identifying features. Her scarf's up." Jenna turned in a full circle. No movements from the crowd. The students were waiting for her to address the student who had challenged the White Light Infraguard's authority. The unruly student stood with his hands outstretched. An obvious defiant gesture. She would drop him later. "On three. Three, two, one. Move, now!"

The left flank broke away from the other three rows, spreading out in a half-moon.

Crap. The woman broke from the crowd. Jenna shouted into her wrist radio, "We've got a runner. Row one, continue. Apprehend. Rows two, three, and four quarantine area. Neutralize troublemakers." Jenna sprinted across the courtyard, trying to cut the girl off. "Jenna Voit. Commander. White Light Infraguard. Seal perimeter," said Jenna. Her internal radio commands went to UNSI. There were guards who could help at Campus Wall.

Jenna had been in decent shape. She was a soccer player on a club team. But Theo's command had been firm. Worship God, the White Light, and the temple that carries it. Within two weeks Jenna had ripples on her abs and could flex her small firm biceps. Yes, she was in the best shape of her life, but this girl she was chasing was gaining not just ground, a *lot* of ground. Jenna grew frustrated as the girl got further away and closer to the gap at the security fence. Still pressing, still pushing herself harder, Jenna saw the security gate pull together and shut, and knew she had this rogue criminal. She again drew her Taser. Five blasts ready to go. She would use them all.

A man stepped in front of the running girl. His weapon was real, but she sprinted anyway. Then the shirt tore, and the body morphed. Two black wings tore through the fabric. "Fire, now!" Jenna yelled. She did not officially command UN security but called the order out anyway. "It's a blackwing. Fire your weapon, now!" she screamed.

The UNSI guard froze, looked up, and watched helplessly as the blackwing lifted into the air.

Jenna did not slow.

"Open the gate. East entrance," she huffed, running forward. Nothing happened. Jenna was furious. The man should have fired. Sure, it was not her call, but he should have fired regardless. His gun was still strapped. "Open east gate, damn it. Jenna Voit. Commander. White Light Infraguard. Open east gate, now!"

Jenna could not wait. Rather than slow her momentum, she climbed. She was surprised to see that two White Light Infraguards were right behind her and were hitting the fence as she neared the top. Jenna grabbed the razor wire. It dug through her gloves, tearing into her hands. She pushed the pain out and pulled herself up, a fabric seam tore as she went over, taking some skin with it.

The gate was still closed. *Damn them to hell.* Jenna looked up. The blackwing was below the clouds. She could still see it. "Need angels. Blackwing airborne. Two blocks south of 45th. Just outside the University perimeter fence. Infraguard leader in pursuit." Jenna turned at the next block, jumping onto and running over a car's hood, sliding over its roof, hopping off the trunk. Her lungs and legs burned. She flung her helmet off as her warm breath started to suffocate her. The blackwing was getting farther and farther away.

Suddenly, it turned and flew back toward Jenna.

"Come on, you bitch. Bring it on." Jenna fired her Taser at the renegade blackwing, even though she had no chance of hitting it from this distance.

The blackwing slowed and watched, as if curious or taunting Jenna. Then it turned and swooped down.

Jenna followed it into an empty alley and onto a bare street on the other side with only two cars going in opposite directions, leaving the street empty.

The water of Lake Union was below and the I-5 bridge spanning it was nearly overhead.

The blackwing touched down.

Jenna quickly looked over her shoulder for support, but she had lost any trailing Infraguards. They had either tired or had taken a wrong turn.

"You just ruined my life," the young student blackwing said. She still had her hoody pulled up, but Jenna's bodycam would sync with the school ID system. Jenna took in the facial features as best she could in case there was a technical failure. The small ski-jump nose, brown eyes, light brown hair. A mole on her left jaw. This blackwing would have to kill her if she ever expected to return to campus. Jenna was prepared to die for the cause.

"You ruined your life when you broke the law. When you didn't turn the devil inside you into the proper authorities. Now, under the laws of the White Light, as Commander..."

"Commander?" The blackwing laughed.

"As Commander of White Light Infraguard, University of Washington Chapter, I place you under arrest. On your belly. Palms touching the asphalt."

"Why didn't you just leave us alone? It's not a demon. She cares about people. She cares about me. She warned me about the White Light. The evil."

"You've got that one wrong," said Jenna. "Do not trust your inner-Satan."

"Satan?" She laughed again. "I guess you'll believe anything. Have you seen the siccums? The White Light brought them here. Have you seen what they do? What they do to people when they can't find a blackwing to suck on?"

"Siccums? Creatures conjured from the depths of hell by vile, evil beings like you." Jenna raised her Taser. The four red bars on the back indicated how many blasts she had left.

The blackwing pulled something from the side of its leg—concealed in fabric. It flashed in her hand, and as she moved, it grew longer.

At first Jenna thought it was a rod, but then realized it was a strange coal-black sword. "With God and the White Light, everything is right," Jenna said. And then she charged. Her first shot was blocked by the sword, her second as well. Her Taser was ineffective against the armed blackwing. After firing the third of the four shots, she realized that the fourth would likely be batted away. Jenna had not been trained in hand to hand combat, but she was not afraid of it either. She threw the Taser to the ground in front; it skidded to the feet of the blackwing.

Jenna put her head down and charged the blackwing. The

blackwing drove the butt of the sword into the back of Jenna's head. Jenna fell. The blade sliced into her back, even through her hardened bulletproof plastic armor.

"Now, the next time you chase blackwings out of the shadows, especially a peaceful blackwing, remember this day."

There was another burn. Jenna realized what the blackwing had done. A second slice on her back, like the wing pouches, like the scars Jenna was told to look for.

It was not over, though. Now, Jenna was right on top of her Taser. Jenna pulled it out from beneath her and then fired it into the blackwing's foot as the blackwing struck down on the back of her head.

Then there was a bright glow, and Jenna could no longer see. Her eyes blurred. She felt so much pain; but she felt so at ease.

Jenna came to face down on a gurney. The angel stood over her. He glowed like the moon and smiled down at her. Yes. She had pleased the White Light. Was she dreaming? She tried to sit up, and with some struggling, finally managed to get up on her forearms.

The blackwing was on the ground. It was dead.

"You should be proud," said the angel, his long blond hair spreading behind him like extra wings. "The electrical jolt disabled the blackwing and just as I showed up."

"I only did my duty," said Jenna. "I shouldn't be proud for doing what's right—what the White Light—what angels command."

The angel placed his hand on Jenna, pushing her back down onto the thin white mattress. "Rest. The White Light Infraguard needs you well. Now more than ever."

Jenna pushed herself up again, her back in pain, wet with blood and sweat. "UN security failed," she said. "I know the

White Light Infraguard is a newly formed unit, but the UNSI on campus shouldn't just work with us, they should answer directly to us. We have sworn oaths. We are Holy Followers of the White Light."

"They shall," said the angel in his beautiful harmonic voice.

"Another thing. Off subject." She did not get many face-to-face meetings with angels. "I was thinking, well, not just now, but earlier. Data mining. We need traits and statistics for all known blackwings. See if there's a connection."

"Yes, of course. Now, rest and heal," the angel said. "The White Light needs your service."

Jenna relaxed, or more appropriately, collapsed, with a smile, full of pain, and in complete bliss.

Chapter 35

The hoolies snipped open a chained gate and found their way into the parking lot, and then into the offices of an abandoned warehouse. They had regrouped, but it would only be a matter of time before they would have to either disband the gang or fight. Cameras and drones filmed every inch on clear days. *Thank you Seattle weather.* Garrett figured that if UNSI troops and angels were not flooding the abandoned parking lot and warehouse, it was only because they were too busy killing Mila. Garrett, more than anything, wanted an explanation. His heart felt crushed, but he knew he was confused. Did he even know her? What was a blackwing anyway? Was it something she had wished for or because of something she had done? *Oh, Mila.* He shook his head. Just his luck.

And if he had not covered his face well enough, it would only be a matter of time before they identified him in surveillance footage and traced him, though he could always claim the hoolies took him as a hostage. After military service and his temporary incarceration, face-recognition software would boot him up in less than three seconds on a slow computer. He would need to report his motorcycle stolen.

"Thinking about your chick?" asked Chookey.

"I'm thinking about a million things, but yeah," Garrett said. "Not sure if she is mine."

"Yeah." Chookey smiled. "You're likely *hers.*"

Garrett shrugged. He practically was. He hoped he was because that would mean she was still alive. His heart, even with all the action, sadness, and drama, still ached to be with her. But how could she be okay? Three angels? Helicopters?

Hundreds of UNSI officers? And she had been shot. He saw it. His sanity rattled loose a little at a time. He tried to hold his anger in. He fought to regain control. Veterans do not always fall apart and shed tears, sometimes they shed blood. Garrett took a slow deep breath and tried to hold it all in, but the pressure was building. *Maybe she's just a prisoner.* That was the best he could hope for.

"Boy, you *are* her bitch," said Chookey. "Don't worry. We're all bitches to someone. I'm sure she got away. I've seen her fight. She's good. She's got lots of friends, too. She's a street hero. Saves babies and all."

"I've met some of her friends. They're not that great. Stuck up university kids."

"You haven't met her street friends. She helps people. She's like a *real* angel. Even I'm her bitch cause she saved my life."

Chookey told Garrett about the Rose City Hatchet Club's ambush, and Mila, a young university girl smashing rabid hooligans armed with small hatchets. *Holy shit.* He really did not know her. Yet, he remembered a sensitive Mila sipping bourbon on his rooftop, how she could barely take a drink, how she haunted his coffee shop with shy smiles and a timid crush, how she cried when the blackwing was killed, and how a missing father ripped her insides open. She stood by, but also stood up to her fascist friends, and she read *Confessions*. Human or not—whether she chose to be a blackwing, or the blackwing chose her, she was the type of person he respected and the type of person he wanted to be with. Unless it had all been an act.

"Chookey, what now?" he asked.

"The leaders make a plan. They think we need to split into smaller groups for some time. We're outlaws."

"They'll just hunt you all down. This is when you should band together. Or...join another group." Garrett stood, heading for the circle of men who hovered around a small flashlight, cussing, conspiring, and throwing their hands up.

"I wouldn't interrupt their meeting. This isn't a democracy—and even if it was, you're not a citizen."

"I don't care. We're lying to ourselves. Mila's dead, and so is your gang." Garrett had learned on the battlefield how to push grief aside, but he had also learned how to turn that grief into something else. "I know how we can get stronger, how we can fight back, and how we can get revenge."

Chapter 36

The wind blew frigid sheets of rain into Mila. Although her clothes were sopping wet, and her hair was matted against her face and no longer moving with the wind, she was not cold. Mila had tried to hold on to at least some negative senses, like cold and pain—it somehow made her feel more in control, more human—but she had finally acquiesced to Diabliss's offer to make her feel numb, feel less. It had taken less than a week for Mila to find the hoolies, still hiding from the law. Garrett eventually peered out, but she was too afraid to make contact with him. UNSIs would eventually find this band of renegades, especially after the thick impenetrable gray clouds cleared, and the roving satellites and drones again combed the surface. Hopefully, they were smart enough to only come out under low cloud cover. Mila had recognized a gang member and had followed him to this location. At first, she wondered about the lack of light, but then realized that they had lights inside but had draped blankets and tarps over the windows so that the light would not show. Well done. If a small amount of light from their meager lanterns did escape, it would only look like a hiding family or a rogue squatter, likely not enough to warrant an investigation.

She shook her head as a bakery truck pulled up. Two men jumped out the back and several ran from the abandoned building to the back of the truck, quickly unloading its contents. Within two minutes the vehicle they had obviously just stolen was pulling out, stopping only to unchain a gate and again drape the chains so that from outward appearances their hideaway would seem locked up and empty. They would abandon the vehicle in another part of town.

Go in now. Find him, said Diabliss, growing impatient.

It's not that simple. He might not forgive me. He might not want to be with me. Yes, I love him, and I know, to you it's all about receptors and brain chemistry. To me, love is so much more.

She did not want to just fly down and enter. Shit. The EC Elite had to have known that she was a blackwing. She had fought members of their gang as well as fought alongside them. They had accepted her. But then again, they were hooligans—rogues and criminals. Reaching deep inside, Mila discovered either fortitude or a way to dull sensations, and before the clouds could part, when there was no traffic nearby and the hooley activities had stilled, she swooped down, pulling her wings inside as she landed. She shook her head like a wet dog and wished she was closer to a restroom with a mirror so she could freshen up first. *But this is who I am…*

Enhanced hearing allowed her to determine the knock code for a front door made of thick sliding plywood, so she knocked three fast and then three slow. She finished the code with a low kick. She heard some argumentative whispers, along with her name. They were unsure if they should let her in. "*But she knows the knock*," one man hissed. Another said she would just bring more trouble and then they would be scattering to a new place. A third man said she was there to kill them all. We can take her, said yet another. Good luck with that, said the original whisperer. Just let her in. We all die some time. Those were the final words as the sheet of plywood slid open, scraping on the ground, and Mila slipped inside. Unrecognizable figures swarmed her.

"Follow me," said a man, motioning with his arm. His voice was tough but tinged with fear, possibly due to Mila, but just as likely as he was the one who would escort her to their leader and would have to explain why they let an outsider, a blackwing at that, into their hideout.

A dim lantern blinked. Most interior office windows and doorways were boarded up or missing. The floor had been stripped of carpet, while the walls showed gashes where the electrical wiring, and anything with metal, had been stripped out. Mila's escort knocked on a temporary plywood door, the outline of the light inside barely breaching its perimeter. The light faded and then the door slid back. A head, barely visible in the darkness, peeked out. Mila could see in darkness better than she could before Diabliss had entered her. She recognized the gatekeeper immediately as a gang member in the inner circle. She had even fought alongside him on her way to Portland. They owed her for saving Chookey. In a way, she became one of them when she joined them in their fight, but when they realized their similarities ended there, that she was stronger than anyone, could outfight or outcompete them all, they began to fear her. This was long before she had officially revealed that she was a blackwing. Maybe they would not only remember her final demand, to care for Garrett, but that her fight had allowed them to escape. The plywood sheet slid to the side. Once she stepped inside, they shoved the plywood to its original position and their light brightened back to full strength.

"Oy. Mila," said Pumpkinhead, the fat, balding tattooed man she had once bested in the train. She was glad to sense that he was indeed happy to see her, regardless of her status.

"Oy," she patted him on the arm. With his immediate acceptance, she wanted to wrap her arms around him. He was a brute, but a huggable one. Once they had bonded, she understood that he was a true loyal friend.

"Oy, Mila," said Uno, but his "oy" was not endearing at all.

The light was on, but perhaps the room was best kept dark, though its smells gave away what she saw. A bucket in the corner needed to be emptied. Food wrappers and garbage were strewn about. Some of the food was moldy. The air, lacking circulation, was still cold, but thicker and warmer than the halls and rooms outside. Mila's senses were so much more attuned, rat droppings, mold, mildew, mystery stains, and a layer of moisture that forced them to bleed together. If Mila had entered this room only a year earlier, she would be on all fours retching.

Mila liked Uno as much as she liked being inside the room. Uno had a vicious side, and even though this gang had opened a side to her that she did not know existed when the battle erupted with Portland's hatchet-wielding hooligan army, she still believed fighting was wrong.

A new person outside the room knocked on the plywood. Again, the light cut out and the board slid open. She gasped as she saw through the darkness, Garrett escorted by two men. She wanted to run to him. She wanted to hold him, hug him. She knew if he recoiled, that she would fly away and maybe even turn herself in. She would never come back. She would never be Mila again either. The door slid shut and the lantern again turned up, hissing and spitting propane. Garrett squinted and rubbed his eyes. How much of his time had been spent in this dark warehouse? She knew why he stuck his head out of the building occasionally, light and air. A peek and a gulp probably helped keep him sane in this musty, rancid rat hole.

Mila looked him in the eyes, trying to read his expressions. She smiled, but then just as quickly frowned.

"Garrett, I guess we'll see you soon," said Uno. He turned to Mila. "A deal's a deal. We kept him alive, now you leave us be. There's no stopping them from coming after us, but I think you bring the angels, UNSIs, and those hideous creatures faster than they'll come without you. I'd prefer to fight them on different terms." He looked to Garrett, who nodded.

"Thank you," said Mila. "They'll come, though, and when they do, you'll wish I was nearby. More than a bunch of you would have gone down in Portland without me by your side." She faced Garrett. She was always so firm and in control when speaking with hoolies. She had to be. If someone showed fear, they would pounce on it.

Uno stepped forward. He nodded at Garrett, then Mila, and then he smiled. "Now, you two lovebirds need to fly the coop. May we escort you outside?"

"Yeah," Mila said. "Can you give us a ride into town?"

"Of course," said Uno.

Uno took them to the front of the building and practically pushed them out the door. He told them a car would be out shortly.

Her nerves made it difficult to create words. She looked to her feet, but as she did, Garrett moved forward. He put his arms around her and hugged.

"Mila," he said, "I thought I'd never see you again. You were shot. I thought you were dead."

"I was shot. I nearly was dead."

"But you're okay?"

Mila nodded. She wanted to show him where she had been shot, to show how she had healed, but thought it might scare him too much. Who wanted a practically invincible inhuman girlfriend?

"My only thoughts were of saving you. I wanted to tell you. I tried."

"I know. That would be a tough secret. A lot of risk. I know a little about that. I guess we both have secrets."

A warehouse roller door opened, and a small blue car drove out.

"Garrett, I have to ask. I'm afraid to know the answer, but I need to know. Are you still here for me?"

"Yes," Garrett said. "And I always will be."

267

Mila again looked at Garrett. She could not believe that he still loved her, but she could see in his eyes that he did. She pressed her head into his chest and wrapped her arms around tighter. She could never let go. Ever.

"You still want to be with me?" she asked unbelievingly, her voice cracking.

Garrett nodded. "Of course," he said.

Chapter 37

Jenna leaned over her desk in the new White Light Infraguard headquarters, studying the campus map. She was surrounded by small screens covering each wall, with a White Light Infraguard stationed at each one. Her computer chimed as another phone segment had been ushered to her. All cell phone and internet traffic within a three-mile radius was swept up and monitored for a long list of key words associated with crimes, terrorism, atheism, and any other anti-government rhetoric. One to two key words within a conversation and a recorded segment went to a junior Infraguard field agent. Three or more key words, and it went directly to her, the White Light Infraguard Commander. Yes, she was not only the youngest commander in the White Light network, she had also succeeded in certifying the first campus as blackwing free. In fact, she had created the first certification program period, a model now flourishing on campuses worldwide. Even elementary, junior, and senior high schools had adopted similar programs. Of course, the elementary Infraguard units were run by parent volunteers. News agencies broadcasted her capture of the blackwing, her video of various chase points, but especially her final lunge at the beast from her body camera. Yes. Vital information. Electrocuting blackwings disabled them in the same way it did a human. A young girl had even asked her for an autograph. Jenna nearly refused, as she did not want to feed her own pride, but then reconsidered, realizing how having heroes strengthened the cause.

Her heart jumped a beat when the last name Sadis appeared as the subject in an email. It was from the national

White Light Network that had recently assumed the responsibility of guiding UNSI. Mila, was she dead? Jenna clicked it open. It was a list from a worker rehabilitation camp. Sadis appeared in an admission form along with a transfer order for redistribution. Jenna jumped out of her seat. Bradley Sadis. *She had located Mila's father*. Jenna printed the paper and then found the pertinent information. Redistribution Camp jurisdiction was under UNSI. For the most part, UNSI answered to the White Light, but there were still UNSI officers who were unsure of or challenged new chains of command. It did not matter, though. If she ran into political infighting, she would report suspected resistance to the White Light.

Jenna again tried to justify her investigation. A missing student in her domain? That might seem far-fetched, especially considering Mila was likely shacked up with Garrett Webb, but what if Garrett held Mila by force? No. Jenna had promised to leave Garrett alone, even if she was still convinced that Garrett was a subversive. She had checked more than once; he was not a registered White Light follower. With absolute proof of God's will and the White Light here on earth, anyone who had not registered was so stubborn they were likely evil-minded or a terrorist. Jenna always believed that terrorism was not limited to blowing up buildings. It could include thought—anything that hindered progress, threatened God and their nation. For now, leg work. She dialed the commanding officer in charge of redistribution at Washington Trade Camp 7. "Jenna Voit here. I'm the Infraguard Commander at University of Washington Campus. Yes. I'm flattered you recall that glorious incident. I was just doing my duty. Anything for God and the White Light. Yes, sir. I'm glad you feel that way. In fact, your service and dedication might encourage you to assist me in an internal investigation involving a missing student who would be a great service to the White Light as well. I need anything you've got on Bradley Sadis preparing for redistribution in WTC7. I understand you generally do not give this information to student leaders. It might be better if I request this directly through my White Light connections as I know you have no reason to assist in a simple campus investigation. I'm sure you have many more important things to do... Wow. Not necessary? You'll send what you've got today? Anything will help, sir. You're a strong supporter of the White Light Youth Movement as well as an inspiration. Thank you for your service."

Jenna spoke into her wrist phone. "Kathy. Your presence is requested down at Infraguard Center. Your security level has been raised for two hours. Come down immediately."

After a few taps on her computer screen, a map appeared. A satellite photo where the camp was likely located was blurred out, as were most government buildings and critical infrastructure. She did not have the proper security clearance to zoom in, but the general area, along with more information, would hopefully tell her all she needed to know.

Now would be the more difficult part, finding Mila.

Chapter 38

Chookey dropped Garrett and Mila off across town, within walking distance to Garrett's apartment. The rain had stopped an hour earlier, the clouds had blown away, and a rare sun was out. Chookey had likely been told to drop them off as far away as possible, a difficult and risky task, especially considering he was only fifteen years old and an unlicensed driver. He had to navigate side streets since the GPS locator had been removed, disallowing travel through major thoroughfares.

All Mila cared about was the fact that Garrett not only held her hand, he held it tenderly, his pulse quickening and blending with hers. And his eyes? Radiant. No suspicion, but instead assurance and sincerity. Few words had been spoken, but they looked at each other with a firm resolve to not let the thousands of unsaid things get in their way. Perhaps best of all was Mila's confidence that there would be time, time for them to learn and relearn each other.

"Thanks, Chookey," said Mila as she stepped from the car.

Garrett leaned in. "Remember what I said, Chookey. You're too smart for this, and you still have heart. You know how and where to find me."

Chookey nodded to Garrett. "The cause above all else? I'll see you soon."

Garrett nodded. Mila perceived that there was something unsaid there as well.

Garrett and Mila walked down a sidewalk in a residential neighborhood as Chookey drove away.

"I think we'd both take Chookey under our wings if we

could," Mila said.

"Under our wings?"

"I know." Mila shook her head. "Poor word choice. But you know what I mean."

"I do. We both see he'll die young."

As they walked, Mila waited each time their hands fell apart for him to grasp hers again, and each time their fingers and palms were apart, she yearned to reconnect. Again, though, he would grip her hand, and it was as if the recognition of new fresh love had begun all over again.

"Garrett," Mila said. "Are we together?" She finally had to ask. Only because she had enough confidence that what she believed had been broken and impossible was now possible and complete.

"Yes," said Garrett.

"In spite of everything?" she asked.

"Yes. But I have a lot of questions."

"I'm sure you do."

"I have…confessions as well."

"Okay, with secrets, even secrets that can't be spoken, we're still together?"

"Yes, especially those that can't be spoken. If you'll have me."

"I will," Mila said.

They were still several blocks from Garrett's neighborhood, passing alongside a residential neighborhood with roving guards around its gated perimeter. The two guards wore casual clothes, and not security uniforms. The neighborhood was not gated because the inhabitants were upper class. The protection that these men and their connections offered were likely mafia-like and scraped together through sweat and going without, unlike rich neighborhoods that used corporate security. It was a simple racket. These men "protected" the inhabitants from robberies and shakedowns that they themselves would impose if the people inside did not pay their fee. What the guards did have on were white armbands, symbols of registering and offering their devotion to the White Light.

"That would make our traveling easier," suggested Garrett, nodding toward the armbands.

"No," said Mila. The escaped word was more a product of Diabliss, though Mila was beginning to share her distrust and disgust with the White Light. "I'm sorry. It is a brilliant idea, and it's only a piece of white cloth, probably torn off an old bed sheet, but I can't. At least not yet. Wearing the symbol would be too bold of a lie."

"I understand, I think, but this is not a country where non-believers are welcomed. The White Light Infraguard is self-regulated and has been granted immunity from prosecution by Congress through the Loyalty Act. They search who they want, where they want, when they want. If you refuse, they call in UNSIs. Freedom of expression and freedom of religion here only means you are free to believe if you follow. But, shit, it's always been that way."

Mila looked at a decorated Christmas tree in a yard. A little early. The first she had seen. Wow. She might never be a student or soccer player again in this world, and Garrett might never have a normal life. They were renegades. She gripped his hand harder. At least they were finally together. Garrett and Mila had discussed where to go. Walking endlessly, finding a tent city or a private place under a bridge had been suggested, as did returning to Garrett's place, with perhaps Mila scouting the neighborhood first. Garrett told Mila he was fairly confident his coffee shop was opening and closing, but he was less confident that the business aspects would be intact. A health inspection, tax audit, or UNSI raid could occur at any moment and would likely result in a closure.

274

Mila told Garrett about stealing medication for the poor. He liked that.

"Can you tell me more about Diabliss?" Garrett asked.

What else could she say? Diabliss likes to drop people from the sky? He made her even more skeptical? Diabliss had an explanation for nearly everything, and his explanations made sense to her. What else? She had been fighting with a gang and liked it. She had killed and burned angels. Technically, according to world standards and morals, she harbored evil inside, which perhaps even qualified as demon possession. Mila shook her head. "I don't know. Maybe if you promise me something first—a trade. I give up something and then it's your turn."

Garrett laughed and nodded.

"And it has to be something really good."

Garrett, again, nodded, but she doubted his secrets could come close to hers.

Their walk took them close enough to Garrett's apartment that they decided to risk going inside. Maybe not the safest place, but Garrett was mostly concerned about Mila, and Mila assured him she was safe as could be. She wanted to tell him she would do anything to keep him safe. She would burn a dozen angels and drop UNSIs from space for him. "I'll help you escape," she said. "Unless your trade is totally lame."

"I have a lot to live up to," said Garrett.

"Well, I did help some people, but I'm afraid to tell you everything. You might not respect me."

"Mila, I think I know exactly how you feel. Remember, I went to war," he said. "I'm going to risk it all and let some things go."

"You do that, and I will too."

Garrett put his arm around Mila, reaching inside her jacket and around her waist. The comfort. The warmth. The thrilling chill when he went over the skin pouch with her razor-sharp wings tucked within. He kissed her on the top of her head. Oh, how she wanted exactly that and so much more. Diabliss stirred again, urging her to procreate. Tonight, she just might.

Garrett had been away from his apartment for several days now. He half expected it to be rented out, even though he was not behind with his payment, or his door blown to bits, but the apartment was just as he had left it. He grabbed the bourbon and glasses, as well as a thicker jacket to put over Mila, even though she said she was not cold. The sun shone bright, a clear winter day, but as soon as the late afternoon sun set, a chill would settle in fast and the world around them would plunge as if falling through broken ice.

Mila stood on the roof deck, waiting. She had wanted to sit up top before going inside. Garrett's usual trips up top were usually accompanied by a bottle, cola, glass with ice, a warm coat, and a book. But this time, he had traded the book for company, signified by the additional glass tumbler. Mila did not need a drink to find the courage to speak, but he did. He plugged in a radio and turned some music on. He found an AM station that was not running live broadcasts or pre-recorded loops of Theo, but instead played holiday songs. Normally, he abhorred popular songs, especially traditional ones, but they needed the sounds to cause static and disruptions for any listening devices. The clear sky made him nervous, as did being in the open. Satellites and drones would be combing the space above, and even with hoodys on and chins down, a glimpse at a bird or a glance at the right angle and face-recognition software would be juxtaposing he and Mila's faces over millions of others until a match was found—and if the match aligned with a warrant, then the sky would erupt with a spatter of black helicopters, and the street

276

would swarm with weapon-clad UNSIs.

Garrett sipped pensively while Mila curled into him. How the hell did this happen, and why to her? She was so nice, even helping save the lives of strangers in need. He did not mind her being a blackwing—but this did complicate things more than either of them could likely realize. He knew more than to believe the reports that blackwings were vampires sucking blood and severing heads. The decapitations could be explained by the red beasts. When he looked into her blue eyes, he saw the innocence of a true person whom he loved. Intelligent, kind, and most of all open-minded. Most people could only believe what they were taught or told, most people were incapable of original thought and doubt; he could see her consider, and then even question. Shit. She not only read *Confessions*, she loved it.

He took a gulp. The acid in the cola stung his throat, the bourbon burned as well, both just the way he liked. "Well, Mila, you went first last time. I guess it's my turn to start." He took a breath and then paused for another. "I spent three years in Syranistan. I hunted people, and if they were deemed an enemy combatant, I killed them. I was so good at it I won medals. While under enemy fire, in a hostile combat zone, a friend ran across the line of fire." He shook his head. "Everyone should question war, or nothing will ever change."

"Everyone says you fight for freedom—theirs and ours."

"Maybe. It's also about pipelines and minerals. It's about acquiring resources, stopping economic coalitions from forming, and a military industrial complex, a greedy beast that's always hungry, always has to be fed. It's about breaking open territories so there will never be a legitimate competing world superpower or an alliance that might create one."

"Then why did you go?" Mila asked. "Didn't you volunteer?"

"I went for freedom."

"I thought you said it wasn't about that."

"I went for *my* freedom. I went into the system so I could disappear. Becoming a veteran took me off the radar. I killed for money. Twenty thousand Ameros. A signing bonus that got me the start of a coffee shop with enough left over for a motorcycle. But mostly, I did it so I could be left alone. I'm a subversive. I've stayed out of their reach for the most part, but if I ever find myself in their clutches, with my background and training, they'd sign me up for another tour in a heartbeat. With my record as a true killer, they'd take me back."

"I see. You get ignored when you're a decorated veteran. But you're left with scars."

Mila's eyes glazed over, as if recounting her own kills. She had them, too. He knew that blank stare. He had lost himself gazing into a mirror or looking at his reflection in a window so many times. He would snap out of the trance just in time to see his own soul flutter back in. Yes. If the gods were real, and hell was below, there was probably a hole for each of them.

Garrett continued. "I was a student, like you. Only in my day, my professors organized the students. We studied the erosion of our rights by night, fantastic laws and parchments that are rarely used but every generation bleeds for, keeping the dream close and alive. When the professors disappeared, I tried to write the story. I tried to locate them, too, but they had simply vanished. Dissidents. I would be next. Given the choice between conformity and my own abduction, I chose the unexpected path. None of the above."

"Sounds like my life," said Mila. She added, "This is a none-of-the-above life situation. Sometimes there's no right answer."

Garrett gulped at his drink until Mila put her drink down and placed her hands upon both of his. He finally realized he could not hold her hands and keep them warm, while holding an iced glass so he put his drink down.

"You make what you think is the best choice at the time. I still don't know what I could have done differently." Garrett shivered. Even with a blanket, a drink inside him, Mila snuggling against him, it was still winter and cold out. How did Mila stay so warm? She emitted heat like a furnace. "I did end up with a coffee shop, and because of that, I met you."

"Coffee," she said. "It's been weeks since I sat indoors and had a cup. Most shops are running out."

"Yeah. You're not missing a lot. There's a shortage. Only cheap crap. Mostly it's a food-grade brown dye with artificial flavor. The tea's not much better."

"Great. I hope they at least add caffeine."

"Of course. We're a medicated nation."

"I guess it's my turn." Mila sighed. "There's some things I won't share. Maybe someday. I have helped people. Homeless families, but there's more that I'm not proud of."

Garrett considered letting himself off the hook, but Mila had been more than fair and was way ahead when it came to giving up dark secrets. He was about to do something he promised himself and his cause he would never do. Not only disclose an underground movement to an outsider, but he was going tell her everything, or almost everything. It was important that she understand what he was about, especially since he had made another commitment, a commitment made when he thought Mila was dead, slain by angels. *Too many secrets*, he thought as he rubbed his temples. *Flo-Rite*. He might never drink the chemical again, yet Flo-Rite could still kill him. Why did he even care? The rest of the world certainly did not.

Garrett interrupted. "I don't have to hear it. At least not today. Tell me when you need to let it go. Until then, there's more that I need to tell you. Some things that may change the way you think about me. And a plan. A plan that may change what we've started. It makes my course, our course, complicated."

Mila looked up, surprised. He knew how she must have felt when she took him to a dark, abandoned garage, hoping to pop wings that would show she was an illegal creature, wanted and hunted by angels and UNSI, feared, hated, and hunted by nearly everyone. She had a secret, and a secret life, just like he did. Garrett, though, was not so naïve to think that just because he had a similar secret that he had kept from her that she would understand and not be angered over it. It is one thing to love reading an underground newspaper when you are a sheltered student; it is another to love someone considered by most, a terrorist. Garrett knew too much about politics to believe that just because someone is a member of a hated class, the person or group will automatically relate to or empathize with another hated class.

"I need to get something," said Garrett, standing up.

Inside his apartment, he opened his silverware drawer, and reaching in from the cabinet beneath it, felt for the slight ridge of a sticker. There was a section of wood that was hollowed out just enough to hold a memory stick. The cabinet manufacturer's label covered it, and it was just close enough to the drawer glides that it would pass the sweep of a metal detector. A memory stick that would send him to prison for life was inside. He grabbed his backpack with his laptop off the table, examining the location of his zippers. He always zipped to the exact position. Always. Sure enough, it was off by a quarter inch. He did not have to doubt that in a hurry he had left it in a different position. He did not do that. He left it in the exact position so he could always be one hundred percent sure if someone had searched his stuff or his place. Of course, secret searches were as much a part of UNSI-led investigations as cameras and data collection. It did not matter. It was a routine follow-up search. The type of evidence they were looking for he held in his hand. If they considered him a high-priority threat, they would be swarming the place already. The fact that they were not made him breathe easier. It meant they did not know he was the Agorist or that Mila was a blackwing.

Sure, a door-exploding raid made him hate the premises, but that was before spending a week in an abandoned building without light, heat, adequate food, or clean water—with or without Flo-Rite. Plus, sharing rooms with a hundred men who had not showered in weeks or maybe even months was something he experienced only in military service. Back then, like here, it was the civilians who smelled. Hoards of homeless, unemployed refugees living like rats in alleys and holes, waiting for a raid by foreigners in uniform. That was what he had become over the past week, a rodent and a refugee, awaiting a raid by foreigners in uniform.

He slung his pack over his shoulder, his sweaty palm gripping the shiny red memory stick. He feared sharing what was on the memory stick with Mila as much as he feared another arrest. He did not think he could go through losing Mila again. He would beg for death, but death came easy in this world.

On the deck, he turned on his laptop, running a viral sweep, making sure it was not transmitting or scanning for information. It was, but he quickly disabled the program. Nearly all electronic devices had sweep and transmit programs built into them, and all antivirus software did. Since it was corporations collecting data, the government kept their hands clean. The corporations got tax rebates, subsidies, or just sold the data. This data-sweep program was new and easily found with a black-market comp scan. He pushed the memory stick into the port. He got nervous every time he did this. He could say it was old issues that he had collected. And they might even believe him.

"*Confessions*. You have all the issues." Mila leaned over his shoulder and hugged his side. "Wait. Some I haven't seen before. You have the health and safety data on Flo-Rite?" Mila scrunched her nose. "Interesting molecular structure."

"It is."

"It looks like medication."

"Yes."

Garrett did not want to say it. She loved his underground paper, but would she love it with a dark secret attached? Would she love a loathed liar?

"Mila, I haven't been completely honest with you," Garrett said. "I have a hobby. I'm the Agorist."

Mila's nose un-scrunched. She had a look he did not recognize or understand. She pushed the laptop off his lap. It slid onto the rooftop's wooden decking. The blanket at their legs braced its fall.

He closed his eyes. He had never regretted anything before in his life as much as he did now. And then he felt her lips and mouth on his, and a forceful pressure as she pulled him closer to her, climbing on top of him. As she kissed him, he felt her smile.

"I love you, Garrett Webb," she said. "And that will never stop."

Chapter 39

Someone knocked on the door shortly after Garrett and Mila returned to Garrett's apartment. Mila had stopped him from finishing his confession. Maybe one dark secret was enough, for now, but his respite would be temporary. His other dark secret was time sensitive, and he could not wait much longer. In whispers, Mila and Garrett decided they had to know who was at the door. If it was UNSI or Infraguard, at least they had knocked instead of just blowing the door to pieces. Garrett checked over his shoulder so he could make sure that Mila was out of sight and then he opened the door just enough to see out, wedging his foot into the bottom of the door in case somebody leaned into it for a home invasion.

It was one of Mila's friends, Kathy, dressed in the White Light Infraguard riot gear, with two additional White Light Infraguards at her side.

"Open up, Turkey," said Kathy.

"Do you have a warrant?"

"Not even sure I need one. No, really, I don't know. But do you think for a second I can't get one transmitted to me within thirty seconds?"

"No," said Garrett. "I'm sure you can."

"I might also consider your impoliteness as suspicious behavior. I've been trained to spot those who might have NCD. Would you prefer a mental health evaluation?"

"Non-Cooperation Disorder? That's definitely not me." He shook his head. "I'm like the opposite of that. Do you want coffee and a home-cooked meal as well?" Garrett checked over his shoulder one more time before opening the door about six more inches.

"Coffee. Real shit, or cheap shit with brown dye?" Kathy shook her head. "Dumb question. Jenna will shit on my uniform if I don't hurry back. This plastic can protect me from a lot of things..." Kathy slapped her chest plate.

"But not Jenna's shit."

Kathy pushed the door open and punched Garrett on the arm. "No," she said. "Not Jenna's shit."

Garrett resisted rubbing his arm, but he wanted to. Shit. How could Mila take that all the time, especially before she was a blackwing?

The two guards with her were students. Their right hands rested on holstered but unclipped five-shot Tasers. Each had one foot forward, ready to change direction or block his attack, and each scanned their surroundings for any movement or sound. Garrett only hoped that Mila would not peek out. Just because they had not arrested him, did not mean they did not have something on her.

"You seen Mila?" Kathy asked.

"No."

"You sure?" Kathy stared, unblinking, into Garrett's eyes.

"Yes."

"You're lying, but we'll pretend you're not. I need to reach her," said Kathy. "It's not about me, Jenna, or you. It's about Mila and her dad. You see her, you tell her to call Jenna. She can call me, but Jenna has the paperwork. Here's a pass. Her old card won't get her on campus. Jenna's done her a huge favor."

"You know where her dad is?"

"No, but Jenna does. All I know is there's a closing window. He might be moved if he hasn't been already. If that happens, she'll never see him in her lifetime. So, pass it along." Kathy hit his arm again, only this time lighter. "'Kay?"

Garrett nodded. "Sure. I will."

"If I find out you saw her but didn't pass it along, I'll have you slinging coal in China. I don't need Jenna for that, but it's nicer than what she'd do."

"Mr. Cooperation. Takes orders." Garrett pointed to himself and nodded.

Kathy turned to leave, but as she did Garrett called her back.

"Listen. I don't know a lot," he said. "I try to keep my head low—you have to in this world. I hope you understand that. I don't know Mila's entire story, but I know she would appreciate what you and Jenna have done for her, and because of that, so do I. I may have misjudged you both."

"Not bad. I think I see what Mila likes about you, Mr. Cooperation Disorder. You know I'm not as zealous as Jenna, but I appreciate what Jenna does and respect her accomplishments. Somebody has to care enough to do the dirty work."

"I guess I know how that feels."

Kathy did not nod or acknowledge anything. She instead snapped her heels together, and in unison the two men with her straightened. "White Light's Right," they chanted together, with both hands closed they thumped their chest. *White Light's Right. Thump.*

Kathy and the men stood, unflinching and unmoving.

"White Light's Right," Garrett said, pounding his chest with both fists.

Kathy smiled. "You're probably not so bad. Join the fight. You'll hold your head high."

"I will."

In more ways than one. Yes, he had a lot to tell Mila. Not just about her father. A plan had hatched when he thought she had been slain by angels, UNSI troops, and red monstrous hell hounds. Mila had to find her father, and she still did not know that Garrett had volunteered to lead a military attack with Uno and his hoolies, joined by anarchists. One last act of freedom-fighting, an act that would get Flo-Rite on national television, *and me dead.*

Would he have agreed to a suicide mission had he known his true love had survived? Shit. His worst lies were the ones he told himself. Agreed to a suicide mission? No. He had organized, planned, and implemented the motions for an attack when he was holed up with the hoolies. He had lit a fuse that could not be unlit, and he certainly could not sign people up for their deaths and then walk away or never show up. His heart sunk in his chest, and he reached inside for the strength to do what he had to do. Pull his heart out just long enough. As good as Mila was at survival, Garrett would not knowingly lead her into the suicide mision he had committed himself and a resisting force to. How could he lead her into a pit of angels, especially if it stole what could be her only chance to reconnect with her missing father?

Chapter 40

Mila left the bedroom in a daze. The sound of her dear friend had nearly brought her out of hiding. When she heard Kathy mention her father? It took Diabliss to hold her in place. He was right. Kill the emotions when necessary; bury them in order to survive. The effort overwhelmed her.

Your brain has always had this battle. Now, you're just aware.

You're right, Diabliss, but it doesn't make it easier.

It thinks you should stay with Garrett.

Look deeper, Diabliss, and you'll see it's not that simple. My father. He might be shipped away. I can always come back.

No. Not always.

It's not like I'm searching randomly through alleys. Jenna has his location.

Jenna is dangerous.

She's a good friend.

She's blind. She bases her decisions on perceptions and not the truth. That's dangerous.

Garrett's eyes were fraught with deep concern.

"Don't worry. It'll be okay. I can handle Jenna." Mila tried not to get her hopes up too much. She had gone so long without seeing her father she was still in disbelief. "My father." She smiled a little girl's smile. Mila fought Diabliss off as her tears spilled out. *Sometimes, crying's all you can do*, she told him.

After whipping up two lattes, Garrett set them on the counter to cool. He held Mila in his arms. They were inside

Sweet Perk, just steps away from Campus Wall. He did not know how long Mila would be gone. Would she go straight to her father? They did not even know what city her father was in, or even what state. If she left Seattle, it would be for the better. She would be safer elsewhere, he thought. The likelihood of Mila leaving Seattle gave him solace.

A coffee-seeking student peeked into the closed business through the front window. Garrett held open both hands. "Ten minutes," he mouthed.

Garrett had planned to tell her about the upcoming attack. But that was before she found out her father was still alive. Garrett had even tried to tell her, but they were interrupted. First by Mila's kissing attack, and then by Kathy. Now he did not know if he needed to tell her or if he even should. It would force her to choose between a suicide mission and reuniting with her own father.

"I can't imagine this taking more than a day or two," said Mila. "I don't know why I got so upset. I guess because I finally found you, and you complete me in a way nothing else can. You should go with me."

"I wish I could. The business is hanging by threads. I also have a meeting with friends later."

He wanted to tell her. She would want to fight by his side. But, no. He could not bring her into this cauldron, and yet it was one he could not walk away from. Yes, in the end, some causes were greater than his life, even when it became complicated by love, but especially when your actions might save the one you love.

"Being away from you will feel like eternity," Mila said.

"It certainly will for me," he said.

"I'll try to hurry." Mila gazed at her campus. "I'm not as afraid as I used to be."

"Yes, but you should be. More and more blackwings are being caught and killed. More and more are being turned in.

The UNSIs, the White Light, Holy Followers, the Infraguard—they all want you dead."

"Diabliss says you're hiding something from me. I told him you fear for me. He doesn't always understand human emotions."

Garrett did not answer.

"He says you're trying to calm yourself."

"I'm in love with a super-strong, possessed criminal. I have to calm myself. I'm worried about you, me, everything." Garrett squeezed her tighter. "Go meet Jenna. Try to find your father. And be careful with Jenna. She's very likely to be more fanatic than friend."

"Do you want me to stay?"

"Yes, but I also understand that you can't, and you shouldn't."

"You could go with me," Mila suggested again.

Garrett shook his head. No. She had to meet with Jenna, and Jenna had to somehow keep Mila away.

"No," Mila said. "You're right. You can't come. Jenna can be complicated. I'll hurry back. I promise. We have our whole lives to figure this out. I just need to find my dad. He's the only family I've got."

"Will you tell him about Diabliss?"

"I've pushed that decision back. I might have to. I've never been good at keeping secrets from him. I could never lie to him growing up because he could always read me."

"You don't have to tell him. He doesn't need to know. It only endangers him."

"I guess you don't exactly tell your parents you're the Agorist."

"I don't. I don't know what they'd think or do."

"Don't you want to know?"

"I'm too afraid I know the answer already."

Garrett grabbed their two coffees sitting on the counter

and handed one to Mila.

"Time?" asked Mila.

"7 A.M.," said Garrett. "You have to go?"

"Yeah. You give me an incentive to survive so we can spend more time together. Diabliss' thinking is wearing off on me. He's right. No matter what, just survive. Garrett, don't look so upset. I won't be long. I won't last long without seeing you anyway. Maybe we can see my dad together? God, pulling away from you, even if it's just for a day or two, feels so wrong. Am I doing the right thing?"

Garrett wrapped his arms around Mila in front of the fake painted fire, not wanting to release her soft, perfectly fitting comfort and warmth for even a second. His hands shook as he cupped her hands in his. He tried to remember how to turn the light switch off that was his soul like he had done every time he pulled a trigger in Syranistan. "Mila," he said. "Sometimes, there is no right answer."

Chapter 41

Mila crossed through the Campus Wall security gate, shaking and nearly in tears. Several workers were adding an X-ray machine with a conveyor for bags. One looked up at her and then went back to work.

Mila had not carried her phone or an ID card for some time since they both gave away her information or location. She had stashed them under the freeway overpass several weeks earlier, but it seemed more like years. Since her departure from school, she had left her friends, fought angels, UNSI troops, joined a hooley gang, lived under a bridge, practiced street medicine, and had fallen in love. She had the new card from Kathy but grabbed her phone and old card just in case she needed them. She messaged Garrett.

Diabliss told her she should stop thinking about Garrett. She had to be ready for whatever would come. Diabliss also advised her not to seek out her father. Diabliss knew his own existence had to be hidden from her father as well. And Diabliss said he would miss Garrett, too. He was more social than he realized. Maybe he had acquired the trait through her. Diabliss had tried leaping into conversations with Garrett, wanting to know more about his underground movement. Diabliss was pleasantly surprised when he realized what Garrett and Garrett's Agorist alter-ego did in the night. Diabliss savored the idea of being in a resistance movement, especially against a government allied with angels.

It's ready to take over.

I know, Diabliss. No matter what, though, do not hurt a student. I would rather die.

This shocked Diabliss.

Diabliss? PROMISE.

Mila had become more attuned to Diabliss, especially his thoughts and processes. After all, Diabliss was utilizing her biological synapses to compute, even though he was also trying to find portions of the brain that she was unaccustomed to using or a way that would allow him to think without her knowing. She had given up on trying to keep things from Diabliss. More important was that he did not influence her thoughts or constantly interrupt, especially when she was deep in conversation. Mila could sense that Diabliss was trying to find a way to make a promise not to hurt students, with a loophole that would allow him to back out of the promise if he needed to. She even sensed his embarrassment or anger at her catching him being manipulative.

If we are attacked, maybe it will just wound them.

Oh, Diabliss. Maybe? Is that the best you can do? Oh well, I guess that's fair. Just try your best. I don't know how much I give a shit anymore anyway.

Walking between austere buildings full of majestic arches, stained lead glass windows, brick, chiseled and carved faces, the awe of the campus, and even campus life, reminded her of what she missed. What she had not counted on, were the little things, like the purple and gold. With Mila being an athlete, she had more loyalty and a stronger competitive drive than most. She wanted Huskies to win, and she did not care if it was her sport or any other. She had always thought of herself as somewhat rebellious, but not when it came to school spirit and unity. This campus, filled with friends, had become her family when her father disappeared. She even missed the faces of strangers, students recognized from passing by them hurriedly at the same times each day, the nod from each acknowledging this pattern. But most of all, Mila missed her friends, Kathy, and yes, even Jenna. As much as she had despised their unflinching religious devotions, Mila missed her time with them. What she really longed for though, was the innocence their time together represented. No blackwings. No White Light. She was more aware than most students, but she was somewhat amused by and not fearful of eroding civil liberties, anarchy, domestic terrorism, war, and the UNSIs that surrounded them all. A month earlier, Mila's only worry was for her father, a soccer game, and money. Her only goals were to be the best student and soccer player she could be. Jenna had her worship and Kathy had her boys and midweek "Friday" beers that just never seemed to last until the weekend. Coffee time outside the campus wall while flirting with a handsome mysterious barista was her only crime. Her sadness for Garrett turned to anxiousness.

Why did you have to pick me? Mila asked.

"Mila-chick!" a female's voice called out.

Mila turned to see a White Light Infraguard running toward her. Just before impact Mila saw Kathy's face. Mila braced herself for a hard punch, but instead Kathy grabbed Mila into a hug and lifted her into the air. The hard white plastic panels of Kathy's white riot gear dug into Mila's chest and arms.

Diabliss, feeling the shortage of air, urged Mila to strike out. *Not an attack, Diabliss*, Mila said.

"Kathy," said Mila. She burst into tears.

Kathy was not letting go. "I was so worried about you. Some said you weren't coming back. Coach said your father was ill, but he doesn't know you've been looking for him without any luck. How are you? Are you back for good? You're staying, aren't you?"

"I don't know much of anything," said Mila. "You don't know how much I need you and Jenna. I've missed you so much." She sobbed some more, and then finally mopped her tears with her forearm.

Kathy's tears spilled as well, only her arms were encased in hard white plastic. She shrugged and laughed when she realized how ineffective dabbing them would be. Mila used her shirtsleeve and forearm on Kathy, but this only caused Kathy to cry more. Then they both cried more. Kathy slowly and softly punched Mila on the shoulder.

"Of course, I care. A lot of people care, Mila-chick. You're the future of the women's soccer program here, but most of all, I miss *you*. Your room isn't the same. Jenna doesn't even loan fridge space anymore. It's so good to see you back on campus. I thought you had dropped out. You haven't been in class for weeks. Some professors might let you make up the tests. A missing father affected you deeply, and that isn't your fault. Oh, Mila-chick, I'm so sorry for what you've been through. I should have been more understanding. I take my parents for granted. Sometimes I wish they'd disappear, but I don't really think that through— like what you have been going through."

Kathy grabbed Mila and embraced her once again. This time much lighter, making Diabliss feel less like killing her.

"I appreciate you helping by getting the message to me. I'm here to get the information on my dad from Jenna."

"Of course," said Kathy. "There are a lot of people who will help if you need it."

"Thanks," said Mila, turning to leave. Maybe she had been living the wrong life. Maybe she had misjudged her friends. "I have to find Jenna. Do you know where she is?"

"That's right, you haven't heard," said Kathy. "I won't spoil your surprise. White Light Infraguard. We're set up in the HUB." Kathy slapped her plastic chest plate. "You'd better go. Call me later. I've got an interrogation. How long have we known Jenna? She's just now raised my security clearance and entrusted me with responsibility."

"And responsibility is a lot of responsibility," said Mila.

The saying was one of their many inside jokes.

"Yeah, it is." Kathy laughed. "She only lets me go on night patrol with women."

"It's probably for the better. Until you find the right person."

"Are you sure you're okay?"

Mila felt Diabliss bristle as two rows of White Light Infraguard passed by. Mila straightened and turned so she could watch them. "Yeah. Thanks," she said.

They hugged again and then walked away in different directions.

The HUB was the Husky Union Building. The center for school spirit would be appropriate for Jenna. No one had more spirit than Jenna.

Mila veered off toward the building. She jogged. What if Jenna left early?

What if this is a trap? asked Diabliss.

Then you'll get what you want. A fight.

It only wants to fight enemies. Besides...

I know. I fought for fun against the hoolies in Portland. Rub it in. But you're the violent one. I had never even thought about fighting before I met you.

It was always in you.

Mila had never thought of herself as a warrior, but her desire to win would always prevent her from giving up without a fierce battle. And with Garrett she had somehow found that strength inside her again. Not a strength that came through Diabliss, but one that really made her want to stick around and survive. She wound down the narrow asphalt path toward the brick HUB. Outside, two guards stood dressed in white riot gear, wearing helmets with tinted faceplates. The White Light Infraguard gathered in clusters and marched in lines throughout the campus. Each had two sets of weapons holstered, one on each side—a real pistol and a thicker Taser.

The sidearms were real though. They had been outlawed on campus years ago after a police officer shot a student. But now a White Light Infraguard, made up of students, was armed. And if she needed to bolt, if there was a fight, or even worse, if she or Diabliss had to kill to escape, her uncovered face would reveal her identity. She would never be able to return. Cameras were around before the blackwings, but now they were so much more abundant and ominous.

There were two guards posted outside the heavy double doors of the HUB. A Husky dog statue had been replaced with a statue of Theo. One guard glanced at a reader on his wrist that scanned the information transmitted from her ID. Mila remembered the pass. It had the details embedded. She was dazed, but still sighed with relief as her access was approved. She did not even know if she had been kicked out of school, and although she still thought her invitation could be a trap, nothing from either guard intimated that she was a threat, or that there were ulterior motives.

The air inside the student building was warm, but the atmosphere was vastly different from her school days. No longer did scurrying college kids fill the halls. Nobody was studying, eating, flirting, or doing any of the various activities that would normally fill this building, especially on a cold, wet day. Instead, a double row of students in White Light Infraguard riot gear marched out the door. A young man, a senior football player with a clipboard in hand, Infraguard uniform on, a helmet tucked under his arm, and a serious look, walked by, clipping her with his elbow. He glared at Mila, narrowing his eyes, directing them at her shoulder lacking a Holy Follower armband, and then looked back at his clipboard, shaking his head. The idea of volunteer students armed and marching through campus worried her. Garrett thought the school was unfair to free-speech advocates before. If the Infraguard leader was anything like

Jenna—closed-minded, zealous, and suspicious—the school was no longer a learning institution but a system of brainwashing. *But it's still the only home I have.*

After passing an information desk, Mila hesitated, staring at a touchscreen office map, until the lady at the desk called Mila's name and directed her down the appropriate hall. Mila had been off the grid so long that now she felt uncomfortable walking under constant surveillance. It was like walking naked. She had rarely thought of her identity being public back when she had first learned the true nature of her phones and radio frequency IDs. She was still thinking mostly about classes, friends, soccer, *and Garrett...*

Maybe she should run back to Garrett, screw this school, and forget her forgetful father.

Yes, Diabliss whispered.

No, she said. She loved Garrett, but she could at least be happy that he was currently free from harm. Anytime he was with her she put him at risk.

The walls were adorned with pictures of the White Light from magazine covers and newspaper reports. There was a large framed picture of Theo standing next to Jenna in a main foyer that Mila crossed, and there were White Light Infraguards, UNSI soldiers, and plain-clothed Holy Follower students with white armbands, making her feel like a honey bee in a wasps' nest. Most of the Infraguards and UNSIs glanced at their wrist readers as Mila passed by. Maybe she stood out because her arm was bare. A few more Infraguards, reading her dazed look, mistaking it for confusion, pointed down the hall, always knowing which direction Mila was headed. A sweaty-palmed Mila with a racing heart paused as she read the title on the door before her: White Light Infraguard Commander. Jenna Voit. Holy crap. Jenna had not only taken this as seriously as she could, she had excelled, and now controlled it all. Mila felt relief and fear at the same time. As Mila rapped on the door, Diabliss urged her to be ready. He was making his dislike for all the White Light memorabilia and tributary items known, and he reminded Mila that each person in this building was an enemy.

The door swung quickly open, and Jenna met Mila with a huge grin, and then a strong hug. Mila worried that Jenna would feel the wings on her back, but somehow thought that she knew already. Only, Jenna could not know. Not with the look in her eyes. Jenna was truly relieved and happy to see Mila. Jenna's eyes welled with tears, forcing Mila's to do the same.

Subterfuge. Yes. Make the enemy think you care.

I do care. Now, be quiet. I need clarity.

"Jenna, you've been busy," said Mila once they had their cryfest out of the way.

"Yes. It's a different world. One I've embraced wholeheartedly. I've been wildly successful. Me. Can you believe it?"

"Of course, I can."

"But I miss having you here."

"I've missed the three amoebas," said Mila.

"Kathy was the only real amoeba," said Jenna. "I think we were pretty solid."

"You were," said Mila. "You think I was solid?"

"Of course. Athletics. Grades. You're at the top. Just not spiritually."

"It was only doubt. There are worse things to be guilty of."

Jenna smiled kindly. "Yes. You could be a blackwing or an anarchist."

Mila nearly choked. She hoped Jenna could not read her too well. Mila calmed herself. "That would be challenging."

Jenna shook her head. "More than that actually. I'm still holding out hope for you. I'll never give up on you, Mila. You had no family. Family is like a leg on a stool when it comes to the Lord and the White Light. It's something that holds us up."

"Because we can't stand up on our own?"

"No. Because we need to rest our butts eventually."

Mila allowed Jenna her final metaphor. She was tempted to argue that stools and sitting down make great metaphors, but they still did not mean anything. *And legs on stools sometimes break.*

Jenna sat down and looked at her computer screen. She held her finger up. "One minute," she said. She rattled on her keyboard, shook her head and nearly cursed, and then looked to Mila again. "As we used to say, responsibility is a lot of responsibility."

Mila laughed. "Yeah, it is." Mila looked around at all the notes pinned to walls. "You've been more than busy," said Mila.

Yes. Jenna filled her in. Schoolwork aside, Jenna had created the first Blackwing-free campus. She had single-handedly created a uniform model that was being adopted across the country. She had built the White Light Infraguard—again another model that was emulated nationally, and from there things grew quickly. Within two weeks they had uniforms, and in another they were armed. Now, it was no longer just a student movement. It was spreading outward. Block by block. City by city. Police communicated with the White Light Infraguard. UNSI troops answered directly to the White Light and most people suspected that even the president served angels. There was a flat-screen digital picture hanging on the wall. It flashed pictures of Jenna. Jenna receiving a medal from Theo. Jenna and her White Light compatriots. Jenna and Theo, an unending crowd beyond. Various stills from Jenna on duty. Jenna and a blackwing?

Mila's hatred surged, or more precisely, Diabliss within her erupted, projecting hatred and a violent side that wanted to tear into Jenna and the White Light Infraguard.

"Oh, that?" Jenna asked, following Mila's gaze. "I was awarded the Medal of Light."

"For your work here?"

"Yes, that and a little more." Jenna stepped up to the flat screen on the wall. She held her thumb on a panel to the left, a fingerprint security feature, and then a different screen appeared with various menus and still pictures. Jenna tapped several spots on the screen and stepped back. Mila moved next to her.

"This is the easiest way to explain what I did, what I do, what the Infraguard does."

A film clip played. Troops marching on red cobblestones in the courtyard between the two main libraries came to a stop. "Watch this girl right here," said Jenna. "I had read intercepts and suspected her of being a terrorist. She was also reading subversive media on the Internet. When we went to pull her in, an informant told me she was in the courtyard. Watch."

The girl sprinted across the courtyard. She was much faster and more athletic than the White Light troops chasing her. Mila gasped as the wings emerged and the female blackwing easily cleared the perimeter fence. Jenna pointed to a running figure in white armor. That was Jenna. An assembly of cuts from various security cameras gave angles in addition to Jenna's body camera, eventually narrowing the chase to Jenna and the girl. Different stationary camera angles, a body camera, and a drone camera caught the rest, Jenna's short battle, and how Jenna tricked and electrocuted the blackwing. Mila eyed Jenna's hip holster nervously. A Taser. Yes. The voltage would disable her momentarily. Is that why Jenna brought her here, and why she was so calm?

Had she distracted Mila just long enough to get within reach? Jenna's hand rested on her Taser.

Diabliss, furious, clambered for possession of Mila.

No, said Mila. She severed connections as quickly as Diabliss built them so he could take control. *Is this what you've become? The possessive demon Jenna warned me about. You said the White Light steals souls. You said blackwings are different.*

This isn't possession, this is survival.

Diabliss was right. Here, a blackwing attack would strike at the heart. Here they could set back a force that was trying to kill her and other blackwings.

No. I have to learn about my father. I need him. Now, more than ever.

Diabliss finally retreated.

"Mila?"

Mila shook her head. "Yes. I'm sorry. My mind wanders."

"Your father."

"Yes."

"He's at a factory camp." Jenna lifted a piece of paper off her desk and handed it to Mila.

"I thought factory camps don't exist," Mila said accusingly, wanting to remind Jenna that this was an argument they had had before. Jenna had sworn there was no such thing: Our government would never allow it.

"Okay. *A trade camp.* Factory camps don't exist the way you think they do. They're here to help people find a trade, and to help the country. He was being lined up for redistribution. I think he was headed to a trade camp in Mexico that needs workers."

"Did he try to contact the school?"

"No. I found his name in a database."

"You searched for him?" Mila asked. "With everything

going on in your career, you did this for me?"

Jenna nodded and held her finger up to her lips.

"Serving White Light is like that," she said. "You strive to be selfless. Skeptics see the uniforms, weapons, and conformity. I see a glowing light with enough brightness to bring us out of the shadows. I know you and your heart will find the White Light someday. You'd be perfect for the cause. Really. You're an athlete. You understand winning and team dynamics."

Diabliss chimed in, *Yes. Trickery. She's trying to convert you. Kill her now.*

Damn it, Diabliss. She found my father! I owe her! She might be a friend. A true friend.

"I don't know how to thank you," Mila said.

"He's in southern Washington just north of the Oregon border. I've requested that they delay any transfers for twenty-four hours. I don't know if they'll honor my request. Some think of me as a celebrity. Some fear my connections. I've met Theo personally. I've been invited to see him again. He called me his pride and joy."

"Jenna. I don't know what to say. Thank you."

"But…" said Jenna.

"Big but or little but?"

"Big but. Before we go any further. You have some tests to take," said Jenna.

Tests. Of course. A blackwing-free campus. Mila was on campus again, and theoretically a student. "Jenna, it's not that I don't want to. I just don't want to waste time."

Jenna looked at her quizzically. "Mila," she said.

"It's not that I don't want to take your tests, it's the principle, too."

"Yes. I suppose. Special favors were done so I could make this happen. That's not really fair, but it's a minor principle. I know it takes time, but I just don't see you throwing away a decent education over things beyond your control."

"Maybe when I get back."

"I don't believe you. Garrett dropped out. He probably told you to drop out too."

"Jenna. Garrett and I…are a thing." Her jaw quivered as she spoke the words. The only reason she did not grin was that she was still in disbelief.

Jenna winced. "He's a fool. I warned you."

"He is," said Mila. "I can see you're upset. I should just leave."

"No. You're not leaving without taking these tests. These final exams save your semester. Even taking them will keep you off probation. You were already doing well." She picked up a stack of papers and slammed it on the desk in front of Mila.

Mila was about to sprout wings and summon strength, readying herself to break out and away. Then she saw the title of the first test. It was from a micro class. Mila quickly rifled through the stack. More tests. All exams from classes she had missed. Diabliss squirmed inside, but Mila could tell that Diabliss, too, was surprised.

"Jenna," Mila said, clasping her shoulders. "I love you, my dear, dear friend."

Chapter 42

Mila gazed at Jenna, still at her desk, eyes intensely focused on her monitor, occasionally covering her earphones, intensely listening to something, closing her eyes as she did when thinking something through that was difficult or required concentration, and then rapidly clicking on her screen as if whatever she had just seen or heard had led to a series of revelations requiring searches.

Mila had tried to mimic Jenna's look of deep thought and concentration while taking the make-up tests Jenna had collected from her professors. She purposefully missed several problems, even though she knew them all. The intense reading she had done, along with a newfound ability to analyze and solve problems, made the tests simple, like basic single-digit addition or multiplication, but she could not let on that it was this easy. Did all blackwings have superior test-taking abilities? Would Jenna suspect something if Mila not only passed every test, but aced them? She certainly would if all answers were correct and each essay perfect. She eventually pushed her neatly stacked pile of tests toward Jenna and looked up at the clock. How much time did she have before her dad would be shipped overseas? Not much. Sure, she might find him after he transferred, but that came with too many risks, and the world was too big and too easy to disappear into. And she needed her dad. She was extremely grateful to Jenna, but she had to leave. As each second ticked by, she felt her father drifting further away.

"Mila," said Jenna. "I know how you want to immediately rush to your dad, and I appreciate you allowing me to take care of you in this small way. You're too selfless.

You throw everything away too easily. Soccer? You just walked away. You're our star. Your coach says he'll take you back next season if you promise him a championship ring, but for now you'd best find a seat on the bench if you want to make next year's team and keep your scholarship. I'm not saying you need to be more selfish, but your dad, even a boyfriend, Garrett, or whoever, if they truly love you, they'll want what's best and safest for you, and that's a higher-level education and your soccer scholarship, and even better, university as a Holy Follower."

"You're right," Mila said. She had to put Garrett out of her mind if she could, and now, walk away from him. "I don't know what to say, Jenna, except, thank you. And tell Coach he'll get that ring. Tell him I'm stronger than ever."

Jenna shook her head. "But you're not. You just don't get it. It's why you're so perfect for the White Light, not just Infraguard, the whole movement. It's about selflessness and turning your life over to a higher purpose."

"Jenna..."

"I know. Doubt."

"I don't doubt that it's not right for you. Maybe in another lifetime, if there is such a thing, it will be right for me." Mila put the cap on her pen and pushed it toward Jenna.

"Mila, you don't have to be certain today. The White Light will love you until you can love yourself. It's a dangerous world, but there are limits, and that's my fear. The White Light is forever for those who accept it—those who find it. Don't be too late." Jenna's eyes watered and then tears dribbled down her face. "Remember my love for you Mila-chick, and don't be such a stubborn fool."

Mila grabbed Jenna and hugged her. Mila's tears fell as well. Diabliss did not try to hold them back, perhaps he knew this was a battle he could not win.

"Train leaves at noon. You'll make it if you go straight

to the train without stopping and then you'll be there early afternoon. Show this card. Any problems, call me." Jenna laughed, shaking her head. "I'm a hero, and that comes with special privileges."

"Thank you, Jenna. I owe you."

Jenna walked Mila out of the building. She confided that she had a meeting with angels, and a few select UNSI and Infraguard officers. Jenna guessed it was something big and tried to conceal her excitement, and somehow, she managed to regain composure enough to chastise a passing Infraguard, who according to Jenna's reader was late to his post. Jenna found and directed a different Infraguard to escort Mila immediately to the train station.

Mila was grateful that she and Jenna had mended the differences separating their friendship. Diabliss despised Jenna and her work, but Mila struggled with her desire for Jenna to succeed and her loyalty to Diabliss, herself, and other blackwings. Mila just wished that Jenna used her zealousness in other ways.

It took about thirty minutes for Mila to get to the the train station, though without the personal service provided by Jenna and the White Light Infraguard, it would have taken nearly three times as long. Still, she barely made it. The train was not the same one she was used to riding on, the one with a roving flea market and rabid hoolies. It was a separate, dedicated line used to haul corporate and government freight. It was next to the soccer and baseball stadium. The lone passenger car in front was filled with high-ranking officials and important businessmen. She overheard a conversation and gathered that many were nervous about traveling in the sky, where a blackwing could bring down jets like a cat batting down a low-flying moth. She did not have the heart to tell them that a blackwing could just as easily derail a train.

From her window, Mila could see freight being loaded. Human and machine. A line of unemployed and homeless men, faceless wanderers, were being packed into box cars like livestock. It would be a cold ride. It was in the mid-forties and wet. The wind would whistle through gaps in the unheated steel boxes. Mila wanted to trade her comfort for theirs. She wanted to set them free, but to what avail, so they could wander? Most likely, even free they would not have heat. She had seen the life of the transients. Water, food, restrooms, heat, sanitation, dry clothes, and medicine were lacking. If they did not find a group, they would have to turn criminal, or quickly succumb to becoming a victim of that same element. Animal-like fearful eyes showed sheer desperation, while their sullen faces showed surrender. Was that what her father had become? Was this how he ended up near the Oregon border? She had always imagined him working, or looking for work, but had he turned away from the humanity that had raised her and filed into a boxcar? Her missing Garrett, her not being able to see him again before she left, her problems as real as they were, paled in comparison.

A pair of UNSI soldiers climbed into her car. They were Chinese and said something to each other that she could not understand, and then they each took an aisle. They had wrist readers, and as they walked by each person, they confirmed the photo on their small screen with the face in the seat. Mila's card had a radio frequency sticker that would tell them what she was doing and where she was going. Her identification card fed them her picture, student status, and other details. The soldier looked at her quizzically, perhaps wondering who the young female student knew to get a ride with the military and corporate elite.

Mila waited anxiously, trying not to garner attention, and trying even harder not to look out the window at what she now labeled the invisible march. She detached a tablet from the back of the seat in front of her and sifted through the news. *Theo's Mass.* That was what they were calling the growing multitude at the Sounders' soccer stadium and neighboring baseball park. Each day saw a new world's record, the largest public gathering ever, and it was growing at an alarming rate. She scrolled through the headlines as the train inched forward, glancing out the windows at the soccer stadium, now headquarters to the White Light as well as home to Theo's global broadcasts. She paused from reading and watched as several glowing white spots, angels, flew down into the stadium. Black helicopters buzzed in and out. As far as Mila could see, Holy Followers clustered around small channels of smoke from warming fires and makeshift outdoor kitchens. A large transport helicopter larger than a city bus hovered and flew away from the stadium, but within seconds a replacement arrived. The amount of food needed to feed the rapidly growing population would be overwhelming. After living on the streets, she had learned that hungry people became cranky and desperate.

Jenna's unbending smile finally dissipated after reading the fourth intercept. She only had a minute or two before she would have to leave for her meeting. Her team had read the Agorist's newspaper articles and had run seven different author identification programs without finding a match, though they did verify that the works were indeed written by one author, but the style was continuously altered. The profile did not matter. A young male in his twenties. *Wow.* It narrowed it down to ten percent of the population. Should be easy. At least that is what she kept telling herself.

She decided to narrow the focus. She plugged in the age range, allowing an additional five years on either side. The break-in was at the Seattle Water Municipal Building. She excluded all regions except Seattle. Then she added a new field. Aptitude. Who could write this kind of material? The writing would likely require an education, but it would definitely require aptitude. The UNSIs had searched for high technological training since the Agorist had the ability to avoid leaving an electronic footprint, only they had not screened for high test scores and aptitude in communications, particularly reading and writing. These could also indicate someone qualified to write this kind of propaganda. She added the field. Okay. Even more. Next. Anyone who had taken a college-level writing class.

It could have been a female, but a break-in? A file cabinet had been pried open. Lights had been shot down. Criminal theft. No, it was a male.

Her list shrunk again but was still too big. She tried unemployed and the list shrunk further, but then she changed her mind. The Agorist was not a wanderer. He likely had a cover.

Library records. Books were ranked on their level of subversiveness, though Jenna disagreed with many of the choices and labels. Huckleberry Finn was a level 4 out of 5, and it was required reading. 1984. Obviously a 5. It was not only a premonition, it was one-sided. It never explained why the government needed the control. It never described the terrorists, because yes, there had to be terrorists who drove a democratic world government to a system of hyper-control.

Finally. The list got noticeably smaller. How many had sent letters to an editor? Too small. The Agorist had cited constitutional law. How many had read the constitution on the Internet? How many had ever taken a law or a political science class or read a law book or visited related sites?

Finally, the list became manageable.

She began punching up profiles. The first man, a former student, had moved to Seattle, allegedly looking for work.

That is what his online habits showed as well, frantic job searches. Not unusual. On the night of the break-in? He had visited his parents on the wrong side of the state. She moved to the next person.

They shot down a traffic light. She put her hands on her head. If she went through every profile, it would take two weeks she did not have. If she delegated researching the evidence, she would never feel confident that vital clues were not being missed.

Arrests. Most criminals, whether convicted or not, had been arrested before.

Still too many.

She combed through the list again, and then stopped at a name and laughed out loud. "Really?"

A near-perfect match, even though his single arrest was because of her mistake: Garrett Webb.

Garrett sulked in his apartment, thinking that the hardest question to answer was one where there was no correct answer. Sometimes none of the above was the best answer. Garrett had suggested an attack on the White Light leader and his growing hoard of Holy Followers, something to show those who were cowering or mumbling in the corners that there was a dissenting voice, and it was all right to rise up, seek truth, and make decisions based on thought and facts. At the time of his plan's evolution, though, he was holed up in cold dark tunnels with stinking hoolies thinking that angels and UNSIs had killed Mila or had her in a torture cell. He wanted nothing more than to hurt them like they had hurt her. Now, though, he would hurt her. Sometimes, even doing the right thing was the wrong answer.

The angels will eventually find Mila. If he could disrupt this growing force and ignite a revolution, it could save her life. The White Light was a movement intent on ridding the earth of blackwings through absolute control and inhumane acts, and Garrett loved a blackwing. And there was the cause. If everything went according to plan, the anarchists would broadcast a warning and a message of hope to the world. But it was more than the cause. So much more. There were so many reasons why he could not and should not run back to her and tell her he loved her and always would. *And that soulful look in her eyes.* One of so many bullets he would fire.

If only he had known that Mila was alive, that he would see her again, he could have run away with her instead. Oh, what a coward and a hypocrite. His country, human rights, morals, and beliefs were all worth dying for. He could have forsaken it all, but he had not. He not only volunteered for a suicide mission, he had unified two groups, hoolies and anarchists. The anarchists wanted to bring the government to its knees. The hoolies just wanted to be left alone and have their soccer stadium and games back. Both forces had signed on for what Garrett knew was a suicide mission, and there was no way to turn the mission off. As many times as Garrett had run various scenarios through his head, he could not find one that allowed him to back out and stop this mad attack. It was a collaborative attack, the wheels were in motion, and he was the gear that had moved them forward. *And still, we might save Mila.* The vision of her fighting UNSIs, siccums, and the White Light reminded him what she was up against, and what he was going to attack.

Someone knocked on the door. Then footsteps scuttled down the stairs and away. He moved to the door and picked up a thick book placed outside. He brought it to the table and slowly strummed the pages. He knew that it was hollowed out. He knew that inside was a pistol, a 9mm police issue with four ten-round magazines. He knew it because this was the first step in a long string of deliveries across Seattle. Some at doorsteps. Some under park benches. Some dropped into open car windows. Orders had been placed, some, like his, carelessly.

Garrett placed his fingers on his temples.

The love of his life was back in school or reuniting with her father, and Garrett would most likely never see her again.

I love you, Mila. I'm so sorry, Mila.

Chapter 43

Mila exited the train. She smiled anxiously as she passed the various UNSIs comparing their readers with each passenger. Each UNSI had a hand on a pistol or a Taser, and their wrist pad turned toward their faces. She thanked one who, after analyzing the language translation from Chinese to English, gave her directions.

She got to the raised platform and looked over the precipice, seeing the people from the freight cars below shuffling down ramps. UNSI guards opened one railroad car at a time, and the shivering homeless were herded into a fenced area, entering through a security turn-style built into the fence. A UNSI guard tapped her on the shoulder, signaling for her to move on. For a fleeting moment she imagined her dad huddled with the masses and channeled into a cattle yard, but this was a processing system, and he had already been processed. Her dad was nearby, and she was going to save him from this horrid ugly existence. Mila lifted her chin and pretended she had seen this a thousand times. Perhaps in a way she had, but what she did not want was to draw attention.

Mila held her wrist up and looked at the screen on her phone and a street sign, trying to follow the digital map. Two blocks and two minutes. She found a large blue industrial building at the appropriate coordinates. There was a steel fence with barbed wire facing in. Most security fences kept people out—that was what the Campus Wall did back at school. When the sharp points and razor barbs faced in, it stopped people from escaping. Mila swallowed. She looked up, counting the cameras. They would know who she was, what she was doing, and where she was going before she even crossed the street.

Jenna's face was flushed as she arrived in the University conference room that was usually reserved for the University of Washington President and board members. She did not usually arrive late to anything, especially a meeting for a privileged few with an angel. After bowing to the White Light at the center, her face turned from rosy and embarrassed to pale. Theo himself, in all his majesty, towered over her. As Jenna trembled, her legs nearly buckled. An endearing smile from Theo allowed her the strength to find her seat.

Theo spoke. "Now that we have everyone here, and your complete attention, we'll start."

Jenna had gotten caught up in datamining and was so close to finding the Agorist. As she had worked, time had slipped by. She needed to verify some things with her friend Mila. Mainly, she had to verify that Mila did not know about Garrett's secret life.

Jenna's angel hero pulled down a screen and touched it as the lights dimmed inside the small conference room. Theo read through the statistics. Another record gathering. The masses were getting more difficult to feed, and the surrounding sanitation systems were maxed out. The security perimeter had to be enlarged. There were too many gaps. They had reports that anarchists were planning an attack. It was likely on a Sunday, because only godless terrorists would try to stain God's holy day.

Jenna's mind raced. *Theo is speaking.* She tried to concentrate. *Stay focused.* She was not only a Holy Follower; she was a holy warrior. How could she not control a simple thing like her concentration? She wanted nothing more than to serve the White Light with her ability to organize and implement systems that even an angel told her had to be a gift from God. Theo himself had said her inspiring zealousness and passion for justice would be replicated.

"And we've saved the most important for last," Theo said. The lights came back on. "Jenna once again has amazed us with her foresight. I, Theo, came here today to commend you personally."

Jenna looked around the room. Sure, the other attendees, all important officers, were also faithful servants, but they were human, and she could see the jealousy in their eyes.

"Yes, Jenna has been datamining and giving us helpful leads in the war on terror. She suggested we use data to locate likely blackwings. We did. We used datamining for all known blackwings. We interviewed family and close friends, analyzed personal histories, Internet searches, book downloads, social networking, and movies. As we analyzed the data and metadata, we began to see a common thread, and that is how we found out that blackwings do choose their hosts. The possession is not, I repeat, not random selection."

The angel's eyes locked on Jenna. Jenna immediately looked away. Theo's assistant had said it was disrespectful as well as dangerous to look an angel in the eye when up close. She hoped Theo would grant forgiveness. It had only been a glance. He had to understand.

"Jenna, please rise," said Theo.

With her eyes down, Jenna stood.

The angel flew into the center of the room. He spoke again. "Jenna's suggestion has led us to find the common strand of code. The solitary binding human flaw that leads to demon possession and a place under the wings of Satan."

Jenna could not have breathed if she had wanted to. She looked up for a brief second, just long enough to see Theo's smile.

"It is doubt," he said.

Jenna looked at him, slightly confused, forgetting her

place. And then it hit her. *Doubt.*

"Yes. Doubting authority. Doubting religion. Most humans can follow the White Light without any doubt. We call it faith." Theo again smiled at Jenna. "Now, not all humans who doubt are blackwings, but they are all potential suspects and are susceptible to possession by demons. We will turn this world upside down with this revelation and shake Blackwings out of dark clouds."

Doubt. Jenna's mind flashed to Mila. Doubt. No one doubted more than Mila. No. *Mila-Chick, a Blackwing?* Jenna nearly burst into laughter. *Naïve and susceptible, yes. Blackwing, no.*

But she had never absolved Mila. Mila had avoided Jenna's blackwing-Free Campus Initiative.

Doubt. Faith conquered doubt.

Only, Jenna had signed for Mila and absolved her of being a blackwing. That simple moment of trust was a forgery, and it could ruin everything. What kind of credibility would the White Light Infraguard Commander have if she had not only allowed a blackwing into her midst, but had checked her off the list as well? She had to absolve Mila personally.

"This is a new beginning that will lead to the end. Datamining for traits and information that leads to doubt. Within a month, we will have a genetic trait identified and a DNA test that we will use to summon those with this serious character flaw for an interview."

Arrest. Yes. That is what an interview summons meant. Jenna's mind filled with the possibilities. They could round up all blackwings, or at least keep them in hiding or on the run. But again, the solitary word crept in. *Doubt.*

It was a word that defined Mila and her thought process.

Theo finished, taking Jenna's hands in his. His fingers were soft, slick, and the perfect temperature. He squeezed and then let go. A white chemical coated her hand where they had touched. An angel's dust. Her heart pounded. Her skin burned. Her breath quickened. She should have felt pride, but somehow, she felt she had let Theo down, and she was afraid. Jenna had to absolve Mila, but more importantly, she had to absolve herself.

"It's an honor to serve the White Light," she mumbled nervously. "With God and the White Light, everything is right." She thumped her chest with her fist.

The people in the room repeated the mantra and pounded their chests.

Jenna had already planned on going straight to Mila to question her about Garrett, and she had travel permissions imbedded in her reader when she realized that she may have been right about Garrett all along. She had to know how much Mila knew about him, and more importantly, if she knew if Garrett was the Agorist. His profile was a perfect match.

Her mind reeled with questions. Her face burned. She tried to focus on the meeting. Again, Theo praised her efforts. Again, her comrades' eyes winced, stung by jealousy.

She would be able to tell by Mila's reactions what she already suspected. Why not just pull Garrett Webb in? No. She had promised Mila, and no, they had already tried that. On paper, Garrett was a nearly perfect citizen. He had left school in order to serve his country. He watched Fax News Services nightly, as he should. The Fax News agency was full of obedient volunteers and servants in the decades-long war on terror. Garrett had been interrogated by UNSIs, and they had coercive methods. Had they gone far enough before she had called in to admit she may have been mistaken? She would never truly know.

And Mila's doubt…

Jenna bowed as the handful of people clapped, and then she took a moment. She prayed. *White Light, God, please don't let it be so. Please don't let Mila-chick be a blackwing.*

Garrett filled his backpack and tucked his pistol in a holster strapped to his belt, along with the extra clips. He was going to mingle and work his way into the White Light gatherers, a pack of fervent pilgrim Theo-worshippers camped in and around the two stadiums.

Tonight, he would either be a martyr or riding the fast slide to hell. Theo's back-up angel was on the news again. Yes, he glowed. Yes, his voice sounded musical. At times, it nearly brought tears to Garrett's eyes. The entire experience was mesmerizing, but it did not mean they had been sent by God. If fascism was God's only tool for compelling the masses, then Garrett had seen enough and had chosen the opposing side a long time ago. He looked down from his balcony at the street. No UNSIs there, though that did not mean they were not hiding. He looked up at the sky. Black military birds cruised in the distance in and out of the stadium area. They always did. The sky above him? It was clear. So why did he feel like his doors were about to be blown in? Why was his skin crawling? Then he saw movement down the block. Yes. A shadow shifted on a rooftop. Two White Light Infraguard. But were they watching him or someone else? Garrett closed his eyes, trying not to smile and break into laughter. Who else would they be watching?

The lobby reminded Mila of the registration center at the University. There was a long counter about stomach high, a plastic glass window with sliding steel exchange drawers like banks had at their drive-through windows, and a small square speaker where the countertop met bullet-proof glass. The floor was scuffed linoleum. Mila wondered if the security measures mattered much. Everything was recorded and they were next to a train depot full of UNSI soldiers. Only a blackwing could really commit a crime in a place like this and get away. *Only a blackwing.* Mila hoped she would not have to break her father out. She was doing her best to stay focused and ignore thoughts of Garrett, but it felt like a chunk of her heart had been torn out whenever she was away from him. And if something were to happen? *He'd be better off without me.* She had to keep reminding herself of that.

She inched up to the woman behind the glass, who looked at her screen and then again looked at Mila. She nodded toward a chair without saying a word, punched a few buttons on her keyboard, and then spoke into her mouthpiece.

Mila sat in the corner of the waiting room, facing the woman, an interior door, and the exterior entrance. Mila shook her head and grinned nervously. Diabliss' instincts were wearing off on her. Even with the jumbled emotions of finally seeing her father, Mila still thought about where to sit in order to have the best chance of escaping or surviving an attack. A TV in the opposite corner showed Fax News. Mila tuned out the sound. A man stepped out through an interior doorway and signaled for the woman behind the glass to turn up the volume on the television. She nodded and Mila looked up to see what he was so interested in. It was Seattle. There had been an explosion.

The commentator returned. "This just in. Another horrible act of domestic terrorism. An attack on the White Light. In all appearances, it looks like hooligans, but our sources at UNSI tell us that it's indeed both anarchists and hooligans. Perhaps the two criminal factions have even joined forces."

The camera shifted to a smiling woman. "Seattle has a history of domestic terrorism."

Back to the man who was touching his ear. "It's been confirmed by the White Light Infraguard. A massive attack by domestic terrorists."

The interior door opened again. "Mila Sadis."

Mila nodded and jumped up, looking to the television nervously one more time. Her heartbeat quickened. Emotions swelled. Diabliss was trying to tell her something but was afraid to turn the chemistry down. He had better not shut down the emotions of reuniting with her father. She would just as soon turn herself in. A daughter's love for a father? This was her humanity.

A foreign UNSI guard led her into a room, leaving her alone with a tall, thin stranger in an orange jumpsuit. He had a mustache and a crooked dirty-gray beard. She looked around. He was not holding a reader. She looked for a mop and bucket thinking he was a janitor. Then she saw his jaw was quivering. Her emotions exploded.

"Dad?" she asked. Her tears exploded.

Chapter 44

The door clicked shut behind them. The gray room resembled a jail cell more than it did an office. There was a table and two chairs in the middle. Mila and her father faced each other, neither moving, until his palms opened ever so slightly. She grabbed her dad, and they hugged. She had to refrain from lifting this frail lighter version of him off the ground or squeezing so hard that she would end up hurting him. The anger she had felt from him not calling her for so long and the emotions swirling with thoughts of Garrett dissipated. Instead, she felt guilty for ever wanting a penny from him. Here was a man, starved, or at the very least half-starved. His diminished size told stories. His arms were thin, and his back was slightly hunched. His chin protruded and his cheeks were sunken, as if there were only a thin stretched layer of skin resting directly on bone. The top of his head showed through thinning hair. That was new.

He held her away and grinned as he looked into her eyes. He then pulled her back into a hug and held her tight. "Oh, Mila."

"Dad."

He told her stories of wandering, seeking work, and finding only random part-time jobs, where all earnings went to taxes, debt, and a mat to sleep on—not even a bed—too often not even food.

"You've grown," he said. "They must be feeding you well." Only, the way he said feeding, she could sense that it was awkward, as if it reminded him of his own suffering or possibly even made him jealous. He placed his arm around her again and squeezed, his hands patting her back. "But that's good. You're taken care of."

Mila had not thought about her own appearance. She had been starving herself since arriving at college, but he would not know that by looking at her. She was not only healthy and strong; she was physically bigger. In fact, she probably looked like she had overeaten. It did not matter, though. She would do everything in her power to make sure he never went hungry again.

"I put on some muscle," she said. "Coach made us add weightlifting to our workouts. Doesn't want us getting knocked off the ball."

"I could feel muscles in your back. Nearly as hard as my bones." He gripped his left forearm with his right hand, finger and thumb touching.

He asked about soccer and she told him all the details. They laughed together at her account of the techies practical joke with the exploding soccer ball.

They embraced once again. Mila could not let go, nor could she hold back her tears.

He knows, Diabliss whispered in her head. *He felt the wing pouches.*

Her eyes were still blurry when they opened wide.

Jenna checked the data reader on Mila and traced her route. Mila had waited for thirty minutes in the factory camp lobby, an additional fifteen added per Jenna's request. Now, Mila had had fifteen minutes with her father. Whatever she was, whatever she had done with Garrett, she deserved to see her father, alone.

After double-checking her Taser, Jenna leaned forward, reciting another prayer.

"Don't like flying?" the pilot asked.

"Some trips are easier than others." Jenna looked down at the warehouses and fenced courtyard below as they hovered.

"Your landing request has been approved," the pilot said. "We're touching down inside the compound."

Jenna watched as the buildings grew closer. She looked to her reader again, determining which building she would be entering and through which door. She knew she should be positioning Infraguard or UNSIs at the exits. Sure, Mila might not be a blackwing, but she at least qualified to be interviewed. Jenna's heart skipped a beat. She had personally checked Mila off in order to attain the blackwing-free campus status. *Why did I do that?* At the time, the thought of Mila being a blackwing was absurd, but that was before they knew about doubt, the creeping thoughts that fertilized a demon's seed. Blackwing or not, Jenna had been a fool.

"Open," said Jenna. The side door slid open, and Jenna jumped out. UNSIs looked at their readers and then away. Yes, she could pass. She could pass wherever the hell she wanted to. The steel door clicked open and Jenna entered the hallway. Mila's ID card indicated she was one hall down with her father.

Jenna stopped and controlled her breathing. There was no sense in confronting Mila in front of her father. Only, Jenna was so furious she was not sure she could refrain herself. She unclasped her Taser. Just in case. She tried to hold back her emotions. *With God and the White Light, everything's right.* She whispered the mantra, reminding her of her duty, strengthening her resolve. She had broken so many protocols, regardless of whether many of the rules had been created and instigated by her or not. As soon as the Infraguard had asserted authority over the UNSIs, Infraguard members were no longer volunteers, they were military. They might not receive paychecks, but the rules of angels and God were not meant to be broken. Jenna would pay for her own misdeeds.

Oh, how war caused so many pains. If Mila was in league with Satan's minions and refused help, Jenna would have to take Mila down. *No hesitation.* She would drive the doubt right out of Mila personally. Outside the doorway, Jenna again steadied her breathing, then she opened the door and stepped inside.

The hoolies had proved their expertise by acquiring the extremely rare items—weapons, explosives, gasoline, and most importantly, UNSI and Infraguard uniforms, and the too-easy-to-replicate armbands. Even if at close range they looked out of place, it was more than enough to get in and infiltrate the masses.

Garrett, the Agorist, put on the white armband, pulled up his hoody, and then lifted the kerchief over his face. It was cold and rainy enough that he might not stand out too much, though he had yet to see a Holy Follower with a covered face. UNSIs covered their faces, but that was mostly to conceal foreign features. A lot of people, even if medicated by Flo-Rite, disliked foreign troops on American soil. His armband would get him close enough. If a citizen questioned him, it would be easy to pat his side arm and intimidate them. If an UNSI or Infraguard approached, it would be their last human act. The White Light armband had black fabric on the inside, and as soon as the first explosion went off, they would be flipped over so that hoolies and anarchists could distinguish themselves from the White Light hoard.

Garrett's backpack was heavy in so many ways, but his soul was even heavier. Theo, his Holy Followers, and UNSIs had formed an alliance and were creating an illegal system of government intent on ridding the world of people like Mila, but what if the White Light were angels sent by God, and those following them were not only Americans, they were the chosen people. There was a fine line between being a civilian and being an enemy combatant. The White Light was arming this legion. If Garrett waited any longer, the transition from confused civilian to rabid soldiers under fascist rule would be complete, intent on killing Mila. But it still left a gray area. Garrett and his small army might be attacking *civilians*, even if they were now armed civilians. Shit. That place in hell indeed had a Garrett-sized hole there, empty and waiting.

Theo had thought about Jenna more than he knew was healthy for a leader. It was the humanity creeping in. The humanity craved this woman, and even craved her in the flesh. But Jenna had rushed away after uttering a mumbled thank you. Something was amiss. Theo had wanted her by his side. Theo had to make sure she was ready, and willing. He had been so sure. It would serve so many purposes. The world needed heroes, mothers and fathers, Kings and Queens. The world needed Jenna more than she realized.

He would fetch her personally. He would bring her to his side.

Both Mila and her father turned as Jenna stood just inside the doorway. Mila grinned and rushed to her, distracting her momentarily from Diabliss's words.

Remember, she worships the White Light. She hunts and kills blackwings.

Yes, Mila knew all that.

"Here on official business. I'm Jenna," she said, turning to Mila's father.

Mila raved about how generous Jenna was, how many times Jenna had helped her. Mila told Jenna's story about the blackwing and her position in the White Light Infraguard. The words were awkward and sporadic, with pauses where she was not supposed to pause and straightforward rambling where commas should have slowed her speech. Mila's thoughts raced. She tried to read her father's eyes as she had done nearly all her life. Something was indeed wrong. He was disappointed. She knew that look.

Diabliss, almost as frantically, tried to regulate the chemistry, but he had been letting it run too free so that she could experience the reunion with her father unfettered. The red flags Diabliss threw out burst in her brain like fireworks. Diabliss was commandeering parts of her brain, trying to sense if there were heartbeats on the other side of the concrete and steel ready to storm the room. Jenna's official business and sudden appearance was meant for her.

"Jenna," Mila's dad said. "Being a member of the White Light Infraguard, you probably know some things. Is there a way to medically extract a blackwing from a body?"

Mila's heart repeatedly slugged into her chest until Diabliss was finally able to moderate it. She was perilously close to losing control of her body and fainting or throwing up.

Jenna looked at Mila. Her lips turned down, as if she were about to cry. "No." She shook her head. "There is no known way to medically extract a blackwing. All efforts have resulted in... death."

Yes, it was in Jenna's eyes. She loved Mila like a sister, but she served a higher purpose. Mila looked to her dad. Sure, he knew that she was a blackwing, but Mila did not want to be arrested in front of him. And she did not want him to see her cede control to Diabliss, who in an effort to save himself and avoid capture might kill anyone or anything in his way.

Her dad had seen so much hardship. He could not know for sure that Mila was a blackwing. He had to have doubts. Would he turn her in?

"As I understand it," her dad continued, "there is a law that requires citizens to report a known or suspected blackwing."

"Yes," said Jenna.

"And a reward?" he asked.

"There is a cash reward," said Jenna. She was not watching Mila's father. Her eyes filled with tears and locked on Mila.

Diabliss begged Mila to escape or fight.

Mila's dad cleared his throat and spoke again. His voice shook. "There is a reward if you are the first person to turn a blackwing over to an authority?"

Jenna turned to him. A fire seemed to dry her tears. "Yes," she answered, incredulously.

"Dad," Mila said.

"Has anyone reported Mila Sadis?"

Jenna shook her head. Her jaw dropped.

"Dad!" Mila cried out.

"I hereby officially report that Mila Sadis is a blackwing." He then ran to the corner and cowered.

Mila fell to her knees, in tears.

"I'm sorry, Mila," her father shouted. "You don't know what I've been through. And it's the law."

Diabliss clawed at her internally, he was furious with her father and wanted to rip his limbs off. Mila did not want that. Mila just wanted to die.

"Daddy," she implored. Mila put her hands out and looked up, crying.

Jenna walked toward Mila's father.

He rose and pointed at Mila. "I felt her back. I knew it right away."

Mila covered her face. Tears bled through her fingertips. "I would have done anything, Daddy. I would have given my own life for you."

"You don't know how hard it is when you lose everything. I do love you, Mila, but I'm a patriot, too," he said. "This is for God and country. This sacrifice is harder on me."

"And the reward?" asked Jenna.

"I claimed it first. There's a reward. It's mine. I've earned it," he said, his eyes empty and soulless. "Money doesn't make this easy."

"Just easier," said Jenna.

"I won't fight. You can have the money," said Mila.

"Yes. Here's your reward," said Jenna, turning and facing Mila. "It's the gift of love to your daughter." Jenna placed the Taser on Mila's father and fired a bright burst of white-light tendrils into his forehead.

Chapter 45

As Mila's father's eyes rolled into the back of his head and he collapsed to the hard linoleum, Jenna pouted for a long second and finally breathed. What kind of a man turns in his own daughter? With all the leads rolling in, Jenna had never considered that before. Patriotism? Sometimes, but not here. She saw greed in his eyes. He had sold Mila out for money, and Jenna understood Mila's pain. If Mila was a blackwing, then maybe a blackwing deserved its dignity this one time.

Mila sobbed from the opposite side of the room, her hands covering her face.

What if I just risked my soul by sympathizing with a Blackwing? She would arrest Mila now, she had to, but not in front of that shell of a man, that soul pimp. He would get his money cleaning Pentagon outhouses in Syranistan, and it would be an Amero a day through blistered bleeding hands.

Jenna punched numbers into her reader, ignoring Mila's sobs. Most of Jenna's tears had been siphoned away by fear and anger; the electric charge into Mila's father had cauterized the rest. If she could only do the same for the pain coming Mila's way. If only she could cauterize the pain she would feel arresting her best friend.

"Are you going to fight me, Mila?" Jenna asked.

"Jenna, I'm so sorry." Mila stood and staggered toward Jenna and her father.

"Stop. Mila, I don't know what you deserve, but you don't deserve him."

"I'm done." Mila stared blankly at her father. "I'll go peacefully."

Jenna was unsure if Mila was speaking to her or a

blackwing.

Mila went to hug Jenna, but Jenna put one hand out to stop her and placed her other hand on her taser. *It will be easier if I charge her right now. Four shots left.*

Mila nodded as if reading Jenna's thoughts. Mila hurt; Jenna could see that much. It was not an act, but that did not make it any easier.

"Thank you," Mila said. It was the same thank you Mila used when Jenna stuffed food money into her pocket. It seemed genuine, but maybe it had always been an act.

Jenna stood over Mila's father. She punched more numbers into the reader, deleting the last sequence from the camera and turning it off for the next minute. She rolled him onto his belly. She placed the taser on the back of his head and punched three consecutive blasts. Mila's father would not remember the past week. In fact, he would not be able to hold memories for weeks to come.

Jenna kicked him over.

Visited acquaintance's father, Brad Sadis. He had a seizure. He has an unfortunate mental disorder. Extreme paranoia. Send medic and then ship overseas immediately. She punched the buttons on her wristpad.

Jenna leaned over and checked the pulse. He was out but alive. She looked up at Mila. "His heartbeat's still strong." Jenna was about to tell Mila not to worry about her father, how he was not worth it, but all she could do was hug Mila. Then the door suddenly opened, and several bodies rushed inside. A bright white light appeared. She shielded her eyes

"Embracing the enemy?" asked a familiar harmonic voice.

Her vision blurred, but the voice. *Theo?* The White Light could detect blackwings, especially this close, and here she was hugging Mila. "I just learned about it. I wasn't absolutely sure until now," Jenna cried out.

"A betrayal for sure. Conspiring with the enemy," Theo said. "'Tis a shame. And I came here for you, for better things." His light flashed brighter.

No. Jenna's eyes burned. The tears did not help. Jenna could barely make out the angel through eyes that felt as if they had been seared in their sockets by a hot poker. A group of men shuffled in and held battle positions. By the sounds of the boots, she was sure they were UNSI soldiers. As her eyesight returned just enough to see it was indeed Theo.

Jenna, now bawling, bowed down. She had failed him, but more importantly, she had betrayed everything the White Light stood for. Even with blurry vision she could make out UNSI guards with their weapons aimed at her and Mila.

Mila was a blackwing. Jenna had to confess to Theo, she had to tell him, only her words stuck and her mouth dried. *Mila.*

Theo, the glowing angel, stood over Jenna with a raised luminous sword. As her vision adjusted, she saw pure hatred in his eyes, a fire like a burning ember smuggled straight from hell.

Jenna turned and faced Mila. "Mila, you're my best friend, and I love you."

As Jenna's head rolled onto the floor, one final thought escaped. *Fly, Mila. Fly.*

Chapter 46

Diabliss grabbed for control. The Mila-chick was done, emotionally destroyed by her father, and now, her best friend was dead. Diabliss even liked Jenna, now. It saw the life drain from her glazed stare. A sacrifice it could understand, even if it went against survival.

An open door? A patch of light from outside just beyond a corner indicated the closest exit. A quick flight and it would be in the sky making its way, only, the angel Diabliss recognized as Theo, turned suddenly and swung its sword of light. Diabliss flew, around and behind the UNSI, and then jumped up, turning belly up, pressing against the ceiling, as a burst of panic-induced bullets rained across the room. The UNSIs dropped to the floor as they fired into each other, but Diabliss could not tell if they were all injured, dead, or playing dead. It did not matter, though. There was an angel, an angel alone. Diabliss liked that. Diabliss hissed at the angel and then crouched for an attack. *Small room. One exit.* Diabliss needed to block the exit. *Trap angel in. Fly out if Diabliss wants to escape instead.* But it did not want an escape. It would give its life to stop this White Light. It had learned from Jenna what Mila understood all along. *Sacrifice.*

The White Light looked down at a small screen on a UNSI wrist reader on an outstretched arm, but it watched Diabliss, too. A siren wailed from the wrist reader's speaker. "It's an organized large-scale terrorist attack. Hooligans and anarchists," said an angel through a garbled transmission. The screen showed a stadium filled with smoke. Holy Followers in White Light robes stampeded as a ball of fire billowed near them. The screen flickered and went blank.

Theo's stadium was under attack, and before Diabliss could block him, Theo flew out the door.

Mila wrestled for control, their feet and wings slowed.

Must fight White Light, Diabliss argued, fighting her.

Mila-chick's head turned to the screen on the dead UNSI's wrist. *I have to look for one second. It's Garrett*, she said. Anarchists and hoolies working together. Garrett's complicated facial expressions at their last goodbye.

Ah, yes. Diabliss understood. Garrett was in this battle.

As Mila rushed through the entryway, away from Theo who had gone out through the rear of the building, she somehow found the strength to wipe and then stifle her tears so she would not stand out. She wanted to run. Diabliss wanted to fly. She hoped that Theo had fled too quickly to issue an alert.

The group around the flat screen in the lobby had grown, but they were not interested in Mila. She knew she had to hurry, the UNSI bodies could be discovered at any moment, but she stopped alongside a small group congregated in front of a television mounted on the wall playing a broadcast of the attack.

"Shit. What the hell does soccer have to do with terrorism?" a man near Mila asked. "I don't see the link. Hoolies are terrorists now?"

"It just means the whole world is going to hell," a black civilian woman said. "Have to choose sides."

"Side with the White Light," someone said.

"With God and the White Light, everything's right," several said together.

"Angels are cutting through them. They're rounding them up. It's just a matter of time."

An announcer spoke while the footage played. "Inside, a group has taken over the broadcast center. Angels were burned. The anarchists have human hostages. Hooligans are still wreaking havoc. Honestly, you can't tell who is who. There are too many people. The stampedes literally shake the earth. The White Light has released the following statement. *Dying for God is better than doing nothing in the war against Satan. The death of any Holy Follower is sad, but in war, it is still a triumph.* Brave words." The camera shook. The reporter turned as several explosions rang out. Smoke billowed into the air. The screen blackened and then regained transmission. Gunfire rattled between two opposing sides. There was another explosion, and parts of the stadium interior rained down.

A group had hijacked Theo's broadcast studio. The man, wearing a face mask with an opening for his mouth, dark glasses, and a headwrap, held a piece of paper up to the camera. Mila recognized it as a synthetic molecule. Yes. Garrett had shown this pharmaceutical compound to her with this same Material Safety Data Sheet. It was Flo-Rite, and proof that the population was being mass-medicated.

"This is in your water," the man said. "Do you seriously believe the government mass-medicates the entire population in order to prevent tooth decay in children? Try drinking two glasses of water and see how hard it is to think, much less stay awake." The man spoke again, "The red monsters at night. The drained bodies. They are siccums, brought to Earth to hunt blackwings. Brought in by the ones you call angels. Only thing is, these siccums eat people, too, and they work for your false angels."

The speaker turned and signaled someone. The screen flickered to a shaking handheld video of a siccum lapping at the blood pouring from a headless neck. The next screen showed UNSI soldiers and an angel releasing one from a cage. The siccum bounded off into the neighborhood, disappearing into the darkness. "They call *us* terrorists?

Destroy our country and take away our rights, and yes, face our terror," the man with a covered face said, this same man who sounded identical to Garrett.

If there was a link between hoolies and anarchists, it was Garrett, and if there was any chance of saving Garrett, it must come in the form of a blackwing.

We need to hurry. Yes, Diabliss. Time for you to kill. You'll get your fill today, Mila said.

Must save your love. Must save Garrett Webb.

And you can kill angels. Mila would do this herself, but Diabliss would do so much better.

Yes. Angels will burn.

Mila felt his giddiness. Diabliss loved killing angels. He loved dropping UNSIs from the sky. Diabliss craved the fight.

Two UNSIs entered the lobby with guns drawn. They were frantically looking for someone.

As the group inside dove to the ground, Mila slipped outside, and then ran. The sky had begun to darken as heavy late-afternoon clouds blocked the sun. As soon as she found an alley without people or cameras, Mila's wings shot through the back of her hoody. She tore a strip from her T-shirt, wrapped her face, and flew into the air.

All yours, Diabliss, but I get to kill Theo.

Diabliss took flight but then paused just beneath the clouds over an abandoned neighborhood. The Mila-chick disliked that it had stopped.

It needs help, it told her. Diabliss found the signal, like the heartbeat of a bat, lightly tapping, floating, and dissipating. So many stirs. So many particles. A signal only a blackwing could pick up. Anders had been following them. Anxious. Yes. Attractive and powerful. Too bad Mila-Chick did not see the match. She loved the eyes, but the enchantment did not strike deep enough. *Not yet.*

Diabliss hovered, so it could see, sense, and hear.

Anders was the leader of a small army, his Hatchet Club, and Mila needed an army, and another blackwing.

The White Light has been stabbed in the heart.

Diabliss, Mila. Anders laughed. *You think I don't know this? Seattle's done. The damage will be lasting. We can start a new army of blackwings. Stay with me. We'll gather and build. We'll be unstoppable.*

No. It can't stay.

You're just doing this for the girl, a shell that doesn't even share her body with you equally, said Anders. *She's doing this, not for a cause, but for one ordinary man. Well, you're in luck. A small force is on its way, but at least they do this for a cause. Don't tell me you didn't know what your friend was up to.*

Yes, Diabliss understood now. Anders had been peeking at her life.

Mila interjected. *Spying.*

"I was looking after you, and Seattle, a cause, and us," Anders said out loud. "We have a common enemy. People we care about will die for this cause today, and that sacrifice will help us build. But you don't have to die today. The world will be a better place if you don't."

Diabliss realized it would probably die if it went to Seattle. *Yes, it probably will fight until it dies. And yes, it's okay with that.*

Anders shook his head. "If I go up there to help, and we somehow survive, then she owes me that cup of coffee," Anders said arrogantly. "In person and in Portland. You have to agree."

But Diabliss was off. Anders had enough information to help if it wanted. Anders was laughing at Diabliss and called their plight foolish. Mila fought for control again. She did not want any more delays. She was still mad about Anders.

No, said Diabliss. *Nobody's happy with Diabliss right now anyway. And it's just coffee. It's for Garrett, and it probably won't happen anyway.*

Mila finally stopped trying to take her body back.

Yes. Mila calm. Seattle, now. Yes, air machine. Won't stop to crash it. Just fly. Yes, Mila-chick, just fly.

I have lost my best friend and my dad. I cannot lose Garrett.

Inside the Seattle stadium, Theo had already slain a blackwing and a dozen rebels. The tide had turned, but he was still furious, as he should be. His proud student, one he had had so much faith in, one who had convinced him she held deep devotion, had failed him. If Jenna had only known she could have been Queen in a submissive world. Now, his Holy Followers had lost control of the broadcast center. Terrorists had overrun the small complex, and it was difficult to discern who was an enemy and who was a worshipper. One angel suggested they nuke the stadium. Theo considered it. Not such a bad idea. The battle was lasting much longer than he had anticipated, and there was no end in sight. A nuke would take care of that and send a message, a sacrifice for a higher purpose. Theo calculated this option as well as the alternatives for a moment. There were too many Holy Followers here for that kind of sacrifice. A tactical flaw. His forces would need to be distributed across a greater geographical area next time so it would be harder to strike at them.

"Have we at least disabled the broadcasts?" Theo asked.

An UNSI officer shook his head. "Not yet, Sir," he said in Chinese. "We were instructed it should never be shut down. It should be on an educational loop." He was looking down, but Theo could still see his eyes wince.

"It's not. They have been broadcasting Satan's lies for over an hour," Theo said.

The UNSI officer nodded and shouted a command into his wrist. From the stands above the building and stage, Theo looked down as a troop of UNSIs ran toward the building.

An angel nodded at Theo, acknowledging his actions were correct and appropriate. Again, Theo glowed, trying to convey the angelic strength to the panicking masses, though the moment of inspiration was short-lived as a small explosive mushroomed. The momentum shifted, and phobic particles filled the air. He could use a new Jenna, calm, taking action, in control. But humans, like Jenna, were proving themselves to be too unreliable. Theo roared out loud. One moment of weakness, and the credibility of the people's authority figures, but most importantly, the White Light movement, was in jeopardy.

"Fifty UNSIs, now," said Theo. His eyes locked on the UNSI standing beside him. "No Infraguard. Infraguard has been compromised."

As Theo and two newly arriving angels flew to the broadcast center, bullets rained down, thunking on the steel building and the ground, occasionally hitting random people and soldiers, even striking Theo and his new comrades. Theo pushed the bullets out of his skin and began the internal healing process, a mild distraction. The smoke was thick, making it difficult to breathe and see in Theo's human shell.

UNSIs assembled before the three angels.

Theo, holding his sword high, signaled for them to line up at the broadcast centers main entryway, and then two at a time, they poured into the small broadcast building next to Theo's stadium show stage. The UNSIs in the back turned to run, but the angels flew and landed behind them, shepherding them into the building.

"Go forward and you shall receive eternal life," shouted

Theo.

Yes. Angels understand righteousness. Another angel landed beside Theo. The three angels entered the building, pushing and shepherding the UNSIs before them.

The White Light had won the broadcast center back.

But no thanks to Jenna. No thanks to devotion. Now, it is time for pain.

Late. Yes, there had been another quick detour. The Mila-chick was angry. Best arrive late with dark sword than unarmed and early.

Diabliss quickly flew toward the black smoke.

It surprised the first angel, hacking at a wing until it broke off and ripped away from the flesh. Diabliss liked how the wounded angel tried to fly with one wing on its way down. No. Gravity stronger than the "holy" creature. *Pray for a new limb.*

Find Garrett, said Mila, her mind screaming desperately.

Fair. Fair. Diabliss would have plenty of fun. It swooped down and finished the writhing creature with only seven slices. *No more time for fun.*

Find Garrett, Mila implored.

But it was not that easy. First, it saw the boy Chookey, who smiled at Mila, but when he did a bullet went into his head. After a burst of emotions, Diabliss had to avenge the boy. Mila was okay with that, but then she became overwhelmed with a fear that this had happened or would happen to Garrett. And then the White Light chased and attacked and chased and attacked again. There were almost too many.

Diabliss analyzed the buildings, while swooping, lifting, and dropping UNSIs, slicing several, who now knew to run as Diabliss swooped down.

Mila begged, *Please find Garrett. Please. Please.*

Too many bullets. One more. Diabliss dropped the soldier from the sky. Oh, how the men wished they could fly. Every time. Each one. *Flap. Flap. Fall. Flap. Flap. Fall.*

It was the Mila-chick who spotted the dish on the roof of a small building. Yes. Diabliss could see the White Lights outside. *Too many. No, Mila-chick. No.*

The Mila-chick angered, wanting the body back, but Diabliss was a better fighter. It should have the body.

No, it said.

A bullet struck the Mila-chick's body. Diabliss found him. A solitary UNSI soldier. It pulled the man up and into the air.

Diabliss felt the Mila-chick fighting to take the body back. *Mila-chick is right. Yes. Go down.*

Garrett knew the camera was no longer broadcasting but argued his message a moment longer into an empty microphone. His fellow anarchist shook his head.

Garrett took the UNSI AK-47 and checked the high-capacity magazine with a quick toss in his hands. Full. He aimed his weapon toward the door, and as UNSIs flooded forward, he plugged round after round into the hoard, until a blinding bright whiteness grew, filling the room.

Garrett fired into the White Light with closed eyes, but it was too late. His eyes burned and judging by the panicky screams of his comrades, they were blinded, dying or dead.

The magazine emptied. He cleared the chamber in case there was a jam, but with one click knew he was out of ammo. His ears rang as they always did after battle, but much worse because he did not have ear protection. The UNSIs were on him. Garrett struck out, connecting once, and missing once. There was a hard pain as someone kicked the side of his knee, and then he went down. He was captured, and he felt at peace. This would be his end.

Goodbye Mila. Please be safe. Even if her being safe was just for one more day. *Please be safe.*

Chapter 47

It was losing. Mila screamed inside, nearly commandeering control from it as the UNSIs and White Light entered the broadcast center in the well of the stadium next to the smouldering stage. Yes. Diabliss understood. Her Garrett Webb was likely inside the small structure sending out his message. Yes. If UNSIs and the White Light were entering, the force inside holding them off had been overrun. *Yes*, Diabliss answered Mila. *We're still going to try to save Garrett.*

Garrett was dead, dying, or about to die. Her powerful emotions tugged at it. But death would be the most likely outcome for it and Mila as well. They might imprison Garrett. He likely had information they wanted.

It landed on the green turf field near the building. A group of reporters covering the battle from ground level zeroed in on Diabliss and began following it. They called after it. They wanted an interview. After making a quick visual inspection, verifying that they did not have any weapons, Diabliss ignored them and walked away. A wisp of acrid smoke from a nearby explosion engulfed Diabliss as it stepped over strewn bodies. It wondered if someone would soon step over it and Mila. No. Its enemies would circle and then step in, clip wing pieces and then hold the souvenirs up for the cameras. They would make necklaces and heirlooms.

Death. A slowing and stoppage of particles, and then decay. There had been a time where Diabliss would have gladly accepted an end, only here it had learned to appreciate survival again. This death would be for Mila and her Garrett, but it would not come without more of the White Light tasting a bit of their own hell and finding their own end first.

There were several armored personnel carriers next to the broadcast center. Diabliss tipped one over and pulled the gasoline tank off the bottom of it, snapping the metal. Fuel spilled out as Diabliss tossed the tank onto the roof of the building. A UNSI guard jumped away from the skidding steel piece, repositioned himself, raised his assault rifle, and fired several rounds. He thought Diabliss had been aiming at him. He fired more bullets as Diabliss hopped around until it found cover behind a different vehicle.

And then there was a loud roar, as if a fighter jet had swooped by, as hundreds of wild charging men poured down the stadium aisles and hurled themselves into the crowd of Holy Followers and UNSIs on the field. The Rose City Hatchet Club had arrived from Portland. And a new blackwing circled in the sky. *Anders.*

The reporters ran away from Diabliss, shifting their focus to the renewed battle.

Yes, Mila. It hears you. It's ready to go in.

Diabliss tipped a smaller vehicle, pulled off another gas tank, and carried it through the building's main entrance. The metal tank barely fit through the door. Gasoline sloshed and poured out, leaving a wet trail behind them.

Diabliss rushed and then hurled the gas tank forward at the end of the hall. It entered the broadcast tower's main room. A bullet seared across Mila-chick's skin; another went inside. The body bled, weakening as it drained. Bullets pounded into Mila and Diabliss. More holes. More pain.

The White Light brightened, trying to blind the Mila-chick's eyes. No. The Mila-chick should not have gone inside. *Not good.*

Diabliss scurried and flew. It ran and jumped, relentlessly fighting until the UNSIs, disabled, lay on the carpet, bleeding or killed, mostly cut into pieces, but finally quiet and no longer firing.

It pushed bullets out and internally rushed to heal wounds. Diabliss knew which choice would help it to live. It should leave Garrett behind with the angels. Only, the choice conflicted with what Mila would want. Diabliss also knew what it was like to be left behind with these "angels." If Garrett was lucky, they might execute him quickly, but Diabliss knew what kinds of torture and pain the White Light was capable of inflicting. Garrett would not be lucky.

The three angels stood beside their hostage, Garrett, a quiet man in a mask. Diabliss had not attacked the angels, and now they understood why. They had something of value.

Mila, it hopes you decide to survive. Diabliss appreciates life, but it will understand.

Diabliss placed its foot on a fuel tank bleeding gasoline and returned the body to Mila. This final moment of their shared life would go to her.

Mila regained control of her body. She was inside the broadcast building which consisted of a large room, surrounded by offices that were empty. There was recording equipment, servers, monitors, cameras, and a podium. The only UNSI soldier still standing was next to the angels and had a camera at his side. But they would not be streaming this even though the dark sword in her hands shook, and she was a bleeding mess. Diabliss either was not steadying her or could no longer do so.

Garrett's face was still wrapped, but Mila knew it was him. She wanted to run to him and embrace him. But for the first time in her life, heaven or no heaven, she was not afraid to die. Finding Garrett's eyes, she acknowledged that his resolve matched her own. He was ready to die.

She looked at the angels indirectly; they were trying to blind her with their white light.

The lead angel, Theo, spoke, "Why have you embraced such evil? Why have you forsaken mankind?"

His harmonious voice failed to enchant her. Instead, she wanted to kill Theo. She shielded her eyes with one hand and held her sword up with the other. "Maybe when the White Light loses, we'll talk about mankind over coffee someday. For now, you need to release the prisoner so we can all live. If you don't, we all die."

"Blackwings are never okay with dying," said Theo. "It's one of their many weaknesses."

"This one is okay with it. Maybe we evolved, together," she said.

Mila rocked the metal tank from the military jeep with her foot. Gasoline sloshed out. She saw Theo's eyes flicker and widen as she tapped on it again. His nostrils flared as he detected the floating gasoline vapors. Yes, Theo just now understood that if she struck the metal tank with her dark sword, sparks would fly and the room would erupt in flames. Maybe now he smelled the fumes from the fuel pooling on the roof and dripping down the building's sides. Mila, closest to the only door, would perhaps be the only one to survive, unless she tried to save Garrett.

Theo looked to Garrett. "Will you kill this man you came to save?" he asked, grabbing Garrett by his shirt at the shoulder, placing Garrett between himself and Mila. "And kill yourself and your demon?"

"For the greater good, yes. For love, yes." Mila pointed to Garrett with the tip of her sword and then struck the tank with the tip of the sword lightly, and then harder. She did not want to die, but she did not want to live without Garrett. A spark shot up. The angels sighed relief when it did not ignite the spilled fuel. Theo winced with each loudening metallic ring as she did it again, and again. His two archangels clasped his shoulders.

"My friend and I walk out. You and I live to fight another time in another place. You get to finish your broadcast, with or without commercials. That's the only deal going down."

Theo pinched Garrett's cheek through his thin facemask. "He's just a man. He is nothing. You risk your life for organic particles. Temporary organic particles. If you only understood what forever truly means."

"I've heard about your kind of forever," said Mila. "The forever you spin is a web of lies."

Theo looked to his prisoner and then to the other angels.

Mila again grated the dark sword across the gasoline-soaked steel as if striking a match.

Theo finally nodded, pushing Garrett toward her. "If you only understood that you can't win in the end. The White Light always triumphs." Theo held his hands and wings out. "Humans understand. The White Light has God's will on their side."

"Because you say so," said Mila, smirking.

Theo scowled and then smiled arrogantly. "Yes. They believe it because I say so. And that is why the White Light will win in the end. Because I say so and then they believe what I say."

Theo pushed Garrett forward. Mila and Garrett backed down the hall, watching the three poised angels who she guessed would be chasing after them and trying to kill them as soon as she exited.

Outside, Mila quickly flipped and rolled a personnel carrier, so it blocked the broadcast center's main door. She signaled for Garrett to move back. It would hold the door for one push, maybe two, but that would be enough. She hacked at it with her dark sword. One time. Two times. And the third time a spark finally struck the gasoline dripping down the side of the building from the fuel tank she had thrown onto the roof earlier.

There was no pushing on the door yet. Maybe they were broadcasting. Maybe they were content with her fleeing.

The UNSI soldier jumped off the broadcast center just in time. The flames erupted in front of Mila and quickly engulfed the building.

The stadium screen above the battling crowd flickered as Theo's face appeared. Now, she was not feeling as rushed. The angels were livestreaming instead of coming after her.

Why do I feel guilt for burning these creatures?

You're different, Diabliss said. *Guilt is okay but burn them anyway.*

Theo's voice filled the stadium. "An evil is before us, but God and the White Light will always prevail." Theo's eyes shifted away from the camera and there was an orange flash, followed by screeches and screams as the broadcast center turned to flames, filling the rooms inside like a hot brick oven.

There was a push on the door. If she held the heavy vehicle in place, the angels would burn. Theo would burn. Mila hated Theo. It was because of him, the White Light, that she was in hiding, that she had lost her father and best friend, and he was the reason she had nearly lost Garrett. Mila turned. Reporters and their cameras were rushing toward her. This is what they wanted to see, a blackwing burning their God-sent glowing angels.

It knows what you're going to do, Mila.

Diabliss understood the hard truth. Her father she had lost to greed. And Jenna? It was her blind devotion that had killed her, but her eyes saw the truth in the end. And the White Light was not going anywhere, just like the people's belief in angels.

Yes. Diabliss knew her well, but there was more to it than that. *It's not just about being labeled an angel killer,*

Diabliss.

It knows. It's what they want. If the angels burn, it feeds the hate, and you don't want to feed that hate.

Yes. A blackwing burning angels would only make more people hate blackwings.

But she was still torn. People needed heroes as well. They needed to know that doubt was okay and that sometimes a person had to make a stand.

She moved aside, allowing them to open the door. As soon as she had, three angels burst outside, wings smoking, only seconds away from complete combustion. A few surviving UNSI soldiers crawled out and rolled onto their backs, gasping and coughing, but breathing in fresher air.

The angels coughed and sputtered for only a moment, but upon seeing Mila immediately charged and swung at her with their swords.

Mila parried the assault, but in the process dropped her own sword.

Do you want it to take over?

No. I can do this.

As the flames behind her grew taller, two of the angels closed in. Mila grabbed them and pulled them toward her, turning and pushing them into the building's flames. The sleeves of her hoody caught fire as she held them in place. Fire crawled up their bodies. They both screeched, and in flames, flapped up away from her and into the sky, only to plunge and spiral downwards somewhere outside the stadium. Mila patted out her own flames. Diabliss immediately initiated the healing process in Mila's hands and arms. The blisters were already beginning to flatten. Red skin shifted closer to a healthy pink. She faced Theo.

Theo kicked Mila's dropped sword away as he stepped closer. She would not be able to get enough lift without getting sliced apart if she tried to fly away, but then she heard the voice above her. There was a dark figure in the sky, and a small cylindrical falling object. She nearly dodged it by stepping aside but caught it instead. *Anders*.

She flipped the aerosol can in her hand, pressed the small red plastic button on top, and sprayed the paint into the fire. As the billowing chemicals blossomed into an orange blaze, she whipped the flame toward Theo. She stepped closer.

Theo shook his head, his eyes filled with contempt. Mila dodged his sword and then spewed fire across his front. Theo's wing burst into flames, and the blue-orange fires travelled across his body. He quickly flew into the air.

Anders raced overhead after Theo. Before Anders could reach Theo in the air, though, Theo was already flailing and falling from the sky.

A swarm of cameramen with their reporters and microphones in tow rushed toward Mila, stopping a safe distance away from her and the fire. Mila flew to the top of a smoldering charred truck, the rubber on her shoes smoking as the heat shot into them.

The remaining Holy Followers, the anarchists, hoolies, UNSIs, and the blackwings must have noticed the burning angels. The roar, the screams and cries, the flurry, the bass-drum thump from bodies hitting bodies, and random gunfire nearly subsided completely.

Anders swooped, diving into the same direction that Theo had fallen. Mila half-waved goodbye with her free hand. *Crap.*

Yes, you owe Anders coffee in Portland. An option to consider.

Coffee's fine, but my best option's right here.

You fought well.

I learned from the best, Diabliss.

It learned from you as well.

The gathering reporters hurled questions, statements,

and foul names at Mila. They were here to sell advertising and broadcast whatever spin politicians and corporations told them to. *Masked Girl Burns Angels*. They should be thanking her for making their job so easy. At least she did not gift them the easy click-bait title *Masked Girl Burns Defenseless Angels*. She held her hand up as she sheathed her sword. *Screw their thoughts and labels*. Mila's doubt was her faith, and her life, despite the mask, with Diabliss stirring inside, finally felt normal to her.

A few seconds was all it took for them to jump into a series of questions, most of them ridiculous. Then, someone surprised her.

"Why didn't you trap the angels inside?" A young female reporter asked. "You clearly had them beat."

"I gave them a chance. I actually don't want to kill, anyone," she said. "Even those things you call angels."

You deny these are angels? How dare you…What does that make you? How long have you hated America? Their shouts and questions bled together. She waited until they quieted and then pointed to the kinder reporter from earlier.

"Why are you here?" the reporter asked.

"For love," Mila said, choking up. She really could not imagine life without Garrett.

Garrett, who had been waiting quietly behind her, stepped forward and took her hand as she climbed down.

"And why did he come here?"

"Also, for love," Garrett said. Garrett's eyes peering out over his covered face sparkled as he nodded that he was ready.

Garrett and Mila turned and ran into a dispersing twilight battle in the smoke-filled stadium. The massive sea of hoolies, anarchists, Holy Followers, and UNSI soldiers was spreading apart, the fight, disintegrating. The angels were gone, and the scruffy bloodied people looked exhausted and ready to cry over their fallen friends or find their way home. Mila and Garrett ignored them all. Mila could only think about Garrett, love, and staying in love. Together, Mila, Diabliss, and Garrett pushed their way across the waning tide, into the churning and splintering crowd, until they finally disappeared into chaos and anonymity.

Chapter 48

President Laura Banks scrutinized the battle through dozens of fixed camera and drone lenses, each angle sponsoring a small rectangle on a large touch screen on the edge of her desk.

The angels were clearly losing. And Theo, had been lit on fire by a young lady, a blackwing. Her mask prevented face-cog. An ear had slipped out. The overview narrowed her ID to under a million. They would trace her, and either kick her corpse for damning an entire city or tag her toe with an award in a private ceremony. Either way, this fiery young lady was doomed. A charred and smoldering face pressed into a small frame. The President tapped it so that only his image filled her screen. Theo would have been unrecognizable, but this was his direct feed from his wrist and the only screen that mattered. Theo was nearly dead. He was calling her with his dying breath. His suffering was a testament to his strength and determination.

"I will not say this more than once. You might think you can get away with not following my order due to my…condition." A small section on his leg reignited. Theo winced, but he ignored the small flame. "Believe me when I say the White Light has many angels in place, in key positions. Leadership, along with my wrath, will transfer immediately upon my death to a different angel. My death is imminent, so this will happen soon. So, heed these words, my final order, and you shall have grace as you enter the Kingdom of Heaven." He sneered and then composed himself again. "We might love you someday, but today, *Seattle must burn. Nuke the city. Nuke the state. A human must never stand alive in this stretch of your earth ever again.*"

Laura could see the blackwing land behind Theo, but Theo ignored him.

"Do it now," Theo hissed as the blackwing's dark sword cut his wrist phone from the hand. A swinging arm in the screen indicated that Theo's head had just been severed as well.

She had two Secret Service agents in the room with her. She watched the one she knew to be an angel as his wing's shot through his suit jacket. He reached over his left shoulder with his right hand and pulled out a sword of light. He had been one of her favorite Secret Service agents, but had recently been turned, "secretly", to spy, and just as likely to make sure that any order would be followed. She nodded to him assuredly as she picked up her phone and dialed her most trusted general. "We had a problem in Seattle and Theo is dead. I am initiating my constitutional authority with this order, and these will likely be my final words. *Initiate Angels Burn*," she said.

Her eyes narrowed and she bared her teeth in one final smile, a smile that would show this angel that she was unafraid. And she was not. You do not get to be President of the most powerful nation on earth if you actually experience a feeling like fear.

The angel swung out as the second Secret Service agent behind him drew his gun. The human agent on her side would be too late to save her life, but his sidearm was no ordinary weapon. Instead of a bullet, the handgun would emit a blue flame, a blue flame that thousands of agents around the world carried, blue flames that would be used against every known angel in the world, a blue flame that would light every known angel on fire. Sure, they would not get them all, but it would be a start.

President Laura Banks did not blink. She did not even

flinch. The President just grinned as she met her end.

The End.

Let me know if you liked it. Vaya con Dios.
Barritt Firth
barritt.firth@gmail.com

Afterword

About the Author

Barritt Firth grew up in the Seattle area and studied Humanities and Literature, graduating from Washington State University *Summa Cum Laude*. He has an MBA, is a former entrepreneur, and now resides in Southwest Washington where he writes novels and stories.

Acknowledgments

Thank you for reading in general. The world needs more and not fewer readers. And thank you especially, for reading my first published novel, Angels Burn. If you enjoyed it, please rate it. There are other novels on their way. My goal is to engage readers through writing that is entertaining and affordable. You are welcome to share your thoughts with me at Barritt.Firth@gmail.com. There will be updates at barrittfirth.com. I look forward to hearing from you. Mila's story is a story about doubt. Anything presented as a fact should stand up to scrutiny, and nothing presented to us, even when giftwrapped by authority figures, be they political, religious, media, or otherwise, should be immune from fair questioning and doubt. Now, I will step down and thank some people for supporting me in so many ways. I could not have done this without the support from Cindy, Ashton, and Megan, Jeanie, John, Ian, and Dolene. Angels Burn was professionally edited by Karen Grove, and I appreciate her hard work and efforts, and I am a better writer having worked with her. I have had the fortune of spending time with inspiring, talented authors, who have given me a lot of input and advice over the years as well: T K Gilb, Joel Jablon, Christi Krug, Paula K Perrin, Tiffany Dickinson, and Claudia Smith—Thank you. And to my many other friends, thank you as well- Bardi, Tom, Dimitry, Kirk, Matt, Sean, John, and all the rest.

Printed in Great Britain
by Amazon

15670613R00207